The Dark Road

KATHLEEN RHODES

THE
DARK
ROAD

This is a work of fiction. Names, characters, places, and incidents either are the product of the author's imagination or are used fictitiously. Any resemblance to actual persons, living or dead, events, or locales is entirely coincidental.

Copyright © 2024 by Kathleen Rhodes

All rights reserved. No part of this book may be reproduced or used in any manner without written permission of the copyright owner except for the use of quotations in critical articles and book reviews.

ISBN 979-8-9908030-0-8 (paperback)
ISBN 979-8-9908030-1-5 (ebook)

Published by Type Eighteen Books
www.typeeighteenbooks.com

...for Eleanor

"I am not what happened to me,
I am what I choose to become." —Carl Jung

"After a cruel childhood, one must reinvent oneself.
Then reimagine the world." —Mary Oliver

Part 1

Chapter One

"Should we proceed?" Dr. Frazier-Velli asked. He sat with legs crossed and a notepad balanced on his lap. The sharp line pressed into his gray pants led to argyle socks and deep brown, shiny Oxfords. His head angled down, and he looked at her over the top of his glasses, waiting.

Shelly sighed. "I need to try." She'd made this declaration before, many times.

The room was hazy and darker than usual. She wondered if he noticed the change. Shadows peeked from the corners—behind the gray couch, tucked into the leaves of the drooping plant.

For the last six months, she'd been working through horrible recollections that threatened to fling her into a panic attack during the day or disturbing nightmares drenched in sweat. The window over the doctor's shoulder drew her attention; it worried her that the only shift occurring during their sessions seemed to be the seasons passing outside. Today, the glass streaked with drips of rain. Typical November in Oregon.

"Okay. Let's go back in."

In the slow transition from the present to one of her altered moments, she'd relax her body while the doctor gently prodded her with questions. She'd hold on to his melodic tone, like a rope through a maze, until Dr. Frazier-Velli faded into a blur and her mind would spin. Smells generally came first, followed by obscured images that became clearer as time passed. Then sounds.

She breathed in deeply and allowed her senses to take over. The foul, urine-soaked smell coated the air, burning hot through her sinuses and needling the back of her throat.

Focus. Go forward.

"It's pulling me. The closer I get—" Her voice was near a whisper. "I'm so scared."

"Where are you?" he asked.

A trick question. She was at the beginning, where she always started.

"The hall."

In each session, she began in a darkened hallway, facing a familiar door. Today, the walls were painted an ugly muted yellow that hinted at tobacco stains. Sometimes, the walls were grey or blue. The paint was brittle under her fingers and bubbled in sections.

"And the room?" the doctor asked softly.

"Not the room. The closet."

"Excellent, Shelly! Can you take a step?"

"I don't want to see. I need to hide. I can't be here."

"Why hide?" he asked, slightly louder.

Is he talking, or am I? She gripped the arms of the chair, her breaths quickening, and thoughts jumbled.

"Because someone's coming."

Muscles jumped inside her legs as she bent forward. The effort nauseated her; the walls turned like a kaleidoscope, cascading toward a distant door. In the hall, the carpet was a darker green than she remembered, discolored with murky stains. Mesh showed through, with rough fibers extending like angry fingers, ready to catch a toe and pull her to the ground. Then she noticed the stench. How could a smell be so intense in a memory? It crashed over her like a frothy, churning current of filth, strong enough to wash her away to an even darker place.

Warm puddles lurked in the rug under her bare feet, splashing and suctioning with each step. God, she wanted shoes. Her steps slopped through an inch or so of wetness, leaving deep imprints, and she didn't dare look down. She tried to stay centered and follow the clues. She squeezed her eyes, shutting out the office, the window, the sound of the rain.

"I can sense it in my chest. The tight feeling, like my throat is going to close." She massaged the muscles at the front of her neck. "My palms are sweaty. So sweaty." Her lower back ached, and her breathing grew shallow. She felt the sticky cling of the liquid between her fingers. Then, raising her hand, she saw it—not sweat but blood.

The panic spiraled up from her stomach. "Hide. Hide. Do it now!" Shelly cried out.

She spun around, waiting for something or someone to come for her. As if reorienting out of a free fall, she shot forward, her breathing rapid, her hands trembling. With her head between her knees, she stared at her feet, which were still safely contained in black flats on the doctor's pristine white rug.

Dr. Frazier-Velli caught her hand. "Breathe, Shelly. Breathe."

Tears welled up and coursed down her cheeks. She moved her hand across the green velvet armchair, back and forth. She hated the chair, along with the countless, awkward disclosures that happened while sitting in it. Staring at the soft, plush surface, like swirling, melted chocolate underneath each fingertip—how many times had she repeated this same pensive action?

Shelly looked up to see the doctor's brown eyes boring into her. He really did have a nice face, behind the glasses and sometimes, an infuriating, matter-of-fact demeanor.

"Your expression changed just then," he said. "Where did you go?"

She was used to such observations. The good doctor seemed to notice instinctively whenever her mental dominoes tipped over. "This can't be my life," she said. "I'm tired of being damaged and weak.

Josie deserves more than a bat-shit mother. My head is full of this bullshit. She knows I love her, but she deserves a mother who can sit with her, carefree. I hope she doesn't absorb any of this, my fears. I panic and hide over these violent scenarios, and I'm good at it." She chuckled. "At least I'm good at something."

True to form, only solidarity and quiet compassion filled Dr. Frazier-Velli's eyes. He also knew how to handle her episodes of self-pity.

Shelly continued. "When I hold Josie, I see only death. Her eyes, her beautiful hair, but my mind flashes to her body, dead and blue. The images are dark, and I freeze. These thoughts don't end. They just don't end." She fell back into the chair.

Until therapy, she had fought the memories on her own. She fantasized about attacking anyone who tried to hurt her child, always with the same ending—fighting to the death, ripping out eyes, biting necks in a horrible barrage of violence, her daughter witnessing everything. The rage left her paralyzed, exhausted. With Josie now seven years old, the battle had been endless.

Dr Frazier-Velli scribbled in his notepad. "It sounds like you're trying to affirm safety at all costs." He looked up. "Is this possible?"

Her mind churned. It wasn't just possible, but necessary.

"We'll get back to that," he said after a moment.

Shelly hugged her shoulders. He had never written as much in a session before, had he?

"Are you having flashbacks or panic attacks?" he asked.

"What's the difference?" She shrugged. "The ocean image has come up. That's not a flashback, I guess, but it's scary. Paul wants to go to the beach over the weekend. We haven't gone in a year." She thought back to the last time—when she took a sedative to get over her fear. "Josie should see the water and play in the sand," she said. "She's missing out on so much because of me." She remembered her daughter's golden hair catching the sunset as the chilly water soaked her toes.

"The ocean could bring up considerable worries," Dr Frazier-Velli commented. "You've talked about the fear of water, how uncontrollable it is. Does Paul know the level of anxiety it causes you?"

Shelly smiled. He had used her words from a previous session almost to the letter.

"Paul might know what it means, but he doesn't show it. If I resist or hesitate, he won't let up with the pressure." Her shoulders pinched and tightened, and she adjusted in her seat. "We've talked about what scares me before. I don't think he understands. I'd hate for him or anyone to know what this is like. I'd rather spare them."

It's my burden.

"I see," said Dr Frazier-Velli. "Difficult as it may seem, you should let Paul know how you feel. As you said, he may not understand your level of worry and its effects. Without more context, he might see your behavior as a choice, not one your mind is forcing you to make."

His tone implied it would be easy to talk it out with Paul, and that irritated Shelly. He should know enough about their marriage to know how complicated that would be.

"Have you been sleeping? Any nightmares?" he asked.

"Yes, some." She shifted again, adjusting against the velvet.

"And what about the little girl?" He paused. "What was her name?"

A hot wave flashed through her veins. "Red." Her feet shuffled underneath her. "No, Red's been gone a while, and I'm glad. I'd rather not deal with her right now."

"Red," he scribbled. "Where do you think that came from?"

Did the name embarrass her? Why not something more common, or even a child's name? She imagined the doctor thinking of Clifford the dog, or cinnamon gum.

"I can't remember," she lied.

When he straightened up in his chair, Shelly read the cue. It was time to wrap up the session.

"Let's finish with some closing relaxation," he said. "We've covered a lot." He set down his notepad on the nearby table.

Shelly found his session-ending rituals annoying, an abrupt transition as she sat in the clammy velvet chair with her tear-stained cheeks and stiff shoulders. She fantasized about throwing his always-offered glass of water in his face and running out of the room. But good judgment prevailed.

Reluctantly, she planted her feet on the floor. She took a deep breath and closed her eyes.

"Find the sound of the clock," he said softly. "Allow your breath to go in and out as your mind follows the rhythm."

Shelly complied. Once again, she followed the rain against the window. The clock. The focus. She tried to believe better days were coming.

Chapter Two

"Fuck whoever said it gets worse before it gets better." Shelly turned off her car engine, punched paperwork into the bottom of her tote bag, and banged her elbow on the door as she exited the car. She saw them across the street, waiting for her. Probably parked there for an hour despite Shelly being right on time. She feigned a polite smile and waved.

"The only thing missing from this puppet are strings," she muttered through clenched teeth, not breaking her grin. She had scheduled a walk-through with potential buyers, but her neck felt like a thatch of bound cords, initiating a migraine. Her irritation grew as she wrestled with her purse, infuriated with the foreign keys and unfamiliar lock box. Once inside the three-bedroom craftsman, she opened a folder and thumbed through the listing, tax history, and disclosures, alongside a riot of Shelly Blake business cards. Everything you needed for a real estate showing.

Her day had already been full of annoyances, and it was only eleven in the morning. Aware of looming deadlines, she'd endured her daughter's protests while slathering peanut butter on bread and planning open houses for four different families. After that, she threw herself together enough to get Josie out the door and to school. She'd almost forgotten her psychiatrist's appointment.

At every therapy session, she'd start with the best intentions. Life had drastically changed after she lost her parents, and much of her childhood remained clouded, hidden from her. Even her mother's face was a mystery. At times, she remembered a soft expression or the bend of her smile, but nothing more. Only violent traces—torn images and fragments of sounds and smells—occasionally surfaced.

A voice roused Shelly from her thoughts.

"I love the house! It's exactly what I want—in the middle of everything, and you can't beat the view." Judith Turner, tax attorney and would-be buyer, turned to the window alongside Shelly. She was a tall woman with a thin build. Her peachy complexion suited her vibrant auburn hair.

"It's priced too high," Roger Turner chimed in. Slightly shorter than his wife, he resembled Al Pacino with glasses, short dark hair, and a raspy voice. He straightened up next to his wife, folding his arms in defiance.

"No, we'll do it. Let's make an offer." Judith nodded at Shelly, ignoring his objection.

"Are you sure?" Shelly had been here before, drafting and sending offers only to have them yanked by Judith. "It's the tenth offer, but—" She searched for something encouraging to say. "You've put a lot of consideration into this one, and the house has all your priority items." Shelly struggled for words. These clients often disregarded all logic and were constantly changing their list of deal-breakers.

"I know we've taken up a great amount of your time, Shelly, but it's such a hard decision." Judith crossed her arms.

"Roger, you're rather quiet." Shelly turned to him. "If you think the price is too high, I'm not here to persuade you. However, the offer should be solid. It's a sought-after neighborhood, and the property affords plenty of space."

Roger said nothing, and Judith was probably already planning the paint color. They were on totally different planets, as usual.

She lowered her voice. "Okay, I'm going to be straight with you. The seller has multiple showings this morning, and more scheduled later. This house will be sold by the end of the day. Ready to call it home, or will you give it up to another couple with a taste for teal walls and leopard print rugs?" Maybe she could appeal to Judith's

~ 18 ~

design sensibilities.

Judith's eyes widened in alarm, and she glanced at Roger. Reluctantly, he nodded.

"Okay, I'll write it up." Shelly pulled her laptop from her purse and propped it on the kitchen counter. Her fingers rushed across the keyboard. Then she stopped, her breath catching in her throat.

Blood covered her trembling fingers, now hovering over the computer.

I can't see what's there. Her breath faltered. *The blood, the door, the carpet. It's always the same. I can't leave and can't go in.* She clamped her eyes closed and shook out her hands. Dr. Frazier-Velli's face floated before her, suspended like a ghost, still waiting for answers.

"Shelly? Are you listening?"

She regained focus on Judith's grin. Over the edge of her laptop, she watched as her client held up color swatches and swooped around the room.

"Don't kiss it on the mouth," Shelly warned Judith, a phrase she stole from her favorite Julia Roberts movie. Too many overzealous buyers dive into a purchase only to be outbid and wilt in defeat. Judith ignored her and continued sashaying around the island.

Shelly added the details of the offer on her laptop. It wasn't complicated, simply copying and pasting from the other ten she had filed. Her mobile fluttered in her hip pocket. She pulled it out and answered.

"Hey," Paul said. "I don't know if we were going to—"

"What do you think about the color of the walls along the stairs?" Judith tapped Shelly's shoulder. "It's off-cream but looks like water damage. Needs to be painted."

Shelly ended the call, disconnecting without thinking. She cringed, knowing her husband would be annoyed. Lately, he only called or texted for practical reasons. Usually, reminders and cues for her to

~ 19 ~

prioritize. Thoughtful, sweet calls to check on her and her day had faded a long time ago.

"One more thing," Judith said. "We want to make an offer twenty above asking."

Shelly smiled and nodded obediently. For once, she agreed with Judith. Then, it hit her—she needed to grab Josie from school. That's probably why Paul had called.

"Judith, I'll email you the documents, but I have to run." She flipped her laptop closed. After a few condensed assurances for Judith, she made it to the car. She picked up her phone to ring Paul, but another client's name popped up. She answered the call and pulled onto the street, hoping she wouldn't be late collecting her daughter.

At school, Josie was waiting for her at the curb. Her white pants and green and yellow striped shirt were hard to miss. In a manic, pixie-girl way, she spun in a circle with her arms outstretched, simulating an airplane.

"There's my girl." Shelly smiled to herself, relieved. Josie was right where she should be. "Hey, kiddo!"

Josie slid into the back seat. She also wore a knitted hat Paul's mother had sent last Christmas. Handmade, it had uneven ties and flamboyant shades of teal.

Josie had always been a genetic mystery in some ways, not entirely resembling either one of them. Shelly thought she resembled a young Jodie Foster, rather than her or Paul, with wind-blown blonde hair, light freckles, and blue eyes. Beautiful, of course. Her locks were nothing like Shelly's horsetail—as she called her almost-black hair, secured back on most days to tame the waves. Paul had once referred to her as Jennifer Connelly-esque, but that seemed like a reach.

Shelly smelled bubble gum and heard Josie smacking away in the back. The sound burned into her brain. "Mouth closed, please."

Lately, Josie had become a master of eyerolls. Slouched shoulders and ignored requests were her new norm. Even a trip to Disneyland would probably be met with a refusal—that's how contrary she could be. Although after a day at the park, she might also crumple to the floor until they hauled her back to the car kicking and screaming. Traces of Josie's toddler self still emerged occasionally, as did the snuggles and kisses of earlier days.

The Oregon road ahead, wet for nine months of the year, glimmered briefly as light punched through the trees, creating steam that hung above the street. Shelly squinted and adjusted her hands on the wheel of the car. Everyone in the northwest corner of the United States needed a little sunlight on their face, which made the rays all the more pleasing. But the beautiful colors of the landscape—the greens, reds, and sparkling yellows of early fall—required a healthy supply of water.

As if on cue, the clouds crept in, and specks of rain dotted the windshield.

"Mom! I think I left my tablet." In the rearview mirror, Josie's blue eyes were alarmed.

"You'll have to grab it tomorrow. We need to go home to Dad," Shelly said. She prodded the steering wheel again, reminding herself to send Judith's offer.

"Mom! What will I use tonight? I have assignments. I'm supposed to write something." Josie's voice had raised an octave.

Shelly's shoulders tensed up again. She tried to read her texts while keeping the car on the road. There were missed calls from Paul and several messages from Judith. He had been trying to reach her, but the morning's chaos had spilled into the afternoon. Eyes on the road, she gasped at her car straddling the line. Swerving back into her lane, she checked the rearview mirror to see if others had noticed. Her pulse jumped, and she tossed the phone out of reach on the passenger floor.

"Mom." Another whine.

"Jooosssie." Shelly let out a howl, playfully mocking her daughter. She just wanted to get home without losing her mind. "I'm not sure what to tell you. The school has likely locked it up. We can access your homework on the laptop." She held her breath, hoping that was enough.

"I hate the laptop, and Dad doesn't let me take it upstairs." Josie folded her arms.

Her daughter's upturned lip and furrowed brow gave Shelly a twinge of relief. Josie worried over missing laptops and seven-year-old melodrama. At the same age, Shelly's life had been quite different.

Shelly always thought she'd have more children—until the mood swings and paranoia made her rethink everything. Paul witnessed her dark days, the first six months of motherhood, the deepest of her depression.

They had met in a coffee shop a few months before she became pregnant, had connected over their hatred of Weird Al Yankovic, whose music blared overhead as they sipped their tall Americanos. Shelly recalled beaming in agreement as they established their bond early. They agreed that out-of-towners were easy to spot, and that Oregon isn't pronounced Or-E-gon.

Paul was a hospital operations manager and, sometimes, a consultant; he dealt with complex medical complaints for a hospital district that extended across the Pacific Northwest. He used to talk about his job more but had stopped at some point over the years. Perpetually drained and often in a bad mood, he had become less tolerant with her, less adventurous and spirited in general—much less likely to sit through Weird Al on a random Sunday.

The car music died, startling Shelly as she glanced at Paul's name on the dash display. He had called three times in the last forty-five minutes, each time out-prioritized by needy buyers and a seven-year-old. She picked up.

"Hey. Sorry I missed your call—"

He cut her off. "I thought I was picking up Josie today. Didn't we talk about it?"

She gripped the steering wheel.

"I thought I was doing it," he said, his voice growing louder, "and you were going to take over the rest of the week."

Shelly racked her brain but had no memory of such a decision or conversation. "When did we talk? Shit! Did you go to the school?"

"Don't say shit," Josie yelled from the backseat.

Paul exhaled. "Yeah, that's why I called. I didn't see Josie."

"Hi, Dad. I forgot my tablet!"

"Bummer, kiddo!"

"Sorry I worried you," Shelly said. "I got my wires crossed." She hated giving him more to throw back at her later. Her mind was always so clouded. Had they talked about the pickup schedule?

"I didn't realize I needed to remind you," Paul said.

She rolled her eyes. He wouldn't let it go so easily. She kept her voice steady. "I'm heading home to make some dinner. Is there anything you want?"

"No," he said. "Well, I'll stop distracting you. See you at home." He hung up, no goodbye or check-in, just a click.

Shelly stared through the windshield separating her from a vast sky growing darker by the minute. Rain fell heavier against the glass, and her wipers sped up in response.

Doesn't he know I'm trying? The question lingered inside, yet persistent and deafening. *Does he know anything about me at all?*

Chapter Three

John left work, tired but ready to exchange the cherry red shirt and black khaki pants for sweats and a T-shirt. A longtime bike commuter, he knew all the quick routes that zigzagged through neighborhoods and avoided traffic. The streets between work and home were lined with small bungalows wrapped with broad porches. Three coffee shops with pubs next door were on his regular route. A double shot of espresso in the morning, and a glass of stout in the evening. Very Portland.

It was approaching four-thirty in the afternoon when John walked out the rear door of the camera shop into a service hallway. He tied back his shoulder-length hair for the ride and loaded up his bike. He put on his helmet and clipped on flashers. From October to July, Oregon's weather was perpetually unkind, with heavy rain and gloomy clouds. He'd heard on public radio that serial killers often get their start in the Pacific Northwest. He'd often thought about whether that was true, having lived in Oregon his whole life.

That morning, as he biked to work, John's mood had lifted at the sight of cherry trees lining the streets. It would be months before they'd bloom, but he longed for when the pink petals would fall, and their sweet, subtle scent would waft through the air.

But today, the downpour had not let up, and he expected little change on his way home. As he pushed through the heavy metal door and squinted through the deluge, water dripped from the roof and splashed from the rain spout overhead. *Here we go again.* His efforts to save the environment hadn't been easy. And affording a car hadn't been easy either. Starting off on his bike, he crossed the parking lot of the strip mall—boxy storefronts lined up next to endless concrete.

Eventually, his path took him to a two-lane country road leading to Portland's nicer residential spreads.

He hated biking to work in heavy storms, but using public transport held less appeal. The bus would be full of foul, damp air, drenched passengers, and a guy gesturing and talking to himself in the back.

John gripped the handlebars and leaned into the rain, predicting erratic drivers and white-knuckle turns ahead. Undeterred, he pushed down on the pedals, mentally preparing for deep potholes filled with water and splattering spray. He aimed straight through the parking lot, a diagonal dash to the street. The puddles were massive and by the time he reached the exit, he was soaked despite his so-called waterproof jacket. John spit away the rain droplets hanging from his top lip. Water clung to the lenses of his glasses, distorting his view. He slowed his pace to wipe them, then pushed down on the pedals again, anticipating the hill ahead.

For some unknown reason, everyone in Oregon forgot how to drive when it rained. Cars clustered together, suspended in blackened water over a breached levee that swirled and spun. Some motorists honked; others rushed forward, ignoring the conditions. On his bike, it sometimes felt like a game of chicken, or Russian Roulette.

John and his girlfriend, Sophia, had made plans to meet up with a friend for drinks. He'd been looking forward to getting out of the house despite having to work in the morning—the result of a shift trade with a coworker. A rather tedious routine, working five days a week, sometimes six during the holidays, but it paid the bills.

He'd dropped out of high school and had long made peace with having a GED—even if Sophia's family never missed an opportunity to remind him that working a commission job in a strip mall was a clear indicator of an underachiever.

Today, he wouldn't think about that. John stood on the pedals, ready for the climb, facing a solid mile of steep incline. The payoff was at the top, gliding onto the country road and then arriving home. He pushed past the fatigue in his legs and the burn in his glutes. As his body temperature rose, his sweat evaporated and turned to steam in the cold air.

Once home, John tucked his bike under the wooden staircase in the hallway in the lobby. The complex had the look of old Portland: hardwood floors in each unit, stained cherry paneling, and black-and-white checkered tile spread throughout the landing and the second-floor hallway. He climbed the two flights up to his apartment then passed through the doors into the corridor, making his way along a tired paisley rug, holding his breath to avoid the cigarette plume from unit fourteen and the stench from the many cats in unit twelve. As he often did, he hoped the stains on the ceiling and along the hall were from age rather than water damage or something else. He wondered if his migraines and asthma were caused by infectious dander or mold. On the plus side, the rent was cheap.

John looked up as one of his neighbors approached. Typically, he avoided eye contact and scurried to the safety of his apartment, not wanting to be delayed by small talk.

"Hey, what's up? Are you moving?" the lanky guy in a hoodie asked.

"No. I'm staying put. Why?"

"Oh, maybe it's not your place then." He turned to look back. "I saw furniture moving down the hall earlier. Never mind, man. Take it easy."

With a twinge of worry, John fumbled to retrieve his keys from his pocket. He'd heard stories of moving vans loading up entire apartments, robbers operating in broad daylight. Sometimes misguided neighbors even helped with the heavy lifting.

Holding his key, he saw a folded piece of paper with his name across the front in rushed, chaotic letters he recognized as Sophia's. Sloppy and illegible unless you knew her penmanship, which he did after two years together. The note was mildly alarming. It wasn't her style. She was perpetually on her phone, emailing or sending texts.

He grabbed the note, walked inside, and set down his backpack and keys. The one-bedroom unit smelled of wood, like a cedar chest opened every five years. The room had changed; things had been moved. The light in the closet lit up a gaping hole where Sophia's clothes had been. The drapes her mother had bought were gone, leaving behind a naked wall and abandoned windows.

The only items remaining in the living room were the couch, coffee table, television, side table and chair—all his contributions to their space. He flicked on the light in the bedroom. The blankets and sheets remained on the bed, but Sophia's quilt, the mother-orchestrated original worshipped with every visit, was gone.

John caught the edge of a left-behind table, as though he had suddenly slipped into deep water, with nothing to hold onto. His breathing intensified to panicked gasps. He racked his mind for clues as a pit grew in his stomach. He unfolded the scrap of paper, gripping it with hands damp from the ride home.

John. I'm sorry.

His pulse raced.

How do people do this? I've tried to say these words to you, to your face a hundred times. But never could. I never wanted to hurt you. I know why you act the way you do. But I don't want to walk on eggshells anymore. I don't want to worry about what mood you'll be in. I want to smile again. We were in love once, and I hope we still can be friends.

"You want to be friends?" He spit the words out. Balling up the paper, he threw it across the room and kicked the side table, sending a vacation photo from Hawaii to break into pieces. He stormed into the kitchen, seething, and glared at the empty cabinets and the countertop, bare except for a solitary can opener. He grabbed it and hurled it against the wall.

"I'm so stupid! I could never make you happy. Nothing was enough!" His voice echoed.

Pulling out his cell phone, he dialed her number, fumbling, unable to keep his fingers on the buttons.

"Stupid bitch," he muttered under his breath, as heat rose in him. Voicemail picked up, and her pleasant voice enraged him. At the beep, his mind went blank. He hadn't called to beg. Should he demand an explanation?

"Sophia! Why? What's going on?" His voice broke. "Eggshells! I don't want to be friends. I don't know what you want from me. You want to lecture me on moods—" He caught himself and inhaled, holding the phone away from his ear. "I'm sorry," he said, calmer. "If this is about money, I'm working on it. I know I have stuff to work out. Call me."

He tossed the phone onto the couch. A photo Sophia had taken of Multnomah Falls, rather dull and unimaginative—even somewhat blurred—and encased in a cheap frame, hung above the table. She had insisted on putting it up. John stared at professional photos all day. He knew the difference between a good photo and a bad one. The snapshot sent a message, left on purpose: Here's something to remember me by, to remind you that I didn't care. John tossed the chair aside and grabbed the picture off the nail.

"All I did for her!" The grain of the wood frame was rough against his palm.

Suddenly his phone rang, and he dropped the picture, shattering more glass.

"Sophia?"

A low and throaty voice filled the earpiece. "What's wrong? You sound different."

~ 28 ~

"Mom?" He dropped onto the couch, his face falling onto his open palm. She wasn't exactly a source of comfort, and she tried to pry into his life whenever she could. Still, the words fell from his mouth. "Sophia's left me." His breath was hot against the receiver.

"Oh, John. I'm so sorry. When did that happen?"

He sat up straighter. Legitimate concern did not top the list of her character traits. He was speaking with the Mormon version of his mother. The one early to church with his two sisters, greeting newcomers to the chapel with the all too familiar sweet, disingenuous, soft voice.

"Today." He wanted to hang up. Maybe throw more pictures and break dishes.

Joanne carried on talking, but after a few moments, he stopped listening. His mother confused him. She expressed sympathy and a hope for reconnection, while delivering scathing criticism. Listening to her depleted his energy and disoriented him, like being spun around then pushed down a flight of stairs. His hand pulled at the hair behind his ear, soothing his restlessness—a nervous habit.

"John? Are you still there?"

"Yeah." He tried to focus.

"The little bitch was no good."

He had heard it all before. The weight of her words reverberated in his head like she was knocking them in with a hammer. The amount of time Sophia had spent around his mother over their two years totaled in minutes. Self-absorbed Joanne trusted only herself, and her own perspective and focus.

As pressure rose in his head and pounded behind his ears, John thought about telling her to fuck off, and that Sophia had mostly treated him well, with kindness, but what was the point?

"Mom, you didn't know her," he said.

"Oh, yes, I did. That skinny little bitch. Too good for us, wasn't she, with her rich parents!"

He shook his head, listening to her jabs. Finally, her true colors, the mother he remembered, emerged. When he thought of his childhood, she was a figure in dark glasses with broad, looming shoulders, bellowing in an almost masculine voice while he cowered on the floor. With every call, visit, or hateful outburst, he was on the floor again, guarding himself, frightened and vulnerable. Not the grown man he wanted to be.

"Mom. I can't talk about this right now."

Her voice grew louder, adding a further twist to the muscles across his back. He dropped the phone back on the couch and could hear fractions of her words, her hate for Sophia, the fact that he was mismatched with a girl in her class. He blocked out her voice and stared at nothing, until he noticed the chair against the wall next to the television, cockeyed and angled strangely.

A dusty outline remained of the papers and boxes that had once sat there. But something hung from the back of the chair. A gray jacket, one he had never seen before, with some fraying around the cuffs.

He walked over and picked it up. Conservative in style, not the athletic or casual sort he usually wore. Extra-large size. He held it up, turning it over. He reached into the pockets and pulled out a scrap of paper—a debit card receipt for twelve dollars and sixty cents from Hoagie Bros. The sandwich place was Sophia's lunch stop at least three times a week. Turkey and Swiss with extra-mustard and pickle, no tomato, on wheat. Stamped with today's date, the details were for two sandwiches, a meatball sub, and her unmistakable order. At the top: Order for Hunter.

Blood rushed to his face. Why was Hunter buying her food? Why was his coat here in the apartment? He dismissed the obvious thought, yet it clung there, welded in place.

"She never had your best interests in mind, not like me. What a bitch," he heard his mother still yelling on the phone. His surroundings smeared into lines, as if he were on a train, watching the world flow by at a hundred miles per hour.

He hung up the phone without saying another word, and looked again around the room, trying to take inventory of everything she'd taken. He looked for clues, but nothing resonated. He fell to his knees. Beside him, the blurry picture lay on the floor, the shards of glass protruding threateningly.

Chapter Four

From the glossy wood veneer of his desk, Paul's phone showed three-thirty. Holding a manilla folder, he paced across the office, at each turn resisting the urge to kick one of the piles of papers and folders stacked around on the floor.

As an operations manager, it was his job to read between the lines—sometimes not an easy task with his organizational skills. Sticky notes and papers littered his desk and the shelves behind. The needless trip to the school had sidetracked his afternoon; today, especially, he needed to be sharp. The hospital had dumped a new case in his lap.

Though he often worked in the field, his office was at home, which had proven to be less than ideal. He struggled to focus on his tasks and would wander around the house starting projects. The tiles in the extra bathroom were still missing, and he needed to finish painting the hallway. Everything felt perpetually in progress.

Working on-site in the hospital kept him accountable. He could cram himself into a corner and do his inspection without interruption. After all, no one wanted to disrupt an auditor. Over time, it became evident to him that his job went beyond analysis and mediation. He was a mouthpiece for bad news, the translator explaining why insurance hadn't covered treatments, who would cut off those who still needed care.

Paul wrestled for a memory of when his career had made sense. Trophies, degrees, acknowledgements, and certificates hung framed in his office, but surrounded by files summarizing other people's lives and suffering made his honors and accolades insignificant in comparison.

He had promised himself to change careers after a year. But a new focus came, unexpectedly, in Shelly. Indeed, a life-altering shift, but it was for love rather than a strategic career move. Dating turned into marriage, and Josie soon followed. Having a partner and a child had been on his list of priorities, but the whirlwind pace of it left him without a sense of freedom, unable to concentrate on plotting the course of his career, or his life.

Paul crinkled the file between his fingers. Everything these days was electronic, but with sensitive cases, he liked to have a physical copy as he skimmed initial notes.

"Twins. Complications at birth." He jumped to the comments made by other administrators: "Unfortunate situation; dilemma of unplanned routine procedure versus emergency; heart goes out to the family."

He learned that Olivia Jenner, the mother, was a Certified Nurse Assistant working for Good Heart Hospital. After medical care, she received a bill for forty-three thousand dollars. The insurance company wouldn't cover the whole event, and the hospital challenged that all interventions were indicated as routine and, therefore, the patient's burden due to lack of full coverage.

Words jumped off the page: RN; Twin B; bradycardia consistent with contraction. Fetal heart tones concerning over the last half hour. Moving patient for a routine cesarean.

Then he saw it: Fetal demise.

"Son of a—" He idled, thinking in loops.

So far, his boss hadn't returned his emails asking about the new assignment, but a fetal demise changed the whole conversation. The gut-wrenching calls with patients, the investigation into incompetent doctors responsible for documentation errors. Paul had been there before. He balanced against the desk and laid down the dossier, shaking his head.

His frustration with the medical system did not set him up well for this one. Ninety-nine percent of the time he stood in for the Grim Reaper and denied meaningful treatment, following the policies, procedures, and agendas of his employers. But today, it was a dead baby.

A shudder vibrated the desk. His phone was ringing under piles of papers. It was Will, his boss. Paul exhaled heavily and put the phone to his ear.

"Paul here." He saw his reflection in the window and didn't recognize himself. He'd once had a strong brow line over deep-set eyes and a muscular jaw. He looked old, with ridges casting shadows, as if he was wearing a harsher mask.

"Hey, I got your emails. Sorry to blindside you with that case." Will's voice was low and raspy from twenty-plus years of cigarette smoke.

"Yeah. What's the background? It seems thick," Paul said. "Travis has bandwidth for this level, and his skill set fits. I'm drowning here." He pictured Travis, a nerdy, accountant type who could spend hours reviewing and picking apart three pages in a chart.

"Travis has a full deck," Will said. "This one's yours, man."

Paul felt a tightness in his chest. "Will, I can't handle it. Come on! An infant death? The review needs to be done with a microscope. I already have an ass-high pile of cases." He began to pace again, rubbing his temple.

"I know," Will said. "We cleared them to give you some room. Hansen will take the low-profile ones. This one is top priority."

He gripped the phone tightly. *He's taking all my cases—what the fuck is going on?* He pictured Will slurping coffee and blustering about his teenage sons and country club membership. Was this a setup? Clearing his workload only to throw him to the wolves?

"I didn't have much say in it," Will said quietly. "I can't go into it. Higher-ups want to make this top priority. The patient has been informed of the escalation and who's covering it. They've been given your name."

Paul dropped onto his chair. At his worst, Will had been background noise the last few years, passing along the expectations of others rather than having a pulse of his own. But strong arming was unusual, even for him.

"Will, I don't understand. Over your head?"

"Listen, I'm only going to say this once. They want this one to go away. End of discussion. I've got to go. Call Hansen and update him on the cases he's getting from you."

The call ended. Paul stood silently with the phone against his ear.

Hearing noise from the garage, he guessed Shelly had returned with Josie—something that should bring him comfort but instead brought a churning in his gut. Could he face her? Lately, it was obvious she didn't listen when he opened his mouth. Why would this be different?

He stomped downstairs, passing framed photos of vacations, holidays, and birthdays. Frozen smiles trapped behind panes of glass. Shelly and Josie were in the kitchen, chatting about the day. Both turned and smiled, but after seeing his face, their expressions faded into concern.

"Hi," Shelly said slowly. "Everything okay?"

"Sure." He looked at their daughter. "So, no tablet, huh? I should have asked while I was there." He wanted to say more but instead went to Josie and leaned against the counter.

"Nice job, Dad." Josie laughed, her nose crinkling up. "You could have at least asked."

His daughter had no compass for adult tension, but the barbed comment did not go unnoticed. Shelly stopped emptying her bag.

"Babe," she said. "I'm sorry about the pickup. I don't know why I thought it was my turn today." She looked down at her paperwork. "I tried to answer when you called, but Judith talks nonstop."

He stared at his wife as she pulled papers from her purse and checked her phone. Shelly, like Josie, had her mind elsewhere. Couldn't she read him anymore? They used to look at each other and a connection would be made. He gripped the white countertop until Josie tugged at his arm.

"Can you get me some water?" Josie asked.

"Waste of an hour," he said. "Whatever!" He jerked opened the cabinet, clanking around glasses and cups until he found a pink one with an owl and tree branches.

Shelly blinked, watching him. "Was it a hard day?"

"Horrible day," he said. "Will dumped an intense case on me." He filled the cup with water, splashing some over the top of the counter before passing it to Josie. "It's not going to be easy. Loads to review."

"Josie, honey, no!" Shelly pulled the Winnie the Pooh and Tigger stickers off the granite.

Paul talked over the distraction. "Will's steamrolling me. I don't need this shit right now."

Josie extended a finger in his direction. "Dad don't say shit. I'm not allowed to say shit."

"Don't talk to me like that," he shouted.

Josie was startled, went stiff, and looked away.

"Paul, come on." Shelly inched toward Josie.

He rested on his heels and looked his wife in the eyes. Her expression had hardened. Did she really think he'd hurt his daughter?

"All we did was walk in, and you're immediately—"

"Don't start with me," Paul held up his hand. "I have enough fucking pressure right now. Will gives me a dead kid and rips away the other cases I've been agonizing over for weeks. He gave them to Hansen."

"Dead kid?" Josie's mouth dropped open.

"Paul!" Shelly's eyes were sharp as daggers.

He turned to his daughter. "Josie! Mom and Dad are talking."

"Wait," Shelly said. "Can't you ask Will to take you off it? Maybe he can take the case himself."

An immense weight pushed at the back of his skull, growing in intensity. How could he make it clearer? Couldn't she see? Shelly went to the other side of the island and pulled a box of chicken nuggets from the freezer. He had watched this scene countless times: his wife floating through the kitchen like a detached spirit. He watched her shake several pieces from the bag onto a metal tray, then dust crumbs into the palm of her hand. She avoided looking at him.

Heat welled up in his cheeks. Will didn't care. Shelly didn't care. It was him cradling a dead baby, in a room full of strangers. It would be him telling the mother to get a second job, to sell her car. He'd bring her life to a halt. A tremor formed in his bottom lip.

"I've already spoken to him," Paul snapped. "Do you think it's that simple, or that I haven't thought about it?"

She stopped arranging chicken nuggets and looked at him.

"Don't worry about it. I'm obviously interrupting." He turned and walked out.

"Paul. Wait!"

He heard her but kept going.

***

Dreading what would come next, Shelly pulled back her shoulders and followed Paul up the stairs. His usual modus operandi was to gloss over anything she said, compile it, and fling it back at her later. But she couldn't back off now.

In the office, Paul paced the room.

"That wasn't fair," she said. "I don't like being someone's punching bag."

He pivoted to face her. "Did you ever give me a thought today? Do you remember talking this morning about the plan?"

"Today is not my fault," Shelly said. "I juggle crazy clients all day, then come home to you and Josie. And I—"

"You're right," he said. "I'm mad at Will, but I'm also tired of my words bouncing off you and falling to the floor." He moved closer. "And I'm sick of you brushing off whatever the fuck is going on with me and disappearing into wherever you go, inside there." He tapped her forehead with his index finger.

A shock pulsed through her. His touch was hostile, rough.

Sensing her alarm, he quickly drew his hand back.

Shelly trembled; her hands filled with heat. She seethed from his physical breach. "You are not allowed to—" she started.

"I handle everything," he yelled, hands up and standing taller. "I juggle things too." He turned, shoving the desk chair out of the way.

Anxiety climbed up through her center, bracing for a fight. A familiar, squeezing sensation occluded her throat; each time it happened, she'd vow to power through. This time, she couldn't. She pulled at the skin and muscles under her chin.

"Now you're upset. Shit." With the back of his hand, he whacked a pile of papers from the desk onto the floor.

The sound was like a mallet coming down on her head. An icy chill surged over her body. The room was a trap. If she didn't leave now, someone would come for her. Her vision blurred. Lights flickered in her peripheral.

Paul's image became translucent, obscured by the silhouette of someone else, someone whose eyes were laden with malice. Shelly had stood under this towering shadow before. Cries bounced from the walls. She backed towards the door. The ground moved underfoot, and the walls became fuzzy. She battled in her mind. *Use your skills. Slow your body down.*

Paul called her name from far away, but she couldn't answer. The hard end of the doorknob hit her hip. Her escape blocked, she panted and huffed as she twisted the knob. When it wouldn't open, she pounded on the door. Her flashback took over. She was powerless against the memories and sensations flowing in.

Yelling, so loud. It's still shaking the walls. Yellow above my head. Jars with no lids. Oh, the smell. Pull in tight, knees to chest. It's safer, the smaller you are. Someone's coming.

Shelly pressed her head against the wood, still trying to pull the knob. "Let me out!" she screamed.

Chapter Five

Each muscle felt primed. The rain beat down as the storm hovered over him, his own private hurricane. Alone, John saw no other riders on the stretch. He rode fast, but torrents hit like tiny bullets, seeping through his clothes and into his bones. Tires sloshed spit from the road in his direction. His waterlogged pants were heavy on his knees, but he pumped his legs harder. His knuckles ached from blasts of cold air, but his locked grip remained tight.

Stopping at a light, he made every effort to remain calm, twisting the handlebars as water dripped from the bill of his helmet. A strong orange beacon lit him from behind, like a firework thrown across the pavement. Sophia had helped latch it to his seat, wanting him to be visible and safe—even though she was going to crush his soul in a matter of weeks. His mind went back to that moment in the apartment, the void, the emptiness. Each footstep had echoed across the hardwood. Nothing but blank walls and dead air, except for the shattered remnants of their lives together.

John had texted Hunter, pretending nothing was wrong. It had to be a mistake. The jacket was a coincidence. When he rode up, Hunter would open the garage door and they'd play ping-pong and have a drink. But when Hunter didn't reply, it led to more texts, followed by angry calls.

John racked his brain for signs. He could visualize Sophia's big green eyes gleaming as she smiled between sips of beer, the three of them eating nachos or playing cards or a game of pool. Sophia, with her wavy blonde hair braided and swooped over her shoulder, would sit by John, her smooth fingers on his arm. Everything was fine. Why hadn't she said something, warned him she wasn't okay?

A honk jolted him back to the street and the rain. John kicked at the pedals and moved through the traffic light.

The city street was crammed thick with cars, and he noticed a familiar force—vehicles hovering close behind but hesitant to pass. Other drivers didn't give a shit. They hugged his pocket, his zone, and zipped past with a rush of air and water. John usually adhered to general cycling etiquette, staying close to the edge and waiting for cars to swerve around when they got a chance. Today was different. He narrowed his eyes and dropped his head, pedaling faster, ignoring the three-thousand-pound metal projectiles encroaching.

"Hit me. Go ahead," he yelled as they passed. John sensed another car coming near, the low-pitched hum of the engine behind his left shoulder. He resisted the urge to pull into the lane and spook the driver, forcing him to slam on the brakes and swerve. But who would care? Not his mother or sisters. Not Sophia. How long had she been lying? How many times had she fucked him and then Hunter?

Another car approached; another driver too nervous to pass. In his helmet mirror, John saw a truck, looming like heavy breath on his neck. Something about the truck driver's indecision incensed him. The tension lifted him up off the seat; his jaw clenched, and his hands tingled.

"Idiot, just pass! Why are you staying behind me when there's nothing stopping you?" His leg muscles screamed, but he forced himself to pedal faster. John turned, stared down the truck driver, deliberate enough for his glare to be visible through the rain. As predicted, the driver held his position.

He was filled with visions of violence, of pulling the guy from his truck, smashing fists into his eyes, kicking him in the chest and stomach. John extended his middle finger, and the driver sped ahead, spraying him with mud and water. The pellets showered his cheeks and shins. He tried to steady himself as the truck passed, but adrenaline shook through his frame, making him weave. Tears filled his eyes. Grit and mud itched his skin.

***

John shivered, ashamed to be there.

Hunter's duplex rested in the corner of a cul-de-sac next to a park. The narrow building butted up against two other units, perfect for a college student or, in Hunter's case, a part-time data entry associate with an insurance group. The park to the left stood vacant except for soccer goals and mud puddles on an old baseball diamond. John walked towards the building, drenched and covered in mud. His fingers were cold, and his soaked clothes clung to his body.

When he made it to the porch, he could see Sophia in his mind, cupping her hand around Hunter's neck and laughing in his ear. He started to panic—he wasn't ready. He didn't want it to be true. The possibility of losing two of the most important people in his life in one day ripped the air from his lungs. But then the latch clicked.

Reality hit like a boulder dropped into his gut. Her face peered out, and slowly, she stepped forward.

"Sophia?"

She stepped outside, wearing the shirt she'd bought at their first concert together. The teal color offset her rosy skin tone and brilliant eyes. He recalled telling her that the first time she'd worn it. Today was a different story. She scanned the scene beyond him, looking around the complex. Hugging her shoulders, she avoided his gaze.

Finally, she looked at him. "I think Hunter should be here if we talk," she said. Her foot was positioned to keep the door cracked. "It's better that way."

"Fuck you," he said. "With Hunter? He's my best friend." He squared his shoulders and leaned forward, causing her to step back. "How long?"

She held up her hands in defense. "John," she pleaded. "What difference does that make?"

"It matters to me."

She paused, searching his face until her tense expression melted. "The New Year's party."

"New Year's?" His voice cracked. Ten months? He'd had too much to drink and ended up passing out on a friend's couch.

"Wait. Did you leave with him?"

"It got too hard, John. I couldn't handle you, the paranoia, the jealousy, your constant need to be reassured." Her eyes blazed.

"No. You're not putting this on me. Did you leave with him?"

Sophia looked at the ground; strands of her hair flowed past her lips.

"You're a dirty whore!" His breaths came heavily, but he felt composed. "You wrote that you understood why I, 'act this way.'" He pulled the note from his wet coat, crumpled it, and threw it at her feet. "So—tell me!"

"What good will this do?" Sophia's signals were clear. Her lips thinned, and her brow dipped towards the bridge of her nose. She wanted him to go away, but he was not going to let her off so easily.

"You have no idea what it's like to roll your boyfriend into a tub," she said. "Puke everywhere—in the car, the driveway. Leaving me with the mess to clean up." Sophia leaned in, rocking with each angry word. "Every time you had more than a few ounces of alcohol, you turned into a jealous freak. Always questioning. Always lurking, checking my phone." She paused, analyzing him.

John could tell something gathered in her mouth; words latched to the tip of her tongue. "If you have more to say, spit it out!"

Her eyes flashed wide. "Fine. I'm not going to pick up the pieces of your broken ego. You have things to deal with John, and it's not my job to hold you together." She cocked her head to the side. "You were trashed again. Making sure you're okay—that's all I was there for. I don't want to be someone's mother!"

Her words were like a punch in the face, and he braced himself against the swell of her energy.

"I need to be with an adult, someone who can take care of *me* too."

The corners of his vision darkened, tunneling. *She's throwing you away. She hates who you are.* His body stiffened. *Skinny little bitch and her rich parents. Little bitch, little bitch.* Joanne's obese figure overlapped with Sophia's, hair flowing over her dark eyes. Together, their mouths became one, creating the same psychotic smile.

"I don't need you to be my fucking mom." He fixated on her glare. "You think Hunter loves you? You think he'll treat you right? He does nothing but take advantage of girls. Don't be surprised if he throws you away like trash, like the useless slut you are."

Suddenly, he wanted to hurt her as much as she had hurt him.

"I can't do this, John!" She waved him away and started to close the door.

A fuse lit in him. He kicked the door, knocking Sophia into a side table. A moan collided with the sound of crashing wood and glass. She rolled over to look up at him, panic etched on her face. Pawing at the ground, she struggled to crawl away.

"You can't do this to me," he screamed. "Where's Hunter now?" Foaming at the mouth with each syllable, he moved on her as she continued to kick backwards frantically.

John had never felt like this, being on the other side, towering over someone weaker, taking control. Then, as if something within him released its hold, he stopped and slumped. His vision cleared, and he saw Sophia cowering in a ball at his feet. Tears mixed with blood dripped from her nose. He rubbed his temples as another trickle of crimson leached slowly down the side of her face.

She lifted a trembling hand to touch her head. "John, please don't hurt me." The rose-colored heat left her cheeks, and as her skin became ice white; her eyes floated as if she might pass out.

What am I doing? Look at what you're doing.

His knees buckled, and he held out his hands. "Sophia. I didn't mean for you to fall, all right?" His rage had gone too far, and he didn't want to be a monster. He knew about monsters.

But she wasn't listening. Sobbing uncontrollably, she shrank from his extended arm, her body shaking.

Slowly, he backed out of the apartment. "I'm sorry. I'm leaving. Soph! I'm leaving." He turned and ran toward his bike. What had he done? The rain continued to pour, coating him. John grabbed his bike, hopped on and pedaled fast, trying to get as far away as he could.

Chapter Six

Shelly's eyes closed for a moment—a moment which led to hours. Tears salted the corners of her eyes and rubbing them felt like sandpaper. She had declined Paul's offer of dinner, partly because she was not hungry and partly to avoid him. The den seemed inviting with its windows facing the front yard. A quiet, small space that often went neglected, just enough room for the oversized chair and bookshelves. She covered up with a soft throw blanket, trying to relax and think over what had happened while her husband and her daughter dined without her.

She touched the window beside her, a cold pane chilled by the weather. Outside, large homes with manicured yards stretched in a line. The scene always left her humble. The rundown house she grew up in had holes in the drywall, a patchy lawn, and tire rims and trash bags outside the garage. They'd rarely had a working vehicle. During the last joy ride with her mother, the brakes failed in their Fiat, sending them careening through an intersection. The defective Uno was left abandoned where it died and did not decorate their front yard as others had. Shelly sighed, dropping her hand into her lap. The evening had vanished; the sidewalk was lit by streetlights. Paperwork and emails raced through her mind, snuffing out her energy, like hands holding her down. The long list of things to do was daunting, and as she did with every panic cycle, she tried to trace where she'd left off. Then a stronger urge arose—she just wanted to sleep.

She climbed out of the armchair and tossed the blanket down. Making her way to her daughter's room, she let a hand brush the cream-painted wall, smooth under her fingertips. The carpet was soft under her toes. The smell of lilac and vanilla drifted from scattered plug-ins. No sour smells, no sopping wetness existed. It was a hallway of Shelly's creation yet brought little comfort. Her fingers brushed sections of unfinished paint, left over from Paul's stalled progress. It held the same texture as the bubbled tarnished plaster that haunted her therapy sessions, an image which flashed incessantly with every pass. A stain dotted the light-colored carpet fibers at her feet. Grape juice that Josie sloshed on a scramble to the bathroom during potty training. The view of it looked red rather than purple. The red of her nightmares.

She'd always had some anxiety, but it worsened severely when she became a mother. As she touched the doorknob to Josie's room, she winced with the return of a familiar thought: *It would be easy to disappear, and her family might be better off.* Nausea formed in the pit of her stomach, and she sighed, frustrated with herself.

Cracking the door, she crept in quietly and curled up next to the sleeping child. Josie had become her touchstone on hard nights. Was it fair for Josie to be her anchor, a child who pulled her mother back from the depths? It was a heavy burden to bear for one so young.

Josie stirred slightly, and Shelly remained still. The ceiling was covered with glow-in-the-dark stickers of stars and moons. The room glowed purple, with clouds painted in each of the corners. The little dresser was splattered top to bottom with decals of hearts and flowers. Old dolls and stuffed animals sat on the rocking chair—a teddy bear, My Little Pony, and a pink, fluffy elephant. Next to it, the glow of a tiny nightlight showed the dotted curtains bordering each side of the petite window. A diminutive, pastel oasis.

Draped over the cherrywood rocking chair in the corner was a baby blanket embroidered with bluebirds. The iridescent stitching sparkled and brought a vivid image back to Shelly of standing in the kitchen, holding Josie at six months old. A cloth had been draped over Shelly's shoulder to catch spit-up, while she'd tried to open a can one-handed. She slipped, slicing her finger. Blood wept from the skin. What seemed like a moment later, her hands were on the chain-link fence at the front gate, as the sound of hydraulic brakes expelled from a passing bus. She had no idea how she had gotten there. Worse yet, Josie wasn't with her.

Back in the house, she'd found Josie asleep in bed. Not injured, not crying, not cold. The decorative bluebird blanket, a perfect square beneath her tiny body. Shelly had no memory of how the baby got there, either. The sight of blood had sent her to another place.

Shelly closed her eyes. Josie lay inches from her now. Yet, she seemed just as vulnerable as when she was an infant.

"Mom?"

"Yeah, baby?" she whispered. "Sorry, did I wake you?" She didn't want to disturb her sleep but would much rather stay there than spend another tense night with Paul.

Josie turned over and rested her head on Shelly's shoulder. "Mom, why do you get scared?"

The question caught her off guard. Could Josie have heard them yelling?

"Mom?"

Shelly knew her answer, with all its complexities, would be impossible for Josie to understand. The burden was hers. "Yes, I'm afraid sometimes."

"About what?"

"I worry about you and Dad. I worry about all of us. Why do you ask, baby?" Josie didn't answer, and Shelly watched her drift in and out, snuggled into the gap between her shoulder and the pillow. She eyed Josie's honey-colored skin, her blush-pink lips partially opened, and the blonde strands stuck to her forehead with night-time sweat. She touched her hair, brushing it gently out of the way.

If anyone knew how fucked up I am. Shelly pressed her lips together, fighting a burning desire to weep. *I've thought of all the ways I'd kill them, anyone who tried to take you or hurt you. How it would feel to bite off an ear, and what their blood would taste like. I'd pull the skin from their cheeks with my nails and watch them scream.*

Josie blinked heavily and forced her eyes open. "You looked sad, and so did Daddy." She yawned. "I asked why, and he said you were scared. I don't want you to be scared, okay?"

"Okay, baby. I'll try. Go to sleep. You've got school in the morning."

Shelly rolled onto her back. She'd like to sleep but thought of many neglected tasks downstairs. More than anything, she didn't want to deal with Paul. He had a skewed view of her limits. Despite witnessing her panic and knowing her past, he pressed for some kind of resolution where there was none. He sought a way forward, regardless of her inability to provide it. She resisted and wanted to run from him—an urge she shouldn't have about her husband.

Light streamed in from the hallway, where Paul stood silhouetted by the glow. Shadows ran up the walls—dark figures, outcasts from the luminosity of the outside world.

"What are you doing?" he whispered. "Aren't you coming to bed?"

"Not yet." She held her breath, scared of what his presence in the room would bring. Her body was still as she waited for his reaction. Would he posture or retreat? She hoped for the latter and knew he wouldn't leave her alone if she came out. He would restart their earlier conversation, peppering her with more questions and detailing her many errors. But she already knew she was broken. There wasn't more to discuss. Was it reassurance he was after? *I did it*, she thought. *It was me. I'm to blame for our marriage coming to a halt.*

She gazed at him, her hand blocking some of the light.

Slowly, he shook his head, closed the door, and walked away.

Chapter Seven

Paul stirred against an unfamiliar feeling. Moving his hand down, he discovered he still wore the condom. The chill in the room matched the cold he'd felt the night before. Goosebumps dotted his skin, and the thin, hotel sheets provided little warmth.

He stared at the popcorn ceiling and faux-wood fan. The smell of cigarettes filled the room—musty, yet reminiscent of the smell that always lingered in his grandmother's home, a chain-smoker to the end of her life. Tobacco mixed with rose, floral but faint. A sour taste filled his mouth, and pain bounced between his temples.

Next to Paul, a sleeping stranger stirred—Ellen. *Was that her name?* She was twenty-seven. No, twenty-eight. She drank almost as much as he had. Where did she say she had moved from? He couldn't remember. He turned and stared at her long hair against the pillows. Her chestnut-brown waves traveled over her shoulders and exposed breasts. Air passed through her lips; she appeared to be in a deep and peaceful slumber.

"Shit," he whispered. Inside, he screamed. He slid to the edge of the bed. His skin hung like a stiff crust, dirty and soiled. The room was dark except for a window trimmed with gray drapes. Sparse light drifted in, casting a quilt of shadows. A desk, a chair, and a bed. Each corner filled. The decor, muted orange and brown with a splash of avocado, was straight out of the seventies. His clothes were strewn around, his shoes near the wall where they had been kicked off. He was still wearing socks.

The memories of the night were blurry, but not enough to escape the guilt. The naked body next to him was evidence enough of what had taken place. It was wrong, but he had done it anyway.

Flashes of memory rushed in. The bar was vacant when he arrived, lethargic and dimly lit. The only stimulation came from the sports channel playing on a mounted television. Wood-paneled walls stretched from ceiling to floor. Behind the bartender, a wall of bottles and taps for any persuasion. He wanted to take the edge off and calm down. Scotch sounded right.

Two drinks in, he was feeling more mellow, and his lungs spread, granting him extra capacity to breathe. He'd been able to distract himself with the soccer highlights, but when he finally looked around, people had gathered. Laughter mixed with reactions from the sports fans. His thoughts drifted to the realities of the next day, work and home and Shelly.

I should have left. Quit before anything happened.

For sure, she would leave him and take Josie with her. He would if the roles were reversed.

Across the hotel room, the cheap, plastic clock on the bedside table showed four-thirty in the morning. He picked up his cell phone from the floor next to his jeans and looked at the screen. No calls. Half of him hoped there was a text from Shelly, an effort to check in, even if he didn't deserve it. He grabbed his pants from the floor. Where had he and his wife fallen apart? What catalyst separated them? Ending up in a seedy bedroom with a stranger had never been a temptation or an urge, even when he felt the sting of his resentment. It had just happened. A cliché.

Ellen? Hainsworth. The haze in his brain started to clear. She'd never been to that bar before. She had moved to the area a month earlier.

Paul enjoyed her laughter and warmth. He liked the attention, her undivided attention. She had cute bangs that came to her eyebrows, and a carefree spirit and lighthearted manner that was as intoxicating as scotch. She complimented his hair. She loved rugged Portland men with beards, she said. Her words lingered, making Paul stand taller, more confidently. He felt a sense of reconnection with his old self, the competent, proud self that had been buried deep inside.

Standing in the hotel room, phone in hand, he mourned his history with Shelly. The blank phone screen signaled their lost connection and the ways they had drifted away from each other. He had only distant memories of her compliments or fingers on his cheek, the curve in the small of her back as he slid a hand around her waist. The love they'd once had, their true enjoyment of each other, was fading fast. His grip tightened on the phone. His reflection was tired and pale, haggard.

"This wasn't the plan," he said under his breath, hating the sight of himself. One impulsive trip to the bar could destroy his family. He put the phone into his pocket and looked out the window at the dimmed lights in the parking lot. Watching the sleeping woman sprawled across the bed, he had absolutely no idea what to do.

He gathered the items tossed about in their drunken frenzy. As he pulled on his coat, she stirred beneath the sheets, and a leg moved across the bed, exposing more bare skin. Paul cringed, closing his eyes. Vivid details of sex with her emerged like a sudden migraine. Despite his knuckles pushed into his eyes, the images remained. Her tongue grazing his lips, strips of light shining across her breasts as she moved rhythmically above him. Each second brought more scenes, as though he was watching porn, the sordid images of his betrayal. The air seemed muggy, making it hard to breathe, and his feet were cemented to the ground, paralyzed by indecision.

He tried to convince himself that he could make things right. He'd be home before his family woke up, wouldn't he? He closed the door quietly and stepped into the brisk, early morning air. As he walked towards his car, he thought of ways to avoid the reality of the night. He and Shelly had fought. He went to the bar and slept on a friend's couch. Nothing more.

When Paul crept into the house, it was five-fifteen. He went to the spare room and undressed in the bathroom. The warmth of the shower ran over his body, kicking up the woman's rosy scent and with each whiff, the pit in his stomach grew. As the effect of the alcohol subdued, he tried to ignore sensations on his skin, lips against his neck and fingers trailing across his abdomen. That scent, ever-present, filled his nostrils. Would Shelly notice it; would she track the pheromones of the other woman, now steamed into the atmosphere of their home?

He scrubbed his body and turned up the temperature. The water was almost scalding. He tried to scrub the odor off, but it burned into the back of his sinuses. Between his feet, the current swirled into the mouth of the drain, and he wished his body would dissolve into pieces, disappearing with the dead skin and hair into the sewer. He wanted to free himself of the filth and stench of his actions. The water covered his head and cascaded over his face, cleansing the impurities of his thoughts, leaving a spotless yet harsh reality. These were his sins, and no matter how much he scrubbed or how hot the water, Shelly and Josie deserved better.

Chapter Eight

John stood at the store window, looking at the parking lot of the strip mall. His bloodshot eyes stung from the fatigue of a restless night. He had submitted to insomnia and had gone to work early, not knowing where else to go.

All night, he remembered Sophia's panicked face as she tried to get away; the images repeatedly snapping him out of his REM cycle. His texts declaring his love remained unread and unanswered. He was mindful of saying much more in case she called the cops. He didn't want to provide a written confession about what she'd been subjected to the day before. John felt stifled, unable to communicate his regret. He wanted her to believe he wasn't the monster she witnessed. He wanted to believe it as well.

When rage took hold, things went dark, his eyes tunneled, and everything faded to black. Explosive fights and broken furniture had been a common occurrence in his youth. His mother chastised him, talked about the devil coming from his fingers, his mouth. Based on yesterday's sickening performance, she had not been wrong.

Even worse—many calls and texts from Hunter. Every expletive and degrading comment paralleled John's own self-loathing. At times, Hunter screamed so loudly, the phone relayed the words as a robotic, distorted sound. John deleted several threatening voicemails, all warning of a gruesome death if he ever went near Sophia again. With each vibration, each piercing ring of the phone in his pocket, he was reminded of the harsh reality that their friendship was over too.

His mother's calls topped all others. Since he had hung up on her, her wrath was unleashed. In the past, rejections had intensified her lunacy. She'd act out, repeatedly call him at work or show up at his house.

Once, his mother had arrived unannounced at the fast-food restaurant where he'd been working. He was flipping burgers in the back when he'd heard her loud voice at the front-end cashier. Joanne wore a teal green dress, low cut and exposing the top part of her breasts, with her hair in dual buns on either side of her head and long, hippie-style beaded earrings. Far from her Sunday best, she looked like a total spectacle, given her two hundred thirty-pound frame and five-ten stature.

"My big boy, working so hard," she said in a high-pitched shriek when she saw him. He'd wanted to drown himself in the hot oil. On her way out, she slipped and hit the floor with full force. She screamed and flailed about, all an act. He recalled her fat legs parting and her dress bunching up above her torso, exposing the rolls of skin and the flimsy fabric of her underwear. He had to leave work after she refused an ambulance. In the car, she'd leaned close to deliver the real message.

Just as it had in his youth, he saw his own withdrawn expression framed in her glasses. Past the rims, her round face, flushed blotchy cheeks, and quivering lips, hovered inches away. A stink of stale liquor flicked at his nostrils. "Maybe you'll remember the importance of celebrating birthdays," she had said, spraying saliva. "I could have died today."

He watched her, his mind churning. It was her birthday, and not calling to admire her day of birth had earned him retribution.

Coping with his mother's volatile nature was a struggle for his whole family. His mother professed to believe in purity, complete trust in the Lord, and traditional family values. John called it, Sunday Charades, he and his siblings lined up on a bench to hear God's word—or rather, to hear a random person read the scripture and claim it as a message from a higher power. John, his two sisters, and his parents were at church every Sunday, displaying zero doubt about their devotion—at least, publicly.

John could not say he had ever believed; he'd always seen through hypocrisy and lies. Under the pretense of living as servants of Christ, his family showed faithful constancy week after week. Unfortunately, their displays of violence within the home contradicted their Mormon values. Early on, physical punishments were inflicted by his father, though to a lesser degree, and stopped only because he died early in John's childhood. John's mother took over from there. A bitter and hateful woman, she claimed her abuse was to teach him the importance of respect. Mostly, he received punishments for being a reminder of his father's existence. As he grew up, he started to fight back and ran away often. As an adult, he tried to keep his distance for his own survival.

His two remaining sisters seemed to have made it out relatively unscathed. They went to college, got jobs, and acquired money to run farther than their mother could travel to disrupt their lives. Seemingly impervious to the after-effects of violence, each sister had disappeared. Maybe he had made it out as well? Who could say what elements were required for self-preservation? He knew it would not have been possible if not for Ashley.

John's stepsister, Ashley, was his father's daughter from another marriage. And he considered her the only light in his early life. She and John had been close, closer than anyone else. The only welcome memories he had of his childhood were with her. Until she disappeared. Ashley hadn't been seen by any of them in thirteen years.

Too many thoughts spun in his brain, with no time to trip over family baggage. He shook his head to clear it, waiting for the click of the electronic locks to signal that the shop was open for business.

Two hours later, he was about to make his first sale of the day.

"The most important thing about a camera is the person holding it," John announced with confidence, parroting something he had heard during training.

His customer held a Nikon D3500, an exceptional camera. But true to the monotony at Snap Pros, the person holding it—by John's standards, at least—had limited skills and, surely, would use little of the camera's potential, wasting his money when a cell phone camera would probably meet his needs. John endured the man, who groped the expensive camera like a bowling ball, because even ignorant customers helped pay his bills. Sales meant commission, period. As the customer snapped useless pictures of props around the store, his satisfied nods and nervous fidgets were easy to read. John threw out unnecessary details about the various settings—features the man would never use. Next, he would explain the zoom and lighting, then close the deal.

As he chatted with the Nikon buyer, his boss walked in. Surprise visits were not his style, and John's heart thumped in his throat. Bob worked when he wanted, which really meant never. The store operated with the same, regular crew—John on the closing shift, and his buddy, Allen, during the day. Bob's rotation as a district manager included this store, but no one put out the red carpet or called the news stations. There'd been no hint of his visit.

"Bob! How's it going?"

The boss nodded slightly and walked by.

John smiled halfheartedly, watching the manager walk behind the counter. *Does he remember my name?* Although he tried to appear unaffected by his boss's presence, his eyes darted about, monitoring Bob's location, looking for signs of aggravation. As he pulled out a zoom lens to show the customer, a cabinet slammed. The higher-ups had no reason to be there, stalking him, without a customary call or fair warning. Something was wrong. Could Sophia have called his employer? Maybe she told them a madman worked in their shop.

"I'm going to buy this." The customer jolted him back to reality.

Immediately, John jumped back into his role as a salesman, realizing the man still existed, and closed the deal.

"Good choice. You'll have great pictures, and since it's digital, you can move these to your laptop for easy printing." His pulse quickened as he rang in the purchase. More commission meant more recognition.

John wrapped up the Nikon and returned the displays to their platforms. As he put things back in place, Bob approached, dampening his buzz over the sale. He tried to look busy to hide his nerves.

"John! Nice Nikon sale. Hey, do you have a second?"

"Sure thing." His pulse jumped but he feigned calm, walking light-footed to the back room. Along the way, he straightened merchandise while his heart pounded, and he fought the emotions competing within him. Bob walked before him, his dropped shoulders and wide head like a target. John wondered if he appeared flushed, whether culpability was etched in the engorgement of capillaries across his face. He wondered whether he could keep himself in check.

Chapter Nine

Shelly's eyes focused on the bold lines of the road, the white dashes down the middle, one after the other, like a heartbeat, like a stop motion film. She was in familiar waters, unable to pivot or make decisions, paralyzed by life. Her eye twitched, and her eardrums pulsed. There were too many critical tasks and too many neglected projects. Her vision began to tunnel, distorting everything in her periphery. Just a blur of orange and gold leaves abused by rain. How could she get through this, salvage her marriage, and stop scaring the shit out of her kid?

The rhythmic kick of Josie's foot against the seat, in tune with the gravel pelting the undercarriage of the car, pulled her back.

"Don't kick the seat," she snapped unintentionally. Josie said nothing. Shelly hoped to talk more about yesterday, and what she saw. Her daughter would not hold back when upset. Shelly knew that.

She had ended up sleeping in Josie's bed all night. When her eyes fluttered open that morning, she saw the pale green hues of Mars and Jupiter floating overhead. Her shirt was drenched in sweat, the sheets damp underneath her. Luckily, Josie hadn't woken when Shelly scampered to the bathroom.

As always, they were running late. She had opened her laptop long enough to finish the offer for Judith. Despite her frustration with the buyers, it would be Shelly's fault if she lost this bid. Then she rushed Josie through the standard routine—eat, get dressed, brush teeth—so she could get out the door without dealing with Paul.

He had not come downstairs, even for coffee. A clean getaway. But the sense of relief was followed by guilt, which crushed her lungs like the heel of a boot. She should have gone to him and offered support. But she had not tried. Instead, she'd hid to avoid his all-consuming energy. When had they changed? Better yet, when had *she* changed?

Shelly puffed her cheeks and slowly released her breath as she worked the steps to remind herself of the actuality. Tree—green, road—dark, sky—gray. Not the most uplifting mantra, and on a morning like this, words provided little comfort.

She turned on the radio and found a music channel Josie liked. As usual, her daughter had created a masterpiece with her attire. She wore her grandmother's original teal hat, as she often did, but this morning, the combination involved a purple sweater with a giant penguin on the front. Her blonde hair lit up in contrast, shining brightly against the arctic-themed shirt. A pair of pants dotted with little stars completed the look. She looked like a Monet painting.

"Days you'd run hot and cold," Josie belted off-key. She missed a good majority of the words but sang confidently anyway, mumbling through the lyrics like she was performing for the Grammys.

Then, as it did every trip, the road turned up ahead. Shelly flicked off the radio.

"Hey," Josie protested.

She squeezed the wheel. Eyes peeled. Ready. Every mile exposed the potential for tragedy. Ditches flanked both sides of the highway. A significant drop-off and an embankment on the left was an easy place to crash, sucked in by thick mud.

A large pond around a curve brought anxiety-fueled hallucinations; she and Josie had crashed there—in her mind—more times than she could count. As they passed, she pictured the ice-covered waters of early winter sliding across the hood of her car, splashing over the roof and covering the windows.

In one of their recent sessions, Dr. Frazier-Velli mentioned control. Shelly's anxiety attempted to predict the future, every angle or breach, to prevent Josie's death. There was evidence of this everywhere. Flood lights on the garage. Double locks on every door. In her glove box, a tool to cut seat belts and break windows—useful when icy winter ponds engulfed the car.

Shelly rubbed her forehead. Focus. Go forward. The time to speak with Josie grew shorter; they were only minutes from school.

"Josie, sweetie?" She swallowed hard. "You said something last night. You said I was scared. Can you tell me what you meant?" She glanced in the rearview mirror, scanning her face for any changes.

"I don't know." The girl shrugged, bouncing her feet.

Shelly had a rush of relief, but it was short-lived.

"Mom, why does Daddy yell? He yelled and yelled. I thought he was silly, and I told him." Her forehead creased. "Was he frustrating with you?"

"Frustrated, you mean?"

"Yes! frustrated," she tried again. "Mommy? Did you make him mad?" Her finger drew in the condensation at the base of the window, as the heat around them met the chill of the glass. She twirled a heart in the droplets.

Shelly smiled in the mirror.

"Daddy was mad. I don't like that either," she said. "His boss is being mean."

She wondered if she enabled him. Paul having a scapegoat only perpetuated the problem. Shelly didn't know what to say to Josie about his anger or misdirected resentment, or the fact that he had erupted in front of Josie. A snap of tension shot through her shoulders but loosened as she gave the memory more consideration. She'd been guilty of this exact sin—blaming him for something that wasn't his fault, snapping at him for no reason. She wondered what excuses he'd had made about her. She was the one responsible for their strain, sucking everyone into her illness.

Hearing her phone, which had been buzzing throughout the drive, she moved her purse closer and fumbled one-handed through it while keeping her eyes on the road.

Josie giggled, catching Shelly's eyes in the mirror. "Mom, you were silly, sleeping in my bed. Can we do that every night?"

"No, baby. I—"

"Who's Red, Mommy?"

Startled, Shelly almost slammed on the brakes. "What did you say?"

Red was the little girl who haunted Shelly's dreams. Always hiding, always terrified and pursued. In her dreams, they ran. Shelly trailed steps behind her through dark corridors lined with crates or mounds of garbage. Sometimes they were in a hallway that never ended. When Shelly looked back to see who was pursuing them, she saw only shadow. Red wasn't talked about, not even with Paul. That was a slice of her irrational mind she kept to herself.

"When you were sleeping, I heard you say 'Red.'" Josie cocked her head to the side. "Then you said, 'Red, don't go in there.' Mom! You kept saying it until I pushed you."

In the mirror, she watched Josie hold up her hands, reenacting the push, complete with an intense grimace and elbow shooting to the right.

"I'm sorry you had to hear me," Shelly said carefully. Her insides sank. Red plagued her but should leave Josie alone. It was her ghost, not her daughter's.

Josie rolled her eyes. "It's okay. I have dreams too. You were really scared, Mommy. You hid under the bed." She giggled, covering her mouth. "I told you to come out. A monster could be under the bed. If I was a monster, I'd hide there. Duh, Mom."

Shelly's mouth went dry. *Under the bed.* In her dreams, Red would be dragged out first, then Shelly, while they kicked and screamed, clawing at the wood floor.

"Oh, baby," she said, controlling her voice. "I was silly, wasn't I? What silly adventures we have when we're asleep, huh?" Shelly couldn't think what to say. *Your mom is broken, baby.*

They approached the school, and she pulled up to the curb. As Josie gathered her backpack, Shelly checked her face in the mirror. Her eyes were red-rimmed and glassy. After a few quick wipes, she turned and flashed a grin.

"Love you, baby," she said. "Have a good day, okay?"

"Okay, Mom!"

"Wait, Josie." Shelly reached back, catching her wrist. So much more to say, to explain.

"You know I was only under the bed to fight off any monsters that were hiding, right?" She gripped her arm. "You know that. I will protect you from anyone who tries to hurt you."

"Mom." Josie's soft eyes widened, and her dainty mouth lowered in a frown. "Monsters aren't real." She hesitated for a second, looking into her mother's face, then she opened the door and ran off.

As tears spilled, Shelly looked over at the cars, lined up for drop-off and scattered throughout the parking lot. She partially covered her face, hoping no one would notice her sitting there.

Monsters are real. They're all around us.

Chapter Ten

The house slept. An eerie quiet filled the living room and in the dim light, shadows dripped from edges and corners. Paul pulled at the waist of his black sweatshirt, fidgeting and adjusting with each lap around the couch. The sleepiness he had felt earlier had dissipated. Instead, he paced, desperate for something to soothe his psyche. In each spin through the front room, he muttered under his breath, bargaining for his wife and child with the windows, light fixtures, and loveseat as if they were members of the jury, weighing the evidence along with his confession. He had already accepted his guilt but hoped for leniency.

It was six-thirty in the morning but felt like midnight. Paul had not slept more than two hours at the hotel. When he got home, he tried to nap on the couch, but Shelly's pragmatic spirit oozed from every surface. The gray and taupe wonderland mixed with light pink pillows on a brown corduroy sofa. A leather chair was partially covered by a knitted shawl. He could picture Shelly confirming its aesthetically pleasing position at a forty-five-degree angle from the window.

He closed his eyes, and images flooded in. The lingering sensation of Ellen's touch on his skin, the naked curve of her waist, the stiff, bleached sheets curled under the fleshiest part of her hips. Pleasure and pain in equal measure—then, seized by guilt, he thought about Josie.

Divorced men rarely keep a connection with their daughters; they grow apart. He'd seen it with friends, with coworkers. Josie wouldn't understand any of this for years, how people love and what happens when they stop. Had he stopped? Would his daughter accept him, flaws, and all? He dreaded the day she would ask: How could you?

Paul retreated to his office, the one place he could avoid the eyes of judgment. After picking up the messy pile of paper, he reopened the file on the infant mortality case and sorted through the documents. Leaning toward his computer, he hoped that engrossing himself in someone else's misery would distract from his own.

From the descriptions, the mediation had been tense, leading to zero middle ground. He looked through the documentation of grievances, starting with transcripts of the mother's statements during early discussions. During the latter part of the intercession conference, she had started yelling about her dead baby, cursing at the team and promising retribution. They called security as the mother shouted about litigation and pounded her fists on the table across from the hospital bigwigs.

His hand weaved back and forth along each sentence, hunched over the file as if analyzing a microscopic organism.

Notes from nurses outlined that the birth happened eighteen months prior; the mother arrived through the emergency room in active labor. Circumstances changed quickly, moving from vaginal delivery to a cesarean.

RN12: Mom pushed hard for a long time. She was vomiting, losing energy. I thought she would be a cesarean. With twins it's always possible, but I don't know who made the decision. One of the doctors. I stepped out. I don't recall.

RN18: I got the incubator set up for Twin B, but he was struggling. I set up the incubator, and we had the other baby to deal with. I would say everything moved fast. She ended up in the operating room—I'm sure the record details things, but I can't recall.

RN12: Doctor talking with patient about the birth plan. The baby is showing fatigue. Mother showing fatigue. Patient struggling to stop pushing through the assessment. Moderate pain. Doctor again at the bedside, counseling patient. Fluids hung and oxygen administered. Baby showing changes, decelerations started to level.

Paul summarized what he had read out loud. "She didn't want to have a cesarean, but she had concerning vitals, so they talked with her." Running his eyes up and down the page, he searched for the doctor's comments.

OB: Anxiety is up. Pain moderate but monitored. Contractions have frequency of 2-5 min. 40-60 seconds. No partner involvement. RN support provided. Fear about lack of progression. Provided routine options. Forceps brought concerns for tearing. Cesarean discussed.

He stopped in his tracks. "They called it routine, then the baby died." Calling something routine in the insurance world meant no emergency, and much less likely for the procedure to be covered.

The chart continued with a brief postmortem of the baby, followed by a social worker's assessment. Given the mother's grief and the circumstances of birthing a single baby when expecting twins, psychiatry visited the mother. From the notes: no father involvement; estranged before birth.

He exhaled. "She owes money. The hospital is owed money. She's not screaming about money."

Paul flipped back to the mediation notes: *Mother became irate. Demanding entire chart. Accusation of error in practice. Reminded of policy and procedures of fee for service. Mother removed from mediation.*

He opened his laptop and began drafting an email to Will, his fingers shuddered as they hit the keys. Because Will had cut him off on the phone earlier, offering absolutely no help with the history behind the case, Paul tried to calm his haste and irritation. A good part of him wanted to hand in his resignation and a photo of his middle finger. Instead, he mentioned the pieces that seemed to be missing from the file and asked Will to call him.

As he hit the send button, he heard Shelly's car.

Chapter Eleven

Shelly pulled into the driveway and looked up at the house. From the safe space of her car, it seemed easier to fall into the canyon between herself and Paul than to build a bridge. Nevertheless, she rehearsed what she would say.

Through the front window, she saw Paul sitting at the dinner table. Her heart thumped; heat formed in her cheeks. She closed her eyes and took a big breath. She had put it off long enough.

As she opened the door, silence filled the room. It was like entering a museum, as if someone would punish her irreverence if she spoke too loudly or clattered her keys. Gently, she put her stuff on the counter. Her phone, endlessly vibrating in her pocket, shook the edge of her coat and clicked against the zipper. Probably another client, an inspection or something else gone wrong.

Paul sat in the dark room in his faded Portland State University hoodie, with his hands under his chin. It was an inconsequential yet significant attire choice. When they moved in together, she'd found the hoodie and pulled it over her pregnant belly. He said he loved seeing her in it and would give the sweatshirt to Josie when she was old enough. Something seemed different about this present Paul; he was drab and tired. Puffiness bulged under his eyes. Dark shadows feathered over his nose. Josie's dishes were still on the table, which usually drove him nuts, but he sat calmly, staring straight ahead.

Shelly had always considered him attractive. He was tall with a broad frame, thick brown hair, and a beard. The image of younger Paul floated there, hovering, connected by a string, bobbing in the stale air until it faded to the reality of the downbeat figure before her. He even looked smaller now.

What's going on in there? Shelly could sense the tingle in her forehead again.

She took off her coat and sat down in front of him. He did not react. A sliver of paranoia dug at her brain. She expected his fist to shoot up and catch her in the temple, a foot to kick her stomach as she curled on the floor. The anxiety confused her; he had never been physical with her, not once. She bounced her leg under the table.

Shelly moved in closer and lowered her voice. "I don't mean to be, well, a mess. I'm trying—" She fiddled with her hands. What words should she use? She didn't even know the depths of her trauma. Countless hours sitting in front of professionals and not any nearer to a resolution, "—to find a sense of safety. I need to find security in things. It's not easy, Paul. Every step, every moment—"

"Stop," he said.

The words halted in her throat, and her stomach churned. *He might already be gone.* The thought squeezed her temples like hands gripping her skull. She noticed his chin quivering. When had he last shown such emotion? Then she remembered. Josie. When their daughter was born, Paul wept, saying again and again how he loved his girls. Josie, yes. He loved his daughter unconditionally, but could Shelly be sure of his love for her? They were like two strangers staring at each other across the table.

"Paul, I have to say—"

Before she could continue, he grabbed her hand.

"I know you get stuck sometimes," he said, searching her face. "Like last night in my office, and I know I should help you." He paused. "We need to talk about something." Color drained from his face.

Shelly leaned in, peering into his glassy eyes. He inched forward, his hand loosely holding her wrist, the softest of holds as if she would crumble. Dropping his gaze suddenly, he let go.

What's so hard to say? The question flushed her cheeks. "I want us to be close again," she said. "I'm scared about everything, and it's driving a wedge between us. Last night was the proof, a sign."

Paul's demeanor changed, a swooping release of tension through his frame. "I know I've been angry. That's not your fault." He paused and took her hand again. "I love you. I do. I've been so frustrated. Frustrated at you, myself. I don't know what I'm doing anymore."

Leaning back in his chair, he ran his hands through his hair. She saw a glimmer of the guy in the coffee shop, the confidence of his jaw, the white of his eyes holding up the greenish-blue center.

"I need you to let me talk," she said. She couldn't decide what was worse: Paul hearing the story or having to own it as her tale. "I didn't live with my parents as a child, you knew that." She squeezed her eyes closed, trying to calm her pulse. "When I was little, my father did something horrible." Each word held its place in the air. "Those memories are in bits and pieces, but when they surface, they all do. And it's really hard." Tears spilled quietly. Again, her past raised its head and began to gather, first in shadows, then sounds. Her hands gripped the table.

"I was Josie's age. It brings up things for me—bad with the good. I mean, Josie is perfect." She gave a small smile. "She's everything I hoped for, but she's also my greatest terror."

Paul shifted his weight on the chair and sat up taller. His features softened.

She paused a few seconds longer, knowing he wouldn't break the silence.

The cool table was under her fingertips. She closed her eyes. "I imagine Josie being taken from me, being forced to live without her, to watch her disappear. It kills me." Her head fell to the side with full knowledge of what he needed to understand, what he needed to hear. The concession, however, invited the past to come forward.

Chapter Twelve

Shelly sat on a bench at the edge of a park. Her coat was bundled, and a scarf hugged her throat. She'd been to the playground a dozen times, watched Josie running along with friends. Gold and red leaves swirled briefly in a field to the right as she eyed the soccer goalposts and frisbee-golf chandeliers. She had no clue what they were really called, but they peppered the green grass.

Without warning, a piercing scream shattered the tranquility. Shelly's head snapped back in time to see Josie slide down a large green tube. She emerged at the other end in a blur of motion. Her hair was a wild cascade mirroring the speed of her descent, while her purple fleece vest clung to her flowered tee shirt. Her jeans were dirtied at the knees.

Shelly squinted, shielding her eyes. She'd lost Josie in the glare of the sun. Then, in fractured pictures, she saw a heavy-set man with glasses under a tuff of trees. His clothes were dark and indistinct, and stood out against the vibrance of the earthy leaves and greens of the park. Her eyes narrowed, and as if pulled by a winch, she elevated to her feet.

The man walked towards Josie, his cold gaze fixed on her; he glided at a speed Shelly couldn't match. The sunrays glimmered from his lenses, flickering like Morse code. The message jolted Shelly to the core, like an arrow to her chest. She swallowed air and panted through fear, bringing her fist to her sternum. The man's shoulders widened, and his body stretched and reached higher and higher into the sky. Josie looked miniature in his shadow.

"Run, Josie!" Shelly reached out as her daughter began screaming.

Paul's voice surfaced, as though someone had flipped a light switch after hours of pitch black. She saw her hands, flat against the table. Perspiration gathered at the back of her neck, dampening her hair. Had it been seconds or minutes? What had she said?

He studied her with a calm expression. "I know you worry, but she's safe."

He didn't get it. Smile. Nod. Leave. Her body cooled. He believed her anxiety was so easy to contain, to muffle. This usually closed the door on their conversations. She would get up and walk away, pour coffee or turn on the TV. Anything but talk. Paul was wrong. There was no easy solution, and her worry was not benign.

"Paul! I can't shut it off." The way she said his name made him stop. An inner scream, like hail on a glass. "It's not that simple."

She delivered the brutal details of her past while Paul listened—passively at first, then with greater intensity, as she divulged each horrifying memory. The fractured, slivered images of her mother thrown against the wall, young Shelly trying to stand up and fight back. The attacker was her father, although she could never see his face. She only recalled her mother's pleas for him to stop and the shadows he cast on the walls, the floor. As she told her husband about these episodes, she left out key details—hiding even now as she did then. She'd cower under the bed for hours until it was safe to come out, until her mother came to get her.

Paul took in every word, listening to his wife describe her greatest fears: Josie's vulnerability and unknown dangers lurking in corners, behind trees, beneath waves, ready to snatch their daughter from their lives. She explained how her life was dominated by insomnia, anxiety, and panicked driving, how she only found enjoyment when they were safe at home.

But Shelly had more to tell, so much more. The words cemented to the back of her throat, and she couldn't bring herself to explain the blood or the urine, or how she visualized it, sensed it, tasted it. She felt a sting of deception for not stripping all the way down and revealing everything about her past. But she hoped this small stride would help her husband to understand.

Suddenly, her stomach cramped, and a burning sensation built in the back of her esophagus. She ran to the sink and let her body release into the basin. Paul came to her side, and she turned and hugged him.

Gently, he brushed her hair from her face. "I want to be *us* again," he said. "Don't let my fumbling with words or idiotic attempts—"

Shelly held her breath.

"I wish I had what you needed," he said. "But when you act like you did last night, when this comes over you—I wish I knew what to do, but nothing seems to help." He shrugged. "I'm sorry I can't be what you need. I'm lost, useless."

"I'm not asking you to save me," she said. "You can't. I'm the only one who can get through this." With a rush of courage, she threw out an idea. "But I know something that would help us talk to each other." She hesitated as a mix of sensations fluttered in her stomach, hope dancing with fear. "Come to a session with me. Dr Frazier-Velli knows so much, and it might be what we need."

Every time she had suggested it before, he would blow it off, but to her surprise, he put his arms around her and smiled warmly.

"Yes," he said. "I love you, and I love Josie. I think we need some help, and I don't want to mess things up more than I already have."

Shelly smiled but instead of letting relief take over, a flash of warning surfaced. "What do you mean, already have—" She stopped as she looked at him. Were his eyes watering?

He took her hand.

"Is it Will and the stuff at work?" She put her hands on his chest. "You can talk to me."

Paul didn't speak for a moment but when he did, he seemed to be fighting to control his breath. "I don't want to mess this up. I might lose you, lose Josie."

"No," she leaned back to look at him better. "We're still here."

He pulled her back and kissed her, a gentle brush of lips that quickly increased to more. She had not felt his kiss in what seemed like years. Somehow, they had drifted into parallel lives and were no longer united by anything but their daughter. Her body warmed as an intense, sensual heat moved down her frame, hovering at each muscle. She kissed him back, her hands gripping his neck and sliding into his hair. Soon, they were rushing to the extra bedroom, the closest option.

Chapter Thirteen

Shelly was lying against Paul's chest when she awoke. She heard her phone ring again and having neglected work the night before, she reluctantly rose and crept naked into the bathroom to take the call. Judith's name lit up the screen.

Please let it be good news.

"Shelly?" Judith's voice sang into the receiver. "I saw the paperwork you sent earlier. Believe it or not, we signed."

"Oh, nice!" She looked up at the ceiling, grateful the signing hadn't been delayed.

"I'll send it right now to the seller." She dropped the phone and put Judith on speaker, In the reflection of the mirror, her skin was flushed with post-coital glow, and her glossy black locks tumbled onto her shoulders. They had not had sex in months, avoiding each other's disingenuous embrace when offered. She was in a good place to proceed with her day after a quick shower. Less drag on her body, less loathing of every step.

Her skin erupted in goosebumps as her feet hit the cold tile. She looked around for a robe or a towel. Judith chattered through the earpiece about crown molding in the master bathroom, and her visions of gray and white hexagons to complement the layout of the space, but Shelly was only half listening. There were many hurdles to overcome before hexagons.

Tucked next to the toilet was a pile of clothes. Paul's, obviously—an odd place for them, but she gathered the items for the hamper. As she picked up a pair of his pants, a yellow paper fell onto the floor. She picked up the slip with a glance so fleeting it matched the flutter of a hummingbird's wing, yet something made her stop to connect with the words.

Hotel Corner Side.

Shelly unraveled the scrap, letting Paul's pants fall. At her fingertips was a thin, waxy piece of paper that made no sense. She held it closer to her face, following the words etched in ridged, computerized lettering from left to right:

Date: 11/04

Total: $67.88

Last night? He came to Josie's door then went to his office, right? Didn't I hear him?

Time stamp: 2:33 a.m.

In slow motion, she wandered over to the sink. Her mind raced. She looked again at herself in the mirror, trying to come up with a safe conclusion. No. She was looking at it wrong. Paul had stayed away, kept his distance. It didn't have to mean—

Judith's voice brought her back.

"Yes," she answered. "I'll send the bid, Judith. Let's see what happens." She paused. "Listen, I have to go. I'll call you when I hear from the seller's agent."

She clicked off the call, wrapped herself in a towel, and sat down on the toilet.

In the kitchen he wanted us—he sat there and told me he wanted us to get better. There's nothing here. You're crazy, Shelly.

Even in the face of her paranoia and wounded instincts, Shelly needed to know the truth. She listened for noise from the next room. The edge of the bed was partially visible, but he was still fast asleep. Slowly, she searched his shirt pockets but found nothing. In the back pocket of his pants, she touched something circular with a serrated edge. Pulling it out, her heart sank as if dislodged from its ligaments and descended into the pit of her stomach. Three condoms emerged. The sheen of the foil packaging highlighted the red wording with a black eight-ball in the center.

Her breathing became small gasps. She pulled the jeans close to her body, shivering.

I always wondered how it would feel.

All around were parts of him. Clothing, pants, and cold, white tile. A hole formed through her center, an experience she would later recall as indifference or numbing. She felt empty. Tears fell as her body told the story even as her mind closed.

Shelly heard his feet hit the ground before he appeared at the bathroom door. He seemed unsteady, off balance, as his eyes darted from her hands to her face.

Clutching the contents of his pocket, she examined his features and soon realized her worst fears were true.

Shelley raised the wrinkled piece of evidence. Her mind slowed, and the room angled wide, circling three hundred sixty degrees. Boundaries distorted, and her arm extended beyond its natural length. Her stomach turned like air correcting in fluid, lifting to the top of her diaphragm. The room swirled, a nauseous dissociation like intoxication, the spins pulling at her stomach.

She was no longer standing on the frigid floor of the bathroom. Instead, it was the threshold of a pine door. The carpet beneath was rough under her feet, its dampness soaking through to her skin. The stark white bathroom walls clouded into darkness; moist air and an increasing scent of foul urine took its place.

Shelly's spine stretched as if pulled upward by a noose. She couldn't bear to look and discover which part of the rabbit hole she had tumbled into. Her arm, still held up, gripped something different. Not paper or condoms, but something squishy and uncomfortably cold as if she held chilled, raw meat. Her shoulders twitched, and each breath became a tremulous inhale.

The thing in her hand had been there before. Familiar remnants, details of something forgotten, spreading in her mind like ink hitting water, conjuring images of her childhood. The cold object, about the size of an orange, scared her. It meant something, although her brain held its secret.

Shelly lunged forward, and Paul stumbled back. And the carpet vanished, along with the smells, aside from a drift of a sickening, rose-scented perfume.

The forgiving wife part of her wanted to defend him, but the cheated-on woman part of her wanted to hurl herself against him with all her strength and knock him into the counter's sharp edge. She bolted from the bathroom.

"Shelly! Wait! I went to the bar," he stammered, tripping over his words.

She avoided his eyes. "I don't want to hear it." She wandered around the room looking for her clothing, looking for focus.

"For fuck's sake," he said sharply. "You don't want to hear me now? After your speech about wanting me to know what's going on with you?"

She continued pacing. Her steps were less about the clothes and more about indecision.

"Maybe I wanted this to happen," he said bluntly.

She stopped. The comment hung in the air like dense steam, making it difficult to breathe.

"You wanted what to happen, Paul?" The pitch of her voice plummeted to a baritone, a growl.

He held up his hands. "I wanted us to change."

"What part, Paul?" She faced him. "What part was going to change us? When you fucked someone else?" She stepped closer. "Or when you fucked me just now?"

He blinked, watching her.

"Nothing matters." She tried to move past him, but he grabbed her arm.

"Shelly, it wasn't my plan! I didn't go out to get laid." His grip on her arm tightened, and a flash of spit landed on her forehead, hot from his breath. "I needed to escape! Surely that's something you can relate to?"

He cut into her, knew where to aim, excuses at the ready. Paul often fought dirty, highlighting her weaknesses and flaws to avoid blame.

"So, I had a few drinks," he said, then looked down. "It didn't mean anything."

It didn't mean anything. You don't mean anything.

In all the sessions with Dr. Frazier-Velli, she had never figured out the exact cause of her mind and body split. Like a seizure, these episodes were spontaneous and terrifying. As she disappeared inside herself, her core shriveled, uncoupled from actuality, and her body flipped into autopilot. Paul's yelling grew fainter; his movements slowed before her eyes. A silhouette overshadowed him. A figure with broader shoulders and a taller frame.

He knows. Leave them and run. Run!

Panic choked her like a fist, and she couldn't get enough oxygen. Her lungs struggled to refill. Lights formed at the circumference of her vision, and she was dizzy, hyperventilating. Something was coming for her. Footsteps on hardwood radiated with thuds up her legs. Her surroundings diminished, leaving a gray curtain between her and the outside world.

The embodiment emerged. A checkered shirt over a fat barrel-like stomach. A muted but stern and furious expression, hidden behind oversized glasses. Shelly felt fear and rage in equal measure. Her muscles tightened, and she curled her fists into balls. Her forehead and brow line crowded as her eyes narrowed.

Screams echoed around her. Who was screaming? Shelly tried to move away as the space closed in like a dark blanket thrown over her body.

A faceless voice yelled from somewhere: "Run, baby. Keep going! I'm behind you."

Shelly turned to see where the voice was coming from, but someone held her arm. Her legs stiffened down to the balls of her feet, and blood coursed through her body, boiling in preparation. She clenched her teeth so hard she thought they would crack. Every primal part of her brain unified to protect and survive.

Take control. Escape. Kill.

An overwhelming compulsion took hold; she wanted to tear into flesh, shredding the muscle fibers at the soft point of his neck, ripping it away with bare hands.

"Shelly!"

Fight! Kick, get away. You're free, baby. You're free now. Run and don't look back. Run far away.

"Shelly!"

Her head shot up, and her body lurched forward, fists ready to strike. Like the animation of a flipbook, images flashed between Paul and her assailant. Shelly's brain struggled to differentiate.

Fight. Kick.

"Shelly!"

Through the tunneling of her vision, she identified the voice as Paul's. Stopping herself in midair, she was like a train trying to stop forward momentum. Adrenaline pulsing, she found it hard to contain the raw anger coursing through her body.

"Let go of my fucking arm!" she said, inches from Paul's face. It all flooded back to her. The cheating. The betrayal. "Let go, or I'll kill you!"

He released her arm, stepping back with hands held up.

The chill of the room covered her bare skin, making her shiver.

She detested the sight of him.

You coward. You didn't fight for us. Instead, you fucking gave up.

Sobbing quietly, she got dressed. In their shared bedroom, she threw together a bag for her. Down the hall, she packed some things for Josie.

At the front door, Paul tried to block her path.

"Get out of my way!" She glared at him.

His mouth fumbled through words, forming none, and he held his hands up again, as if bracing for her to walk through him. "What about Josie?" he asked.

With some effort, Shelly hesitated, determined not to be distracted. Determined not to let Josie be the bait on a hook tethered to his fist.

"I'll pick her up from school. Go fuck who you want. I'll take care of the hard stuff like I always do." She pushed past him.

She didn't know where to go, but she needed to get to Josie—nothing else mattered.

Shelly backed out of the driveway and headed across town. Her focus, like sunlight seeping in and out of fog, loosely connected her to the surroundings. Only the humming in her purse anchored her to the road ahead; her phone rang continually, like an incessant, mini power drill.

Early by thirty minutes, Shelly pulled into the elementary school lot and slid into the strip where waiting parents would eventually cluster. As she sank deeper into the seat cushion, the glass fogged, obscuring the view of the parking lot.

She wondered if the woman's hair had copper tones like hers, or whether her eyes held the light the same as Shelly's did. Or had Paul's tastes changed? She forced the tortured images out of her mind and replaced them with thoughts of Paul's demands. In recent months, she had acquiesced to his pace, his work schedule, and *his* expectations of their relationship. The feeling of betrayal returned as she shifted on the seat. She still smelled his scent and sensed the friction between her thighs, the results of their lovemaking so soon after he had touched the same intimate parts of a total stranger.

Had she pushed him so far away? Was the burden to remain loyal too heavy? Perhaps coping with her demons was too high a price to pay for love. Such thoughts came and went like bullets through her center.

She pushed against the steering wheel, pressing her body into the back of the seat. It was all a lie. Self-preservation. None of it was genuine. *Work on it, do better, I don't want to lose you. Lies. I knew there was—I just knew.* And there was probably more, hidden.

Her phone rang again. Paul. She quickly hit decline but scrolled down to read his messages. They were all the same, asking for forgiveness and mercy. She swallowed hard and threw the phone against the seat, trying to hold back tears for Josie's sake.

Would it be better for them if I disappeared?

Attempting composure, Shelly assessed her face in the mirror, noting her puffy eyes and the dark circles beneath. She'd try to disguise her sadness before Josie came out.

The clock on the dash read three-fifteen p.m. School had let out, and her heart began to pound and the sound of feet hitting pavement reached her ears. Where would they go from here?

Chapter Fourteen

Shelly needed time to figure out her next steps. She needed time away from Paul.

The model home—yes, that's where they would go. The alternative, a hotel, didn't sit right. A rented room was bad enough with a standard-issue, AstroTurf carpet, peach and teal decorations, and the smell of mold or toxic bleach on the sheets. For Shelley, it went deeper. Hotels terrified her.

She told herself this was different. Josie would see the situation as an adventure. Something unexpected, something exciting. Her departure with Josie did not involve running, scrambling, or darting to the car. Josie was not in fear for her life. A complete contrast to the many memories of the escape Shelly had from childhood.

Mom had yelled something about a belt, and Shelly had known exactly what that meant. A two-inch wide, chestnut strap with a large pewter buckle. She had sobbed in the corner as her mother ran back and forth in the hall. Eyes wet and nose running, Shelly clutched her Raggedy Ann doll, with its frayed nose and red yarn hair. When her mother grabbed her arm, Shelly dropped the doll. She screamed for the toy, but her mother dragged her away and lifted her onto her feet.

Once outside, she was thrown into the passenger seat, and her mother scrambled to get behind the wheel, not even bothering to fasten either seatbelt. Her mother's body shook, and she drew breath through quivering lips as she fought with the ignition of the unreliable Fiat. It sputtered alive, to their surprise, as her father bolted from the door. Shelly saw the belt in his hand and hid in the seat well. Her mother hit the gas, and the car jolted backwards. When the car bolted forward, they heard her father yelling.

The motel reeked of cigarettes, which tainted the walls and furniture with a yellow dinge. The meager light and threadbare blackout curtains shielded them from the outside world but created a cave of shadows. Her mother sat on the edge of the bed, hands on either side, staring at the parking lot. Hugging the pillows, Shelly whimpered and waited, listening to her mother's silence.

Slowly, her mother stood and gazed at her. In the minimal light, Shelly could see her engorged skin, the purple mound like a fresh plum around her eye. The white part surrounding her pupil was darkened red and her upper lid was mangled like chewing gum. Shelly had not seen him hit her mother, but she had watched her mother crash into the wall, which had sent Shelly to—a safe zone? These memories were still clouded. Where had it been safe?

The corner of her mother's mouth was swollen, with a slit through the pink of her lower lip, glistening red from fresh blood. In the dim room, her features were almost unrecognizable. She winced as she spoke, bracing her mouth with her fingers, visibly in pain.

"Don't you dare leave this room," she'd said.

Shelly knew this meant she would be left alone, but she didn't know why. Panic sent her heart racing, and her body squirmed as her mother turned and walked out. Was she going back to him?

She touched her ripped jeans, rolled up at the hems because they were too long; the folds covered her worn, gray sneakers. As the headlights of her mother's car flashed past the window, her small body wilted, slid down the pillow, and curled into a ball.

Shelly did not move from the bed, not even to use the bathroom. She had not dared. Her eyes hadn't fully shut since her mother left; the warning still echoed in her ears. Fixated on the break between the curtains, she waited, terrified her mother would never return.

When the Fiat pulled into the hotel parking lot, dawn was approaching, exterminating the darkness with light.

Her mother appeared in the doorway, and her face was still swollen with bruises, but there were no signs of anger or sadness. Shelly let her body go limp. Her mother's hand was cold and trembling on her cheek. She spoke the same words Shelly had heard many times. He didn't mean it. Outside his control. His job, traffic, bills, back pain.

Deep down, Shelly knew he blamed them for everything. Voices too loud, a toy left out, dinner served late, an unflushed commode. In the event of the latter, the bastard had once hung Shelly over the toilet bowl by her ankles, threatening her with her own excrement. Leaving reality behind became her method of survival.

Her mother's voice faded. *Hide. Until it's safe. When the yelling stops. The yellow above you. A hiding place. It's a forcefield. Just until the yelling stops.* Shelly visited places in her mind, like the green hilltops she saw outside the car window, or a big city where no one could find her.

The cold chill of her mother's touch brought her back to the room, the night, the bed. Shelly deflated, widening the hole inside herself, finding peace within, and still, after everything, loving her mother.

Chapter Fifteen

Oregon fall, in full swing, continued its barrage of inclement weather. Shelly accelerated into town. Rain obscured her view as the road narrowed. Like clockwork, the wipers kicked on, spreading the first droplets across the glass.

A flutter of movement: something caught her eye. A biker to the right, riding through the storm's peak. He was too far away to get a good look, but gradually, he moved closer. His flickering bike light danced across Shelly's windshield like lightning in a thundercloud.

Her disordered mind refocused, with a mother's genuine concern. Lord, be careful.

"What are you doing out here?" she muttered, squinting to organize his warped form, the yellow helmet and orange flasher. He was pedaling hard, his legs thrusting diligently.

"Mom, where are we—"

Shelly's body suddenly lurched as a sudden boom lifted the car. The entire front end of the vehicle thundered to the right. The shock triggered a scream from Josie. The surge from the vehicle's underbelly found its way into the steering column. The leather grip bounced between her fingers like a machine gun.

"What! Stop!" Shelly grasped the wheel, trying to keep control. In fight or flight mode, she moved by instinct, eyes fixed on the center yellow line.

"Josie! Hold on!"

With her eyes wide, the road suddenly abandoned her. The front end of the car slipped to the right as the back end drifted left, propelling across a sheet of water on the road. The car was skipping, like a rock thrown at the surface of a pond, bouncing Shelly and Josie within its belly.

Horns blared. A car headed toward them.

Helplessly, she spun the wheel, but their direction didn't change. An oncoming car barely missed her left side. Gears screeched, and headlights shot past her window. She kicked down hard on the brake, but the out-of-control sedan continued its path.

Josie screamed, and between jolts, Shelly looked back. Her daughter gripped the door, her little body pressed against the belt. The car heaved again, snapping Shelly's head forward. As the car's front end dropped down, a rasping, grinding noise reverberated with an unmistakable, high-pitched scoring—the metal rim against the grit of pavement.

We've lost the tire, Shelly realized.

Shelly saw a flashing orange light. The biker, pedaling through the storm. Images came like the churning of a movie projector. In a blink, the man bobbed pell-mell against the hill, his yellow helmet and the flash of his reflector casting flashes of light through the air.

The car moved toward him, driven by nothing but the descent of the hill. In full slide, Shelly tried turning as the car's antilock system clicked under her foot, unable to catch the moving earth.

His head turned in the rainfall, his eyes illuminated by bursts of orange and the car's headlights. His mouth dropped open.

Another flash of orange. Another blink.

"Look out!" Shelly yelled.

"No. Jeeesus!"

On impact, orange light exploded into the cabin as his body shattered the windshield with a loud, hollow crunch and then disappeared over the roof.

"Josie!" Shelly's shrieks were cut short, sucked back by the force of the car vaulting into the air. The moment her body became weightless, the hood hit the ground, causing the car to kick back and roll. Her body floated in a bubble, a void of gravity. She could smell both Josie's sweet hair and the searing chemicals released from deep within the engine.

Glass shot into the inner compartment as if fired from a cannon. Her skin tingled and then burned with the spray of shards against her face. She braced for more, squeezing her eyes closed, seconds before her body hit the side window.

Pain erupted at her shoulder but fired into the back of her neck and up into the lower part of her skull. More agony pulsed through her body as she tumbled like clothes in a dryer.

The car twisted again, and the ceiling dropped down, causing her muscles to seize in unison. It took an enormous effort for her body to respond, to press up and away from the crumpling metal. She braced for impact, incapable of finding direction and flailing at the whims of gravity. Her left leg jammed into the dash, sending a wash of searing heat up her side; the bone jerked inside her flesh. An unbearable, deep ache drove in the muscle, squeezing her groin and pushing into her stomach. Nothing could release her long enough to look back for her daughter.

As quickly as it began, it stopped. Her body was still.

Chapter Sixteen

Paul watched as she drove away from the house. His texts had been ignored. He didn't know what he had expected—maybe more angry words, another rip at his character. He slid to the ground, cradling his face. Until that day, he had never witnessed Shelly's glare so targeted, like knives cutting into his body. This was not the wife he knew, but then again, she could make the same claim. The Paul she had married would never have cheated.

The room was silent; every subtle creak in the house echoed. The stillness seemed to be a prediction of his future.

He didn't want it to be over between them. He craved their earlier selves—laughter down the hall as they chased and tickled Josie, the calm moments alone. Shelly's childhood had wounded her spirit, but it couldn't last forever. There was so much to be happy about. Why couldn't she see it? He missed her smile and laughter. The woman in the bar had been totally different, offering something exhilarating right now, in the present. No part of her was shackled to the past.

His phone rang, and, reluctantly, he answered.

"We have a major problem with your case."

He didn't know what to say to his boss.

"Paul? Are you there? We need to meet."

He fought the urge to slam the phone against the floor. "Listen, I can't come down. I need a pass on this one." He hadn't asked for time off before, he'd always been a team player, had always accepted whatever they asked of him.

"Can't do it," Will said. "The hospital administrators are requesting an emergency meeting. There's no way out of it. Get down there by four. We're under a lot of heat."

Paul held the phone away from his ear. "Will! Listen to me," he said. "What the hell is going on? This case is a disaster, and I'm a mess right now. None of the transcripts make sense, there are missing notes, and the RNs changed what they remember. Too many holes to fill." He covered his eyes. "Are there addendums to this rat's nest? How can I write up a report when the documentation is half-ass?"

"The patient is demanding a meeting today. That's the truth of it." Will exhaled loudly. "She wants hard lines to be set, or she'll take this to the media and court. They're announcing today, and the parties are meeting. After this initial proceeding, they'll insist on our report, so the half-ass documentation is your problem to fix." He paused, letting the weight of the matter settle in. "The findings will be turned over to our lawyers, who will likely continue reviewing documents. They'll need a liaison for the data, and that's you."

"Will, I can't do this."

"I'm not going over this again!"

"Shelly walked out on me," he said and immediately regretted it, because he didn't really know for certain. "I don't have it, man." Paul closed his eyes, waiting.

Will said nothing for a few seconds. "I'm sorry, truly, I am. But you're going to need to get it together. After today, we'll try to phase you out."

Paul couldn't believe what he was hearing. *After today.*

"Just show up today with the synopsis," Will said. "I wish we had an easy way to kick the can to the next department. But this woman has all sorts of people stirred up. There are accusations on the hospital side, and the whole thing is a mess."

Paul snapped, "What do you mean, on the hospital side?"

"Keeps changing her angle. If it's not the money, then it's the doctors. Her demands keep changing. What can I say—she's a bitch on wheels."

"Is she right?" The question slipped out before he could stop it.

"What do you mean?"

"I mean the chart lists 'routine' throughout, but Will, the kid died. What's routine about that?"

"Paul." His boss paused, then spoke slowly. "It's not our fault the services weren't covered. There's nothing indicating other issues with the care. End of discussion."

Other than a fetal demise. Paul knew he had no choice. Telling Shelly he had lost his job was not an option, on top of being an adulterous ass. "I'll show up today, but I can't guarantee beyond that."

"Okay," Will said. "Showing we are present and engaged will go far. And I hope things get smoothed out between you two."

Paul hung up. He wanted to believe his boss, that he might actually care something about Paul other than his productiveness and acquiescence. Will was human, after all, but only marginally.

He looked at the clock; Shelly would be picking up Josie in less than thirty minutes. Should he call her again? He stood up and looked outside. He had to get ready, but his feet were cemented to the ground. If only he could rewind, go back, and undo the last eighteen hours. He would have cleared a path out of his office, thrown himself into family life, and skipped the bar and all the mess that followed.

Chapter Seventeen

Shelly moaned like she had vomited up her insides. She had envisioned her death more times than she could count. A car accident, drowning, being impaled by a tree, head-on collision—the list went on. The oatmeal-like substance of her brain had splattered many windshields over the years in the deathscapes of her mind.

In her horror-filled imagery, her corpse would be found outside, implying death had come through other methods. She had often pictured her body in a field, legs sprawled, naked, although sometimes she was clothed. She had died several times swimming in blades of grass, a bloody heap thrown away like trash, broken and left to die. In some scenarios, death came via a murdering psychopath, after she threw herself at his mercy to save her family or even a demanding client. But in all the times she had imagined it, death certainly had never been a surprise, catching her off guard after a ruptured tire.

Her pain abated, hovering outside her consciousness like Novocain-drunk nerve endings. She had no physical awareness of the car, no pressure on her skin to signify she was huddled against a surface. Her eyes wanted to open, but the fear of what she might see paralyzed her. The muscles around her eyes quivered and pinched shut. She drew a shallow breath through trembling lips but heard only the passing of air over her tongue. An icy bite brushed Shelly's cheek, and the chill seeped through her body from the tip of her toes to her scalp.

She found it impossible to reach into the void, to touch the space below or above; it would be like checking a doorknob in a fire, expecting it to explode. Instead, she slowly turned her head, and her cheek scraped the rough ground. The gritty surface pulled her skin, and the bitter taste of dirt dusted her lips.

Righting herself on her back, she peeled open her eyes to distorted images and shapes, spheres and blurred circles swimming together like a spun prism, still casting a glimmer despite the overcast sky. The mess of shapes mutated into objects. She knew the car must be somewhere, and she looked for a plume of smoke or steam.

None of what she saw made sense. The car was gone. The rain had stopped. As she looked around, she spotted no scraps of metal. There were no flames, black smoke, no odor of burnt rubber, or the faint wobbling quiver of gasoline fumes over puddles seeping from a break in the fuel line. Her eyes opened wider, and she suddenly felt microscopic. A miniscule creature, as if she was the only living thing left in the world to be scrutinized. The silence grew louder, her ears flooded with vibration of the wind rushing over the dust of the ground. She detected a waft of soggy leaves and moss, like cold nights on her back porch, the smell of an Oregon fall. Panic gripped her by the shoulders.

"Josie?" The name caught in her throat. Her vision shifted to the passenger side—or where it should have been—but she saw nothing but emptiness, a jumble of light and gray. No Josie. No sparks of colorful clothing or remnants of a bouncing, gleeful little girl.

If Shelly had been ejected from the car, Josie could have been too, her body tossed like a rag doll and disappearing into brush. The image horrified her, Josie's eyes grayed over and lifeless in a bed of newly snapped briars.

She called out again, "Josie. Josie?" Her voice was a whisper; she was too weak to force more air through her vocal cords.

She heard nothing. Stuck in her useless body, she squirmed like an animal trapped in a predator's jaws. The distance between them could be a mile or inches, and every second without Josie provided more proof of tragedy. Life without her daughter held little meaning.

Failure as a mother brought a sense of helplessness without end. Shelly's mind played the movie, like a child watching shadows dance across a wall. Only screams accompanied the images; fragments in the back folds of her brain were pushed aside like books on shelves in a decaying library. Was she lost in her mind again? Was the car accident real, or had her psychoneurosis altered things so severely that her brain had simply split from reality?

Wake up. Shelly, wake up.

Paul had been right, and the concession jabbed her rib. She had deserted them and disappeared inside herself. All her bullshit, her efforts to fight off death, had amounted to nothing. She had become a child overrun by ghosts, shielding herself with a blanket, a powerless onlooker. Despite all her efforts to protect Josie, their daughter was out there somewhere, all alone.

"No," she croaked against the cold ground.

Please, God, let her be alive. She wasn't religious, but maybe something in the ether could help her. Hear her prayer.

Determined, she placed her hands under her chest and pushed herself off the ground. In a state of shock, she felt only numbness.

Positioned on all fours, she sensed the texture of gravel and concrete under her hands. Her fingers parted, exposing black rock or pavement, and her palms ran over its surface, scuffed by the porous indents and crumbling edges. It would have been easy to convince her she crouched on a sound stage, with a false light barely arousing the space. It was a road. The scene before her mirrored the endless asphalt stretched behind her.

Her arms tensed as if weighed down with pounds of sand. She looked down at her fingers, sprawled against the blackness, and the quivering muscles of her forearms in a battle to stay upright. Red droplets slowly wet her skin, then began to drip continuously, splattering as they formed puddles. *My head. My blood.* In disbelief, she tumbled backward, touching her face. The area around her eyes and the bridge of her nose was thick like clay. Each finger jumped nervously as it approached the tissue along the ridge of her cheekbone, and her breath quickened to a pant, her lips shaking with each gasp.

The folds and lines of her brow warped and her swollen skin, taut like a balloon, radiated heat as voluminous, cell-rich fluid accumulated under the surface. *My face is torn. My eye.* Her fingers told the story, moving across her ravaged face, with injuries spanning from the right side of her head, disrupting the tissue of the eye in its path.

Nerves came alive. An ache kindled as if a hack saw had dragged slowly across skin and bone, and abruptly, she became lightheaded. Searing pain pulsated behind both eyes. Clutching her temples to brace for the explosion of brilliant pain, her hand froze. Her skull felt oddly shaped, and she traced the edge of what had to be yawning flesh. Her hands swept jagged bone jutting through her scalp. Here and there, skin hung loosely, like the lifeless hide of a turkey over its missing neck. Shelly's moans erupted into a scream.

Tracing the lower perimeter of the skin behind her right ear, she touched an oozing substance; it ran over her knuckles and neck. A thick, syrupy texture moved between the cotton fabric and top of her breasts as she touched her upper body. Blood spread across her chest, soaking any remaining hope.

I'm not ready, Shelly thought, *It's not time.*

Revulsion hoisted her shoulders forward despite the stabbing pain and she feebly slapped her hands to rid them of her body's tar. Shelly panted, her chest heaving in sync with her heart. A deep stain, diminishing to pink, covered her palms, collecting in the creases of her skin and around her nailbeds. It wouldn't come clean; it dyed the surface burgundy and kept falling from her face. The burn of vomit stung, and her abdomen jerked to a gag, but she spit only foam.

At the same moment, a snap rang out, like an axe against a hollow stump. The boiling ache from within her leg was unimaginable. Shelly's body took impact like sniper fire, one arm held to her face and the other groping for a sense of balance but failed. Gasping through screams, she looked at her leg. Torn flesh surrounded a splintered bone jutting from her thigh. Blood pulsed through her jeans, like something from a horror film. The lower part of her leg was awkwardly limp and bent to the side. She touched the skin above the break and let out a wail like a wounded dog at the side of a road.

"Help me," Shelly screamed. Although she feared she was close to death, her desire to find Josie was all-encompassing.

She had heard of people cutting off limbs with Swiss army knives or breaking their own pelvis bone to free themselves when pinned under currents of water.

Gathering all her strength, she called out to the sky, "Somebody help me!"

Whether it was a flashback or a nightmare, there was no letting go. Not yet.

Chapter Eighteen

Shelly dropped her head to the side, wilting onto the hard street. She willed hypervigilance and waited for the first hint of motion. But she heard nothing, not even the coo of a bird or the horn of a distant car.

She was filled with frantic confusion. She thought of all the bullshit stories of divine intervention, spirits talking through people or coming to their aid while they lay dying in ditches or lost in the woods, starving and dehydrated. Stories of the afterlife and being turned away at heaven's gates by Jesus himself. Perhaps these accounts were real? An angel, a burning bush with words of hope, all intoxicating one's mind to believe the pain didn't hurt and someone was watching over us.

But she was alone. She had only herself to depend on.

Roll over!

The thought of moving anything made her tired. But she relented, not knowing where the impetus had come from. She rotated to her side. The throb in her skull intensified with the shifted weight, and she collapsed to the surface with a view of her mangled limb.

Try again.

Pulling herself up, she paused, waiting for a surge of painful protest from her body. Instead, the area around her leg tingled with pins and needles. Looking closer, she noticed her wound had stopped bleeding, and the bloodstains on her pants were becoming smaller, disappearing. Her skin quivered as it surrounded the hole, like a cocooned larva beneath the surface. Shelly couldn't look away but also couldn't comprehend what was happening before her eyes.

Without warning, the bone shrunk back into her flesh. The jolt of it sent her body forward, not in pain but in disbelief. Helplessly, she watched the transformation, her femur withdrawing, leaving the flesh to seal.

An electric current violently clamped down on her skull in a vice-grip and hoisted her into the sky. Shelly's scream died in her throat. She grabbed feebly at whatever held her suspended but felt nothing. The force shook her vision and produced a course hum, like pulling a knife across spit-stone. Clicks and crunches filled her eardrums as the skin of her face and temples pulled tighter. Then as quickly as it had started, her head tossed free, hitting the pavement and sending her body into a roll.

Once more on the cold asphalt, Shelly felt her lungs expand. Her back arched, as if breaching the surface of water. She stiffened, anticipating pain. Yet her leg went silent, and the pressure surrounding her skull was released.

These events were only possible in a dream, and Shelly wanted to wake up. If she stood, would she float or drop through the floor? Shifting slowly to push onto her hip, she anticipated snapping limbs or eviscerated bowels. No pain. Each movement came easily. She rolled into a crouch, then stood without hesitation. Her legs held.

Free and no longer shackled by physical ruin, she bolted forward like a runner entering a sprint. "Josie!" Shelly wasn't sure the word materialized. With every muscle regenerated, she almost tripped over her own feet, unable to limit her momentum. After a few steps, filled with frenzied excitement, she spun several times, scanning for anything, an anchor, an explanation, for her daughter.

The cold air hung thick. She had left the house before four o'clock, but now the moon hovered above the trees. It dusted the branches with a sheen, enough to fight back the darkness. Alone in the haze, Shelly sensed her insignificance, a minuscule figure etched on a contemporary canvas, her human structure lost in the grays, blues, and blacks of a cloaked road. There were no turns or breaks in either direction; the yellow dashes of the center boundary stretched into an unknown distance. Beyond the shoulder of the road, ditches emanated a soup of gloominess. Withered grass waved in a slight breeze.

The trees on both sides of the road were large oaks, with substantial limbs and clusters of clutched moss. The shadows devoured their trunks, revealing a sinking tree line where the branches drew away into deeper shades of black, hiding what lived beyond.

A few yards away sat the Lewis and Clark Expedition signpost with a depiction of an explorer, hand extending toward the road leading to the ocean.

Her body softened. Josie often recounted the history of Lewis and Clark when they passed the sign. It had come up once, Shelly recalled, Josie asking curiously what the men were doing. Ever since, Shelly would grin at the sight of it, waiting for Josie to proceed with her slightly inaccurate version of the story.

This was our route. We traveled here together. Shelly realized she was standing only five minutes from school and seven minutes from the house.

"Josie!" The sound bounced in the air and fell dead, carrying only inches. "Josie! I need to know you're okay!" She strained, listening for the slightest noise. Something broke through—a whisper, a breath in her ear.

"Shelly."

She spun around and found nothing but the road. Then, tumbling in like a storm meeting the shore, mist flowed from both sides, merging before her. She froze.

"Shelly!"

She stepped back, moving away from the thickening vapor as her thoughts crowded in. *Run. Something's alive here. It's with you, all around.*

Turn, run. Do it now. The foggy air enclosed her, wrapping her in white and gray feathers of smoke. Where could she escape to? Her hands came up instinctually.

Deep in the center of the encroaching fog, flashes of light, orange then blue, flickered amidst the swelling moisture. Shutters of darkness drew her in. A pull wrapped her shoulders, like an underwater current, a wave. At once, immense pain ripped through her leg. She screamed and fell to the ground, which disintegrated beneath her. The change in position happened in a fraction of a second as the world around her—dark shrouded trees, water-filled ditches, the endless road—spun into streaks of mossy Oregon green.

Voices echoed in the distance, as though from the bottom of a well, rolling and muffled. Through fractions of eyesight, she visualized the hard metal of her car roof pressed against her head. Water fell onto her face, dripping across her eyelashes.

Did I imagine it all—the road, walking without pain, the mist?

Her eyes closed again, and a warmth beckoned her to retreat from this world. But she knew staying in that cocoon could be the end, a sleep she wouldn't wake from. In and out of consciousness, she felt soft rain tapping her skin.

When Shelly woke, someone in a uniform was bent over, gaping at her with lips moving at half speed. A ringing in her ears prevented her from hearing him, and despite the increasing number of faces in view, her mouth stayed limp. Was it one person or several? She could only hold her gaze forward, as if her head were taped to a board. And in that narrow view, the puzzle pieced together.

The car had flipped. Through the imploded driver-side window, she saw the hillside, the flashes of emergency vehicles clustered at the scene. Their glow woke up the lethargic field, highlighting muddy ridges the car had traversed on the way down the slope.

Shelly tried to move her arm but found it pinned. Above, shards of glass glowed against the black lining of the roof, flickering with the tiny reflections of blue and red lights.

Struggling for air, an animal instinct pulsated in her chest. She needed to move, to kick, to get away from the roof, the seat, the broken glass, the strangle at her throat. A violent jerk sent excruciating pain to her right leg and shoulder, and she couldn't be sure if her scream stayed inside or erupted from her mouth.

The wave of pain intensified to a halo of fire at the tip of her skull. A weight pressed against her back; perhaps the seat, broken from the frame. The belt hugged her, pulled her back against what she assumed was the leather cushion and its support. Her leg, the one she could see, was up on the dash, but the other was concealed and silent, numb of sensation. As she contemplated this missing limb, her brain sent signals to her other lower extremities for details. A burn like a red-hot poker tugged up her side, fired through her nerve fibers, and slowly crept up toward her hip and into her shoulder blades. Shelly moaned.

With her shuttered vision, she saw blue laces—a sneaker. The sight of it blew her eyes open, and her body squirmed, ever so slightly, moving in its direction.

She's right there. I can see her. Shelly wanted so badly to bury her face into the crook of Josie's neck and breathe in her sweet scent. But the pain cinched down on her leg like an animal protecting its meal, causing her to wail and move backward.

Her words were barely audible. "Baby, I'm here. Josie!"

Her words echoed and trailed off. The pain moved out of her like a sliver expelled from flesh. As her vision ebbed, she was lost in the hypnotic flashing of lights. Red. Blue. Red. Blue. Against her will, Shelly submitted to an overwhelming sense of fatigue, and her body was shrouded in blackness.

Chapter Nineteen

By the time Shelly regained consciousness, the grass and the glow of emergency vehicles had disappeared, leaving only the long, yellow line of the highway. Her brain felt heavy, like the ache of a hangover.

Again, she found her body healed. She could move without pain. She shot up, trembling. Moments ago, the car seat was behind her, resting at her back. Josie was within arm's reach. Was that right? Yes. She'd seen the wreckage. Then she awoke to the road, in limbo, in a dream. Or was the car crash a dream? What was real?

Each muscle tingled with worry as trees swayed in a steady breeze, and she noted the change in energy. It was like static lifting hair. The wind intensified, creating a hush of movement, and something caught her eye—a darting mass of color, like the passing of an animal through the brush. She watched as a figure slowly shifted across the hillside beyond a bank of vegetation. The movement continued, cutting diagonally through her eye line. She could make out the ridge of a nose, the angle of a jawline framed in shadow. The figure dipped out of view.

"No wait! Don't go," she pleaded. Her body responded, and blood coursed to her muscles. The distance between her and the person shrank as she followed the side-to-side movement of the figure, who would shift position and double back, then continue. The petite form drew closer, with long blonde hair blowing behind vivid shades of violet.

"Josie!" Shelly screamed. Her body took flight, bolting into a sprint, her heart pounding in her ribs. Yards away was the warmth of her sweet child, the one born in a rush of pain who then curled on her chest and turned a crimson hue. "Stop! It's Mommy. I'm here." She shuddered to think of how scared Josie must be. "Stay still, baby! I'm coming."

The small figure stopped moving, but her back was turned. Josie was wearing her grandmother's hat still, but her hands were at her sides and her head was tilted down. The profile seemed familiar, but with each step, Shelly grew cautious, listening to warning bells sounding in her head, each tug of intuition at the nape of her neck. She thought about the spirit-like flow of clouds, the whispering voice in her ear.

At last, she stood before the little girl, who had the same deep set oval eyes as Josie, along with the trio of freckles on her left cheek. But there was a dullness in her expression, a lack of childlike vibrancy. Josie didn't look up. Her shoulders gleamed in the glare of the moon. Stray hairs not pressed down by the weave of her cap, flowed across her brow. Once white and dotted with stars, her pants were now covered with stains. The arms of her shirt were ripped. Rust-colored fluid soaked through breaks in the fabric and dripped down her little hand.

"Oh, my God. You're bleeding." Shelly sank to her knees, and together they crouched in the dark field in the mist. Shelly's hands stretched out but stalled, hovering close to Josie's wounds. Something about her made Shelly want to pull away at the same time her heart swelled to see through the blonde strands and her sweet face.

Josie didn't look at her mother but extended her arms as if bracing against a fall. In doing so, she revealed the full extent of her injuries. The twisted, ripped skin exposed her elbow joint, but the child stared off, oblivious, her arm bent awkwardly.

Shelly's tongue went bone dry and stuck to the top of her mouth. A familiar, salty sting tugged at the lower lids of her eyes, but no tears fell. She finally managed to speak. "You're hurt, baby. It's going to be alright," she said. Would it be alright?

Taking her by the thinnest part of the wrist, Shelly looked at

Josie's face intently. Her eyes darted from side to side, and her mouth opened but no sound came. Her muscles twitched under Shelly's hands. Josie leaned toward her mother, the broken arm dangling at her side awkwardly. The lurch of her little body caused Shelly to jump back and fall onto her hip.

Josie stared at the ground. "It's bad. I don't like it here. You should be with Daddy and me, Mommy."

Shelly paused, trembling. "What do you mean? I'm with you." The hair on her arms stood. This wasn't right. The Josie in front of her had pieces missing. A mother could tell. Shelly knew it like her heart knew to beat a hundred times a minute.

Josie brought her hands to her chest. Blood dripped from the bend in her arm and pooled on the ground. "Mama, please." Her face grimaced like she was talking in her sleep. "Mama. I can't stay here. I can't stay." She shook her head, first slowly, then furiously, hair spinning with the jerks of her skull.

Then Josie froze. "Do it." Her voice had become deep; a tone that would crawl from a thundercloud. "You have to walk through!"

With the last word, a transformation began. The skin of Josie's cheeks peeled back and drifted away like dried, cracked paint. The tissue beneath glittered as the moist surface caught the minuscule light. Flecks of its brittle shell collected before Shelly, still frozen to the ground. The air grew heavier, and the light slowly died. Soon, the Josie-figure's body was covered in shadows.

Shelly's movements were frantic as her hands fumbled into a crabwalk. Kicking at the dirt to get away, she stared at the silhouetted, ominous creature. Without warning, the disfigured face pushed close to hers. The mouth held only a hint of pink as the lips cracked and fell away to expose ivory teeth extending from the meat of the jaw; holes in the skin etched over bony protrusions of her skull.

The thing's head cocked to the side, and in a childlike tone it spoke.

You're broken. At least you're good at something. She's just like you. Show her how fucked up you are.

Shelly felt the air leave her lungs as all her strength was devoured. The words could have been ripped from her brain and held in front of her. No sooner did her hand cover her mouth in horror than a searing pain shot across her chest and into her limbs. She screamed in agony. Light exploded all around, enveloping her.

In a single thrust, Shelly's limbs and her trunk were pulled in unison and dropped flat. People rushed around her, yelling in broken sentences she couldn't understand. A medicinal odor wafted past her nose. Around her, white walls; above, more spheres of light.

Shelly attempted to speak but the words were garbled. Her gut seized, and her body jerked with a wave of motion sickness. A churning heat climbed up her throat. Hot liquid erupted over her lips. The world flipped.

Somebody yelled, "Fluid now." Churning wetness came again, hot and thick.

Sleep summoned. A peaceful warmth hugged her shoulders, and melodic sounds pulled her mind. A hiss of ripping fabric, a smooth, thin edge rolled over her skin. She could taste vomit and chemicals as something thrusted into her mouth. Her stomach contracted, gagging with the reflex at the back of her tongue.

The pain increased, unabated. Her head and limbs throbbed. She heard a voice far away, saying her name; murmurs, calling her to open her eyes.

Chapter Twenty

Grit caked his lips, and his body rested against something hard. John coughed deeply, with a sensation of lungs stretching against his torso. Had he been asleep for hours? The light penetrating his eyelids was a less urgent hue, as if the sun had made the journey from east to west. No, it couldn't have been hours. Sweat from his bike ride still dampened his forehead, and he felt winded and strained. The rain had soaked his clothes, and goosebumps rubbed against his shirt.

A stitch in his side twisted, like a kick ordering him to move. Something was undone. Think. The urgency idled under his skin, an electrical current irritating enough to keep him from sleeping. Even after several dry blinks, his vision remained blurred. His ears rang an incessant chord. John finally rolled onto his back to see gray sky above and fog in his peripheral. He rotated onto his knees. Black soot and pebbles clung to his palms, and all around were green trees: a lifeless forest, olive tones bleeding off branches into fields diluted to gold and contrasted against black tarmac. John analyzed his surroundings. He was in the middle of a road. But where? Nothing looked familiar. At the same time, nothing looked natural; everything looked painted with muted, dull colors that were slightly off. A strong gust of wind cooled the side of his face. Through squinted blinks, he looked at the stretch of pavement, an endless black road with no obvious purpose other than splitting the distant horizon. A dizziness overtook him and led to nausea as the space around him twisted and swirled.

He couldn't remember where he'd been going, and his bike was gone. Something knocked at his temple. A notion. A goal. Then he had it, and latched on to this vague reference, as it materialized from the back of his mind: Sophia. He needed to see her, to tell her, to explain himself. His promotion—he remembered.

John had been at work, selling cameras as usual. His boss had asked to meet with him, and John prepared for the worst. Bob leaned his pudgy elbows on the table, and his shirt buttons strained against his size.

"We are looking to restructure," he began. "I'd like to hire you as manager and bring in a replacement sales associate. It's a good opportunity. The folks at the district office are impressed by the sales coming out of this store." He clicked his pen and grinned.

John's eyebrows reached his hairline in astonishment. He rubbed his hands, tacky with sweat, over his knees. A promotion would be great for them. For me and Sophia, he thought. She would finally see his potential. But then what?

Once again, he lost connection with the beginning of the day and the present moment. His brain was floating, heart pounding, uncomprehending the gaps in time. Was he half-awake, half-asleep, or somewhere in between?

John's ears twitched with a static buzz. He stared at the silhouetted tree line and gripped the course ground. He strained his senses for anything to latch him to reality. Suddenly, tires screeched, and a horn blared as though right in front of him though he saw only the vacant field. John's head snapped around; the noise, a rush of air, passed by in a woosh of mist, then faded quickly. An unease climbed up his spine, an intuition that something had shifted. Tension ricocheted between his bones, matched by the speed of his pulse. John touched the outline of his ribs beneath his skin, almost to check whether he was real. The heat of his body passed through the red shirt as his finger slid over the Snap Pros logo.

Suddenly, his mind flashed in a series of still images, like shrapnel slamming across his skull. A vehicle with smoking tires. The car. The crash. He began to hyperventilate, and his energy drained.

John had straddled his bike. The road beneath had glittered with water after a pause in the rain. Sunrays battled the clouds for a split second, shining through the overcast sky and illuminating the tips of grass with gold flecks. Then the heavens opened again, sending sheets of water to the ground.

A sound to his left had broken his concentration. A pop, then grinding metal. At first, he hadn't thought much of it—the noise was almost drowned out by the hammering of the rain. His attention had honed on his turn. He'd seen the road unfolding and a break to the right coming up. But the black car lurched toward him, unrelenting. He'd seen the car fishtailing and wrenching to the right. Rain had blown off the hood, spraying everything in its path. Braced for the impending impact, he'd gripped the handlebars and clamped down on his brakes, but the front end of the car had hurtled toward him. His lungs emptied, the bike had lurched from his hands, and his chest took the hit. Another wave of imagery brought bending chrome and his wheel, crushed like an aluminum can, bowing inward as it hit the side of the car. He remembered a black hood and front window, then a deep sensation of snapping bone.

The energy around John bloated larger, swelling the space. He began to crawl, as drool and sweat dripped from his chin. Then the drag of his lower limbs seized his attention. His body lulled, and everything below his hips was numb. Looking back at himself, the scene blew his eyes and mouth open. His legs dangled limply, each broken above the knee. Yet he felt no pain, despite the muscle ripping through shredded flesh and the pale bone protruding from the thickest part of his leg. Unable to control his shaking, John couldn't comprehend what he was seeing.

John managed to roll to the side of the road. The distinct color of blood speckled its surface, and he recoiled sharply from the sight, as his face leaked crimson on the ground. Wobbling and resting on his hip, he instinctively reached back to investigate his head, now heavy upon his shoulders. His fingers met warmth, and a lather of fluid hung over his hair. He slowly let his fingers drift along the skin until they paused over a large indentation.

He could only imagine the details of the wound, using his fingertips to paint the picture. The laceration was long; he could place his entire finger-length into the space. As he did, he felt the gushy wetness of hair matted with blood, and the slippery, ripped meat surrounding fragments of course stone. Or was it his skull? Pulling back, the ridges of his knuckles were stained with rust-colored fluid. His hands trembled as red drips fell from his fingers.

Sophia dumped him, the car hit him, and Bob promoted him. A chaotic order of prominent points dotted the timeline, which had curled and overlapped like the ramblings of a lunatic. Was he a lunatic? He wanted to believe he'd drifted into a dream, rather than separated from his sanity.

Suddenly, his skin moved at the base of his head, a prickly sensation of a hundred fingers dancing across his scalp as flesh moved on its own. The stimuli caused him to jump, and he quickly reached back and felt the skin receding around the opening. He screamed. His legs moved about like snakes, as the same drumming sensation at the surface of his skin grew and grew until his left leg snapped straight, followed by his right. The form under the fabric of his pants finally laid still. Was he seeing this? It felt like a movie. He wanted it to be a movie.

"Am I dead?" he asked.

If this was the end, his dying wish would be to see Ashley's sweet face, lighting up this dark place. Imagining her leaning over, waiting to soothe him, he reached out a trembling hand.

Chapter Twenty-One

Paul arrived five minutes late for the debriefing. He raced down the hallway in his button-down shirt with no tie, wrinkled khaki pants, and the dress shoes he had not worn in over a year. His clothing was like him—haggard, tired, and dirty. He tried to smooth out his pants and organize the pile of documents he had shoved into his bag. Checking his phone every two minutes all day hadn't left room for even a shower.

He hoped to sneak in and find his boss. He gripped the long, iron handle attached to an immense and heavy wooden door. As he pried the thing open and walked in, half the attendees in the room raised their eyebrows, knocking him back with their shotgun glares.

Twelve people circled a large table. Some he recognized as various hospital administrators, quality management, and others he assumed were attorneys. Paul tried to navigate toward his boss without disrupting the session. Will sat on the left of the table towards the back. Paul took his place next to him quietly and surveyed the room.

The air smelled of coffee, with a hint of paint. The stark windows reached from floor to ceiling and spanned the length of the space.

He whispered to Will, "Sorry I'm late."

His boss scribbled in his notepad, seemingly impassive to the interruption. "They haven't said much yet. Just how-do-you-dos and all that mutual interest, ethical practice shit."

Paul smelled the rot of cigarettes and tried to avoid Will's breath. "So, nothing about litigation?"

"Not yet." Will's soft voice was slightly more assertive than he must have intended, because several people looked over. He leaned closer. "I want to see what their angle is. I mean, I get it. She lost her child, but the cost and the death—totally different issues."

Will's ability to compartmentalize came from within. He had advanced professionally by nodding his head to everything the higher-ups requested and saying no to everyone else. He was the kind of pet you liked to have around; an amoral, undriven vessel who protected the bottom line.

"Did you read my draft?" Paul asked, stomach queasy suddenly.

Will continued looking at his phone. "Yeah! Yeah, I read it. A synopsis, simple, but might need more than 'this is the timeline and what happened.' Look for details that discredit what the patient is alleging." He waved his hand toward the table. "The hospital treated the baby and did what was needed. Unfortunately, some actions were unplanned, but routine care, and some fell under emergency classification. The only reason we're in this room is because she used to work in a hospital. Like we need to kiss her ass."

Paul studied Will as the comment hung between them. Suddenly his place in the room reminded him of the motel—seedy, with the rough sheet pulled over his naked body. Goosebumps erupted down his back.

The people at the table started to sway and chatter. Everyone talked in monotone voices, and Paul strained to hear. Finally, the hospital administrator launched the first attack. She listed interventions and costs generated but not reimbursed. The words were Paul's. She read parts of his synopsis outright. The presentation was robotic, nothing about human lives, just decimals and responsibilities of cost. The dynamics pulled his stomach. He'd been training for these events for years, directed by Will to feel nothing and get paid. This brainwashing had stalled his progress on the report, writing and rewriting the vague details, hearing Will in his head. They want this to go away.

The energy intensified and Paul turned his attention back to the speakers. One of the quality management attorneys stood. "The hospital shouldn't be fighting this battle. We can all agree that the patient and the insurance rejecting the claims are in dispute. It's clearly stated in our patient care agreement that partially covered care is not the hospital's burden to justify." He crossed his arms.

There were vociferous reactions around the table. It was evident how far apart the two sides sat. Paul kept his head low, waiting for his portion of the circus to end. Yet, no one mentioned the holes in documentation, or what he called the *necessary remedies* he'd outlined for the hospital. Neither had Will.

As the chaos ensued, he noticed a short, round-faced man with wire-rimmed glasses. His jacket gaped open, pushed forward by his slouched shoulders. The man stared at the center of the table, displaying no reaction to the yelling all around him.

Paul blinked, looking away from the man. How long does it take before someone turns to stone in this job?

The arguments raged on for ninety minutes; then both sides retreated with plans to review in fourteen days. People began milling about the room, chatting in opposing corners. Paul made his way to the hall, looking down at his phone. No missed calls or messages. He dialed Shelly's number, but it went to voicemail again.

Will appeared at his side, breathless. "That's the mother. Holy shit, she came."

Paul angled his head, peering through the crowd of black and gray suits exiting the conference room. Several gathered around a small figure, and his eyes widened as she came into view.

The patient, a young, slender woman, stood talking with one of the men. She appeared agitated but held herself confidently, spine straight and shoulders back. Her fists were clenched. The man held his hands up, as if to soothe with no effect. The woman had large, intense eyes framed by square bangs. As Paul watched, she met his eyes, then stiffened, slowing her mannerisms while holding her gaze on him.

He waited for her to react, to share in his panic. But nothing. Nothing changed in her demeanor. Instead, she stared back as if a contest had begun. He waited amid the hospital big-wigs and legal representatives as the blood left his head, and the muscles in his thighs jumped.

"Hey, man. You, okay?" Will caught his arm. "Go home. Sorry I put you through this. Just go home, and let's talk tomorrow about what to do."

Across the room, the woman stared, knowing full well their connection. The bar, the hotel afterward. Without so much as a fidget or wringing of her fingers, she walked away, hair flowing over her left shoulder, accompanied by one of her attorneys down the hall.

Part 2

Chapter Twenty-Two

Miranda watched as a stretcher pulled into the trauma bay and skidded to a halt. Doctors and nurses circled the room. The smell of gasoline or antifreeze trailed like a fallout cloud behind the gurney. The team, each one draped and gloved, surrounded the tiny body.

The emergency tech reported on each case with a machinelike delivery. His stern monotone was detached but effective. Miranda imagined he might order breakfast with the same metrical chant.

"Seven-year-old female. Restrained passenger of a road traffic accident, initial loss of consciousness on scene. Heart rate is stable at one-ten, and blood pressure one-twelve over eighty-eight. The patient has deformity of the right arm and a laceration on the left side of the forehead. She is awake and alert now."

Working extra shifts always sounded like a good idea at first. But the weight of the room pressed down on Miranda's shoulders. Her eyes stung with the desire for sleep. It was easy to rationalize being on your feet for twelve hours, skating through blood and vomit, for double the pay. Unfortunately, it took days off your life, and fatigue soaked to the bone. Miranda had become adept at zooming in. At first, the job had drained her, and the rush of chaos rocked her to the core. She'd scurried the halls, eliciting eye rolls and barks from older nurses and doctors. Then something would click, like a searchlight turned on in the pitch dark.

The burnout was only realized later, a raw and emotional edge, like crying over sentimental commercials, or uncertainty about whether yogurt containers went into the recycling or trash. How were the whales going to survive if she had that level of confusion with every trip to the trashcan? Miranda didn't bother with answers; she cried under the weight of exhaustion and pocketed the money. After numerous emergency room shifts, she could decompress, but the more hours she piled on, the harder it was.

The girl's body lay hooked to several monitors. The undulating rhythms of green and blue lights flowed over computer displays. Sounds filled the space: fingers on keyboards, opening and closing drawers, machinery humming.

With the girl's form squarely under the lights above, the team had a clear visual of her injuries. Fresh tears glistened on her cheeks, exposing her pale skin in finger-width lines against the smeared dirt. Glass shards clung to her blonde hair. Her eyes flicked from side to side, and her breaths came clustered. The girl's left eye was covered in white gauze, soaked red in spots. Emergency crews had wrapped and braced her arm on the scene; it looked like a boxing glove that started at her elbow. Staff on either side approached, cutting back her pants and shirt.

"Stop! I need to wear clothes! I'm not home. I can be naked at home but not here." Her cry broke into a shriek. Chest heaving, her head squirmed under the belt across her forehead. Doctors orbited the room like satellites. One checked her neck, another called for X-rays and medication.

The crew shifted her small frame from the gurney to a hospital bed. The move brought panic, and she lurched her shoulders. "My arm. My arm, please don't touch it. Mommy!"

Miranda closed her eyes and took a deep breath, not fully prepared for the piercing sound. She tried to draw from the IV, which had been placed enroute to the hospital, but it wasn't working. A new one would have to be set, something she hated doing with children.

Leaning forward and holding the child's arm, she had to yell to be heard over the electrostatic of the room. "Okay, honey. My name is Miranda. There's a lot going on, and I know it's scary." She watched as the last pieces of clothing were pulled away. "Can you tell me your name?"

The girl didn't answer; her eyes darted around the room. Miranda zoned in on the blue-green shadow at the base of the girl's wrist, a vein bobbing under the milky surface, a nurse's landing strip.

When the ambulance crew loaded up to leave, one of them caught Miranda's eye.

"The child's mother is still on scene," he told her. Broad-shouldered, in dark blue overalls and a hat stitched with *Ameribus,* he paused with a fixed stare, dropping his head slightly—a look that said things didn't look good.

"Where's my mom?"

Miranda turned back to the girl; her face was filled with trepidation.

"I saw 'Josie' on your backpack," Miranda said. "Is that your name?" A bag of belongings was tucked onto a side table waiting to be collected and stowed.

The girl continued staring at the ceiling. Miranda pushed the needle into her vein. When a flash of red appeared, she placed the line and secured it. The child showed no reaction, too dazed and fearful to feel a pinch of the needle.

Miranda realized she had only practiced on kids in trauma rooms. The scuffs and bruises or wiping tears would *only* be in trauma rooms. Plans for her own children had been put firmly on the shelf. The idea of being a mother was a can she'd kicked down the road since her twenties and had since given up on. The possibility died the day Eli died. It suited her better to focus her attention on other people's pain.

"I want my mom. Please get my mommy!"

Josie's brain made the connection with her injuries, and she started to thrash as the staff held her down.

"Push the meds please. We need her out," said a doctor.

Miranda complied. Josie needed sedation.

"Is my daddy here?" The girl's eyes were pressed shut. When she tried to turn her head, blue-gloved hands clamped on, but the restraint increased her fight.

Without skipping a beat, Miranda followed protocol—complete orders, process the patient, and repeat.

"Do we have a name yet?" Dr. Charles Stevens barged into the room.

Miranda loathed Dr. Stevens. He was handsome, with perfectly straight teeth, wavy black hair, and high cheekbones—attractive enough to trigger ovulation in any woman. Rumor had it he had cycled through most of the nurses. This was part of nursing culture she tried to ignore. Miranda steadied her aim, holding her eggs to the confines of her ovaries and staying focused on the task at hand.

"Not sure of a name. They are pulling the mother out now. The scene looked—" The charge nurse shot a glance at Josie. "—complicated."

"Fine," Dr. Stevens said.

Miranda watched as the doctor approached. His dark blue scrubs were a size too small—all the more loathsome for how they complimented his physique.

"I'm Dr. Stevens. Can you tell me where you're hurting?" he said to the girl. He listened to her heart and moved to probe across her belly—little pleasantry, just business.

"I want my mom. Please! Where's my mommy?" She stared at his face with the longest fixed attention Miranda had seen since she'd arrived.

"Does this hurt?" He positioned his hands, looking into her face. "When I press here?" He moved his fingers along her lower abdomen.

"Um, no. My shoulder hurts. I don't want you to touch it." Her words came out rapidly.

He unwrapped her splint, exposing an obvious fracture; the skin stretched at an angle, and her bone bent sharply to the right.

"It hurts. Not my arm. Don't touch my arm!" she shrieked, attempting to roll away from him.

"Okay, sweetie." Miranda stepped closer. "Your arm is hurt, so the doctor wants to make it better. He only needs to look." She held her hand to the girl's forehead.

Locking eyes, she stepped into a memory. Her fingertips, touching Eli's face, running her hand through his hair. A familiar haunt since returning to work. His eyes were groggy slits, almost asleep as she rested on his chest with her black curls drifting onto his collarbone. Their lungs shared a rhythm, the same comforting air.

Miranda quickly pulled her hand back as if an electrical charge had passed through the child. She realized she was holding her breath and sucked in the air. Briefly closing her eyes, she waited for the current to abate. *He's not here. Her pain, not yours.*

"What's your name?" Dr. Stevens asked.

"Josie," she whimpered.

He started to pull at the wrapping around her wrist to have a look at her forearm.

"Ouch. Please, don't," she said, moaning louder with each touch as he pulled away the dressing. "Stop, it hurts so much."

Commotion washed the room. "We've got another one," the tech said.

Miranda hoped it was the girl's mother, with an urgency that surprised her.

"Twenty-four-year-old male, John Proctor. Car versus—"

"Left side, thrown up on window of car—"

He trailed off as nurses and hospital staff filled the other side of the room.

"Head trauma but wearing a helmet—"

Through a field of workers, Miranda caught sight of him. Torn athletic pants and deep abrasions to the right side—leg, arm, and face. An orange light glimmered from his shoulder reflector, blinking against the white sheet. The helmet stuck out, and Miranda saw red-tinged smears coming through the holes in the top, highlighted against the silver plastic. The emergency tech continued to work, soon relieved by a surge of staff. They meticulously cut his clothes and peeled layers of fabric from his tattered limbs.

Miranda had witnessed the same scene a thousand times.

Chapter Twenty-Three

Paul sprinted through the sliding doors, tripping over his own feet, briefly airborne. His muscles twitched, head darting, as he tried to find the right place and the right people to ask what had happened to his family.

The emergency department, congested with patients seated in chairs and on the floor, idled in a low whine. Windows lined the walls, but the light seemed to shy away from the space, leaving the room hazy. The air was filled with the smell of rain-soaked bodies mixed with bleach. Somewhere, a baby wailed. Phones rang with a piercing shrillness.

Paul pressed through the middle of the crowd, past a man with a sprained wrist arguing with his wife about insurance, and finally descended upon the reception desk.

His heart pounded as if he had run a mile in four steps. "My wife and daughter—they were in an accident," he said, gasping. "Josie and Shelly. Are they here?" He looked around, searching for a familiar ribbon or a lock of blonde hair.

"Okay, last name?" The young woman behind the glass partition wore a headset and a brightly colored scarf, her hair secured in a bun exposing her high cheekbones and triple-pierced ears. Paul squinted to see through the scratched and clouded plastic.

"Shelly," he repeated, suddenly forgetting his last name. "Shelly and Josie Blake. Someone called my phone. They were in an accident. They wouldn't tell me anything."

Paul's phone had rung while he crouched over the toilet basin, vomiting. The sight of Ellen, or Olivia, whatever her name was, had twisted his gut sending him to the bathroom. The only significant words he remembered from the call were: Good Faith Hospital. Accident. Shelly. "They were brought here. Please, I need to see them. Are they okay?"

The young woman seemed to move in slow motion. Paul tapped on the desk impatiently. His spine felt wired, plugged in to a current. His eyes bounced from the receptionist to the screen, the backroom, and the automatic doors. The woman didn't flinch but continued typing in a rhythmic way, each click of her finger excruciating.

"Please! Are they here?"

"Yes, yes, but only your daughter at this moment," she answered. "But you can't go back just yet. They're trying to move her." She looked at him with leveled, patient eyes.

"She can't move? Why—" He pressed closer to the window.

"No, sir." She held up her hand. "She needs to transfer to a different space, away from another trauma."

"Trauma! She's in trauma?" His voice rose, and people turned their heads. "Is that my wife or my daughter? I don't understand."

"Sir," she said and sighed. "Okay. Your daughter is the only one here. You can go to bay four. Head through the doors." She pointed.

"What about my wife?" He stared at the blurry screen.

"Sir, just pass through those doors there." She ignored his question and extended a finger.

He hesitated. The push to move failed him when an instant before, he'd not been able to stand still. Did he still have the privilege to be here? Did Shelly want him, need him? The door opened automatically, allowing him to pass. Paul shook the thoughts from his mind.

A new smell slapped him in the face, a strong disinfectant with a scent of oranges. As he made his way down the hallway, the beeps and chirps of machines, motors, and fans filled his ears. Air seemed to circulate overhead, shuffling the tips of his hair.

"Help me! Help me," a feeble older woman extended an arthritic hand. Her skin was blotched with age, and her fingers seemed to glow white under the fluorescent lights.

Doors opened to rooms where nursing staff arched over beds and typed at monitors. A blonde woman seated at a desk looked at him with questioning eyes. "Sir, can we help you?"

Paul approached timidly, an unfamiliar feeling—he had spent so much time in hospitals. "Bay four. Number four," he said. Before she could respond, a familiar sight seized his attention. Paul clutched his chest, his heart fluttering. Josie lay on a gurney, face pale, shadows around her eyes. Her feet were turned inward unnaturally. A flimsy white sheet covered her, tucked under her chin. Paul saw no colorful clothing or hair tie; instead, she wore a pale green cotton gown. One eye was swollen, and her forehead was streaked with dried blood. Josie looked miniature, toddler-sized, in comparison to the stretcher and the enormity of the room. Reality started to settle in for Paul as her monitors beeped a heart rhythm while the nurse appeared to be in no rush, going through steps as if she were cleaning out a drawer on a casual Sunday. Two men in scrubs passed Paul like he was invisible, a wandering spirit haunting a room.

"Oh, baby, my little girl." His fingers floated above her. "Josie, sweetheart. Can you, can she—" He looked up for anyone to tell him something or give clarity on her condition but realized he was alone with her now.

Her eyes were closed as her chest moved and air drifted from her mouth. He held his hand out to grab her exposed wrist, unsure where to touch her. A large portion of Josie's right arm was wrapped in a bloodstained dressing. The sight seared his eyes and dropped puzzle pieces one at a time, compiling an alarming picture.

"Honey, it's Dad," Paul whispered. Josie didn't stir. Fear turned to anger, and his head twisted around locking on to anyone within earshot. "What's going on? Please tell me what's happening." His voice grew louder as his body curled down closer to his daughter.

"Mr. Blake?" A different nurse walked in behind him. A surgical mask hung from one ear, and another was tied near her chest. Beyond her, a frenzy of staff moved back and forth. "Mr. Blake, I'm Miranda. I've been working with Josie." The nurse held his gaze. "Your daughter's been sedated for her pain and will be leaving for surgery soon. The doctor will explain the correction to the arm."

She disappeared in the blink of an eye, leaving him breathless, pivoting in place as his eyes filled with tears. Looking back at his daughter, he watched the rise and fall of her chest and the green line floating across her monitor. He lowered his shoulders as his tension slightly faded. She was, at least, alive. Paul stroked her hair, wishing for her to smile or giggle. To do something that his Josie always did. As he bent over, he winced seeing the red smears across her skin, her usual sweet scent was overpowered by an odor of gasoline and burnt plastic.

"Sir?" A different nurse spoke. "We're taking her now. You'll want to go to the waiting area on the second floor. They'll find you there."

"Please," he said. "What's wrong with her arm?" The nurse gathered tubes and turned off the monitors.

"Compound fracture. Two fractures, one below the wrist and one above the elbow."

Paul turned as a man approached.

"Are you the father? I'm Dr. Stevens."

"Yes," Paul said. "What's happening?" he said. The side rail of the bed clicked, vibrating through his skull.

"Mr. Blake." The man spoke louder. "We need to stabilize the breaks. We'll know how extensive this is once we operate."

Shelly. What about Shelly?

"Is my wife here?" The space next to Josie held a cavity, an impression where Shelly would naturally have been. Always doting over their daughter. Always there.

"I don't have any details on that. I'm sure you'll be updated." He turned, then paused. "Do you work for the hospital?" He asked. "I noticed the chart had some restrictions."

An ache in his temple expanded around the back of his head. "Yes, but non-clinical." Paul kept his response intentionally vague. The title of Auditor didn't need to be thrown around.

"Oh, gotcha. Well, we will see you after the surgery." He said and followed the gurney out.

Paul stood in the empty treatment bay with the powered-down tubes and monitors. Paper scraps littered the floor and smears and drops speckled the gray tiles. Blood. Josie's blood.

"She won't be coming back here."

Josie's face filled his eyes as though she floated before him. Paul shuddered and stepped back to see Josie's features blur and dilute away. A young woman stood there instead, wearing blue scrubs and hair covered by a cap. "Sir? Up on the second floor, there's a waiting area. Go out these doors, down the hall, and take the blue elevator up."

Of course, he knew. He knew hospitals.

Down the hall, the elderly woman called again for help.

Chapter Twenty-Four

At the ridge of the endless road, Shelly awoke curled up in a ball. She looked at the asphalt, the extending yellow lines. Why return to this listless place? She strained to remember which direction would lead home. A wrong choice might land her even farther away. Reluctantly, she rose to her feet and looked out to where she had seen Josie running across the field, the only break in the branches, evergreen and heavy with hazelnuts ready to fall. Josie's agonized face had said everything, pleading for Shelly to return. She started where she'd last seen Josie but after a few steps, froze. Had it been Josie, or something conjured by Shelly's mind—or by the road?

The air smelled like home. The historical marker pointing into the distance anchored her to this point, anchored her to Josie. Yet to take a step was like a tightrope across a canyon. A voice had called out from the darkness. Mist had enveloped her. Events she'd not composed.

Then her ear twitched.

The trees began to move, responding to a strong breeze. Shelly's eyes lowered and aimed at the hillside. Something was brewing. This type of certain paranoia, she understood well. A similar shift happened when Josie appeared in the dead space.

Move. Yes, but where—toward the trees or away from them? Her pace quickened, but the wind gained intensity, whipping against her body. She squinted through the gusts of deep gray, the thinner wisps of white lingering over the ground. Danger. Her instincts fired and she attempted to move parallel to the grass. Stick to the road.

She'd not gone two steps before a stationary figure became visible. Crouching, its shoulders curved over thin arms extended to the ground; it was too large to be a child. The figure pulsed an orange glow, consistently timed. On, off, on, off. Another strobe brought details into sharper focus—a young man with a gash across his head, oozing blood, the skin warped and torn at his scalp. Shelly's muscles tensed at the sight of his wounds. The strength of the gust bound her arms and legs, forced her closer to the exposed skull and sagging flesh. The gruesome scene faded to black as the light clicked off.

"I don't want to see! Stop!" Shelly yelled. The shine of fresh blood was like fire whenever a gleam of orange caught its surface. She turned away, digging her heels into the ground and pushing against the wind. Then something clamped down, like a vice at her temples turning her head, against her will, compelling her to regard him.

Look, Shelly. Look. A woman's voice, harmonic and buoyant, echoed around her.

A red shirt, black pants, and a familiar curve over the shoulder. A thought shook free from the back of Shelly's mind. Details rang familiar. First, rising to stand on his pedals, his head scanning to the left, briefly checking his blind spot, then a view of him with rain spraying off his tire. Shelly had seen him before. In synchronized rhythm with the orange strobe, pulse by pulse against the mist, she remembered: staring anxiously through the windshield at his drenched and exposed form, the front of his coat unzipped and billowing behind him.

The car is spinning. *We're going to hit him.* Shelly sobbed, turning her head side to side. It played again; the moment of impact flashed in full clarity.

His head shot up abruptly, his back arching as he let out a pain-filled wail. She screamed as he contorted no less than a foot away from her.

The blood started to drip against gravity, returning inside the tissue, which curled back over the crumpled skull; bones fluttered together like playing cards. Unseen hands held tightly to her shoulders, forcing her to face his convulsing body. Muscle fibers straightened like snakes slithering through mud. Shelly felt the urge to vomit and teetered on her feet, only to be shoved closer.

He clutched his skull and with the final jerk, the young man dropped to the ground, heaving, while his arms trembled under the weight of his torso. Shelly also dropped, crumbling to her knees. They faced each other on all fours, and she stared at him with utter confusion. He must have been in his mid-twenties. He looked fresh, not quite a teenager and not quite an adult with a low-positioned ponytail. His eyes were frantic, deep-set under a creased brow.

Shelly stared in utter disbelief. "We're all here," she said. The three of them. Shelly, Josie, and this man had all arrived at the same point after the accident. A place that healed but supplied no direction. She wondered if this place, this endless road, was only traveled by the dead.

Slowly, the man pushed upward, first on all fours, then back to his knees. Suddenly, he flinched.

"Can you see me?" he asked. Trembling hands came up, still bloody from his wounds though his skin had smoothed. "What's happening to me?"

Shelly's eyes shifted from the red-tinted fingers back to his aggrieved face; he was desperate for an anchor to reality. She wanted to tell him it was okay. She wanted to be okay, but they weren't. Their togetherness was unnatural.

"I think I had an accident," he said. "Everything went black, and I came here." He steadied himself and stood.

"You healed," she whispered. "I saw you. Your head healed in front of me." She considered telling him she had healed too but held back.

"Yes." His hand touched his hair. "It happened before. The first time."

"You've been here before?" she asked.

"Maybe. I don't know. It felt like someone switched television channels. I moved away from here, away from the road." His eyes glossed over as he considered the sequence.

"It's the same for me, waking up here after—" She didn't have the courage to finish. After the accident.

The young man's head swung back. "There was a loud noise. I can't remember it all. I got hit by a car." He started to laugh with a miserable hilarity. "We must be dead, right? My body fixes itself, and I've been floating in and out of events that already happened. We must be dead." A cascade of emotions washed over his features. He paced back and forth. "Are you seeing things? I mean, strange things happen here, don't they? He paused and covered his face, shuddering. "I need to talk to Sophia again."

Shelly tried to organize a reassuring answer, but she felt drained and at a loss for words. Instead, she stared at the dry rims of his eyes.

"No tears," she said under her breath.

His breathing stalled as her comment registered. A hand brushed his face, then pulled it back for inspection.

It was happening to him too.

He looked at her. "What does it mean?"

She shrugged. "No wounds. No tears." The rest she didn't know.

***

The bike rider stood with his hands at his sides under an artificial twilight. A blue hue floated around them like the lights in a photographer's darkroom, ambient instead of rays cast by the moon. Both stood in their own lane on the road.

"What's your name?" Shelly asked.

"John. What's yours?"

"Shelly," she said, unable to look him in the eyes. Instead, she shuffled her feet. "You asked if I saw things. Why?" She wondered if he had seen Josie—or anything hopeful.

His eyes twitched and seemed to click in pace with his thoughts. "I saw the crash and after that, everything got jumbled. I remembered my boss sitting on his fat ass telling me about a promotion. He made me a lead. I swear it happened before—before the accident." His brow creased. "It happened, right? They gave me the job. I was going to tell Sophia about it."

"You mean, your boss was with you, on the road?"

"Not here. I mean…" He shook his head. "I heard things in the mist. God, this sounds crazy," he said.

"Is that your wife? Sophia?" she asked.

Suddenly his chest stiffened, and his features solidified to stone. He spun around and his eyes seemed two shades darker. "No. She's not my wife."

Something about him told Shelly that anger came easily. Wounds not mended, a trait she recognized.

"I wanted to tell her the good news," he said, "then bam!" He beat his fist against his palm like a crack of wood in a fire, sending Shelly's shoulders to her ears. "I'm in some drug haze on a road to nowhere."

It took a few seconds to calm her pulse. If he saw the crash, how much did he know? Goosebumps rose and Shelly's hands rubbed at her shoulders as a wave of grief rippled through her. If only she could change his story, take away their misery.

"With everything I saw, I should be dead," he said. "My bike hit the front of the car. My face— I saw my reflection in the hood. I keep seeing it."

Shelly's insides twisted. Watching his youthful eyes cloud over, she could only imagine his mind, flooded with scenes of shattering glass and a massive object bearing down.

"I'm so sorry." She wanted to drop to his feet and plead for absolution. Grief and fear clawed from the inside of her skull, like fingers digging under her eyes. "I saw my daughter," she said.

He looked at her. "Your daughter."

"I was scared to reach out or comfort her. Something—I don't know—didn't feel the same." She had not moved closer to answers, only to chaos. They were in the same desolate place, with their own personal ghosts. She hated what she had to say next. How do you tell someone that you killed them?

"My daughter and I were driving today on this road. Just like you, we crashed."

"You crashed today?" His eyes widened slightly.

"I think a tire blew, and my car lost control. We started to spin, the car, it kept—" she couldn't say the words. "We rolled." Shelly watched his face. "It was an accident. I tried to stop. Believe me—I'm so sorry. I'd do anything to take it back."

John's mouth hung open. "It was you?" He leaned back, swaying a bit. The orange safety light intensified, seemed to pulse brighter. "You were in the black car. You knew the whole time. Do you understand what you've done?" His face filled with color. "Didn't you see me? Or did you only see my face shattering your windshield?" He walked towards her, stopping an arm's reach away. Spit covered his curled lips. He seemed to have grown two feet in stature as he loomed over her.

"I tried to stop," she said, "but the brakes wouldn't grab. Each way I turned, the car—"

"Shut up!" John screamed.

The wind turned slightly, weaving through the trees. The hair on her back stood. "John, stop. Something is changing here." She could feel electricity in the atmosphere, then in her hands, which she extended toward him, keeping an eye on the hillside. "I need to find my daughter. I saw her in the trees. She tried to warn me or tell me something about this place. I don't think we have much time."

"Fuck your daughter," John snapped. "None of you care about anyone but yourselves." He towered over her, his hair whipping out of its binding. He came at her slowly, fists clenched, the muscles of his forearms taut. The look in his eyes matched the escalating fury of the atmosphere. "I'd tell you to go to hell," he said, "but we're already here."

An alarm rang in Shelly's core, telling her she needed to retreat. "Wait. I—" Slowly, she backed away.

A voice came from behind her, drifting to a whisper, waning next to her ear.

"It's bad, I don't like it here."

"Did you hear that?" she asked.

John paced in erratic circles. "I had a life. Don't you see what you've done?"

Outside the corner of her eye, something moved. She stared, transfixed. A pale, undulating shadow rose from the ditches at the side of the road. The thickness of the churning haze intensified, becoming less transparent and more human-formed.

Again, the air hissed next to her ear. "We are waiting."

Suddenly, something broke free from the haze. Eyes emerged first. The pupils were marbled with threads of black and an ice blue center, giving off a demonic gaze. The surrounding cloud drew back, and it stepped through, face, then shoulders. A woman. Her pale skin was mottled and patchy, with ashen lips; her white hair was like spun wool.

Shelly! The lips moved, while a hand stretched over John's shoulder like a spider; knuckles bulged through paper-thin tissue.

"It's there!" Shelly screamed, falling backward.

John, reacting to her panic, spun around and fell beside her.

Her heart thundered through her chest as her eyes darted in all directions. The figure had vanished as quickly as it had surfaced, until not even a wisp of her cloudy visage remained.

"A woman. I saw a woman! She stood right there."

"A ghost?" He huddled close, momentarily forgetting his animosity toward her.

"I don't know, but she looked dead."

Shelly scrambled over to the grass. "I need to find Josie."

John followed her. "How do you think you'll do that?"

"Wait." More sounds. Giggling, coming from the woods, like children playing.

"What is it?"

Shelly strained her eyes but saw only blackness in the field. Her head twitched when she heard the sound again. "There!" With every inch of her body trembling, she pointed to a patch of tall grass. Two small shapes stood together, holding hands. Paper-doll silhouettes cast by the moon, with petite legs and small slender frames. Silken, light-colored hair fluttered over the shoulder of one. Without thinking, she clutched John's arm and whispered, "What do we do?" Then more giggling. The light, playful tone reverberation moved around them. A childlike plea followed. It seemed miles away and met Shelly's ear.

Mom. Come here!

Shelly's grip tightened on John's arm. "Tell me you heard that."

His chest heaved next to her. "How do you know it's her? I think we should stay by the road."

Shelly didn't know what to think; her mind betrayed her daily. *Is it a trick?* One of the figures leaned close to the other, as if telling a secret.

Mom, it's me. Come play with us. I met a friend. Mom, come see.

Suddenly, the pair of figures turned and ran away. The thought that Josie had someone pulling her, taking her away, caused adrenaline to shoot through Shelly's core. Nothing else mattered—whether they were ghosts or Josie in living flesh, she had to know. With frantic energy, she exploded forward.

"Don't leave!" She scrambled up the slope. But with each step forward, the figures moved farther away. They disappeared into the trees.

Shelly slowed. The atmosphere changed. Each step forward was heavier than the last. The nerve endings along her back and arms pulsed in alarm. She entered a dense vapor, so thick her lungs couldn't expand. She coughed and gagged, gripping her throat. Slowly, she fell to her knees. Her head began to cloud, then the world went dark.

Chapter Twenty-Five

The elevator smelled different this time, and the disinfectant made his nose burn.

Paul had been to The Good Faith Hospital several times conducting compliance reviews. In the past when he reviewed charts or clicked through records, the people didn't seem real. They were doctors, nurses, and patients. His role was identifying accountability, and he would dehumanize them to names on a page. They fit into categories—founded, unfounded, or case closed. As he hit the button on the elevator, he envisioned his own chart on some burnout administrator's desk, shifting easily to one stack. Sexual misconduct—founded. Exiled by wife and daughter—founded.

Between the emergency room, and orthopedics, Paul was called with an update on Shelly. The words *critical* and *straight to surgery*, made his urge to vomit resurface. They told him he couldn't see her before she went in. All he could do was wait.

He exited the elevator. His legs quivered as if they'd fail him, dropping him to the floor. Paul weaved to the front desk where a woman talked on the phone. Seeing him approach, she ended her call and greeted him with a smile.

"Mr. Blake." She stood. "I'll get the manager. We didn't know you were coming today." Her laugh was nervous. "As far as rooms, I have—"

"No need. I'm here for my daughter."

She dropped both hands to the desk. "Oh, Mr. Blake, I'm so sorry." She shuffled some papers on the desk, lost for words.

"It's fine," he said. "My daughter is Josie Blake. Has she arrived?"

"Let me see." She turned to the computer screen. "Yes. There she is. She's been assigned to room 214B. Just use the phone to—"

"I know."

Hanging on the wall before two large swinging doors marked "Caution" in shiny yellow was a cream-colored phone that looked like something from the nineteen-eighties. The curled cord, likely six feet long, draped below. Paul pulled the phone to his ear and waited. A storm was moving in; thick clouds loomed outside the large windows directly in front of him. Rain slashed through his reflection. On the phone, a steady tone continued, on and off like a power drill to his temple.

"Hello, Ortho," a man finally answered. Orthopedics—specializing in bone and joint reconstruction. People trained for countless hours perfecting their skills sawing apart and rebuilding bones. Of course, Paul could only think of stories he'd heard through hospital channels: doctors high on pain medication, nodding off with a scalpel in their hands.

"Hello?" the man repeated.

"Yes, I'm here for Josie Blake."

"Hold on." Paul could hear clicks of keys in the background along with muffled voices. "She's not here yet. They stopped at X-ray. We'll come and get you."

"Do you know if—" The line went dead. He held the buzzing phone to his ear a few more seconds, then returned it to the wall.

Wandering to the center of the room, he couldn't shake the feeling the world was passing by at hundreds of miles per hour. He rubbed his arms, fighting a chill, as his thoughts ran wild, reviewing the last twenty-four hours. Josie had undergone so much trauma—the accident, her arm. There was no telling what she'd seen in the car. Paul could not imagine having to say, "Your mother died."

He sat down and thudded his head against the wall at the back of the room. The thump of the impact reverberated through his skull. Looking up, he saw photos and reminders, hospital mission statements pasted to anything nailed down. From his experience, missions changed like diapers on a newborn.

One affirmation depicted a child with a glee-filled family—mother, father, and child gathered around a new baby. Paul's eyes ran up and down the phony photo, noting the parents' smug self-satisfaction and the kid's big grin, missing the obligatory teeth.

Paul could visualize Josie's face on a poster in a vacant lobby. Her smile would appear forced, and bruised, her eye bloated, with her mauled arm clutched to her chest as Paul stood behind her with a full grin. Would Shelly join them, he wondered?

The bottom of the poster stated, "Your health is our mission," a message that riled him. The picture of the fake family had a similar energy to his own family portrait on the fireplace mantel at home. Each one concealed lies.

"Mr. Blake?"

He jumped and sat up.

"Josie's out of X-ray, and they're moving her to a bed. You'll be able to see her in about thirty minutes." A unit nurse, teal scrubs this time, spoke quickly and turned to walk back to the unit.

"Wait." His mind went blank. There was more to say. Will she ever use her arm again? Did she hurt something else?

"The doctors will be around after she's settled to update you on the surgery and next steps." She made a hasty exit, a pro at dismissal.

Paul slumped back into his seat to wait. Eventually, the nurse made her way back into the room and waved him over. He scrambled to his feet and followed her through the large doors.

"This way, sir."

He knew where to go and started heading toward the room. The board on the wall to the right listed active patients, coded for privacy. Josie had become patient BL214JO* COMPOUND FRAC. The small asterisk tacked onto the end signaled that the patient or their family worked for the hospital.

Paul picked up the pace, moving past the nurse to Room 214. He placed his hand on the doorknob, closed his eyes, and took a deep breath. If she asked about her mother, what could he say that wouldn't scare her?

The room chilled his skin, and the hair on the back of his neck stood up. Josie lay on her back covered with a blue blanket. Her arm rested on a pillow, wrapped from the shoulder down. She breathed steadily; her face was neutral.

Paul moved closer for a better look. The bruising around Josie's eye appeared darker, and Band-Aid-like strips had been applied over stitches in her forehead. A shot of panic ran up his spine when he noticed a bulge under the blanket. He made his way over to the corner of the bed. He lifted the blanket and saw her leg also had a cast and was elevated on pillows.

"Mr. Blake?" The curtain next to the bed was moved noisily aside. "I'm Dr. Andrews. I performed the surgery on Josie." He gave a small smile. "Don't worry. We got things set up for good healing. The bone should fuse straight."

"What?" Paul's eyes moved from Josie's leg back to the man. "I thought she only broke her arm. What happened to her leg?" He stared up at the young doctor. He couldn't help being annoyed by his calm demeanor.

"Yes, the arm is the more severe injury of the two. She required plates to stabilize the bone, so we'll need to monitor her to rule out infection. She will experience pain. It's a serious break, requiring several layers of repair."

"And her leg?"

"We found the fracture along the tibia on X-ray, but it's not as serious."

"Will she wake up soon?"

"She'll be sleepy through the evening. We'll assess her in the morning. Hopefully, we'll avoid infection, and she can leave in a few days."

"Her mother, my wife, is here too. They took her to surgery. Do you know anything about her condition?" Paul couldn't help but ask.

"Oh, I'm sorry." The smile fell from his mouth. "From the same accident?"

Paul nodded.

"I don't know about her. If you need to check in with that team, go ahead. Your daughter will sleep most of the night, I think."

"Thanks. I'll check in over there."

After the doctor left, Paul sat down next to Josie, taking her uninjured hand. "I'm so sorry, baby." He held back his tears. "This shouldn't have happened." He listened as she breathed softly.

A whining hydraulic sound startled him. The cuff on her upper arm slowly inflated, clamping down on her narrow limb. He heard it pulse and release, little by little. Josie stirred. Paul watched her face for signs she could hear him. Her eyes fluttered and tiny slits appeared. But then her eyes closed again.

"Josie, it's Dad." Paul brushed her forehead with his lips. "How are you feeling? It's Dad, baby." Her eyes moved and opened slightly. She grimaced, started to whimper, and moved her head to the side.

"Josie, are you in pain? Josie, honey. I'll get the nurse." He stood and slapped at the bed buttons, trying to find the call light. He heard a barely audible whisper and leaned in closer, watching Josie's lips intently to make out the words.

"Mommy shouldn't be there, Daddy." Her chin quivered. "Daddy, she can't stay."

Chapter Twenty-Six

Miranda sat at the nursing desk, a half-moon shape with a clear view to most of the patient rooms. Inhaling the bitter aroma from her third cup of coffee, she hoped for a secondary high.

The Intensive Care Unit had scooped her up for a shift, which always intimidated her, particularly the level of illness and potential complications. Most of the time, she tried to avoid their offers of work, although today, she hadn't had the strength to say no. In the early stages of grief, you needed to stay busy. That's what people told her. So that's what she was doing.

She hung over the keyboard reading patient notes, squinting as the blue screen overwhelmed her vision. Buzzing with the hit of coffee, she flipped her blue ballpoint between her fingers, moving it side to side and tapping the tip against the desk in tempo with her anxiety.

Often, she reflected about continuing with nursing as a career. When her sabbatical had neared its end, she'd thought about quitting and selling off her belongings, essentially gutting the home she'd shared with Eli, and sending furniture and memorabilia to strangers for a few dollars. She even contemplated taking down the drywall, leaving a skeleton of boards.

While moving old clothes, she had come across Eli's favorite hat—billed, solid gray, cotton. Holding it up, she felt numb for the first time; no thoughts came. She stared at it like she would a stomach drain or vomit on a bedsheet, emotionless. With defiance, resentment even, she had placed it on the *free* pile, dropping it like an old sock, turning away from their past, and freeing herself from emotional prison.

After she moved into a new place clear of memories, the hollowness left her chest, shoulders, and space in her head. She'd buried it deep beneath the surface.

Several weeks later, Miranda walked through the park near her new home. Every day, she'd stand in the gazebo at edge of the central pond, watching the water shimmer with the wind. A man approached, his round body shuffling across the grass. He was disheveled and wearing a long black trench coat—strange in such warm weather. A long, gray beard hung from his chin, so thick that it made the rest of his features obscure.

Miranda's body stiffened. This park had become her oasis, far from the hurt and the drugged and dying she saw at work. The sight of this man brought fire to her cheeks. He wore a baseball hat oddly perched on his head, out of context with everything else he wore. The sight of him swirled like a lost name, and each time it churned, the process slowed.

Eli?

The resemblance to his hat was uncanny, the curve, the frayed threads at the bill, the oil stains along the sides from when he ruined their car. She could not have been more surprised if the hat had jumped off this man's head and onto hers. Eli's hat had followed her. No, that couldn't be. How likely was it that this strange man wearing Eli's hat would cross paths with Miranda in a new town?

She stared intently and then started to laugh, softly at first, then uncontrollably, for the first time in many months. Tears spilled down her cheeks, and she gripped her face, watching through sobs as the man lumbered out of sight.

Energy pushed from the middle of her chest, against the top of her skin, in a sense of exhilaration. She didn't believe in signs, the afterlife, or God; normally, she clung to science and real-world results. But the encounter stood against logic. A message had been sent, carried to her with the man's trundling gait, and it meant something to Miranda, coincidence or not. Eli had spoken, perhaps to tell her she was on the right path, or that he would always be with her.

Since the hat sighting, there were fewer dark days and more views of the future. Bean, the faithful hound she found soon after, became a focal point, her new life partner. Their connection filled a void and gave her something to love and nurture. He helped her transform grief into movement. They were often outdoors, rain or shine—which, in Oregon, meant mostly rain.

When Miranda went back to work, she still felt Eli, despite her best efforts. In the breeze, in a sealed room, or standing outside elevator doors opening to an empty floor, or in her blurred vision after a double shift with no sleep. But life went on.

The desk bounced as a gurney bumped into the side. Miranda braced, reorienting herself. Monitors circled her, their black screens watching her every move. She scrubbed the sleep from her eyes. Shelly Blake, a patient of concern in a medically induced coma after a severe head injury, was Miranda's patient. Miranda's problem. Two family members of someone in administration—not a good situation.

Weekly, it seemed, the higher ups added notation requirements for the nurses to include in their workload. If Miranda missed a memo on some stupid rule, it could lead to trouble, especially with high profile patients. She slumped in the chair, frustrated with herself for not keeping her focus on what needed to be done and her proficiency as a nurse. She knew the job. Her confidence had wavered after the time off, but Eli's death had marked a change in her. She admitted as much to herself. Before going on leave, remediation was the furthest from her mind; she could place a catheter in her sleep. But since her return, things required more concentration, more effort. Living without Eli required more effort.

Miranda took a deeper look at the new patient's files. Several injuries, including a possible leg amputation given the extent of the injury. Toxicology came back negative, but she had lost a large volume of blood. She'd come close to death, coded twice before they got her back. Shelly Blake was currently intubated and deemed critical.

Miranda's unconscious tapping resumed and suddenly, a hand slapped her pen flat. She looked up to see the charge nurse. The silver-haired, full-faced woman in wire glasses glared. She took the pen from Miranda and sat back down without saying anything.

"Sorry," Miranda whispered.

Thinking it best to leave the nursing station, she walked into Shelly's room and pulled up the computer. During surgery, the patient's head had been wrapped and sections partially covered her eyes. A mass of wires and tubes were connected for her supportive care. A machine to the right performed Shelly's breathing; visible chambers expanded in tempo for her oxygen needs. For the moment, her status remained teetering between serious and stable.

The room remained void of flowers or cards. Her bag of belongings sat on a chair in the corner. In the last thirty-six hours, she had been in and out of surgery or having scans or X-rays multiple times.

Glancing over her body trends, Miranda noticed that Shelly's temperature had started climbing and her heart rate had followed. Her leg was a worry because, with the plates, fasteners, and incision length, there was a risk of infection.

A man came into the room while Miranda was preparing her shift report. He blocked the light from the doorway, and two steps in, he stumbled back, holding his hand to his face. It must have been his first glimpse of his wife.

"Mr. Blake?"

His eyes squinted. "Yes. I'm her husband." He exhaled. "I'm Paul Blake."

"I didn't mean to surprise you. I'm Miranda. We met before."

"We met?" Concentration pulled at his brow.

"It's okay. You've had a lot going on. Are you hanging in there? This place can be overwhelming."

"I work in hospitals. That part isn't scary," he snapped.

She quickly moved on. "She's just come through surgery. The doctors are down the hallway and will be checking in to update her treatment. Did you want to sit, maybe have some water?"

"Her head is wrapped. Do you know how bad it is?"

"Talking to the doctors would be a good idea. They can tell you more about how she's doing and the next steps."

"Next steps?"

Miranda paused. "The doctors will determine if she is going in again today for more surgery." She could sense his tension.

He touched the bed gently. "Her leg too. This shouldn't have happened."

The sadness in his voice and his gentle stroke of Shelly's blanket made Miranda's throat tighten. She let her hand fall to her leg and pinched it as she listened to him, trying to stop Eli's legacy from entering the room. *It's not your pain.*

"Okay, I'll grab that water."

"Could she die?" he asked softly.

"Sir, I think we need to—"

"I didn't think anything could be worse than her leaving me."

"Knock, knock."

Both Miranda and Mr. Blake looked toward the voice as the tall doctor filled the doorway.

Chapter Twenty-Seven

"I wanted the car to hit me. Before it happened, I actually said it out loud." John searched through the foliage. With a shudder, a sense of culpability crept up his arms. He slowed to a stop in the tall grass as the woman dipped out of sight into a section of trees and disappeared. His fight or flight instinct continued to flare, and the paranoia of being pursued pushed him to trudge through the hillside faster.

"Hello?" The sound of his voice made his loneliness all too real. He gazed back at the road, undecided whether he should stick to that path or go after the woman, this Shelly. Neither seemed like the right call. He hated her for the life she had taken from him, but a part of him felt at ease with her there. Both were traveling the same road for a reason, and he couldn't deny that staying together felt right. Or at least, it felt strategic to keep her with him.

The hillside wasn't inviting; it didn't boast a celestial warmth of light and angels. Having been taught ad nauseam about the hierarchy in heaven and the plan to reunite with true family in the afterlife, this dark road and forest didn't come close. Instead of kin, he had united with a woman who chased after dead children and saw ghosts. So much for the steps leading to salvation. He scoffed at his stupidity. He'd been gullible enough to accept his mother's belief in God and eternity, and that a person's place in the universe had meaning.

He pulled at the back of his hair, his anxiety growing as the night drifted in like a veil drawn over the moon. His unease started to mesh with anger. Perhaps, at one time, he believed he had been heard on those Sundays lined up in the pew, as he folded his hands to pray. Clearly, all were lies. They should have been honest about where you go when you die. A blank, fucking world.

John stomped through the field. Joanne came to mind, and he imagined the moment she would realize her son was dead. The same face he had stared into his whole life, the never-ending frown, devoid of affection or caring. Estranged for some time, his biological sisters would find his death convenient. They would be freed from the fear of his showing up on their doorstep, looking for a handout or a couch to sleep on. John's dad had died sixteen years earlier, and much of the details surrounding his death were vague. They didn't speak about him.

Straining to find a path, a faint glow appeared ahead, shining through the black. Spindles of light drifted through the branches, a hue of gold flickering briefly on, then off. It was the only life he'd seen since the woman. Everything else had been a rabbit hole of delusion. His feet moved forward—they apparently had a plan—and the rest of him followed.

The inside of his mouth went dry, like after eating day-old wheat bread in the chapel on Sunday. Little cubes given for the body and a tablespoon of water to signify Christ's blood. Hand to hand, passed to each member, the bitter paste sat at the edge of his tongue. He could hear the choir too, a hymn in harmony, high then low. A buoyant song.

We go there someday...temple is a place... spirits pray.

John was unsure if the song came from outside or inside himself, and he held his hands over his ears. No exalted god or burning demon manifested, only echoes of would-be churchgoers praising false idols. The singing continued, and blood flushed his cheeks.

As John got closer to the flicker, the singing increased in volume. A cloud circled and thickened, and he struggled to see his hand held before him. Suddenly, he lost connection with the ground, and his chest lurched as he dropped.

He submerged in warm water rushing past in a garbled roar.

At first, he panicked, and frantically pulled for the surface. But that quickly dissipated. The bath held him in comfort, a soothing cocoon of liquid. He was floating. It was a restful place, neither cold nor too hot. Were hands massaging him? He didn't care. Maybe he'd stay there and sleep. But then the impulse to breathe ignited a frantic whipping of arms. He felt strangled, unable to inhale.

With no clear direction, he saw waning light through the bubbles around him. A whooshing sound filled his ears as he kicked frantically and clawed for the surface, moving away from the darkness towards the light. Finally, he broke the surface, slapping a hand down as his face shot up; he coughed and sucked in air. He was in a chamber of milky walls, like the texture of lemon juice hitting cream, covered by corkscrewing ribbons of light that danced off the pool's surface. On either side of him, nothing but stone.

John groped at his chest. The fabric on his body changed to white, a garment rough against his skin. He'd felt its texture before, a weighted suction against his torso, pulled down by the chunky cotton swallowing up water. It pulled down on his shoulders and the back of his arms.

A baptismal font. It was a baptism. It would free him of sin—that's what they said. The water slapped his face; he was eight years old and wanted out, like the water burned his skin. Then came guilt for hating the plunge. Looking up from under the surface, he wondered whose sins were cleansed. No one in the chapel knew his father's knuckles were scabbed over from hitting him or his mother. Did the water wash those transgressions? How would this font wash John's spirit and evil deeds?

Find the stairs. John swirled about, looking for a rail or foothold, as the water turned icy cold. The lights around him started to move away, lower, and lower, and the room dimmed. His breath quickened as he swam toward the side. Each finger curled over the porcelain edge of the tub, and he started to pull and grip the side in unison with his bare toes.

Spirits don't cross over, John. They stay.

Initially, the words sounded like one saintly voice, but soon several overlapped. John trembled, closed his eyes, and hugged the sidewall. To look meant he would know who was speaking.

Your body is the gift, a righteous gift.

The sound of singing, high and youthful, like a children's choir.

John, our bodies are the vessel.

Over his shoulder, ten rounded, pale shapes hovered above the waterline. As the water ebbed, a swirl of light passed over each of them, refracting off the surface. They were heads, each angled down, hair spilling into the pool. All wore the same white cloth.

Clamping his hands onto the edge of the tub, John held his breath, lips shivering in the icy water as panic surged. The bodies floated in his peripheral. Then, in a burst of energy, he levered himself up and lunged forward to escape. The hands of each figure jerked toward him, their fingers pulling at his head and forcing him back into the water.

Take us through, John.

One on top of the other, their blue eyes and ghostly faces beamed through strands of wet hair. Heads squirmed. Mouths moved, but their words were muffled through sloshing currents. Under the weight of their hold, he dropped below the surface again and again. With each plunge and lift upward, more hands gripped his body, leaving him to gurgle screams while he swung his arms. Once, John saw his mother seated to the right above him. She wore the same flamboyant green dress and spectacles she'd worn to his job. In her lenses, light flashed, and his thrashing glared back like fireworks.

Plunged again, foam drenched the light over his head. His eyes never left his mother. Up again, she remained, but she wasn't alone now. A petite figure stood to her left, a boy wearing only underpants, chewing his fingernails.

"Mother." Water filled his mouth.

John, be renewed. Wash it away.

They spoke in unison, holding him down. Fingers and hands clutched his face and chest, quickening his descent until his ears popped. The need for air pried at his clenched lips, and a reflex pushed him to inhale. His lips parted in a final thrust, and fluid rushed in.

Chapter Twenty-Eight

Wake up.

Shelly's eyes fluttered open.

A green carpet, reminiscent of rotten avocado, lay beneath her. The course fibers needled her cheek. She vaulted to her feet, jumping around as if avoiding a scurry of rodents at her ankles.

Something flexed in her mind. The room had been locked countless times, in her dreams or in her sessions with Dr Frazier-Velli. She would stand on the other side of the door, desperate to know what was happening inside.

Past the threshold now, she stood spellbound, transported back in time. She was in her mother's room. A sewing machine tucked away in the corner held pleasant memories of quilting with her mother, passing the needle back to her from underneath the throw. She visualized her mother hunching over the machine, an appliance the size of a clothes dryer, smoothing fabric under the churning needle. Really, it was the size of a microwave, piled high with cut fabric and unfinished projects. To the left, a dining chair held yards of cloth; some had fallen onto the floor.

The room had dark wood molding and yellowish walls, with a patch of carpet in the middle circled by dressers and side tables. Pills and bottles were sprinkled on every surface. *Smacking lips. On his teeth. White paste, chewing pills without water.* Shelly turned away. The flashback fired off in her brain. A large hand, with tablets clutched in the palm. The remnants of addiction, fragments of her father lurked, and she worried she would be sick.

Each stick of furniture was covered in junk. A thin, bare mattress was piled with mismatched blankets and uncovered pillows. The

~ 150 ~

drawers of a dresser tucked in a corner were open, with clothing hanging out.

Then she saw it: her father's belt. The fear only a child could know surged within her. She wrapped her arms around her shoulders. *I did something wrong. He doesn't see me. He doesn't see. Make him go away.*

The belt, dangling from a nail, told a story. The wall looked like a bleeding ulcer beneath the leather strap. Layers of paint had been eroded away by soiled hands in a hurry to grab it off the wall. The sight of it resurrected an old fear. The band would wrap around his palm, while the other end dangled. The belt was the only thing in its proper place in the chaotic room.

Shelly had little recollection of her father, but as she moved through space, memories tucked into nooks and crannies whispered to her. She remembered only that he would eventually find her, though details of the before and after remained inaccessible. An internal buzz, something programmed inside, told her to stay on alert. She strained to listen for anything else alive in the room. There was only silence.

As she stood there, the room filled gaps in her memory. But it wasn't until she took another half turn that **Shelly** came face to face with her mother's closet.

Not the door. Not the room. The closet.

The focus of many psychiatric sessions stood before her. It had become a gateway of sorts, where phantoms and echoes rushed forward, puzzle pieces to decipher. She put a hand on the door and leaned in. She could only guess the contents of the closet, but a feeling of sadness gripped her. Grief and pity lived inside, locked tightly away. Pity for whom? **Shelly** didn't know, but she felt the crater of missing space, and this angered her. Days and days of flashbacks and nightmares out of control, all dictating her life, but when it was time to call up her history and put the pieces together, the voices stayed silent.

She closed her eyes, hoping to hit the play button in her mind and bring forward an answer or clue. As lights can shine through closed eyelids, Shelly saw shoulders and arms beneath a quilt of shadows. Two people, a pair, one larger and taller than the other, were fighting. The dominant one held their frame rigid and squared off, while the other shuddered, and then was tossed aside.

"Mama?" Her hands slid against the cheap wood grain, too scared to yank on the doorknob. In an instant, she saw the place as seven-year-old Shelly. The walls were taller, the room larger, and her confidence retreated.

Under her palms, she felt an oily substance. She pulled back from the door and noticed it was smeared with blood. In shock, she stumbled over a box and onto the floor, falling onto her elbows and twisting back on all fours.

Shelly!

A cool, massaging sensation slid up her shoulders, so faint that at first, she thought it was a breeze from an opened window. Then a hard squeeze descended. Something had her. Each arm wedged closer to her torso. She contorted and tried to raise her hands, but its grip was strong.

Several voices came at once, high and low volume, moving ear to ear.

Glossing over whatever the fuck was going on. Fucking useless. Disappearing into wherever you go. Who could love you?

Familiar haunts talked over one another, each stronger than the next, filling her head, only this time she wasn't tethered to Dr. Frazer-Velli's melodic tone. Paul's knock to the brow buzzed on her skin as if it had just happened, and she felt eyes drifting around her. She grew dizzy. Shouts echoes from all sides. Shelly's mouth seemed taped shut, and her body was paralyzed, unable to fight the hold on her bicep.

It's bad. I don't like it here. Mommy, who's Red? Monsters aren't real. You're crazy.

Without warning, something flipped Shelly over from her back to her stomach and pushed her to the ground. A glistening pool of urine hovered above the algae texture of the green rug. She screamed and tried to push away, but sour ammonia splashed across her face.

She writhed along the floor, a weight still pressed to her spine. Dr Frazier-Velli's voice boomed in her skull. Instead of hope and validation, he had a darker message:

Don't go in there. Not allowed. Don't open. They will find out. You're weak. This isn't going to fix you. You created demons.

The voice mixed with Paul's, Josie's, John's, and her father's. Others, which she could not place, joined in.

None of them are moving. Blood on your— It won't wash off. Hide from me, you little fucker. Don't you ever hide when I call for you. This is for you, Shelly.

The force abated, and she tried to get up, but the lights went out around the periphery. Her lungs were clogged with dense air, and she swerved to the left as a firm grip on her neck caught her and lifted her off her feet.

Don't you dare leave this room.

Just as swiftly, she was released. Her body crumpled to the ground, and she held up her hands in surrender.

Then Shelly heard giggling down the hallway. She was not alone.

Chapter Twenty-Nine

Miranda bustled around the unit, trying to wrap up. Patient handover would start in forty-five minutes, when each nurse would pass off their patients to the night shift team. She couldn't be happier; there would be no bells, alarms, or people chattering at her for status. Three days off would start with a few ticks of the clock.

At the nursing station, the bay door opened, and a hospital bed rolled in. Miranda did her best to repress her anger. "Hey, who accepted this patient?" She stood and blocked the gurney, staring at the staff escorting it.

"I don't know. They don't tell us shit. It took a while because they weren't sure if she needed ICU or ortho."

Her heart sank. The blonde-haired little girl she had treated the day before, lay asleep. Before she could take out a week's worth of rage on an innocent staff person, she heard her name. Spinning around, she saw Mark, the nursing manager, running over.

"It's okay. This is our patient." He stared at her sheepishly.

She and Mark shared an irreverent working relationship; both had started the same year at the hospital. Mark stood six-foot-five, with a short beard and a strip of manicured hair down the center of his bald head. He had attention deficit disorder and took pills for it. Everything that came out of his mouth was sass or catty one-liners. Nothing was too lowbrow. Their relationship had formed over his lurid stories of ejaculation while being playfully choked or Miranda's judicious caregiving of herpetic ulcers or labial abscesses.

Miranda teased him that she knew two versions: Mark and his alter-ego. The alter ego, she called HeteroMan. The person who showed up in meetings spoke firmly, wore gray scrubs, and offered concrete solutions. This was the part of him that existed above the waterline, comfortably sharing his role as a nurse with administration duties. But the beautiful, colorful layers of his personality were often pushed out.

The paperwork and belongings exchanged hands, and both porters backed out the door.

"What the fuck!" she whispered angrily. "It's thirty 'til end of shift and this is a post-op ICU. Are you kidding me? I've still got charting on my regular patients to do. Why is she on this unit, anyway?" She walked down the hallway, leaving him with the gurney. In a rattle of clicks, she heard him gather the bed and push it forward.

"Miranda!" he called, shooting a lower lip out in exaggerated frown and gesturing for her to follow. She sighed and gave in, resisting the urge to jump up and down in frustration like a little kid.

She followed Mark and the bed, grabbing hold of the side, but not giving him the pleasure of eye contact. They scooted the gurney into a room.

"This is Josie Blake," he said. "You saw her in the ED yesterday?"

Miranda sighed, fuming, gathering tubes and hooking the patient up to monitors. "I remember the fucking patient, Mark," she said while multitasking the setup. "A compound fracture. Quit talking to me, and let's get her checked in." She turned on autopilot, wanting to be done with the week.

Miranda's hands shook from a surge of aggravation. Through a long exhale, she gently placed the stethoscope down on the girl's chest. She noted the normal thumps and gurgles, and the whooshing of inhalation. Although there were stitches across her forehead and bruising around her eye and the side of her face, her insides were clicking right along.

"Listen," Mark said sympathetically, reaching out to touch Miranda's arm. "This guy's wife and daughter were both in a car accident." He clicked down one bedrail.

"I know! I have the wife—or I did." She looked at the wall. "What day is it? I can't even remember." She pulled out flushes for the IVs. "They shuffled after yesterday's discharges, and I didn't get her back."

She paused, looking at him distractedly. "Are you wearing eyeliner?"

"Fuck you! It's Stonehenge gray, and I had a date." He smiled and leaned in, talking at low volume. "You didn't get her back because they went in again. She spiked a fever, and they were worried about her leg and did a little squish and suck." Mark had a talent for highlighting the disgusting, using crude slang for debridement of dead tissue. He hummed while arranging blankets around Josie's upper body. "There's some odd energy with this one."

"What do you mean?"

"I guess the dad works for Provident. He's like a QI guy. They also said he's involved in a staff investigation."

Miranda stopped typing and considered the information. "It doesn't sound like anything different from what he normally does. How is that suspicious?"

He clicked his tongue against his teeth. "It isn't, but I got a text from the nurse administrator. The mother and the daughter were supposed to be on this floor. Mandatory." He scanned the door to the hallway. "Why would they need them together? This girl is clearly orthopedics. You're not brilliant with that. We all know."

She glared at him.

Mark smiled. "She's doing fine. External fixtures but probably outpatient in two days. Also, the reason she's here so late—" He slipped around the bed, speaking quietly. "She's being hot-potatoed between two units. They kept getting mixed confirmations about her acceptance. That's coming from management quarreling, not the floor." He looked at her with wide, smoky eyes. "Why is management bouncing a seven-year-old unit to unit?"

Miranda scrutinized him again. "Glitter too? You're thirty-three!"

He recoiled, his mouth open, as if she'd slapped him.

"Mark," she said. "Shit happens all the time. It's probably some conflict of interest, or the guy has the potential to tattle on nurses. Unfortunately, I'm the bitch who keeps ending up with these people, so I guess I'm the one they can tattle on." She connected the flush of saline to the IV on the child's arm. The port ran fine, and she hooked the pump to administer pain medication.

"It's strange, all this pressure," Mark glanced into the hall. "I'm not even sure the mother will transfer out to Neuro ICU, where she should be." He looked back at her. "I think this is a fucking liability mess and a bit of favoritism."

Miranda couldn't help but wonder if the emergency services team had argued over Eli. Did his care team bother to see past the hospital bed, past the monitors and red tape?

He'd kissed her goodbye on a Wednesday morning and left for Florida. Eli boarded a boat with friends that Friday, then died in the ocean. He disappeared forever. Since that day, Miranda had been trying to crawl back into some resemblance of life, one uncomfortable inch at a time. Were Eli's nurses and doctors also people whose shift had run over, people as jaded and exhausted as she was? Had they shown any empathy for his circumstances?

The bed burst into life as Josie shot up wide-eyed, sucking in the air like someone drowning. Miranda knocked against the computer as she rushed to bedside. Josie's arms lifted, pressing against the limitations of her casts and fasteners, and her legs squirmed under the blanket. She lunged to the side and would have flipped out of bed if Miranda had not caught her. Mark ran over to push the call light and then put a knee on the bed, angling to get behind Josie.

The child continued to push forward, held back by Miranda, who nodded at Mark to pull up from behind. Josie's eyelids, half open and heavy with sedation, stared forward. Her lips were moving, mumbling, and then a panic-filled cry emitted. She continued to thrash, trying to leave the bed.

"She's not awake, Mark."

"No. No!" Josie screamed, while Mark pulled her back onto the mattress. "They are dead! It's cold. Why are they dead?" The girl shrieked in nonlinear chunks, her eyes shifting from wide open to slits.

"Sweetie, you're here with me. I'm Miranda. This is the hospital. Calm down." She glanced over to Mark. "We should page the doctor for some medication."

"You got this if I go?" He looked at the child swaying at her side.

"Yeah, just come back with a helpful cocktail."

Josie turned to stare at Miranda and then her hand slid up Miranda's forearm, petting it slowly like you would a sleeping cat. "I don't like it. My mommy's in the woods. I can't like it." Her eyes started to droop.

"You're in the hospital, remember?" Miranda studied her face, attempting to gauge her level of consciousness. "Your mom is in surgery, honey." She held her shoulders. "No woods. You are both here in the hospital."

Josie looked down and seemed bewildered by the cast on her arm. "Red. Red came. She was taking me to my mommy." Slowly, her face grimaced. "They were all dead. Did you see them?" She locked eyes with Miranda.

"See what? Who's dead, honey?" Miranda felt uneasy as she spoke, knowing the brain can do powerful things when it's asleep. Scary things.

"Did you see the dead kitty? I don't want to go there anymore. I want my mom to come back. She doesn't have to stay there."

The child looked tired, with a hunched posture and foggy eyes.

It must be so frightening to be without her mother. This was a loss Miranda knew all too well, an emptiness that hung off her own back and breathed into her ear.

"Where, honey? Where would Mommy have to stay? Tell me."

Josie was falling asleep, so Miranda supported her back into bed.

"With the dead things," the girl murmured, before her eyes closed completely.

Chapter Thirty

Shelly scrambled to the other side of the bed, trying to hide. The sound of footsteps grew closer. Crouched behind a dresser, she saw Josie and someone else run into the room. Her heart surged, but this energy quickly died with the sight of Josie's companion, a petite little girl.

The girl's hair was pulled into a disheveled ponytail, and some strands hung down the sides of her face. She wore the same cut-offs with ink stains on the knees, and her tee shirt sagged off one shoulder. Her slip-on shoes had frayed edges, and the white soles, discolored by use, were cracked. Shelly couldn't help but inch closer to get a clearer view. Josie's companion smiled with her arms folded, then dropped them nervously. Shelly followed the lines of her features like a map. A baby-like nose, round at the end with a youthful fullness. Shelly stroked her own cheeks and cupped her chin, smoothing the lines and ridges of her face, comparing herself to the young girl. The girl's eyes were round, with a dusting of pink around the edges. Someone had said they were like rose petals, smooth and sweet, a place for smooches. The thought struck as if it had been called out in the room. Unmistakable now was the figure from her nightmares: Red.

Like every encounter, Red looked the same. The shirt was her mother's, a favorite in gray cotton. The pants were new, a rarity, but an ink pen had broken at school covering them in stains, and the pants had been cut. One distinct trait burned into Shelly's brain was Red's hands, covered in blood from the elbow down to her fingers. In all the dreams, the blood was fresh. They shared the same childhood. They shared the same tragedies and when Shelly reached adulthood, they shared dreams. Red was Shelly as a child.

On good days, Mother showed kindness. She might get up from bed or even make dinner. She would hold Shelly's face, kiss her forehead, and for a short while, they were safe. The good days were hard to let go, and Shelly had craved them like a drug. Only Red understood this longing.

"Josie," Shelly whispered, her chest twitching with the instinct to grab her daughter and run. Her daughter wore the same outfit from the crash. Her arm looked severely broken, although as she bounced joyfully, it flopped at her side. Then, as Shelly stared, Josie's arm slowly healed. The blood vanished from the child's shirt, the withered arm shuddered and snapped into proper form. During the healing, Josie giggled and chased her playmate around the room, completely unaware that anything was changing.

Red turned her head, pointing at something to her right and revealing more of her face. Her delicate highlights were not the same on both sides; when she turned, she displayed a dark and swollen mass around one eye, and her blush lips were split with a large gash.

Shelly muffled her scream, slapping her hand over her mouth, as she huddled next to the bureau. His rings. The wedding band and class ring. She saw the image of hands dangling beside a man's hip, and a leg, tensing and clenching. She longed to run and crouched, ready to sprint.

"Hey, I want to show you something," Red said to Josie.

Show her what? Shelly focused on nothing but the girls' next move, the hole in the door, the scattered pills, the belt. What were they doing here?

"What is it?" Josie asked.

Red stepped forward and touched the edge of a gold doorknob. From her spot on the floor, Shelly arched her neck, moving forward slightly to see. She heard the shutter and click of the door opening, expecting a release of pressurized air or a hanging body. Something dark had been kept there, and Josie stood at the threshold.

I needed to look, make sure they were okay. Further messages surfaced from the depths of her awareness, like sticky notes on a white wall, yet remained obscure. The anger surged as her brain betrayed her, retained its secrets. As soon as the quarrel surged in her mind, her body bolted from the floor.

"Josie, no! Don't open the closet," she screamed, moving toward the girls. "Josie, sweetie. Take my hand!"

Neither of the girls looked in her direction. Shelly tried to reach out, but her hand stopped short like she'd hit an unseen barrier.

"You can't touch her," said Red. "You're not allowed to. Stop it." Her childlike voice now sounded mature.

Shelly snatched her hand back to her chest. "You see me?"

Red didn't flinch. She'd known Shelly was there all along. Rather than a satellite piece of recollection, Red surely held power here. Shelly's eyes picked a spot on the floor while her mind raced.

The closer she came to unscrambling her thoughts, the more real it became. She was reluctant to accept this room, this place. The repetitions of her abuse, re-runs of painful traumas, were inflicted on her frequently, but now, being in her mother's room and watching Josie—all this was orchestrated. It was different from her flashbacks.

"*You're* doing this!" she said.

Red showed little reaction as the hold on Shelly's shoulders returned, as if she were constrained by a binding rope drawn taut around her form, rendering her immobile. She twisted and kicked at the hidden binding, arching her back and crying out.

"What are you doing? Let me go," she yelled, her body hanging above the girls now. Josie sat on the floor at the base of the closet while Red, covered in blood, glared at Shelly. She looked like no seven-year-old should, domineering and parental.

"I want to see. What is it?" Josie tugged at Red's arm, smearing blood, unaware. She then turned her attention to open the closet. Inside hung a blue dress with white trim, and next to it, a paisley blouse. The clothes dangled above a cardboard box with ripped edges and newspaper folded over the sides. Shelly could barely breathe under the grip on her chest.

"Let me go. Josie, run!" Her words squeezed through a clenched windpipe.

She wanted to look away but at the same time was desperate to see, so she allowed her eyes to trace the blue dress down to the box on the floor. Then, somewhere mixed with the color of the clothing and the rigid black slashes of the print on the box, her mind started to shuffle the memories, like playing cards in a game of poker.

The box. Oh god, they're in the box. It's cold. Curled into a ball, in my hand. She remembered the squishy and smooth feel at her fingertips. Even with her eyes clamped shut, she could visualize the kittens. One white, two orange-striped, and one with long gray hair had made up the litter. At first, they were hard to make out, other than outlines of palm-sized circular shapes. Some clustered to the left corner and two in the bottom right. They likely curled together to stay warm.

The mama lost her milk. We didn't have money for food.

Red smiled and joined Josie. She giggled and pulled at the box. Released by what held her, Shelly fell to the ground. Although she had been let go, her limbs were still held tightly.

Red took a step toward her. "This is for you, Shelly."

Shelly started to scream and kick with no benefit. Her head rolled down as she sobbed. "This happened to *me*," she said to Red. "It's not her life. Let it stay mine," She jerked against the invisible restraints as sweat ran down her brow. "Josie's never seen death. She can't live with this in her head." Fatigue pulled at her skin; she was powerless to protect her child.

Red ignored her. "They're right here," she told Josie. "She had them three weeks ago, and they are so cute."

It had never occurred to Shelly that the kittens weren't moving. The excitement of holding them overwhelmed any hesitation. Josie would feel the same. Helpless babies, hungry for their mother's milk. What could be more innocent than a child holding a small, fragile kitten?

"I want you to name the gray one. It's a boy," Red said to Josie.

The gray one. Shelly's body twisted and rolled like a cocooned fly under the eye of a spider. *Stay out of this room. Mother said we can't*—She remembered her mother's warning. She couldn't see the kittens unless her mother was present. *I went in anyway. I wanted to see.*

Red shifted the box between them and chatted with Josie, all the while smiling. Shelly rolled side to side, overcome with fear and desperate to fight. She flexed her arms against a stiff cold band, invisible to the eye. Looking at her lower half, the skin indented her limbs and clothing, outlining the straps. In a final roll, she was able to see under the bed. The blanket hung low on one side like a canopy over a tent and a pillow was tucked haphazardly. Random jars, plates, and rags were strewn along the floor. Shelly's eyes tunneled at the still-life scene she had not witnessed for years. She gazed at the light filtering through the thin red weave of the blanket.

"I come here at night and bring the mama cat water and cheese," Red told Josie. The details called Shelly back into the moment. "That way, the babies can still have milk. I hold the kittens as gently as I can." Red looked into Shelly's eyes, regurgitating her childlike reasoning exactly, mocking those few moments of happiness as a child.

Shelly watched, transfixed.

Without dropping her eyes from Shelly, Red said, "Go ahead, Josie, pet one."

Josie reached a hand into the cardboard box.

"No," Shelly screamed in a frenzy of body movement as she tried to escape. *She mustn't see. It's mine. I hid it away. The colorful clothes and the ribbons. Be happy and fearless. This isn't her burden.*

Josie lifted the gray cat out of the box. Suddenly, her expression turned to one of confusion, studying the kitten, stiff in her hand. The cat's limbs were tucked under itself, and the tail encircled the feet. It could have been a paperweight purchased at a beachside store, or a velvet knick-knack of a sleeping cat. Josie gasped and her face changed to fear.

"It's cold!" she whispered.

Shocked, she dropped the kitten and stepped back. Her mouth opened but nothing came out.

Shelly studied her daughter, wondering how she'd react. Shelly had screamed. Yelled for her mother and kicked the box into the back of the closet. Then came the shock of cold water. Her mom had dumped water on her head to stop the screams. Now, Shelly watched her sweet daughter change. Her fearless spirit dissolved into heartbreak. Her glassy eyes filled with tears as she pointed at the box.

"None of them are moving," she muttered.

Red was expressionless.

Shelly, still powerless and held hostage, rolled back and forth on the ground. For Josie, this day would linger, a thorn deeply sunk, and she would try to scratch the images out of her thoughts for years to come.

"It's wrong," Shelly yelled. "She's just a little girl. How could you?"

Red turned around with angry eyes. "This isn't for you to decide."

Shelly's limbs flexed, leaving her sprawled. Her body was filled with mind-numbing pain, stabbing sensations at every joint and tendon. The bones in her leg started to crumble, cracking under the skin, which shook with each fracture. Blood returned to the surface, oozing onto her pants. A deep ache at the arch of her foot and at the back of her knee culminated in the thickest part of her thigh. Slowly, as she cried in agony, the tip of her jagged femur broke through the surface of her skin. She gripped the bone in misery.

Through clenched eyes, she watched Josie above her, looking at Red, then down at the kittens, covering her face and sobbing. Then her vision blurred. Her skull split and cracked with a hollow thud, dulling her consciousness. The last thing she saw was the dead kitten at Josie's feet.

Chapter Thirty-One

Go fuck who you want.

Paul felt his feet drop off the edge of the windowsill. He almost lost his balance and rolled out of the chair. Startled, he jerked his head toward Shelly, fearful he'd missed something, or—a worse thought entered his mind. He dismissed it straight away. She was still here.

Josie's condition remained stable, so he'd been focused on his wife. He got up and walked over to the bed. His fingers hovered above her cupped hand, unsure of her level of awareness. Even in this state, she may loathe his touch.

Aside from the beeping machines and flashing lights circling her bed, the room was still. Her body was covered in tubes and bandages. The ridge of her nose and the lower part of her eyelid peeked through the wrapping around her skull. Even that small patch was discolored and bruised. A tube protruded from her mouth, and the gauze dressings around her head made it look swollen.

The doctors said her prognosis could go either way, and he should prepare himself for the worst. Paul found himself staring at their mouths but hearing only a high-pitched buzz. As the words fell through their lips, he saw black lettering hitting a page, a concrete and emotionless story of their tragedy, like the ones he had dripped coffee over and crammed into piles around his office.

He wanted desperately for Shelly to hear him through her coma. "She said she was new to town. I could have just told her restaurants to try. But I didn't. I don't know why I did this to us. I wish it had been me." He lowered his voice. "You need to be with Josie. A girl needs her mom." He covered his eyes, unable to stop his morbid thoughts from taking over: Josie's gentle features losing color, the light in her eyes dimming as he explained where people go when they die—something he couldn't even explain to himself. *Be here. She's still alive. Be here.*

After some deep breaths, he gained his composure. "Josie's doing okay," he said to Shelly's sleeping face. "Her arm is banged up, but they fixed it. She'll be able to go home in a few days, maybe a week. I need to—"

The front of his shirt vibrated, and he stared at the screen of his phone. It showed a number in the hospital.

He flashed with anger that quickly turned to fear. Did Will know? Fumbling at the smooth edges of his phone, he almost dropped it. "Listen, Will," he said. "It's Shelly—she's been in an accident." It was the first time he'd told anyone.

"You sound awful," a female voice replied. "I heard about your wife and daughter. I'm truly sorry."

A boulder landed at the bottom of Paul's gut, and he swallowed. "Who is this?"

"I wanted to tell you I never intended to sleep with you that night. I didn't go there to do anything but talk." She paused. "I'm sorry it went further, truly. I don't usually drink like that, and I'm guessing you don't either."

Paul rubbed his free hand through his hair. Alcohol wasn't to blame, and he knew it. Guilt pushed the boulder deeper into his abdomen. "I shouldn't be talking to you," he said.

Without answering she continued. "Listen. I'm out of options. No one will help me, so you're going to help me."

Paul pressed the phone to his ear. "What—"

Her voice lowered. "They said it was a routine cesarean, and my son died. The nurses were telling him we had to move, get the baby out. He wouldn't. He held us back." She paused. "I found something. Gossip travels. Doctors might not like being on record, but they talk to nurses, and nurses talk to each other."

Paul knew she worked in one of the local hospitals. A detail that shouldn't factor into the case and would likely complicate matters.

"Save it!" He spat into the phone. "I'm not going to be part of this game. I had a life before this! Three scotches, and everything is falling apart. Do you think my wife and daughter deserved this?"

"Do you think *my* son deserved to die?" she snapped back.

Paul held up his hand, sensing the conversation imploding. Hang up, he thought. Don't go any further. "I know it's a significant amount of money," he said. "I know it's crippling to lose a child—"

"You don't know the first thing about losing a child!" she yelled. "Fuck the money! The money is a smokescreen. They want a medical error to disappear, and they'll throw me to the wolves in the process. If I pay, this all goes away and no one knows what really happened."

The words rang familiar. Paul heard his own rants in her anger, rants of the bottom line and self-preservation.

"Do you like where your family is?" she asked.

His hands were sweating under the clutch of the phone. "What?"

"Why do you think they moved your family to one unit?"

"I don't know what you're talking about." Paul's mind was racing. She knows where Shelly and Josie are. "Is this a threat?" His breath was on pace with the blood pumping in his ears.

"I'm not going away. You're in bed with me now! This is not a disagreement over a bill. It's deeper than that."

Paul dropped into the chair. The room became smaller, and he found himself on an island alone as his family floated away. The anger inside had nowhere to go. Blood pressed into his sinuses. "What are you going to do?" he croaked.

Silence.

"You knew, didn't you? The moment you entered that bar. Are you blackmailing me? Is that what this is?"

"You assholes are all the same," she hissed. "You're going to help me find out what happened, or well, I guess it ends up being about money."

Paul jumped to his feet again, pacing through another flash of anger. "Did you follow me?"

"I was assigned a representative,'" she said, "a useless staff member appointed to review the case. Pathetic!" She scoffed. "I easily Googled you, looked at the hospital website, and figured it out."

Something told him she had left out details. It seemed too simple. "You're lying," he said. "There's something else going on here." He was cut short by rustling and background noise. Talking broke through. More commotion. Muffled, broken voices and pieces of sentences, like a television or radio.

"Hello?" The heat of the phone seemed to reach into his ear canal. More sounds came across the line, much clearer now. His heart sank, and he fell back on his heels, his knees giving away. It was *his* voice at the other end, jovial and drunk, mixed with rhythmic breathing and two people speaking the language of pleasure.

"You recorded me—us?" This was less a question than an acknowledgment. He gripped his neck, trying to release the pressure of the panic blocking his airway. Paul stiffened, and looked over at Shelly, broken and battered. He remembered Shelly's tic, something she'd done for years. His hand, again, found his neck.

"I didn't want to go down this route," Olivia said.

He started to ask what his options were, but a cluster rush of shadows approached the door. A nurse entered. "Mr. Blake? They want you down the hallway. It's your daughter. She's distraught." She raised an eyebrow and stared at his phone with disapproval.

"I can't do this now," he said into the phone. "I don't see a way out of this. I don't." He hung up the phone and hurried after the nurse.

***

Miranda stood over her small patient, watching the monitors and her vital signs. She'd been resting for some time.

Slowly, Josie's eyes fluttered open. "Dad!"

Miranda turned, and Paul Blake stood in the doorway.

He rushed to the bedside, and she nodded at him and stepped away.

Josie winced as she strained to move. Leaning back, she touched her cast, then her eyes closed under the weight of the anesthesia.

"I'm here," Paul said, putting a hand gently on her head.

"It's dark," Josie said. "Mom should come home. I can't get to—"

"It'll be okay." He looked at Miranda. "Is she in pain?"

"I'm getting medications now." She stood at the computer, checking the current amounts.

"They're dead too," Josie said.

He patted her arm, and suddenly the little patient sat up, grabbing onto the bed railing and straining the reach of the IV in her arm.

"I'm going to go get Mom," she slurred. The cast banged against the upper rail, causing her to gasp. "Ouch, it hurts."

Miranda rushed to her side. "Hey, hold on there, young lady. We can't have you doing that."

Josie eased herself back down, riding the waves of ache through her arm.

"I don't know what you are saying, sweetie," Paul said, then to Miranda, "How long has she been like this?"

"She woke up talking this way."

"Mom?" Josie murmured again. "We need to drive—you and me, with Dad." Her face contorted. "What happened? The car—" Her eyes reached for her father. "She can't find her way out! If we drive back, we can get her. Like when Lady ran away. We found her because Lady came to me. No one else."

Mark came in, holding an orange-capped syringe and small silver

~ 171 ~

pouches. "How are we doing?"

Miranda took the syringe from him. She still felt annoyed; he'd made this her problem. She could have been home with her feet on the couch in thirty minutes. With a last-minute patient, she'd still be charting.

"I also paged the doctor about the little gal's confusion," he said.

"I don't need this shit," Josie blurted.

They shared glances.

"Oh sweetie, this isn't shit. I promise," Mark said.

"You can go," Miranda told him.

He frowned and moved toward the door, giving her a final look.

"We need to get Mom," Josie said.

"Mommy's in the hospital, just like you are," Paul said. "When she's better, you can see her. Right now, she's resting."

Miranda moved to the bedside. "Josie," she said softly. "We need to get that arm better so you can give Mommy a big hug."

The girl sluggishly turned over; the corners of her mouth sagged in a flattened, melted expression. "My mom's leg is broken. In the woods, she walked funny, but she didn't see me. I played hide and seek."

Miranda stopped. "Did you hear about your mom already? It can be scary when we know someone is hurt," she said.

"Did someone tell you about her leg?" Paul put his hand on the bedrail.

"No! I hid for the game. I didn't want to. I wanted Mommy."

Miranda had seen the hallucinations patients could have from pain medications. She'd met angels and batted away shadows clinging to curtains. Josie's trip, however, held some accuracies, which was strange. Her own thoughts about seeing Eli's hat on someone else often surfaced—but that was different. Josie was drugged up, pure and simple.

"I don't know what to do," Paul said.

"I can up her pain medication, which will help her sleep. I have another med for her nerves if you think she needs that."

Josie began to cry, first quietly then louder, as she seemed to watch a scene happening before her.

Miranda's knees shook, something that hadn't happened in years. The pain felt close. The sound brought back the nights she sobbed into her pillow and woke with a migraine, her eyes swollen to slits.

It must stop. Shut her up, give her the pills, and go home.

"I'm sorry, I don't know," the girl's father said.

"I think we should do both," she said. "It will help her rest."

"I don't want to sleep," Josie said between sobs. "It does mean things to Mommy. I'm scared."

"You're dreaming, sweetie," Paul said. "Mommy is down the hall. She's here, getting better like you."

"Dad, that's not her," she cried. "What if Mom never comes home? What if she's stuck there forever?" She rocked back and forth, in a woozy daze between sleep and agitation. "That's not her. It's not her."

Miranda sat down and patted Josie's shoulder. "Shhh, I believe you."

The girl shuffled a few more times, then slowed.

Miranda could see Paul's discomfort in her peripheral, but she focused on Josie. "I can tell you love your mom very much." A knot formed in her throat. "I think you saw things when you closed your eyes. I'm so sorry you're scared your mom is in that place."

Josie started to cry again quietly.

Miranda took her free hand. "I want you to get better enough to help your mom. There's no way to help if we are exhausted." She smiled tenderly at the child's badly bruised face. "Is your arm hurting now?"

Josie nodded, breathing in cautious swells. "It hurts so much."

"Okay, let's make that better." Miranda cleaned up and scrubbed Josie's fluid port, then administered her medications. When the girl was settled into the nest of blankets, Paul looked at Miranda and nodded toward the door. She followed him out of the room.

"Why did you say that to her—*that place*? Shelly is here." He pointed down the hall. "She's in that room!"

"Lower your voice! She needed to know that we had her back." Miranda looked toward the nurses' station. "Discounting what she said is only going to make it worse. I simply told her I understood. Her dream is scary!"

Paul crossed his arms. His lips thinned.

"Your daughter has experienced a really scary event," she continued. "Her mom is hurt." She took a half-step closer. "So, don't yell at me. I don't need to be corrected for doing my job." Heat rose in her face, and her muscles buzzed with adrenaline—a sign that she needed to leave the situation. "Now, excuse me. Your new nurse is starting in five minutes." Miranda walked away, leaving him in the hall.

She was still stewing as she finished her notes, her fingers pounding the keyboard. She stepped back into Josie's room to make sure she was calm and comfortable. The girl's face had smoothed, and her eyes drooped sleepily.

"Will you be my nurse tomorrow?" Josie asked.

"No, honey, I'll be at home getting some rest too," she whispered. "You need to sleep now. I'm sure your nurse will be great. Better than me, even," she said.

"I think I'll see you tomorrow," Josie said in a slur. "I think I will. In my dreams, there are nice people too, not just mean ones. Red is nice sometimes. She has a funny laugh." She managed a crooked smile.

Miranda turned to sneak out while Josie let out another yawn, taking one last look at the monitor.

"Eli too," Josie said.

She stopped cold. A tightness moved through her chest, and goosebumps formed on her neck.

"There are nice ones there too," Josie trailed off, falling asleep.

Chapter Thirty-Two

As his vision returned, John saw clouds of mist above dark blades of grass. Gasping for air, he pushed forward, unsure whether the attackers were gone. The pounding of his heart muffled all other sounds.

The humidity draped its thick, sauna-like weight over him; each breath moved over his tongue like dense vapor. Fear crawled up his arms, spread over his scalp and raised his hair. The ground below was coarse and uneven, and ahead of him, shoots of hay extended like long, thin fingers. He looked back to see if anyone was following him, but the lifeless road was empty.

Haze took over, encircling him in a blanket of white. John froze. Under his feet, the crunch of the field kept him grounded but soon, even that anchor faded. Then, as quickly as it arrived, the fog pulled back to reveal a clear, dark night.

A neighborhood stretched ahead. His heart sank, and his hand found the familiar place behind his ear. A center strip of trees separated a pair of one-way roads. Cars hugged the curbs, and streetlights spotlighted the tucked-away houses; some were maintained, and others had been left to decay. Swatches of grass choked abandoned lawnmowers and deserted walkways. Waterlogged newspapers littered the porches. The scene was still—not a flash of television from a dimly lit window or even a barking dog. Dead like the road.

John's paranoia swelled. He stood on the lawn of a house he knew well. He'd been led from the road to the watery crypt, and now to his childhood home. *Skinny little bitch. She thought she was better than us.* Each word spiked his heart. Maybe the road knew his fate, and the house was a trap. He stopped, dreading whatever was ahead.

On each visit to his mother's house, he'd prepare for her verbal barrage of disappointments, the blatant attacks followed by scotch and some type of casserole. At the tense dining table, John would stare at her broad hands, the black hair growing from a birthmark. The fear of being hit with a fork in his mouth haunted him still.

Avoiding her was never an option. To do so would mean endless, unpredictable attacks. Stepping into her house made him a hostage until dinner was finished. Afterward, he could live in peace for a few months. He should have moved or run away years ago like his sisters, but an invisible shackle was locked around his ankle.

The house looked like a brown, two-story bread box. A low-pitched roof covered the square frame; matching windows were at each corner. The faded tones of a dark orange door glared against the wood siding like a bruise, a gaping mouth or stretching keyhole, as in *Alice's Adventures in Wonderland*.

A dated hatchback sat in the drive, a blue Toyota with rust corroding a dent on the side door. The yard was uneven and patchy, inferior to others on the block, with plain green shrubbery and a few stray flowers. Neighbors often complained to the city about their yard, though they never offered a helping hand. The grass grew ass-high during the early summer, and their push mower didn't stand a chance. Trash cans were tucked next to the garage, filled to the brim. Likely, his mother had forgotten to take them to the curb again, maybe for weeks.

At the door, the paint peeled around the knob, splintering along the frame's molding, scratched from ancient dogs, long dead. A black plaque hung: No Soliciting. He put his hand on the doorknob and turned it, feeling the cold under his fingers. The door opened and swung freely. His whole body froze.

The front room expanded to the left, with a hallway down the middle and the kitchen, tucked out of view. Normally, his mother would be in front of the television in a long sleeveless dress, no matter the season, a chilled drink in hand, nursing the glass like a newborn at a nipple. But the chair and room were vacant. Her paisley-covered couch and a recliner in the center obstructed the flow from the door to the back of the house.

The television sat squarely under the window, lighting up the darkness. He stared at the flickering silence for a few seconds, at the glow flowing over her chair. Something didn't seem right; there were too many inconsistencies. He stepped back outside, searching the street, then looked down at the lawn.

A white stain, the size of a soccer ball, broke up the uniform sidewalk. There, John had smashed a jar of ash from Mount St. Helen against the pavement. The scars under his shoulder blade started to tingle as a noxious sulfur smell filled his nostrils. John's father had kept the ashes—a strange souvenir that held some attachment for him—and in an angry fit, John had broken the jar. This act ignited a rage in his mother greater than any other episode.

A rubber hose slinked through a tree: a makeshift rope swing. John had many rubber burns from summer nights with the neighborhood kids. Below the tree, a crimson bike lay on its side. His mother had insisted on a side mirror on one handle. The sight of it left him baffled. She had gotten rid of that bike years ago. As he kneeled next to it, he saw now it was a cheap bike with chipped chrome, yet similar enough to the 1996 GT Performer he'd wanted.

Goosebumps dotted his arms, and he resisted the compulsion to pull at the hair behind his ear. The red paint on the bike had a lustrous glitter, which sparkled even at night. The velvety metal felt cool as he ran his hands over the frame. The mirror was cracked in the center, with a missing triangle-sized piece. *I didn't mean it. Mom, don't hurt me. I didn't mean it.* John pulled his hand back, losing balance and falling back over his heels.

The bike mirror had caught the edge of the curb, a simple mistake. The splinter of glass had spun like a prism, catching the sun as it turned in the air. One thousand ten-year-olds had done the same thing, but the hell he encountered when his mother discovered his clumsiness was unforgettable. The stabbing pain as she hit him on the ears. The following day, there was a dry crust and blood on his pillow and in his hair. The feel of dried clumps between his fingers never seemed to disappear. A burst of anger clutched his chest. It was all wrong. The road was controlling him, controlling what he saw.

He rushed back inside and stood panting in the eerie living room. His chest burned. The burrowing ache knocked him backward. He clutched the smoking fabric of his shirt as his chest was peppered with circular burns. His abdomen flexed with each snap of flame, and the scars reopened one by one in a ring of red glow, then turning black and blistered. They lit up against his bare, pale chest like a spreading rash of torment, boils left to fester and heal slowly.

The heat pulled away from his skin as quickly as it had started, and the burning stopped. Only his frantic breathing remained, and the sweet and putrid odor of burned skin. He coughed, trying to expel the stink. The old scars returned; a daily reminder of his childhood morphed into white, glossy rings of healed tissue.

Down on the floor, at the eye level of a child, the view matched that of his nightmares. A dark room, a throbbing heart, the flashing of the sinister television—murmurs mixed with the canned laughter of *The Price is Right*.

Chapter Thirty-Three

An amber-colored drink sat on the end table—evidence of Joanne's lies about her Mormon faith. The glass dripped with condensation. John moved cautiously from the wall and stepped around the recliner. The seat of the once-blue chair looked ashen, broken down from the corpulence of her rear and hours spent in the same position.

In the kitchen, he stood at the sink, which was oxidized and rimmed with cracked sealant. Decaying dishes were stacked on the Formica counter, giving the surface a coating of disease.

You think I have money in the bank for you to fill your face? Waste of skin you are. I'll tell you when it's your dinner time.

The slightest glance, scent, or texture brought back a barrage of memories: pleas for food, hiding scraps under his shirt, praying to return to his room before she noticed. Her rage had never had a pattern. The mental maps he drew, trying to navigate to safety, always led to a trap. Like the road's unknowable deceptions, Joanne always veered off course.

On the ceiling, a recessed box light flashed menacingly, adding an unnatural glow. Framed photographs caught the glare of the light's random bursts. One had a blue marbled background with his family standing stadium-style, donning superficial smiles. He pressed a finger to his own face in the photo—sunken cheeks and fearful eyes above dark circles. In a strange way, his image, frozen in time, reminded him of the picture on milk cartons. He looked like a lost child.

Next to him in the photo sat his butterball siblings, carbon copies of his mother. His sisters were out of the house before he turned ten, and before that, they were barely home.

Then John stared at his father. *You have to remind me of him, don't you?* His father had a broad face, rounded chin, deep-set eyes, and prominent cheekbones. John never saw the resemblance. Nevertheless, she repeated the same accusation over and over.

Down the hall, someone began yelling and arguing, and he was startled. His body was fired with adrenalin. The voice was confusing, more high-pitched than her brash tone. Before he could think or move, Joanne crashed into the room. John instinctively dropped into the formation of his youth and curled down, covering his head with his hands.

"You did it this time, boy. Not a tear, pussy," she yelled.

Every part of Joanne's body told a story. The hem of her skirt brushed past, thick hips swinging under her waistless, cotton tarp of a dress. The sway in her gait was likely due to the scotch; she could shotgun three or four in a sitting. Muttering under her breath, she slammed cabinets, but John couldn't get his body to respond. He was stuck to the floor, thoughts of survival racing. *Get on your bike. Go, now.*

Suddenly, she moved closer. His shoulders rolled down towards his ankles into a tight ball. A crackling of plastic, then pretzels sprinkled the floor. Her body jerked, and she cussed under her breath. She dropped a bowl, and it shattered at her feet sending a shockwave through John's core.

"Look what you made me do," she yelled.

John covered his ears. His skin ran over with gooseflesh. *I asked nice. I wanted something to eat. I asked nice.*

Suddenly, a force pulled his arm, exposing the pale underbelly of skin. Again, jagged cuts slowly opened to the elbow, oozing blood.

"Please, I—" With a firm yank, he was able to free his arm and brace it close to his chest. The pain sucked his focus and strength, and he waited, trying to think clearly enough to plot an escape. Run to the bike, get to the grass or the hills where Shelly had gone. Yet the sequence of images and sounds linked together. He couldn't leave. More had happened within these walls—what was he meant to see? The memories leeched from the plaster all around him.

The glass, the broken dish.

John nodded slowly. "It happened. Joanne ripped into my skin."

Get to the bedroom. Beat her there.

His sneakers squeaked as he stepped through his own blood. He ran from the kitchen, flung open the bedroom door, and his heart dropped at the sight of a frail boy, wearing only underwear, lying curled up on a bed. He slept fitfully, flush-faced and shivering. John moaned softly, clutching his sliced forearm. Drops of blood surrounded his feet, and John flashed instantly to his state of panic as a boy, bouncing on his toes and checking the hallway with his hands flapping. "She's coming. She's coming! We have to leave." He went to the bedside. "Um, kid?" He wasn't sure how to address himself.

John's first thought was to pick the boy up, cuts and all. But he decided against it, not knowing what would happen, not knowing what he symbolized—a ghost or an intruder?

Vomit stained the pillow next to the boy, and some had spattered onto the floor. Then it hit. Heat exploded in John's cheeks; nausea curdled his gut. John touched his lips as a faint, sour burn radiated under his fingers.

He'd been sick in the night but hadn't realized it until his mother smeared the vomit on his face. His muscles drooped, and he looked up at the ceiling in defeat. They weren't getting away. The door flew open, crashing into the wall.

"You done making a mess?" She fumed at the little boy. "Hey, you listening, boy?" She approached the child like a boxer edging from a corner of the ring.

John's rage boiled within. As if living through the anguish once before had not been enough. His shoulders hunched over flexed arms and clenched fists; at that moment, he was confronted with a very different view of his mother. He was no longer a young and scared boy, afraid of the woman who beat him and left him hungry. No. John's perspective shifted and swelled into something else.

"Don't you dare touch him," he said.

Go on. Stop the bitch, stop her now.

The voice tore through his head, breaking his focus, and he stumbled.

Boards creaked under a scurry of feet headed toward the door, and he wheeled around. His mother dropped the shard of broken glass. The little boy lay motionless, too weak to take notice.

"Oh, Lord, I hear the demon! Jesus, save me." Her lower back hit the dresser as she fell. "I heard him, Johnny. I heard him speak." She slid along the wall opposite John, side-stepping and reaching out to the young boy. As she cowered on the floor opposite him, John examined her like an insect under a magnifying glass.

"John, wake up. The devil is here. We need to leave."

The little boy only moaned and repositioned himself.

"Boy! I said get up," She pushed at the bed frame, rocking it. "Satan! He's here, child." Then she started to sing, off-key and tremulous. "Jesus loves me, Jesus loves me. My Father shows me the way."

"You could always spot the devil," John said, rising.

The color drained from her face, and she pulled at the child's arm frantically. Then she paused to look at the frail human in the bed and let go.

"You did this, boy," she choked. "He's talking through you."

John stared at his mother's expression. He'd never seen that look on her face before. Eyes wide, mouth open.

The voice came again. Stop her, John. Stop her, John. Whoever spoke nudged him. Evil lives in her. She stood witness. Sin! Evil! His head spun as the breathy words and swooping energy danced around him. She hurt you, all those times. Burns, it burns, John. She's the one. You weren't to blame. He covered his ears. You can stop her, John. Is there another choice? His expression melted into narrowed eyes and a hate-filled glare; his lip quivered in rage. What other choice did he have?

"I was a boy, just a boy. How could you, Joanne?" A euphoric strength he never thought possible flowed through every vein and capillary, every muscle. There had been a taste of it with Sophia, and he'd retreated from it. The pleasure of being bigger, in control, energized his core. Unable to contain himself, he lunged.

Joanne screamed as his fist closed around her hair and lifted her into the air. His arm was covered in a fresh sheen of blood and wavering lines of ripped skin. It was intoxicating, hauling her evil mass and leaving her to dangle. The size of her should have been impossible to move, yet she lifted easily.

She squealed and scratched at her scalp, and as her glasses turned cockeyed, the reflection in the lenses no longer showed a young face drenched in terror.

John pulled her close and inspected her panicked, twisted expression. Her mouth was open, and she drooled foam as she fought his grip.

"The only demon here is you," he said.

Chapter Thirty-Four

Time skipped. An opaque fog surrounded John. He was no longer holding Joanne or listening to her wailing sermon. His arm had healed and beneath his feet, the road's center line drew his eyes, its coarse surface shined with the moon like scales on a snake's back.

Joanne! Where's John?

His head snapped in the direction of the familiar voice, but the vapor obscured any movement. Circuits fired deep in his brain. *Ashley?*

This might be a trick. The road knew how to capitalize on his weak points. His sister Ashley had been the only source of kindness in a young life that offered little hope. His nostrils gathered another sign of her presence, the recognizable smell of Big-League Chew. She always kept a pack in her purse and a wad under her lip. She could pop amazing pink bubbles.

A memorable yearning emerged: waiting for Ashley at the front window, his forehead resting against the glass and a calico upholstery cushion under his legs. She'd not come home the night before. She didn't return the next day either, but he watched loyally every day, hypnotized by the front sidewalk. The number four bus passed every twenty to thirty minutes. Hydraulic doors opened and shut, allowing commuters to alight; they looked like small action figures in the distance. Each time John would tense, anticipating her return, expecting her to jump from the bus with open arms. But she never did. Without Ashley, Joanne had free reign over him.

John's body tensed. An invisible warmth flowed over his face like hands passing over his lashes and cheeks, past his ear and up into his hair. The embrace made him gasp, but soon he relaxed, basking in its soothing touch. Then the taste came, so intensely that his mouth watered. A caramel-sweetness on his tongue. He closed his eyes, remembering the crisp but mushy texture of the dough mixed with syrup.

Mental dominos fell. *Waffles. I ran from Joanne. They fed me waffles.* Eventually Ashley found him standing with the neighbor and the police. Rain slid over his naked belly, and a blanket hung loosely over his shoulders. He blinked away the drips from his drooping hair as the neighbor tried to shield him with an umbrella. A green and white, terrycloth towel wrapped his fresh cuts, but he couldn't remember any pain. Only the maple, sweet, nutty flavor of breakfast.

John hesitated, knowing the images were delivered by the road's power, and he feared what he'd find if he raised his head. But when he did, Ashley stood before him, looking exactly as he remembered. The goth-girl black hair, with the lower half shaved and the top half in a bun. The same Arby's uniform she had worn the last time he saw her, still too big for her petite frame. The pale skin that gave a ghost-like appearance, and a silver ring glinting on her lower lip.

John's arms came up, hovering in the space between them. He had always imagined what he might say to her if they met again, but his brain went blank, and no words came. Ashley leaving without saying goodbye had become a phantom pain, like a missing limb. Now, its arthritic throb awoke.

"You always gave me baths in the middle of the night," he said. "Whispers and waves, you called it, so we wouldn't get caught." His voice broke. "When you disappeared, I died."

"Joanne!" Ashley shrieked. "He's gone. What have you done?" She stared forward with an angry expression.

John followed her gaze and saw nothing. Slowly, the sight of her grew translucent and thinned, like a signal weakened. Then she was gone. He was alone again.

He dropped to all fours. The road was silent as he rested on his knees—perhaps savoring the loss of his only caregiver. John feared the road would grow weary of his loitering. He couldn't just wait for its next attack. In the distance he saw a shadow, a mound of something near the embankment. Cautiously, he got up and walked closer.

In the overgrowth was a blood-covered flank and a leg twisted beyond the normal range of motion. Ripped pants, with a spear of bone protruding. It was the woman.

John and Shelly must have met a similar fate, thrown back onto the road like crushed soda cans. They weren't going to get out of this; their presence on the road made that clear.

Shelly's chest rose up and down, showing signs, at least, of existing. As John watched with bulging eyes, the blood on her pants faded, and the bone shifted back into place. When her body had mended, she arched her back and moaned. Her arms came up as she rolled over and sat up.

"Hey, hey," he stammered. "Can you stand up?"

She looked at him blankly. "I'd forgotten—" She shook her head, and he couldn't tell if she was even talking to him.

"Forgot what?"

The strands of her black hair, drawn loosely into a ponytail, hung over her shoulder. She wore an oversized sweater and no makeup. She looked to be in her late thirties. The type to go unnoticed in a crowd, he thought, and maybe prefer it that way.

"It's like a terrible drug, isn't it?" he said. "The road."

Her brow creased.

He walked over and extended his hand. "We should get moving."

"My daughter doesn't see me," she said ignoring him. "It's that house—"

"What house?"

"The place where I grew up," she said. "My daughter came to me, she—" Her face crumpled. "The kittens!" She got up quickly.

John inhaled, waiting. This woman had clearly lost her mind. It was obvious from her looping, wavering logic, her rambled speech, and the way she stumbled about, gesturing with her hands. He struggled to follow what she was saying.

"I think this place is fucking with us," he said.

She continued her rant. "Why would she be there with Red?" She stepped toward him. "Josie was hurt, and her arm, it just hung there." She stared at him intently. "Her wounds mended themselves. She's here with us, somewhere."

"She healed, like us?"

She nodded. "It must mean something. Time keeps moving, shifting. But in the house, I wanted to warn her. When I tried to grab Josie, my injuries came back."

As John watched her lips move, the sound of her voice fell to a hum as he realized: they were in the same car crash, and now, they were all here in some state of dead or undead.

"Did you talk with them, your daughter and the other one?" he asked.

"Red was part of—" She trailed off. "I tried to talk with them, but the pain came." She took a few steps along the center line of the road. "Why here? I thought when you die, you go somewhere beautiful." She turned to him. "It's ugly here."

Catching the scent of a past weakness, John fought the urge to expose it, to lean in and rip off the scab. Instead, he studied the hand he'd used to pick up Joanne, flexing it open and shut, experimenting with the response and strength of his grip. Something had led him to fight back. Shelly had not been granted this strength. At least, not yet.

"Are there things here from when you were little?" he asked.

Her eyes widened. "I don't want to talk about it."

John knew he'd have to offer more of an invitation to get her to share. "I saw my mother," he said. "She could hear me."

Shelly's face lit up. "Your mother is here? You talked to her?" She studied him for a moment. "The side of your head—it's not sealed all the way."

"What? Where?" He felt around his skull and found the indentation—dry, without the jagged feeling of bone. A raised section of skin articulated where the injury had been.

"She came to you," she said, "and you could talk to her. That must mean something. Right?"

Heat prickled his face. "Listen." He pointed at her. "My mom is an evil person. No help ever came from her."

Shelly touched her neck and shrunk from him.

"Alive or dead, she would be the boot in the ass pushing me under a tire." He stepped closer to Shelly. "I don't know what the road wants me to do with her, but I'll keep reminding her what she did every chance I get. I'm not a scared kid anymore."

"What do you mean?'" Her eyes narrowed. "Do you think we're here to punish people?"

"Why the fuck not? I'm not going to stand there and take it like I did when I was a kid." His voice echoed over the asphalt.

"Whether I'm dead or not, there has to be more here, some reason," she said.

The brightness around them started to change. John glanced at Shelly; the color was draining from her cheeks.

The light at the side of the road, past the furthest hill, was growing black. A darkened curtain crawled forward, like a scene from a horror film—an encroaching, onyx blob coming to take over. They stepped closer to one another and stared at the steady growth of the shadowy canopy. At first, they moved slowly backward, then simultaneously turned and began to run.

Chapter Thirty-Five

"Shelly!" John yelled as he lost sight of her.

A blanket of coal-colored sky moved in around him. The air was granular like a blizzard and stung his eyes; fragments sheared his skin. In his peripheral vision, he saw a flash. Something was stalking him in the vapor. Weaving through light and the dark, a shifting, gray shadow swam through the softer whites of the mist.

Dear Heavily Father, deliver me from evil. The phrase came out of nowhere, a peculiar urge to pray. As blackness engulfed the world around him, it seemed ludicrous to kneel and beg for help. Faith mocked him, suffocated him in a baptismal font, allowed his skin to burn, and his mother to box his ears. The manipulation of the road continued, but instead of fear, John surged with anger.

The presence took shape. A chest and part of a neck, then a hand that dissipated into nothing. Eyes appeared—hollowed pits over ridges of a cheek. Then the figure drew back. John's body vibrated, heart pumping and hands shaking as he looked around for a way out.

John.

"What do you want from me?"

Forgiveness.

His breath caught in his throat. "Forgive? I don't understand. Forgive who?" The presence said nothing and held its boundary within the cloud.

"Shelly, can you hear me?" She was his only lifeline in this place. "I'm alone and something—" His voice cracked. The center of his stomach knotted; the mental and physical fought each other. His mind wanted to calm the panic coursing through his veins, but his body wanted to fight and claw at the world and hurt those who would harm him. Shelly couldn't help him, and he hated her even more for breaking into his world. She only wanted to help herself, help her daughter. Selfish. Just like his mother, just like Sophia.

Fighting was the only way. John looked at his clenched fist, the same one he'd used on his mother.

"Were you with me in the house?" he asked. Always with you, John. The sound hovered so close he felt the breath on his cheek. There are choices to make, John. We've given you a gift.

"What choices?"

That's up to you. Who's to blame? Who's to blame? The words grew louder and louder, hammering into his skull.

"Stop!"

Johnny. You think you can do it? You'd do it if you love me, baby.

"It's all a game. You're fucking with my mind," he shouted. "You're weak!" He beat his fists against his chest. "Don't ask me about love, you bitch!" Spit flew from his lips.

You think you can do it? You think you can do it?

His mother's chants swirled in different volumes like the radios of passing cars. Something marched forward from the back of his mind. It was faint at first, a similar tone. But more emerged. Joanne had spoken these words before.

The fissure at his scalp ached, breaking his concentration. The murky cloud edged closer until the eye of the tornado engulfed him, cutting his vision. Soon he was unable to breathe. Only sounds came through the thick cloud, and a whisper crawled up his spine like a spider.

You'd do it if you loved me, baby.

Without warning, it stopped. The voices halted, and the air cleared. John had not returned to the road. He was in front of his mother's house again, and the door was open.

Chapter Thirty-Six

Shelly broke into a full sprint, running as fast as she could, forcing energy into her legs as the stress of her breathing ripped at the walls of her chest. Looking over her shoulder, she watched the blackness envelope the grass and the trees behind her. She focused on the horizon ahead but heard John's strained breath and quick feet.

She tried to focus on one point, a hill, a patch of grass, a break in the forest where the light had not yet been suffocated fully. But her body slowed when she realized where she was going. Her surroundings were vacant—behind her, only pavement. She'd wanted to follow the road, to move forward, but it had not allowed that. It allowed them to believe it led to answers, while snatching them up at every turn, throwing their bodies, stealing their tears, and exposing their wounds.

The force had to be close, so she stopped and turned toward the dark wave. A nothingness, a deep, black ocean. In the path of it, she felt as minuscule as a tiny pebble, shrinking by the second.

The void wrapped her, cool against her skin, but not welcomed. There were no sounds; her ears were plugged by a stereo buzz. Shelly cracked an eye open, but it offered little help, her hands and fingers invisible as she inched them toward her face. Unable to control her goosebumps and shivers, she hugged herself tightly, losing all sense of space. The choice to enter had been hers, and she awaited its next move.

He's waiting for you.

Shelly started to speak, but the road took over. Without warning, something grabbed her from behind. She screamed as cold fingers clutched her arm; her entire body seized as if electrified. In the shadow, she couldn't sense up or down but knew her body was being tossed, weightless except for the gravitational jerk on her gut.

Abruptly, she hit the ground, rocking her skull. Lights exploded in her vision. Her limbs slapped the road. She sensed no pain yet cried out against the rocky surface. She waited for the force to hit again, to crush her face into the ground.

When the light began to change over her eyelids, she raised her head. The cloud had dissipated. She'd been placed at the edge of the road, alongside a guardrail, with the pond in view. A chill moved down her spine, and steam emerged with each breath. The temperature was dropping.

The pond quivered and looked abnormally dark. As she watched, the edges started to lighten and crack. From outward in, the pond froze over and turned white to the deepest center. A dusting of snow kicked up, first wisps, then feathering dunes. In the billowing powder, someone stood at the bank, obscured by the storm.

An uninvited thought rushed in: *Go to her. Be with Josie.* And the urge that followed hit her strong, creating an ache across her forehead.

The voice spoke again, this time unmistakably from outside her mind.

You're not lost. He's waiting.

Shelly remained still, intoxicated by the mirrored surface of the water, until a jolt raced through her body. Josie stood near the deepest center of the pond. She seemed terrified, hugging herself and shaking. Shelly took off from the guardrail.

"The water! You can't go near the water," she screamed. As if the road anticipated her move, a smoky haze filled the space between them. "Can you hear me, Josie? Run to my voice."

"I can't see you," the girl called, her voice faraway and faint.

Shelly moved forward, running blind. Her foot caught on something, and she tumbled forward and fell. Instead of the grit of dirt, her shoulder hit a frigid and wet sheet of ice. She heard a plopping and gurgling sound, then a courser sound, like a shovel against concrete. The ice broke apart.

She was plunged into the wetness, and an ache wrapped her body as the water leeched heat from her bones. Restrained by the undercurrent, she sank as the pull became unbearable. Her lungs jerked for air as oxygen drained from her body.

A shadow crept closer, swirling strands of ash-colored hair with fingers reaching through the black until a woman hovered above. She was a ghastly, pale color, her skin discolored from the effects of death and submersion. Decay circled her mouth and forehead. Shelly watched the approach of mortality's messenger.

The figure's mottled hands seized her. Together they flowed, jettisoned backward. *Let it in.* A voice spoke in Shelly's head, but the emotion that followed confused her. She wanted to linger there, her lungs no longer thirsty for air, her body warmed from within.

Let us in. We'll lead you. Don't fight.

If she resisted, what would become of her?

No—I won't go. She channeled this mental message to the ghost, noting a shimmer of light above. Her foot responded and kicked with all her strength, but the woman held tight, putting a frozen hand over Shelly's mouth.

Then she saw it. As if somehow in sync with the dead woman's thoughts, a scroll of images from Shelly's youth appeared. An outstretched hand, light passing through its open fingers, silhouetted like sunrays through a window. White window trim and the dingy, sheer curtain swaying through its gaping center. Shelly was no longer drowning, but back in her childhood home. The pictures in her mind's eye cascaded, one on top of another: blood-covered skin, the porcelain color of her neck, Red, puddles on the hardwood floor.

The dead thing pulled her lower and lower into the darkness. The light at the surface was now a pinpoint, and Shelly kicked furiously.

Her leg snapped, succumbing once again to the injuries from the accident. Rapidly, her wounds returned in a wave, sprouting like pustules and leaving unbearable, searing pain. Blood billowed around her in the water.

Spreading like diluted ink, the dark aura of the spirit closed in. Shelly couldn't move. The woman shifted into her peripheral, a hand making its way up under her jaw.

The dead woman's hold loosened as her lips pressed to Shelly's forehead. The soft pressure stayed there a few seconds, followed by a subtle brush and swoop down to her nose, then her forehead and over her cheek. An affectionate touch, as if to comfort her.

Shelly's heart surged, not in disgust or fear; warmth permeated her body. In an instant, the woman vanished, and Shelly allowed the water to take her. In the swirling pool, her pale arms floated above her head, as if in reverence, and she drifted in the current.

John stared at the disheveled house with less apprehension than he'd felt during his last visit.

The bike was missing from the front yard and this change prickled a warning in his mind. When he went through the front door, he found himself not in the living room but the den, towards the back of the house and past the row of bedrooms. The room was square, with wall-to-wall, mustard-colored carpet and a corduroy brown couch that held a heavy fold-out. It was where Ashley slept, and before that, where his dad had watched heavyweight boxing, hoping to avoid his mother.

The room was void of energy but suddenly flashed into life. Like a movie projector firing up, Ashely and Joanne arrived.

Ashley looked about twenty-three. This was around the time her ties with the family had died, along with their father. Joanne was animated, on the balls of her feet, moving in jerks with nostrils flaring. From her posture, Ashley showed no signs of backing down.

"He died the day he met you!" Ashley yelled. "The best thing for John would be to come with me. You can keep your precious daughters!" She accented each syllable with her pointed finger. "You hate him. There's no love in this house. He deserves more, and I can give him that."

Ashley stood upright, her petite form David to Joanne's Goliath. This pleased John, and he leaned against the wall and folded his arms. He wanted to see Joanne put in her place. Hurt to the core.

"Fuck you, you little whore!" His mother lunged forward. "I never wanted you around here," she spat. "Your daddy was useless. It's no wonder you're stupid. John too." She lowered her chin. "That boy stays here."

Why would Joanne fight to keep him? She didn't want him. It was Ashley who wanted him. Her presence brought back a happiness John had forgotten, like a bear trap concealed under leaves. Ashley would come to him after their parents went to sleep, carefully and quietly—they'd catch a beating if they awoke. She'd change his clothing and give him some toast with peanut butter. Sometimes, there'd be honey, a sweet dream amidst hell on earth. She would brush his teeth, and her voice would be the last thing he heard before closing his eyes.

As he watched their argument, John's body swelled with manic energy as if he were seven again, all passion and reckless action, and little room for rational thought.

"You're the one bringing Satan into this house," Joanne yelled at Ashley. "That energy is following you."

"He's your toy, you bitch!" Ashley hollered back. "You only keep him to have something to control. If I'm Satan—" The five-foot-tall goth girl barreled, shoulders squared, toward the older woman, "then I call you Mother!"

John looked back and forth between the two women in utter deadlock.

His mother raised her arm and slapped Ashley, who collapsed on the pull-out bed. "That boy's full of hate," she shouted. "I know it, and everybody will soon enough."

His sister looked up from her vulnerable position with angry tears in her eyes. She knew Joanne could move in for the kill.

"If you don't leave," his mother said, "I'll make sure he's put in some institution. Everyone will know he's a monster."

Send me away? John thought.

"You'd do that to a little boy?"

"Whatever happens to him, it's your father's fault, your fault. Get out and don't ever come back."

"My father hated you!" Ashley yelled. "He might have been angry, but that's the hate you gave. You sucked out any shred of joy and spit it back at his face."

"I don't think anything bothers him anymore," Joanne shot back.

Ashley's mouth dropped open.

Monster. Monster.

John was pacing. Her words were like shotgun pellets.

"Evil in a child comes out eventually," Joanne said. "Dead animals and burned bugs—these are the signs. I sleep with one eye open, but I can't pass him off, certainly not to you. Leave now or I swear, he'll find himself tied down and electrocuted in some looney bin before your key hits the lock."

John covered his eyes, furious at the voice, the road, the one prodding him, urging him to fight. *Why? Why force me to see this? It's a game for you, watching me tiptoe around landmines.*

Joanne's steadfast refusal to let him leave with Ashley crushed him like a lead weight. He curled forward, legs bent to jump, hands ready to tear out her throat. In a split second, John threw himself at his mother, sending her crashing to the floor.

"Let me go!" He stood over his mother with pent-up sadness

and resentment vibrating through his body. The abuse, burns, and starvation like a sickness flowing from his gaping mouth, reverberating off the walls. Pictures shifted as cracks splintered down the plasterboard, and light fixtures swayed as though a tornado swirled by. Both women clutched their ears, then their heads as if a bomb had gone off. Not finished yet, John grabbed each side of his mother's skull by the ears. He squeezed, and her face flashed into shock—mouth open, eyes gawking.

"You should have been the one to die," he said, and in a final, forceful movement, he slammed her head to the ground. The room collapsed around them. Walls and floor exploded, and debris shot in all directions.

Chapter Thirty-Seven

A loud boom rocketed through Shelly's brain, and she opened her eyes. With a rush of adrenaline, the jolting noise sent her flying backward as she anticipated the violent grip of an attacker. Lightheaded, she squinted toward what had broken her from the icy waters.

"Mom!"

She focused on the familiar voice and found Josie by the car window, pressing her turkey picture against the glass. Children were running around her; adults herded them toward waiting parents. The brightly lit building, yellow with a red door, stood off to the right. When had she arrived at the school? The suffocating water was gone. The woman—where was she? Shelly touched her forehead, where the sensation of the woman's kiss remained.

From the driver's seat, she looked at Josie, cheerful and healed, with an excited expression on her face. The car was upright, not upside down in a field. There was no taste of blood in her mouth. The windshield was speckled with rain, without a chip or blemish, glistening in the sunlight that broke through the clouds. She gripped the steering wheel, still anchored to the car. The world outside carried on, frighteningly normal.

"Mom, let me in!" Josie tugged at the handle. "Mom!"

Shelly looked over.

Josie dropped both arms, and her head fell to the side, an impatient look Shelly knew well.

She hit the power lock button. Her body tensed, waiting for the devastation to appear. One of the teachers, Miss Palmer, peered into the car and waved. Cautiously, Shelly signaled back, still wary of this reality and half-expecting her face to melt away, bone pressing through dangling flesh.

Josie adjusted herself in the seat, squirming into position and fastened her seat belt, carefully preserving her turkey picture. In that moment, Shelly looked for reassurance that Josie truly existed. She analyzed her blue eyes, peeking through blonde strands. Over her head, through the back window, parents were waiting in idle vehicles, exhaust fumes billowing through the air.

"You won't believe what my teacher said!" Josie leaned forward with excitement. "She told us about a book." The child squirmed, removing her coat and revealing a fairy tattoo on her arm. "I don't remember what book, but it was about a dog. And it wouldn't listen, but it followed the girl around. I don't know what kind of dog it was." She paused and looked out the window, distracted by the kids outside.

Shelly took a deep breath and stared at her daughter's beautiful face, absorbing her energy.

Be real. Let it be real. Am I really here?

"Did we talk about the book when I picked you up?" she asked quietly.

Josie didn't seem to hear. She swung her feet, talking non-stop, oblivious to the dark places her mother had been. Her arm was perfect and fully functional, and her face didn't have a scratch.

Shelly reached back and caught Josie's wrist—not bloody or broken, but the lean wrist of an avid monkey-bar climber. "I love you. You know that, right?"

Josie stopped her story for a moment and gave her mother a once-over. "I love you too, Mommy."

Shelly fought the urge to pull her close and kiss her face. Just as powerful was the desire to grab Josie and run, abandoning the car rather than having the accident, or getting lost in another death dream.

As the bustle around the car calmed down, the teachers headed back into the building. Across the parking lot, something caught Shelly's eye. A woman stood alone at the bumper of a Toyota, arms at her side. She had long, light-colored hair and wore a cream-colored dress buttoned up to her neck.

The face was difficult to make out, but the statuesque figure was motionless, an odd contrast to the movements of everyone else. She showed no signs of approaching any child.

Shelly watched as the few remaining kids scurried into cars. When she looked back, the woman was gone. She switched on the ignition, while paranoia pricked the hairs on her arms and neck.

In the back, Josie chattered away, her feet tapping against the seat. "But then, the teacher said she hated the book. That it wasn't, like, teaching us anything. So, then Tammy said—"

"Josie," Shelly interrupted. "Did I drop you off today?"

"Um, yeah! You don't remember?"

"Sorry, baby. I guess I'm a little distracted today."

Did I do this? It could all be a bad dream. Her mind was preoccupied with psychopathic fabrications. Had her mixed-up mind created the road?

"Mom, why are we sitting here? Let's go!" Josie's foot tapped.

Shelly snapped back to reality. "Don't kick the seat," she said.

As they pulled out of the parking lot, her phone lit up in the cupholder. Paul's name appeared. Shelly stared at the blinking screen. It was the first opportunity for connection to anyone but Josie, in what felt like days. She'd declined all his calls after their fight, avoided reality, and planned to run. But his cheating had been dwarfed by everything else. The phone pulsed again.

"Was that part of it?" she whispered.

She answered the phone, but no one spoke. The display went dark, and Paul's name disappeared. Her eyes fixed on the suddenly lifeless rectangle.

She tried to sequence together the pattern of events. *Which came first? He slept with that woman. I left. I came to pick up Josie. There's luggage in the trunk.* Shelly squeezed the wheel and quickly turned onto the shoulder of the road. The tires crunched against the gravel. She jumped out and ran to the back. The lid popped open and inside were two bags of clothes, haphazardly packed, Josie's pillow and some shoes. Shelly stared at the bags, not knowing what to do or where to go.

So many details were still vivid—the woman in the lake, her wounds closing, the suffocating mist, and John. But so was this, her hand clutching a violet shirt that belonged to Josie. Her daughter had turned and was making faces through the glass.

We should go home.

Shelly got back in the car, turned on the ignition, and pulled into traffic. She needed to talk to Paul and figure out what to do. If his infidelity and her avoidance had in some way been fruit from the same poisonous tree, could they make their way back to each other?

She hoped she could look Paul in the eyes and not see that woman. She hoped she could stay here in this reality, with him and Josie.

Chapter Thirty-Eight

The sound of the car moving over pavement couldn't drown out the fight in Shelly's head. All her work in therapy hadn't scratched the surface; her problems were obviously much more serious than she had thought. It was likely the road had been a multitude of hallucinations. She shook her head. Who needs drugs when you can trip out freely?

But John. He existed, didn't he?

Sit up tall, she thought. Take deep breaths. Dr. Frazer-Velli said she deserved happiness but needed to believe it. The noises inside her head muffled his logic.

Shelly turned on the radio. A woman sang in a melancholy voice, and she twisted the dial. Guitars and drums fought the beat on the next station, guttural coughing that sounded more like the growling of dogs. But with the next turn, she found it.

The melody filled her chest. Snaps of fingers and rhythmic cords, and a harmonic, male voice wanting a "day to escape." It made her think of times when her younger self walked barefoot in the grass, dancing like a manic pixie and spinning as music bounced off the rocky mounds of the amphitheater.

Josie looked at her through the rearview, covering her ears. "That song is crap!"

"Josie!"

It was safe in those memories, images of people swaying on a grassy hill, a flashing dome pumping out rhythms.

The radio announcer's voice broke through as he talked about the weather and upcoming hits. A new song played, which seemed to be met with approval from the back of the car as Josie dropped her hands from her ears.

Outside the car, rain clouds billowed, and drizzle speckled the windscreen. Trees waved from the edge of the road, and sunlight dimmed to dusk. Shelly angled a look toward the sky. The weather was changing quickly. She maxed out her lungs in a deep inhale and pushed her foot down on the accelerator for more speed.

Just make it home.

Her back dampened against the seat as she adjusted her posture, and the muscle under her shoulder blade pinched. The somatic tics she knew to be anxiety fizzed up like carbonation over her skin. Despite her best efforts, the road and its curves were taxing. Her hand rested on the silver handle of the glove box; fingers curled under the latch. Before she could open it to find her emergency tool, Josie spoke up from the back.

"There's so much love." Josie's words were too methodical and slow to accompany the tune. "So much love in her heart."

Shelly's hand froze. She glanced in the rearview mirror. "What?"

Her daughter's young face had become constricted and somber. She didn't answer, just gazed at the passing scenery.

Shelly's hair slowly stood up on the back of her neck.

"The love never died. It follows us forever," Josie said. "Do you think we still love after we die? I do." She kicked the back of the seat.

"Josie?"

"She can't tell me if there is a heaven—which is so silly, because she's dead."

Heaven? Who was dead? Shelly attempted to respond but words wouldn't form. Her mind raced. *No. We aren't back on the road. This is the way home. We're going home. The pond isn't real. She's not dead. I'm not dead. We are together and alive.*

"She wants me to hide sometimes," Josie said. "Like you did last night, under the bed. It's silly."

"Josie, what—"

"Who made you sad, Mommy?" Her eyes met Shelly's in the mirror. "All I hear is 'I'm sorry you're sad. I'm sorry you're sad.' She keeps saying that."

Shelly's body turned to ice. "Who are you talking about, baby?"

"I don't know her name," Josie had switched back to a strange, mocking tone as she stared out of the window.

If she stared straight ahead, they'd get home. *You'll crash.* No. The wavering discomfort in her stomach might be hunger and the familiar strangle at her throat fatigue, or the start of a cold. It wasn't happening again. The crawl of electricity up her spine or the prick of tension in her neck didn't mean anything. *He's waiting for you.* No. They made it through. This road takes us home. She didn't want to believe the lies spawned by her brain, decay, and death at every turn, wafting in the air under her nose. She didn't want the road to hold her, and she didn't want to believe the road had Josie.

The car hit sixty-five mph. She pushed on the brake, but the engine surged. Shelly moaned and hit the pedal again, but it did nothing. "The brakes! I've lost the brakes." She pulled at the wheel, trying to regain control. Her eyes flicked to the back of the car, the need to see her daughter inescapable.

In the millisecond it took to cast a glance back, the world paused, everything slowed down, and her vision tunneled. Josie was no longer chatting from the back seat. She had floated somewhere else, and an illusion had replaced her, as though a hole had been punched in the world, where Josie hung unbound. No longer in the car with her mother but in a bed, bandaged and bruised, wearing a hospital gown, her hair pulled away from her face.

Losing all connection with the road, Shelly was watching her daughter like a movie projected against a white wall. Josie's eyes were closed, but she convulsed, yelling at strangers in scrubs. Her chest heaved, and she thrashed her limbs. Her arm was bandaged.

"What's happening to you?" Shelly's muscles twitched as she watched her daughter in terror. It was as if she was balanced on a scaffolding over two realities. Her body was harnessed to the car, but she could also see her daughter in another realm.

Josie can't stay. She's not here.

Shelly lurched forward, and her hand extended to the open void. Then it struck her. History was repeating. She'd reached for her own mother, just as she and Josie now stretched for each other. Someone, something, restrained her from the embrace.

The car swerved, and she slapped at the steering wheel as the vehicle cut back and forth. The wheel ripped through Shelly's fingers with a power of its own. They approached a curve in the road ahead; the center line disappeared in flashes. Beyond the curve was the water and the finality she feared.

More sounds from the back, more shuffling and gasps. "Mom! What's happening to me? I hear voices. They are so scared." Josie was back in the car, holding her ears. "They want me to hide again! They want me to run."

Trees lined up ahead, behind the guardrail with the cardinal tarnish.

"Who's speaking, baby? I hear you. I only hear you." Shelly's heart fell into her stomach like a freefall in the early layer of sleep. No reply came from behind. Josie sat frozen, staring intently at the mirror, both hands gripping the seat. Shelly knew something had entered the car, like a depression in the energy.

"Red's here!" Josie said. Her eyes shifted to her left.

Without warning, an impish child sprung onto the front seat, crashing against the wheel like a wild animal, prying at Shelly's hands, her feet edging towards the pedals. Her body pushed against Shelly's face. Her scent was musty, with hints of urine-soaked carpet and the grimy sweat of a child. Shelly tried to keep control but was unable to see around the figure. The only thing visible was Red's reflection on the chrome detail of the dash, mask-like and determined. The car lurched to the left, and the centripetal force pressed against Shelly's hips and ribcage. Red hit her knuckles, and the car swung again to the right while Josie yelled in terror from the back.

Chapter Thirty-Nine

Red rammed her feet under the wheel and sat squarely on Shelly's lap, like a child would, pretending to drive. The heel of her shoe struck Shelly's shin bone, and then Red's feet somehow took over the pedals, despite her short stature.

"Some paths are harder than others," the small intruder said with no emotion.

The car veered across the oncoming lanes and crashed through the guardrail. They ricocheted until the car bottomed out in a spray of dirt and grass. Shelly's body went airborne, then slammed against the seat. Red collided with her sternum. In the back, Josie squealed. Shelly caught glimpses of her petite frame in the jumble.

A dark slick, like oil over water, lay ahead of her, its center a gaping mouth waiting to swallow them whole. Red pressed her feet against the dash, pressing her full weight into Shelly and obscuring her efforts to steer the car to safety. The nose of the sedan was aimed at the water. Suddenly, they hit the lake with blunt force. The hood sprang up, and white spray flashed over the windshield.

Shelly jolted against the seatbelt, leaving Red sandwiched between the airbag and her chest. Red's ribs crushed between them, while Shelly's chest vibrated with the pops and snaps of what could only be tendons and bones.

When she opened her eyes, Red was gone, and in her place, a bent steering wheel and deflating white balloon. The ringing in her ears drowned out the sounds around her before it quieted and revealed Josie's moans and the rushing currents around them.

The car was bobbing on the surface. Glancing back, she saw Josie wide-eyed, strapped into the harness of her car seat, her fingers curled around the band. The lapping water line outside the window had climbed over a quarter of the glass, sloshing back and forth like hands scratching to enter. The car's passenger door dipped lower, descending faster than the driver's side.

The engine sputtered like a boat idling at a dock. Pine needles and paper scraps rose from the floor, a soup of debris. Shelly pressed at the door release, but nothing moved. Pressing both feet on the floor, she arched her back against the strap, which slinked down and pulled her to the seat.

"We can climb out," Josie said. "You just have to help me." Her side of the car began to dip further. "I'll kick for the top like you showed me. Mom, help! I'm stuck." Over her shoulder, the entire window was covered with frigid water, only a sheet of glass separating them.

"I can't move, baby. Damn it!" Shelly's thoughts circled and stalled as she tried to figure out a way to reach Josie. Their rapid breaths came in white puffs as the cold air filled the car. The crash had happened so many times in her mind, but now she went blank. She tried to remember how it ended and what she had done.

"It's so cold, Mom." Josie's feet were submerged in the spinning water, the flow of it coming quickly up to her hip. She was against the door now as the vehicle leaned, her arm on the window. Shelly feared that her weight would break it. And then it hit her—something she always kept in the car in case her nightmares came true.

"The cutter!" She threw open the glove box and frantically tossed items around. She gasped with her efforts, coming up empty.

"The water!" Josie cried. "It's getting higher."

Shelly had mentally prepared for this tragedy—they broke the glass, got out, and swam away. For so long, she had protected her precious daughter. In desperation, she grabbed her head and squeezed her temples, muffling screams through clenched teeth. She pounded her fists against the steering wheel, sounding the horn, then she elbowed the window repeatedly, feeling as though knives had severed nerve endings from her brain.

Spinning to the right, she saw Josie waist-deep, as the car moaned and creaked with the shifting weight. In horror, she realized Josie would go down before her. The murky liquid rose at an angle into her armpit. Wet hair hung around her pale face in pencil-width sections, stuck to her glistening cheeks.

"Mommy, get me out. I don't want to die!" She reached a hand towards Shelly.

In a moment of clarity, pictures filed away in Shelly's brain shuffled to the front. A mix of images paraded across the void: the angle of Josie's palm with her spread fingers, the way her body leaned in the car. Shelly held up her own hand in front of her, then her arm, totally untouched by the effects of the accident. As if seconds allowed hours, the thoughts joined, sticking together to form something clear, with the last piece, a drip falling from Josie's cheek.

I have no pain, no tears. I never left. I stay. During the split through time, Josie left to be surrounded by nursing staff, in a bed fighting a nightmare. *My nightmare. Yes.*

The road was for Shelly. But Josie can leave. Josie could go again, disappear from this sinking car, turn away from death.

This couldn't be happening. John's ideas of punishment slid into the folds of her mind, engulfing her own sense of hope. Shelly's hands moved into her hair, pulling at her scalp. Time seemed to drag on endlessly as her eyes fixed on her daughter's terrified expression.

"Josie, listen to me. Listen to my voice."

Her fear-drenched face tilted up.

Shelly's throat was tight. "You are such a brave little girl. I need you to take the first steps to get out."

"The water. I'm scared!" Josie's head rotated, looking around for something to pull.

"Just listen to my words, baby. Wake up. Yes, you can. This isn't real. Wake up." She reached out but could only manage to touch the tips of Josie's fingers.

"I love you so much!" she said. "Wake up! It's a dream—but not your dream. You don't belong here with me." The water traveled up to Shelly's chest, coming in through cracks. Papers floated and swirled around them.

"I'm so scared." Josie panted and arched her body to keep above the surface. "I can't breathe, Mommy!" Water cascaded over her face.

Shelly jerked at Josie's hand. "Wake up!" she screamed.

The car plunged forward again, and Shelly submerged, losing her grip on Josie's fingers. She couldn't see anything now, only pieces of debris lit by the tiny lights of the car dash. She was hopelessly trapped, tethered, sinking. Blinded, she whipped her hand back and found nothing, just empty space, a tomb.

Once again, her body jolted, pulled forward as the car rolled and spun. She lost orientation. She was either rising in the air or descending to the bottom.

Part 3

Chapter Forty

Shelly lay sprawled at the water's edge. It felt like she'd been asleep for days. Her face rested in the silt from the shore, and the rest of her body drifted in the shallows. Covered by a few inches of water, she heard muffled sounds underneath the surface. Something was caked on her lashes and down her cheek, porous like salt scrub. Water dripped past her nose, down her lips, and over her teeth, leaving a briny, metallic-tasting grit in her mouth. Reaching forward, she managed to roll over, but her palm crashed down into mud that filled the space between her fingers. She twisted again to get up but sank into clay, her arms buckling as she fell back. She trembled against the bank.

Terrified, she wondered if Josie had made it out. She wept without tears, with only the pond to wet her cheeks.

"Shelly, you have to get up. Get up!"

"Paul?" she asked, unsure whether her words were audible.

Someone grabbed her underneath the arms. "Hey, I need you to help me here. Where did you go?" The man grunted, pulling her body out of the water.

The shift in position left her nauseous, and she sensed the drag against her jaw and throat, a gag forming. Bile flowed over her lips, as her stomach clinched down.

Cracking an eye open, she saw John.

"I died," Shelly whispered, her head falling forward. "It was death, over and over." Her vision cartwheeled as John dragged her from the bank. The grunts of his effort cast spit, maybe mud, along her cheek. He gave a final thrust but slipped in the wet mud.

"Get up," he ordered, "or I'm going to leave you here." He laid her on the bank, and she felt the heaviness of his mass beside her. Shelly hoisted herself farther along in the dirt.

"I don't want to be left behind." She looked up from all fours.

"Something's watching us," he said. His stance twitched back and forth. They were fully exposed in the field, with nothing close to provide shelter unless they returned to the road and down the other side to the trees. "This place isn't giving us much time."

"I'm afraid," Shelly said. "I think it's killing me slowly. I keep trying to get to Josie, but there are things alive here." Shelly looked back at the water, and even at a distance, she felt uneasy. "I can't fight them. They know exactly what I'm afraid of. They're trying to hurt me and—" She covered her mouth, not knowing if Josie had died, trapped at the bottom of the pond.

He stared at her coldly. "What makes you think you're still alive?"

Shelly noted his stony expression, his unprovoked hostility. "Stop." She shook her head. "Stop! There's more to it than the accident. I'm living through my childhood. Things I tried to get away from, but maybe I'm seeing signs too."

"Signs of what?"

"The dead woman," she said, "the one I saw on the road. She was in the water with me. But John, I wanted to stay with her. She showed me things I'd forgotten, and it—"

"Tricks. The dead woman wanted you to stay with her to drown." He started to walk away but switched again, from zero to sixty and back to anger. "The only signs are what this fucked-up place wants you to see. It attacks until you fight back." He kicked at the ground, sending mud over her shins.

"And Josie?" she challenged. "She was in the car with me."

He looked at her, puzzled. "What the fuck are you talking about? Everything that comes out of your mouth is nonsense."

"Wait! There's more than bad childhood shit here. Shut up and listen," Shelly yelled, surprising herself. "My daughter, she travels to me. She's not tethered to this place like we are." Her head cocked to the side. "Then I saw the woman from the road, horrible and dead but it felt the same, the same as with Josie—safe. I can't explain it."

He paused, his breathing becoming more rapid as he looked down at the ground, hands on hips. At times, he appeared vulnerable and open but then he'd become completely unpredictable, leaving Shelly in awe of his erratic nature.

She watched him. "Something happened to you, didn't it?"

Slowly, he raised his head.

"Didn't it?" They locked eyes. "John. I'm here with you."

He turned away. "Just forget it."

She noticed an inflamed gash behind his ear. A sign. The healing meant something. "John," she said, "you're hurting. When did that change? It's worse."

"What?" He touched his head, then pulled back like he'd been zapped, hissing as the sting continued.

Shelly pulled at her black hair, running her fingers along the scalp but detecting no ridge or crevice, not a stitch of pain.

"It doesn't matter. We need to move. Come on." He pulled at her arm like an irate parent.

But she knew she didn't require his company, especially when he wouldn't tell her what he'd seen. "No!" She pulled away with newfound strength. "You hear me? No! Tell me what's out there."

"There were voices," he yelled. "I didn't know who they were at first. Then I saw my mom and my older sister. I haven't seen her in years. She's here." John looked at his feet. "What does that mean?"

"What happened to her?" she asked.

"She left me," he replied. "She left me behind with my mother."

Shelly nodded. "It's happening the same way for both of us, isn't it?"

The muscles in John's jaw tightened. "It wants me to see things, wants me to feel crazy." He raised his hand to his ear. "It's fucking with us. Nothing more. I'm trapped here, just like you!" His eyes grew round. "You hit me on the road. *You* did! Nothing else put me here other than being in the wrong place at the wrong time. I'm not trying to save anyone."

Shelly tried to speak, but her words slipped like shoes in swampy grass. His rant rushed at her, coming too fast. Her vision blurred, and she pushed her hands out, both to steady herself and to ward off John. "Wait. I can't," she said, struggling to form the words.

John ignored her. "For the first time, I stood up for myself. I had power when I was in the house. I could protect myself. Maybe there's something I can change, and I'm going back. It's a chance to make things right."

Shelly noticed a thread of blood at his jawline. "John, don't you see? You're going back there because it showed you something. How is that different? The dead woman, showing me a deck of cards about my life, and you with your sister and mom. Couldn't these be signs— or maybe the way out of here?"

John started up the hill without answering.

"If I fight, my body breaks—" She racked her brain to understand the sequence. The times she had breached some invisible boundary and broken the rules of the road, followed by swift abuse. Memories came in a flurry: *Cold metal on my skin. I'm cold. Taste of vomit. Tube into my mouth. You can't stay. I don't like it here. Her shoe peeked from the backseat. A man looking in. Flashing blue, red, blue, red. Soul returning.*

Shelly's mouth dropped open. She had also left the dark road and come back to it.

"John, I think I'm alive," she said, stopping her pursuit. "I could hear people around me. I couldn't move. But I was in my body." She gasped as more details flooded in. "I saw people in the light, the rain hitting my face. I felt the pain." Why would her spirit stay and Josie's pivot, passing in and out like the moon? Suddenly, dread creeped over her shoulders. *What if I'm pulling Josie away from life?*

"Horseshit." John prodded her back from her thoughts. "I get that you want to believe that."

His incessant pessimism was exhausting her. His temperament matched all the darkness in this afterworld, or whatever it was. "You said it yourself," she said. "You've come and gone. So maybe you're alive too?"

As soon as the comment left her mouth, they were sucked apart, their bodies pulled through the air as if a bomb had gone off. The force of it snapped Shelly's head towards her feet. She was being dragged by the torso with unrelenting speed as a rope would haul a person behind a running horse.

Struggling, she caught a glimpse of John disappearing into the distant forest. She flailed, trying to grab anything to stop her movement, ripping off fingernails as effortlessly and painlessly as a Band-Aid would tug at the skin. Twigs on the ground scraped against her legs, tearing her clothing. The road was angry. It was the only conclusion in her head, followed closely by a question—*What's waiting for me?*

Chapter Forty-One

It was three-thirty in the morning, and the hospital unit was calm. Paul heard fragments of casual, lighthearted conversations between staff members as they walked by—a stark contrast to his state of mind. He couldn't sleep or sit still. His thoughts were consumed by his daughter's disturbed nightmares, searching for her mother in forests, passing through piles of sticks and chasing a shadow. Then his brain betrayed him further by mixing in images of the pale, inner thigh of a woman with chestnut hair, smelling of roses. Each image—her naked breast or the small of her back as he gripped her supple bottom—reverberated through every limb. The next wave of electric shocks would be his imagined scene of the accident, Shelly's open mouth erupting in a scream of agony as the car rolled.

His wife was down the hall, but he felt like an intruder there, so he kept to Josie's room. He'd heard that patients in comas could hear what was happening around them—this notion suddenly became all too relevant. Shelly could be shrieking from behind the veil, desperate for him to go away and leave her alone. The thought chilled his spine.

What would have happened if their roles were switched? Would she be pacing around his hospital room, being blackmailed by a fling? Paul turned toward his daughter, who was resting in a chemically induced peace for the time being. She had a serene expression held in a nest of light from the surrounding monitors.

The answer to his thoughts about Shelly was obvious. She held razor focus on Josie. Every decision she made was always in their daughter's best interest. The idea she might lose herself in lust was absurd.

Paul went to the window and pressed his hands and forehead

against it. His breath disturbed the sheen of the surface. A sting of desire rushed him; he wanted the glass to burst and send him to the concrete below. He thumped his head against the pane. That's right, you asshole, he thought. Run. Leave Josie and run. Coward.

He stared down at the street. There were cars parked in the garage across the street but little foot traffic this early. An ambulance pulled through the center of the complex, and a stretcher popped from the end. He frowned as the small figures hurried through the sliding doors. He thought of Shelly, injured, being extracted from crumpled metal of her car. He backed away from the window, and his hands found the bedrail beside Josie.

"Trapped. Not here with us. What were you talking about?" He reached out to touch Josie's arm. "I've made so many mistakes," he whispered. He thought about the tape, the recording from the hotel. He couldn't even remember half of what he had said.

The walls inched closer, his angst building and building, and he squirmed like a kid in a timeout. Every move he'd made on Olivia's body was by choice. Shelly knew that too, and he didn't tell her when he'd had a chance.

Paul had to get out of the hospital. The walls were closing in on him. It had never crossed his mind that he might be stalked or targeted, but she had known enough to follow him and track his movements. That night had been a ploy, and he'd fallen for it. He pulled his phone out and scrolled through his messages, but it slid from his clammy hand, dropped, and skidded away. He quickly checked on Josie, but she hadn't stirred.

His phone started ringing, and he scrambled on hands and knees to silence the vibration. The screen showed a hospital number, which struck him as eerie. "Hello," he whispered.

"Hello, again."

He gripped the phone tighter. Hang up. Hang up. The sound of

Olivia's voice propelled him straight up like a flagpole. What other person would call him at this hour and under these circumstances?

"Are you at the hospital?" He moved to the door and poked his head out to view the nurse's station.

"No. Don't worry about that," she said calmly."

"What do you want?" He remembered her at the bar talking about her hopes and dreams as her eyes glimmered in the candlelight. The optimism in her voice that night had been intoxicating, but now her direct tone cut through him.

Questions were stacking up. How did she know where he might be? Had she known he would be at the meeting?

Still pressed against the door, he noticed his wedding band and the indent it made in his skin. Paul clenched his fist.

"I told you. This isn't about money," Olivia continued.

"I'd hoped it wouldn't be," he said. "Your message will be lost in the blackmailing. No one will remember you lost a child."

"I may not be a saint, but it's nothing compared to the lies told by that hospital," she fired back. "A month after I'd been home with my daughter, I got a letter telling me Julian died from a medical error."

Julian. All Paul could picture was the kid from the poster in the lobby.

"Error? Who sent the letter?" The idea that she had more on the hospital than improper documentation made him feel sick to his stomach. Falling asleep holding a scalpel, jet skiing after malpractice. Could it be something like that?

"That's not important. But as you said, the message matters. The father of my babies is a physician, a resident who left after I told him I was pregnant. I didn't put him on the birth certificate. The rumors didn't stop, however, and going into the birth, I was paranoid. Everything made me scared."

Paul heard some muffled sniffling. Was she angling for sympathy or some gesture?

"Some people in the hospital assumed I was trying to trap the father," she said. "Doctors sticking together—that bullshit."

"Like you're trapping me now?" Paul couldn't help but push his powerlessness under her nose.

"Why not? Who's gonna listen? I did what I had to." She sighed loudly. "Are you telling me that protecting the bottom line and covering ass isn't the heart of your job? I'm not the one rationing resources here, hitting people with bills high enough to throw them onto the street."

Paul felt his cheeks swell hot with anger. "So, it is about the money. We're back to this, the bill."

"Like I said before, something happened to him. My son left my body crying, breathing. Then he died. He died after the birth, which has been backed up by the transcripts."

"You've read those reports?"

"I read what scraps were handed to me. I asked for copies every two weeks for a year. But I've always been given the runaround. Either no one returned my calls, or they told me records were sent. Guess what—I never received anything." Her voice now moved from calm to pressured.

"That doesn't prove anything," he said. "Hospitals are big. They lose shit and take forever." The sentence left his mouth without hesitation, but he couldn't believe his own voice. He sounded like Will, like Travis. Every horrible boss, doctor, and administrator in the system, for that matter.

"That's where you come in," she said. The sound of her voice scraped like nails on a chalkboard. "The administrators pass reviews through without a thought. I can't do anything with the letter without something to back it up. And if I can, it will be one wrongful death case among many others." Her tone grew distant, undoubtedly running through the strategy as she spoke.

Paul suddenly had a clearer picture of how far she was aiming. "Your baby died—" He stopped himself, realizing how callous it sounded.

"I carried him for nine months, talked to him, prepared to give birth." Her voice cracked with emotion. "You're correct, my baby died, but he should have lived."

"They told you the death was due to birth complications," he said. "Did they say what type of error?"

"The tip, the letter, came from someone who knows, but I need proof. Get me proof."

The call went dead.

Paul's phone stuck to his ear, her demands lingering in the air above him. He went to the sink in Josie's bathroom and splashed water on his face. Looking in the mirror, he saw himself for the first time in days: gaunt features, his eyes droopy. Water dripped from his chin.

"Who are you?" he asked the image in the mirror. "Are you investigating misconduct in a case, or trying to keep your family from dying?"

***

Sprawled on the bed, Miranda looked at the clock: four in the morning. She'd been pacing since she got home from her shift, after walking the dog and eating a meal standing up. She couldn't distract herself.

She thought about the man in the park with the gray hat. How did the kid know about that?

She had never talked about what had happened to Eli, never told the other nurses. Of course, the rumors about her were rife. That she watched him die, became erratic and self-destructive, then quit her job without notice and became an alcoholic. None of which were entirely true. There had been many moments when she had wanted to find and join him wherever he'd gone. It scared her how inclined she had felt about crossing the veil to hold him.

From her nightstand, Miranda pulled out a bottle of sleeping pills, prescribed to her when Eli had first died. She hated taking them, knowing they tended to make her worse, more depressed. But maybe it would be okay to take them now, to shut off the voices in her head.

Bean wandered in and curled up on the bed with an exaggerated sigh, likely annoyed with her restlessness.

"Sorry, buddy," she said, giving him a scratch. She took a tablet out of the bottle and held it in her hand, staring at it. Her mood moved like a roller coaster, and she wasn't allowed to jump off. With a trembling hand, she tipped the pill bottle into her palm, forming a pile of small, blue, football-shaped pills. All of them would deliver milligrams of disconnection.

"It's what we're supposed to do, right? It's part of grieving, to clean up and walk through the shit," she announced to Bean, who perked up his ears for a split second, then fell back to sleep, worn out by her ranting past his bedtime.

"If only we'd never met." Suddenly, Miranda felt like a little girl in a confessional, waiting for a scolding. Her stomach lurched, and she sat up as a wave of nervousness swept over her. Never to have met him. She started to cry. "I'm overworked, and Josie is high on pain medication. She could have said something other than Eli—like Jedi or blue sky. You need to sleep. Sleep, Miranda." She buried her head in the comforter.

The phone rang on the dresser, startling her and scattering a few pills around the foot of the bed. Bean lifted his head to examine the opportunity that had presented itself, but Miranda was ahead of him, sliding the pills over with her foot.

It was staffing, looking for coverage at the hospital. Normally, she would hide under the bed when these calls came in, thinking they could see her, knowing she had time available to work but still avoiding their call. She almost dropped her phone, hitting it to answer. If she went to work, she could ask Josie more questions about the place she saw Eli.

"Miranda Sullivan, there is an open position on graveyard shift on unit 3-B. Are you able to work?"

The ridge of her knuckles jammed into her forehead. Her feet hurt, and she would be crippled by another shift, her fourth in a row. But she had to see Josie and find out more.

"Ma'am, are you there?"

"Yes, I can take it." She regretted the words as she said them.

Heavy with sleep, Miranda curled up into a ball, and Bean adjusted his position to get closer. Her eyes felt the weight of the day, and as sleep began to take her, she recalled something Josie had said.

At first, it had struck her as endearing. The child wanted to see her again. Her eyes popped open. "What the fuck! She knew I'd be back at the hospital!"

Chapter Forty-Two

Driving home, Paul juggled theories, contemplating the grieving, manipulative mother, and the hospital with a bottom line to protect. Running into the house, up the stairs, then crashing into his office, he grabbed the paperwork and spread it out, paying little attention to order or sequence. Some of the folders were still on the floor, in haphazard piles.

If anyone saw his office, there'd be countless violations of confidentiality, and he vowed to shred the paper trail every day. But motivation always dwindled, and the stacks grew larger. Regardless, the litter of pages made him reflect and look back on his early days in the job. He assumed he had proven competent in his new role, because they kept giving him additional responsibilities. Will had been an early frustration, an exacting, sometimes impatient boss. He thought Paul should not waste time on investigating backstory and instead focus on the chronological order of events and the standards dictated by the hospital. Although Paul's expertise was in quality control, he indulged Will since he knew office politics—Will's job was to drive the hospital's agenda. Paul didn't fight it, reluctant to rock the boat, but he promised himself he would turn the train and set limits eventually. Promises unfulfilled.

Paul's hand passed over a file. Timothy York, the first name on the mound of papers. His mother died of a heart attack while waiting for treatment in an emergency room lobby. The case was eventually deemed unfounded at hospital-level and thrown out of court in a malpractice lawsuit. The hospital claimed the patient reported nausea, vomiting, and mild chest pains, so they were not at fault for neglect. It was acceptable that in their standard of care, anyone with nausea would have been bumped to the bottom of the list to prioritize other severe cases.

Sandra Cray had waited eight hours to be seen for a laceration on her arm, only to be told that sutures were not possible because it had been too long. Another claim unsubstantiated as standard practice, regardless of the infection and scarring the patient had sustained.

Reading these accounts evoked a macabre montage of faces that stared back at him. The arms of past apparitions, pulling him down. The extreme anguish of the patients caused Paul a visceral ache; he couldn't understand why he'd kept the documents. His heart sank with the idea of looking through more or requesting more background information. It would take hours, time he didn't have. He felt drained and wanted to lie down and give up.

He noticed a cream manila envelope on the counter behind his desk. Olivia's file. His hands shook as he opened it. Swiping the files on his desk back onto the floor, he opened his laptop and slid into the chair. When the hospital website flashed across the screen, he logged in to the main intranet. Each encounter by a staff person was listed with dates of care. He clicked on the details for December twenty-eighth, the day of the birth, and compared them to the documents under his index finger, sliding across the hard copy, eyes racing almost too fast to keep up.

He leaned close to the monitor, squinting. Blue light haloed his finger on the screen.

Lab reports, dilation, and the health of Twin A were first. Concise and to the point. On December twenty-eighth and twenty-ninth, the doctor listed progress reports, as did the nurses, with twenty notes by a Dr. Ramsey outlining his findings for Twin B. All notes by Dr. Ramsey were dated December twenty-ninth between four-twenty-five and four-forty in the morning.

The hospital notes then became less clear. Twin A had been with the mother, but they didn't mention Twin B for several encounters. Of the notes entered, the only details included led to the movement of the mother to prepare for a cesarean and the events after her return. Paul read on, knee bouncing. Josie was alone, and Shelly's condition remained unclear. He needed to get back.

He read a note from a nurse:

Ms. Jenner is a twenty-seven-year-old post-op from a cesarean at thirty-eight weeks of pregnancy. Returned from surgery about ten minutes ago. I haven't quite finished her assessment, but she is requesting to see her son. Her fluids are infusing at 150 mL/hour, and she has a patient-controlled analgesia pump. Her urine output has been 30–50 mL/hour. No father present. Continues to ask for son. No status yet.

"But what happened before?" Paul spoke to the computer, his head bobbing between the file and the display.

Next, he peered at Dr. Ramsey's notes:

Mother tiring and lacking productive pushing. Rapid cesarean needed. Prolonged labor with unclear impact, stress to fetus. Monitor heart rate.

Paul didn't see the transition or the movement of the patient. She's tired from labor then—boom! No baby.

The notes continued with the mother informed of the death. He clicked the cursor.

The attending physician and anesthesiologist at patient bedside. Mother informed of Twin B's death. Ms. Jenner was extremely distraught, screaming and crying. Twin A was taken from the room due to her agitation. Social work paged.

Paul pulled apart the file, rolling up pages and frantic to compare them. Oddly, only the social worker's notes of the mother's mental assessment were left.

"Where the heck are the accounts between birth and death?" Paul scrolled through the notes, jotting dates and timestamps to get an outline, his pen zipping over the lined paper. Dates were listed under the December twenty-eighth notes, indicating the changes that had been made to a document. Something stood out. December thirtieth, twelve-twenty-five…twelve-thirty-two…twelve-thirty-three again, and again. The notes by Dr. Ramsey and each staff member involved, including the nurses in his services, were signed on December thirtieth. They all had amendments with the same date and time frame. Paul zeroed in on the revisions, wanting to understand if there were corrections versus omissions. The death had been highly scrutinized, yet he had not seen any changes in the summaries, which added to the disorganization of this case. He looked specifically for Dr. Ramsey's notes and clicked on the link which listed any corrections. A box that asked for a username and password blinked across the screen. He stared for a second, finding it strange, but filled in the necessary components. He hit enter.

ACCESS NOT APPROVED.

"What the fuck?" He keyed in the password, then hit enter again, confident of an error.

ACCESS NOT APPROVED in bold red letters passed again across the screen. He'd never been prevented from seeing a chart.

He moved away from Dr. Ramsey's notes to click on the amended notes of one of the nurses at the birth. The same box flew up. His hands hovered above the keyboard, and he took a deep breath, still staring at the dialogue box. Access would need to be authorized by Will—something he'd never had to do before.

He decided to change methods, snapping up the mouse and moving over screens to open the chart on Twin B. The baby was the patient, so the chart should show the details. Hopeful that the file would shed more light on the case, he entered the health record number of the baby and hit enter.

FILE NOT FOUND.

A theme emerged as he delved deeper. Sweat beaded on his forehead, and a chill moved down his back. Paul leaned back in his chair as the office melted away. Simultaneous to Twin B being pronounced dead, every member of that team amended their notes related to the cesarean, amendments he couldn't access. The records for the baby didn't exist.

Paul closed his eyes and dug back into his training before Will, and before he was covered in scales of Teflon. "It's not me," he said out loud. "It's not Olivia, or Will, or the hospital. It's the data." The pace of his pulse rocketed up and down his frame. "What does the story say? Follow the story." When he opened his eyes, scratches of notes rippled in front of him, a diary of his analysis, a form of spirit writing, the information in his brain spit out in sequence.

Twin A at breast. Where's Twin B? Skipped Twin B. December twenty-eighth. Nurse notes. Mother's weakened push. Prep for operation. December 30. Notes, amendments. December thirtieth between twelve-twenty-five and twelve-forty-five. December thirtieth. Blocked access. It was about the story.

"It goes higher than I thought." He stood up and walked to the window, grabbing the back of his head. "Despite her crazy behavior, Olivia could be right."

Chapter Forty-Three

John's body raked over rocks and sticks, the brush tearing at his clothes and scoring his skin. Even as he swiped and clawed, nothing slowed the scene ripping past his face, allowing him to see only a few shards of color amid the dust.

Then, as quickly as he had been stolen, his body was thrown. The experience of weightlessness cradled him, with no drag on his torso or squeeze around his legs. The top of his shoulder hit first, and his back end flipped over his head. He rolled down an embankment, deeper and deeper into the woods. When he landed, his body lay numb under slow gusts of air. He waited for what would come. Every exhale lingered in white mist as the temperature dropped rapidly.

John gave in to his fatigue and let his mind wander. Memories of his many past transgressions floated behind his eyes—thrown fists, fear-stricken faces, and pockets bursting with other people's cash. He imagined himself on a stiff church bench. All heads in the chapel pointed forward, and each person squirmed, contemplating their judgment. They spoke of souls displaced in death, those who rejected Jesus and were destined for some kind of prison for spirits. Lying there in the cold forest with the moist earth under his cheek, John considered Shelly's version of an obscure realm. The road, not death.

Shuffling leaves twitched his ear lobe. His body went rigid, and he sunk lower to the ground as feet shuffled through the undergrowth. Whatever was coming would fail to see him or write him off as dead. Twigs snapped and leaves crumbled, and the pace of the rustling increased. His muscles tensed; John decided to force the issue. He sprang up on all fours, eyes wide, looking for his attacker. There, crouching under a darkening sky with trees dancing with mist, a figure came into view. Suddenly, he stood eye-to-eye with a little boy.

All the tension he'd built up tugged him like a leashed dog. The child was dressed in underwear, with a blanket loosely wrapped around his shoulders. His skin appeared bluish gray, and bruising discolored his forehead. Clutching food in his hand, he ate eagerly as blood dripped from his elbow.

John rose slowly. It was the boy from the baptism, the one who had curled into a ball afterward at his mother's house. Familiar markings covered the boy's chest, and the blanket around him was dusted with tree needles and leaves.

The little boy cocked his head, saying nothing as he chewed his meal. He stepped forward.

John held out his hands in defense then thought better of it. Why else would he be standing there with his young self unless this meeting had a purpose? Slowly, the boy extended a filthy hand. In his eyes, there was a longing John couldn't ignore. John reached out to him. Their hands joined.

John's neck snapped straight, and his head flexed toward the sky. He moaned through a locked jaw while his hand held fast to the boy, although he'd lost view of him. A buzz filled his ears and fizzed under his skin as a surge of heat radiated through his entire body. Brilliant light flowed around him as if he had been plugged in, synced with another.

The forest of trees had gone, replaced by a sidewalk that extended before him. A line of homes stood partially obscured by the light, as though he peeked in from another place, looking through a window to a different time. Without warning, his body dropped, rocking his skull and slamming his shoulder, then his knees landed on the curb with a thud. A painless experience but also an unsettling one that left him nauseous.

John had returned to his old neighborhood. He felt the spray of rain on his cheeks and shoulders, and he was saturated in seconds. Something had changed; everything around him loomed large. He looked at his hands—the flesh was brighter, smoother. The youthful hand opened and closed before his eyes. John's shoulders were wrapped in a blanket. He was a child.

A neighbor had offered the cover of an umbrella along with a warmed waffle to hold off the chill. The sweet taste of maple and vanilla filled him, and his heart rolled in contentment. Water dripped from the umbrella spokes as the neighbor patted his head.

A flicker of red to the left broke him from the bliss. Police lights gleamed against the rainy street, and he felt the cold now, standing in bare feet. Three squad cars lined up at the curb, and the fumes from their exhaust rose in the air. In that moment, John had the same thought as when he was a boy, that the road had caught fire. The red lights from the cars and the rising exhaust under the dark sky looked like a lava bed flowing through their neighborhood.

Dazed, he looked around, squinting through the rain. The police officer, the neighbor, and a few people standing stared at him. Alarmed, he walked in reverse, dropping the waffle and tightening the blanket around his shoulders.

Rain dotted his head as he moved outside the comfort of the umbrella. John couldn't see the curb now, and as one of his bare feet clipped the edge, he fell flat on his back, smacking the pavement and jostling something loose in his abdomen, like a rock falling into deep water.

His belly swirled like a snake trapped in a canvas bag. When the ache started to climb, he watched as a pulsating mound swelled from his gut to his chest. John screamed—a childlike, high-pitched sound. The pain was inescapable as something grew, pushing upwards through bone and tendons, snapping ribs as his skin was stretched by whatever had cocooned in him.

He wiggled like a worm, the punch of something forced up his throat, tearing his esophagus, until his mouth separated his jaw from his skull. It passed over his teeth and slithered forward, and his body deflated into a useless sack.

***

"Hey!" The voice seemed too far away to be bothered with. "I'm out now."

John's eyes fluttered open.

"Get up!"

Then something struck him, a slap as sharp as being tossed into ice water. When his eyes opened, he saw soiled feet, the edge of a soaked blanket, and the boy.

John was no longer a child, but the taste of vanilla lingered on his lips. The sheer shock of what had occurred left him stunned. The boy had slithered out of him. He gawked at the petite human, who now appeared frail and wobbled slightly on his feet.

"She loved you."

"What?" John asked. He was angry and tired of the crazy riddles thrown his way by the road. He concentrated on his old home, where the answers might lie. The boy's eyes held a purpose, and he needed to find out what it was.

The boy blocked his view, then pointed off in the distance, and John's eyes followed. The faithful sleepwalkers also turned toward the house in the direction of the child's extended finger. John felt a wave of adrenaline spiced with anger. The ground under his feet, the red cast of light on the houses, his mother's door—the totality of it crushed him as his vision bounced left to right.

"This means nothing," he screamed. "It's windows and shutters, screen doors. There's nothing here I need. There never was!"

The boy's face was impassive. "She always loved you. She tried to help you."

"Who? Why the fuck do you keep saying that? No one loved me. You hear me! No one." John grabbed the boy's arm, pulling him around, almost lifting him off the ground. His frame was so light it might as well have been hollow. "Love never existed there. That house is a black hole, filled with nothing but her shit. My mother took everything I ever loved. Hate lives there."

"You are wrong, John," the boy said.

John released him and tensed up. He looked at each of his curled fists, then at the boy's already bruised face. Until that moment, the boy had shown no emotion, but now a frown cracked over his lips, and his eyes dropped. Then he slowly turned away.

The crowd of people began to leave too. What did any of it mean? None of this had brought him closer to answers. Did he exist in the world Shelly described or was his soul trapped in prison?

John heard yelling, muffled and distant. Ashley ran from the back of the house, crying.

"John! I'm here." In front of the house, she collided with the outstretched arms of the remaining police. She struggled with them but was pushed back, and her pale arms squirmed, trying to reach him. The sight of her made his pulse jump, and instinctively, he moved toward her. The love he'd held back for so long broke free. Memories of his sister curled up on the floor in his room. Morsels of kindness drowned by waves of abuse and fear.

The fateful night his mother cut his arm and he ran away—it was all happening again, but now John could only watch as a helpless spectator. As a child, he stood barefooted and bloodied as Ashley tried to force herself through the cops. They took John away in a police car and for months, he couldn't understand why he'd been in trouble that night. That feeling, a sense of wrongdoing, lingered.

"Ashley," he called. Fingers held him in a tight and painful grip. A tinge of blood discolored his wrist as they dug in. He looked back and saw Bob, his boss. The hold cut into his flesh, and pain coursed through his frame. Bones squirmed in the tissue as if they'd snap at any moment. John tried to pull away as Ashley continued to push at the men.

"Are you who she hoped for, John?" Bob spoke in a low and sullen tone, nothing like the boring, lifeless employer who wandered through the store. The question burrowed into John's mind and nested there, a seed of an ambiguous doubt that resonated with his already disheartened mind, rejected by all.

"She's fighting for you, but you fight for no one." Bob's head turned slowly in a rotary motion toward Ashley, then back to John. "I think we are headed in different directions, professionally. You should look for a new job."

The words looped John back to a different time, out of sequence. "I don't know what any of this means," he said, as the agony intensified. A warmth of fluid trickled across his lips, the droplets mixing with the falling rain. Looking down at himself, redness darkened the white logo of his shirt. Blood was dripping from his head.

Bob squeezed harder, and the bones shifted in his grip.

John winced.

"You're all the same, just like my mother. You could always spot the devil," Bob parroted him. A rage built in John, and he lunged toward Bob but failed to make contact, instead seizing him around the throat.

Ashley sobbed, reaching for him. "I'm here. You don't understand—"

He stared at her tortured face, the most frantic he'd ever seen her. John began losing energy, life was being sucked from his body under Bob's tether. He saw the overweight man's expression sharpen with annoyance. The transient belief that John had survived the crash, the desire he had to share Shelly's infectious hopes, diminished.

"I waited—" He choked under Bob's grip. "You never came, but I waited." He reached a trembling hand toward Ashley.

With a final thrust forward, she cleared the arms that restrained her. "You don't understand!" she wailed. "He's my son."

Chapter Forty-Four

Shelly's body crashed onto a dirt floor, and grit dusted her eyelashes and cheeks. The walls around her were discolored green and blue; it seemed to be a metal shed. Raw steel was shoved into the mud, held together by bolts in the corners and the weight of a tin roof. Rust encroached from the edges of the jagged panels as if the walls oozed a crimson fluid, left to decay.

As her eyes adjusted, the environment looked foreign, with no resemblance to any part of her childhood memories or even a nightmare. Light fluttered and highlighted the walls, which could only mean a fire. The smell of burning cedar provided additional confirmation. Its natural oils smelled of Christmas and campfires, although far removed from warmth and cheer. As she had with the lady in the pond, Shelly felt a craving to move toward the shimmer, an undeniable and magnetic force.

Shelly ducked under a low ceiling, down a short passthrough. The room beyond, expanded like Wonderland; a keyhole opened to a gaping mystery. The burning wood nested in a stone insert, casting light into creases and fissures, and the walls seemed to vibrate from ceiling to floor.

"Oh, Shelly, wonderful. Thanks for coming. I hoped you were okay. I heard about that accident. Come, have a seat. Let's talk." Seated in the middle of the room was Dr. Frazier-Velli.

A burst of relief filled her chest, and she rose, almost on tiptoes, to see a source of refuge from a distant life, an existence beyond the accident and Paul's infidelity and the happenings of her cracked mind. She stumbled, overcome with gratitude. John had fought her theories of the road and existence beyond death, the idea that life could be possible. But seeing her doctor's face took her back to the land of the living.

A log snapped, shaking her from her thoughts, and her gaze landed on the red-hot center of each shaft of wood. The stone around the fire appeared orange, highlighting the uneven floor. Shelly's excitement tempered at the almost fairytale-like picture. Instead of his familiar, plain office, the doctor sat in the middle of the shack, with a dirt floor underfoot and his books in disarray and littering the floor.

"Doctor?" Shelly analyzed his eyes to see if they might betray him. They held an irreverence, and the way his lips parted over his teeth hit her in the stomach as a warning rather than an invitation. This was no doctor of hers.

The man waited in silence as if he wanted her to sit, but instead, he re-crossed his legs, positioned his writing pad, and stacked his hands on top. Shadows danced over his face, changing it by the second with the fire's glow.

"Why are you here?" She made her way toward the crackling flames, keeping her gaze fixed on him.

Again, he shot her a patronizing smile. "For you. I'm here for you." His head moved along with her, following her to the back of the other green chair.

"I'm looking for Josie," she said. "I see her here, but she slips away." Against all instincts, she lowered her guard. "Can you help me?"

"Josie?" He chuckled and tossed his pad down, flopping back in the chair with a looseness in his joints, almost seductively. "Josie isn't here. No. I'm not here for her. Children don't belong here."

"What do you mean?"

"Shelly." He sat up, more stoic and severe, his eyes focusing on her. "You're smart. Must we drag this on? The exploration. The fucking discovery." His voice sharpened. "This is not fit to live in. It's a pit of death and regret a place to linger after failing all chances to live life to the fullest." He took a deep breath, sarcastically mocking his familiarity with her. "You sit in my office, week after week, diving into the past, but it seems—" He looked around the altered version of his office, "—we're getting nowhere." He smirked, eyes twinkling behind his glasses. "You were not entirely truthful, and the demons are unhappy. The car accident was an opportunity! Something needed to change, and you certainly weren't going to do anything!"

Shelly covered her face, threatened by his edge and harshness. Why him? All those sessions had led to nothing but a sense of failure and endless tears. The notes in his pad might have been deriding denunciations of her weaknesses, stick figure drawings, or emotionless journal entries of wasted time. Was the road parroting his journal from their sessions?

He cocked his head to the side. "Shelleee," he sang. "Sometimes in life, we need a pivotal moment, something to teach us valuable lessons, and we must keep our ears open for these marvelous opportunities. Am I right?"

"Opportunity? Dying is an opportunity?" She locked eyes with him. "Seeing my daughter drowned, bloody, and broken? Watching her witness firsthand every corner of my agonizing past—this is supposed to help me in some way?"

A low chuckle broke from his mouth. He stood up from the green velvet chair and picked up a shovel with a long brown handle and a dark, tarnished blade.

Shelly watched as he stepped across the dirt floor and stopped, half the distance to the hearth. He angled the shovel down and pushed, bringing dirt out of the mound of broken earth. The gold hue of the flames caught the glistening moisture of the top layer of dirt as he moved closer to the surface.

"Yes, Shelly." His breath was labored as he jabbed the blade into the side of the hole over and over. "This is an opportunity."

Chapter Forty-Five

The chart had timed out, so Miranda logged back into the computer, trying to keep up the appearance of functioning normally. At four-thirty in the morning, her body was struggling to cope. Patients were sleeping, leaving her with free time, most of which she spent fidgeting, getting up then sitting back down. A nurse working in such a distracted manner could have dangerous implications. So, with each patient, her attention and emotional energy focused on a new motto: *Pull your head out of your ass. Don't fuck up and kill someone.*

Room Fifteen was down the hallway. Josie's room. That night, another nurse had been assigned to her care, so Miranda had to track her from a distance.

At times, she saw Eli standing by the desk, a vision that could not possibly be real, but the picture played on like a projector. He came alive in the faces of strangers. Dark-haired men on the bus to work, that doppelgänger filling her coffee. It was happening all over again, as it did after he died.

Miranda blinked and the janitor emptying bins with a concerned look on his face became Eli. He waved at her, breaking her trance. Swallowing the rock in her throat, she dropped her eyes as the inner lecture persisted.

"For the love of Christ!" Miranda suddenly heard behind her. "Too many fucking Red Bulls, day shift." Miranda looked at the charge nurse, bewildered.

"Take it from me," she said with a scowl, "you don't look like Allen. Write notes under your own account for fuck's sake."

Miranda pressed both hands on the desk, wracking her brain. It was a huge breach of protocol to use another nurse's account. Chart ownership and access was a regulation nurses were reminded of over and over.

"I must have walked up to an unlocked computer," she muttered.

"Rein it in! You're all over the place. The nurse raised her eyebrows. "Maybe you shouldn't work night shifts?"

Miranda rubbed her face. "Shit," she said, under her hands. "Sorry, I'm a hot mess. She was clearly on edge, and it was disrupting the nursing station. She decided to pace the halls, get her blood flowing. But she hadn't walked three steps when she heard yelling from behind her. It was the charge nurse, hurrying toward room fifteen.

Miranda's feet moved without thinking, and when she rounded the doorway, Josie lay on the linoleum, screaming. Her IV had been ripped out of her arm, and blood was dripping from her wrist. A nurse was kneeling, trying to console her and get a hand on her vein.

Josie thrashed back and forth on the floor. "The water. It's coming," she yelled, wide-eyed. "I'm drowning. Mom!"

"Page the doctor. And can someone call Mr. Blake?" The charge nurse said.

Josie called out, "He's in front of the fire. He knows Mommy's afraid." Her anguish from the dream was heart-wrenching. As blood fell onto her hospital gown and the floor, the tension in the room increased. Miranda grew anxious listening to the chatter of voices coming from all sides. Some nurses wanted to force Josie onto the bed to secure the IV. They spoke about injections and holding her down.

Josie seemed to be fully immersed in a nightmare or trance-like state, marginally connected to people in the room. "They are filling in the hole. They say it's good to do that," she droned, more distant than ever.

Mr. Blake ran into the room and dropped in front of his daughter. "Josie!" His shirt collar was up, and a pressure mark on the side of his face suggested he'd likely been sleeping in his wife's room. "Shit! Baby, you're bleeding. How did this happen?" He reached over, trying to hold her arm for the nurse.

"Get away from me!" Josie huddled closer to the bedframe. Security congregated by the nursing station outside her door, escalating the drama.

Miranda's fear for the child mounted. The poor girl would be pulled onto the bed, secured by nylon restraints, and jabbed with injections to put her out. Energy rose through Miranda's feet and into her legs. A jittery sensation pushed at her temples as she envisioned a train hitting a wall.

"Stop!"

Everyone froze and looked at her.

"Everyone out, except you!" She pointed at Mr. Blake, and he stared back and gave an obedient nod.

Heads swiveled to Miranda and to the charge nurse, then to the patient.

"Yep! Let's see if we can do this another way," the charge nurse said.

Everyone shuffled out of the room.

Miranda took a deep breath and calmly approached Josie. She crouched down next to her, crossing her legs and sitting next to the terrified girl. Josie was clutching the bedframe, sobbing. Miranda looked her up and down, trying to figure out how to gain her trust, what to say that might resonate and allow her to let her guard down. She rubbed her hands on her pants, sensing the father's unease and hearing his tapping feet inches away.

"So, I guess you were right," she said. "I wasn't gonna be here tonight, but some blonde kid made me a bet, and I couldn't let her lose." She waited a moment. "Man, do my feet hurt." She rubbed her arches.

Josie slowly shifted her gaze toward the weary nurse. Miranda studied the young face, knowing the images Josie saw in her head must be worse than anything she herself could imagine. Josie was battling demons, and boogiemen were after her mother.

"You had a frightening dream again?"

Josie sat quietly but didn't respond.

Miranda touched the petite forearm, checking the IV site. Smudges of red tinge dotted the skin around where the cannula had been pulled from her vein. "I'm here with you, honey. I'm just going to cover this, okay?"

She pulled some gauze and tape from the pouch at her hip and carefully secured them onto the IV site. The child studied her closely. While Miranda wrapped her arm, she let out small gasps, the remnants of her frenzy. When Miranda finished, she gave Josie's hand a soft squeeze.

The girl leaned in closer, the color slipping from her cheeks. "The water took our car. Then he dug a hole."

Her tone and intensity sent goosebumps over Miranda's skin.

Josie looked over at her father, who stood nearby with sweat clinging to his brow. Miranda could see the pulse in his neck pounding away.

"What water, baby?" he asked. "I want to help, sweetie." He paused, looking at Miranda. "I know you're very frightened."

Miranda acknowledged him with a nod, recalling the lecture she gave him in their last meeting about offering support.

Josie wiped her nose with the back of her hand. "I see Mommy, but she's trying to get away. She's coming, Daddy." She sat up. "Mommy tried to get me away from the water. I held her hand, and—" Her lips quivered. "She couldn't—" Panic returned, her hands jerking as she shook her head.

Paul tried to soothe her, but she pulled away, visibly agitated.

"She can't be dead!" Josie yelled.

They were going in the wrong direction, and if they kept going, security would take over.

"Hey, Josie!" Miranda said. "Let's go see her!"

She stopped crying, and her father looked up.

"I want Mom," Josie said. "Dad, I want to." She was panting like a motor trying to start, quick sucks in between sobs. "Daddy? Let's go."

Paul, obviously irritated, leaned closer to Miranda. "She can't! Shelly's all wrapped up, and I can't let her see that."

"Mr. Blake, I understand, but your daughter is imagining and inventing an even worse scenario. Maybe touching her mother's hand and talking to her will bring her back to reality."

His frame stiffened, but slowly, he nodded.

After Josie's hair was brushed and she was given a clean gown, Miranda pulled a wheelchair around to the door. Together, they pushed her down the hall toward Shelly Blake's room.

"I didn't know Mommy was so close," Josie said.

Mark's theories of favors begetting favors replayed in Miranda's mind. She focused on pushing the wheelchair. They maneuvered into Shelly's room, allowing Josie to take a minute to absorb this initial vision of her mother. Miranda watched for her reaction, and quickly, her confidence started to crack. A line of sweat formed between her shoulder blades.

"Josie." She touched the child's shoulder. "We can take a break at any time! I wanted you to see for yourself. She's a patient just like you, and she got hurt just like you. She's right here."

"Can I talk to her?" Josie asked softly.

Miranda looked over at Paul. He nodded, so they wheeled her closer. The little girl leaned forward and took her mother's hand.

Miranda's heart hurt for them, remembering Josie's pleas for her mother's safe return from wherever she had gone.

"Josie? We need to go back to your room so you can rest now."

The girl didn't look at Miranda; she stared at her mother with inquisitive eyes then leaned forward in her chair. "The bad man covered me with dirt," she whispered. "But you tried to save me."

Chapter Forty-Six

Seated in the corner of the hospital room, Paul felt a familiar helplessness. Since returning from seeing her mother, Josie lay turned away from him, staring through the window. He couldn't help but think back to when she was a baby. Shelly sat awkwardly at the end of the bed with that trance-like stare, expressionless and unresponsive, holding her newborn as if she held folded towels in her arms. Witnessing Josie so traumatized, Paul was terrified she would follow in her mother's path, showing the same repressed emotions, the same seclusion inside herself, the same pulling away.

He was unsure of so much, except for the years of squandered choices. If only he had seen things more clearly after Josie's birth. Both parts of his life needed him more back then—work and family—both pulling like a finger trap. Instead of realizing the job was the cause of his changing perspective, his resentment towards Shelly grew.

Now Josie kept pulling away and wouldn't let him in. The nurse assured him that kids tend to retreat when they're scared, but Paul knew better. Josie had always leaned on Shelly—and so had he. Shelly wiped away tears, gave words of encouragement, reprimanded and chastised when needed. Paul's parenting skills were more effective in teasing, poking fun, and the run-and-tumble part Shelly shied away from.

Paul tucked the pink star blanket around Josie and her curly-haired ballerina bear, something they used when she was sick or had a hard day. But today, medications might be doing more for her. The truth was, he had no idea if Josie's withdrawn and stoic demeanor was better than her thrashing and screaming.

Since Josie's fall and the journey down the hall to Shelly's room,

Miranda had been assigned as her nurse, and he watched as she made his daughter comfortable before leaving to check on other patients.

Josie was relaxed now, but her tumble from the bed could have done real damage. They would take X-rays later to make sure.

Light started to filter in, and soon the sun would rise, hopefully, with better news on Shelly's status. They needed good news.

"Baby." He stroked Josie's hair. "Your mother is tough, so much tougher than me." He gave her shoulder a squeeze. "I'm sure she wants to be here with you. She knows we love her and want her to get better." His throat tightened, and the tips of his fingers moved along his collarbone to his chin. The motion made him pause and look at his hand. It was the same tic Shelly had, her hands up at her neck. The glint of her wedding ring, fixed under her jaw, had always put Paul on the defensive. He'd seen her do it a million times but had never thought about what was behind it. An uncomfortable squeezing mixed with worst-case scenarios and sadness.

His phone vibrated in his pocket, sending him into anxiety mode. Will was calling, and he wasn't entirely sure how he should feel. Speaking with him could be a double-edged sword. Someone had blocked his access—Will or someone around him. Paul clicked decline. He needed more time. If the hospital had tried to cover up the incident, Will could be part of it. If not, and the staff had tried to conceal details under his nose, there would be tags or trails, which Will could find.

Miranda returned with medication and busied herself at the computer. She sighed repeatedly and pulled at her neck—clearly the signs of a nurse who couldn't wait for her shift to end. Dealing with sick children wasn't for everyone; Paul had read enough complaints to know that. Having dinosaurs or sunbursts on your scrubs didn't necessarily make you a kid-friendly person. Tolerance, patience, and nerves of steel helped more. But he knew Josie trusted this nurse.

Miranda's hands clicked away on the keyboard as boxes and colors changed on the screen. Paul stood beside her, then moved closer. The wheels turned in his mind, like the hovering cursor under her index finger.

She stepped away with quick feet and aimed for the door.

"Can I talk to you?" Paul asked.

She didn't make eye contact, and he knew why. It was likely she considered him an ass. "The oncoming nurse will update you," she told him. Her badge swung as she turned to leave.

"Wait!" He walked after her to the nurses' station.

She stopped. "Did you need something?"

"I have some questions about Josie's arm," he said. "Can you come with me?" He desperately needed collateral and documentation, but his plan crossed all ethics and rules of practice.

Miranda exhaled, dripping with annoyance, but followed him back to the room. Josie was still asleep, curled up with her bear. He was free to fish for more information and confirm his theory, even though he felt jittery from too much coffee and little food and sleep. He knew he wasn't thinking clearly, but without access, he had nothing.

She bent down and inspected Josie's arm as her stethoscope hung down and her hair, drawn up in a tired bun, fell forward over the sleeping child. "What did you want to know?" she whispered.

Without warning, he grabbed the pager from her shirt and popped the battery out. He couldn't have anyone listening.

"What the fuck?" Her face lit up with outrage as she stepped back.

He held his hands out and lowered his voice. "Do you know what I do for a living?"

"Are you out of your mind?" She continued to step back, holding on to Josie's bed.

"Listen!" His head zipped back and forth from Miranda to the door. "Please! I need your help. Something is going on in this hospital, and I need to figure out what."

She loosened her grip on the bed and watched him, waiting.

"I work in this district auditing hospitals," he said. "I've been forced onto a case where all the players no longer work here." He couldn't tell if she was following what he was telling her. Without knowing what information had leaked, he tried to be vague about Olivia's background. "I heard a rumor that a death was made to look like natural causes or secondary to complications during birth—"

"A baby?" Her eyebrows raised slightly.

"Yes." He studied her face, realizing the impact of his words hadn't shaken her. "Do you know it?"

She shifted uncomfortably. "Rumors, yes. Facts, no."

"All I'm getting from the higher-ups is funneling toward the natural causes angle." He leaned in. "The chart is completely void of details. The mother is being charged for the surgery, but there should be more to this case, more of a paper trail." For the first time, he could express his thoughts out loud.

"I can't help you," she said bluntly. "This isn't my problem." In a quick motion, she plucked her pager out of his hand.

"Wait!" Trying not to wake Josie, he dropped down to a whisper. "Let me finish, please."

She shook her head. "Like I said, it's not my problem. I work in emergency, not labor and delivery. I took time off for a while too." She looked away. "I heard about the death, but I wasn't here."

Paul put his hands together in prayer position. "I'm not being clear." His brain strained to find words. "I know how to spot careless records, or records that are inflammatory, but I don't know how records disappear. There's always a trail."

The lines on her forehead rolled into a scowl. "So, what are you asking me?"

"I'm an auditor assigned to investigate a death case, but I'm locked out." He pointed at the computer. "I can't tell if I'm the only one locked out. I need the names of anyone who was there. Witnesses." Paul held his breath. He had made it to the part where she would either slap him or call for security. "I need to go in under someone else's name to see if the record is there."

They were interrupted by medical staff entering the room to take Josie to X-ray. Paul turned his back on Miranda to acknowledge them, then took a seat on the edge of the windowsill.

Miranda gave him a pointed glare as she followed the gurney out.

"Please. Let's talk more," he whispered.

He lingered for a moment in the empty room. He wanted to trust Olivia, but his confidence in Will, the hospitals, and even himself had weakened. The idea that he needed his face rubbed in misconduct to notice it made him wonder if there'd been others. He went to the hallway, pausing at the water fountain to take a drink.

The elevators closed, Josie disappeared, and Paul walked faster to Shelly's room. Inside his wife's room, a few doctors stood around her bed.

"What's going on?" He was surprised he hadn't been called, and he felt heat rise to his face.

One of the doctors, a round-faced man with gray hair and glasses, stood over Shelly talking with another, younger physician. They turned to address Paul.

"Mr. Blake, I'm Dr. Tyler. The swelling and pressure in your wife's brain have increased, and now, she's spiking a fever."

Paul heard the words but lost connection. An unbelievable weight pressed into his chest, so heavy he couldn't breathe. The mumbling continued around him. It sounded like a radio at the bottom of a pool. His hand rose to his throat as he lost equilibrium. He had a sensation akin to tumbling down a steep hill, the terrain kicking him away toward the sky, then rocketing him back down without a view of what he might hit. His eyes refocused on Shelly's placid face, lost in another world, unconscious.

Is this how you felt all those times? Like you were dying?

Chapter Forty-Seven

The rain spilled from the sky. Ashley's words still rang in his ears. *He's my son.* After she broke free from the officers and collapsed at their feet, John lost sight of her.

Bob twisted his arm in a bear-trap grip. Spit dangled from John's mouth as he leaned over, moaning and breathing heavily, his heart pounding in his chest. Blood ran over his fingers. At that moment, his crushed limb was released. Held only by skin, it lay at his side like a hunk of meat. He tried to get up but fell back down under the crushing pain. His injuries were adding up, his reprimand for stepping out of line. But the pain hadn't erased a lifetime turned upside down.

Bob had turned his back on John and approached the little boy. John's younger self seemed frailer by the minute. He was unsteady on his feet, and his features were becoming hollow.

"Ashley!" John wailed into the night sky. "You knew what Mom was like, and how she tortured me. You knew no one would be there to protect me." He crumpled, resting his head against the rough concrete as rain poured over his temples. "You didn't even say goodbye."

The desire to crawl to Ashley was overwhelming, but he stayed in place. The boy and Bob shook their heads in unison—a quiet yet explicit warning. Their collective control of him kindled his anger, the restraint mimicking a pillow over his face, forcing him to thrash and kick for the privilege of breathing.

"Why didn't you tell me?" he cried.

An injection of strength jolted throughout his body, and he lumbered to his feet. Once again, hands manipulated him like a doll and his mangled arm suddenly healed, the large wound zipping closed before his eyes.

Ashley rose and ran over to little John, wrapping her arms around him. Despite her warmth and affection, the child continued his fixation with his older self, staring at John with a mask-like expression.

"They wouldn't let her take us home. Remember, John?" the boy said.

John watched as Ashley stroked his hair and back. He remembered that night when the officers stopped her. Joanne hadn't even come outside. He sat in the police station, swinging his feet in the chair while social workers and officers asked him questions. *Yes, sir. I'm safe at home*, he remembered telling them.

He had such vivid memories, yet he couldn't recall any hint of Ashley's confession. Was this some trick planted in his mind? But what if it was true? Something chafed his brain, the constant feeling of not belonging. Joanne loathed him. Why would she claim him as her own when she could have been rid of him?

If you don't leave, I'll make sure he's in some institution. Everyone will know he's a monster.

John's eyes narrowed as he studied the house. Bob and the police officers stood at a distance, one officer spinning his nightstick while maintaining a robotic, blank stare.

Suddenly, hands clamped down on John's skull, then arms. His head seemed strapped to a board. Whispering came from every direction until it became a mess of hisses and breathy utterances. The sound moved to the left, then the right, circling him.

John! It can be different. John!

He tensed and pulled his arms but remained stuck. "Fuck you! I'm not giving in! She never came back. Is that what I'm here to see?" He tried to break free. "You want it to hurt? You want me to remember being tossed like garbage? You gonna drown me, burn me? Do it!"

He was instantly released, but the road wasn't done. John was knocked flat on his back by a hit to his jaw. He rolled around, struggling to breathe, the air slammed from his lungs. Then came another blow to the side like talons hooking him, sending his body hurtling. He tried to crawl, knowing he needed to move to survive, but his vision spun and shattered into a prismatic rainbow, stealing his sense of direction. His hand tore at the ground, and his knees tried to push his body farther away from the attacker.

Once again, John found himself in the hands of an abuser. Lies spewed into his ear as the apparition beat him. *Keep moving. Get up! You have to get up!* He pushed himself onto all fours, but when he looked up, everything had changed. Each limb flailed, like he'd fallen out of the sky and landed like a feather. Ashley, the boy, and Bob—all gone. The neighbors, fixated on his every move, had also vanished.

"No!" He beat his fists onto the ground, screaming. He was held captive on this senseless carousel, looping him through moments in time without end. He had returned home.

John's muscles were trembling from the fight, and he knew more would come. The house was mostly dark, aside from the television, which pulsated light and rang out with endless chatter. The doors were all closed and overlaid with shadows, except for his old room. John froze, unsure what to do.

Look in there, John. Go!

Something grabbed the side of his head, its fingers digging into his jaw. John screamed as it dragged his body down the hallway and dropped him at the base of the door. His heart thudded against his ribs. From behind, he heard voices. Feet moved under the door's edge; a fluid-filled blob in flip-flops ambulated across the floor.

"Johnny loves Mommy," Joanne whispered.

He strained but couldn't make out all she said. He scooted closer, pulled himself to his knees, and rested his ear against the door.

"Mommy needs your help, Johnny. I don't have anyone else," she cooed, differently than how she normally spoke. "Can you help

Mommy? Then we can get you some new shoes. Wouldn't that be nice? Mommy loves you so much."

Her words made his skin crawl. He heard a quieter voice, another whisper. He pressed closer, his ear as flat as possible against the wood paneling.

"I don't think I can! It's heavy, Mommy. Will Daddy know?" There was a sound, a shuffling and clanging of objects. "I don't think I can hold it, Mommy. Do I have to?" The quieter voice sounded uneasy and shaky—it triggered something in John's memory. He moved away from the door, as if he could see them through the wood and knew what was coming next. It was a piece of the puzzle. The punch line to a story with a bad ending.

"It's heavy, Mommy. It's so heavy."

John held his breath. His pulse beat under his jaw, squeezing his muscles in unison; a burning rage flowed through his limbs. The metal and the smoke. The black hole in his brain. Lights around him flickered, rapidly blinking as he moved away from the door and into the hall. Each had a part in this: Sophia, his mother, Ashley. The one person he loved could have rushed in to steal him in the night. His thoughts raced.

I want us to be friends. Whispers and waves. Friends. Put him in an institution. Maybe remember celebrating birthdays. Little bitch, little bitch. I love you. I don't need to be someone's mother. He's my son. My son. John, don't hurt me.

The warmth in his stomach, the seed where love would grow if nurtured enough, started to decay. In its place was a sour, curdling substance like milk left out on a hot day.

More of his past moved to the front of his mind. His mother, not twisting or hitting him, but caressing his arm with affection. The warmth of her hand drew him in for a moment, but quickly, the vision turned dark as she moved her fat fingers under the butt of a gun.

Tensing his body, he cocked his leg, and with every ounce of his strength, kicked the door, sending it off its hinges and crashing onto the floor. As John exploded through the doorway, his mother jumped back, releasing her hands from the little boy, who also recoiled. A shot fired from the gun, and the boy fell backward onto the floor. At his feet was the answer to every riddle, the bacterial filth at the core of the wound.

John locked eyes with his mother, finally realizing the point of his homecoming.

Chapter Forty-Eight

"Where's Josie? She's also here, but she returns home, and—" Shelly hesitated, not wanting to give up her theory.

High flames lit the room, and the hole Dr. Frazier-Velli was carving became deeper as he removed shovels full of tar-colored globs, chipping away at the festering cavity.

His lip curled back. "Don't you get it? Reaching her now isn't going to help. You've had seven fucking years with her!" The curse word coming from him resonated like a black fly on a sleeping baby's lips, something that brought instant disgust for Shelly. He'd been her most sought-after advisor, her compass, when through life she'd known few. Now he'd become an abuser of trust, an inflictor of pain. Another hurdle thrown down by the road.

"Fuck you. You're not him!" she yelled, fear rising with every shovel of earth. "Is abandoning my daughter a way through my past?" What he was suggesting would be impossible.

His eyes sharpened, taking on a red glow from the cast of the fire. She knew she had limits, and the consequences were unbearable. She took a step back, waiting to be lobbed into the flames or for her skull to split and spill its contents at her feet. As the man resumed his digging, the tension in his brow dissipated and a grin spread across his features. She hadn't pushed too far—yet.

"Every day you lived with her," he said, extending an accusatory finger, "you fucking took advantage of time. We're lost in a place that you've created."

"Living? All I endured was fear, from the start of my life to the end of my mother's—until I crashed." She inched forward, fists raised, pushing against invisible boundaries. "It's not a whole life, but at least I showed up for her, protected her, kept her safe. I wouldn't do to Josie—"-Her voice faltered. "What *she* did to me. Let Josie endure tragedy. Allow her to be powerless and alone."

You failed, Shelly thought. You crashed. She's in pain.

Shelly's hands dropped to her sides, and she turned her head toward the fire, gazing at the burned edges of the logs wrapped in flames. Nothing she had done or prepared for had stopped tragedy from coming.

The doctor rested against his shovel. "Everything you've seen here, everything you fear—it's you! What part isn't your creation?" His nose crinkled as if he detected a foul smell. "You incredible fuck-up. There's nothing different here from the life you've built. Think about it. It's a home away from home."

With a mocking laugh, Dr Frazier-Velli jammed the spade into the ground, where it stuck up straight like a flagpole. Apparently, he was finished with his task. "Your weakness is unbearable," he said. "You haven't walked through or done the necessary work, and we can't wait any longer."

"Walk through. Walk through? That's all you keep saying." Her cries echoed against the shed walls. "No! I won't fall into this trap. I'm tired of this game! And I'm here. I'm confronting the beatings and death. I've shown up. How am I supposed to get to her? I need my daughter. Is this a way back, or my new life?"

"Shelly!" He looked over her head.

She followed his eyes as something moved from the shadows: Red, in the same tattered clothing stained with blood.

"What do you want from me?" Shelly sensed she was running out of time. The presence of Red with her masklike face, her drunk and sluggish stare, intensified her fears.

"Doctor," she said, "I'll do whatever you want, so I can help Josie. These nightmares, the hell. I'll do it over and over." Her voice cracked;

her insides were like a beast clawing to be free.

"Shelly, you've wasted your time, my time. How many chances do you think you have?" He shook his head. "Living is a privilege. What people do with it is a choice you make every day—to live or give in." He walked over, grabbed Red under the arms, and pitched her into the hole. There was a thud when she hit bottom.

Shelly's eyes widened. "What are you doing? She's a child!"

"I know."

Suddenly, his cocked brow and sneer deteriorated. As if flesh and bone burned to ash, the outer layer of his skin cracked and separated, like dust spinning over a dune. In his place was a defeated figure, a face molded by a heavy fist. Shelly rocked backwards at the sight.

They were the injuries she'd seen through her youth, by the light breaking through gaps in hotel curtains or hovering to kiss her forehead when an assault stopped.

"Okay, sweet girl. Time to rest now, Shelly." The embodiment called *her*—Shelly—by name, through swollen lips and a misshapen face blotched with bruising.

The apparition smiled, sending a stream of red-tinged secretion over the chin, the eyes beaming like aquamarine ovals on prominent cheekbones. Now, it was the woman from the pond, the one from the parking lot at school. But more than that. As if looking through a crack in a locked door, it came closer. *Don't you dare leave this room.* It transformed into Shelly's mother.

"No. I don't want to lie down."

Shelly stiffened. Red had disappeared and in her place was Josie, looking up at the revenant whose smile was fading, leaving only a hollow, ghoulish expression.

"Yes, it's time," her mother murmured softly to Josie, as she bent down to gently stroke her golden locks with her frail fingers, like the thin, delicate limbs of spiders.

"I can't let you do this!" Shelly shot forward and hit with full force against the road's invisible boundary. An explosion of power shot through her chest, and she landed on the floor. She lay stunned for a moment but managed to get up. Her mother paid her no mind and tossed dirt around Josie, dusting her shoulder. Tears rolled down Josie's cheeks. She twitched under the falling dirt, groping at the edges of the hole. Pain filled her eyes as the dirt accumulated. Shelly pushed harder, rising to her feet which was, surprisingly, allowed. No crash against the wall or strangle on her throat. If it was a trap, she didn't care.

"Grab my shoulders!"

She dove towards Josie, wrapping her arms around her, and heaved with all her strength. Recoiling back, she looked into her mother's eyes, and she was no longer a corpse, but a youthful vision at the brink of death. The front of her dress was stained in circular patterns, exposing wounds on her chest. Sticky crimson liquid oozed onto Shelly, over her arms, and a warm film dampened her cheek. She drew back, her breath lodging in her throat.

Shelly tried to support her mother as if the strength of her arms could keep her from departing. But as the light of her eyes began to fade, she collapsed further, each breath lost through gurgling blood. Her mother's mortality grew close.

Shelly dragged her mother's body up, angling an ear to her mouth. At first, the hiss of words was indecipherable. Gasping and withered, her mother murmured, "I did not choose—"

"Didn't choose what? I don't understand."

With the dregs of her waning energy, her mother seized Shelly's face and leaned closer, lips quivering. "Don't make my death your reason for leaving her behind." The vise-like pressure intensified.

"I couldn't fight back." Shelly forced out the words. "I should have fought."

"I am not your burden! Don't be hers!" She started dragging Shelly into the pit.

Shelly clutched the side, her hands clawing at the earth. But her mother was too powerful and pulled her deeper. Her throat filled with earth, no matter how hard she clamped her lips together. The silt and grit abraded her skin and squeezed her chest, piling heavily on her body. Every attempt to inhale led to more choking.

The grip on her body abruptly ceased, and movement stopped. Silent and entombed in the earth, Shelly considered giving up, letting the blackness fill her lungs, and decay discard her over time.

No. Push. Do it now. There's more to do. It's not time. For once, her voice dominated the rest. The determination to stay alive gave her purpose, much like Josie kicking inside her womb, a flutter of energy needing out. She scraped through the earth. Finally, she drove through to a void, her hands sensing the freedom of open air. Survival lay inches past a curtain of shit, mud, and rocks impaled by sticks. She tugged with all her might, slowly moving forward. Using her knees and hands against the dirt, she climbed up.

The dirt fell from her face, and she crawled out of the hole. She gagged up a mixture of black coffee-ground-like globs and foam, her stomach retching, pushing out the remnants of the grave. She gripped the ground at the top of the opening. Heaving again, she cleared her mouth and her lungs of the filth, inhaled clean air, and lay on her back. Air moved in and out in a white stream, sounding like a high-pitched harmonica.

Once again, underneath her was the hard surface of the road, and the smell of moss and fungus lingered in the damp air. Shelly was back at the start of her mental prison.

"I'm not your burden. I'm not your burden," she chanted over and over. "Give me my daughter!" She beat her fists on the ground, and the exertion sent her into a coughing fit, bringing up dark froth.

She drove her knuckles into her eyes.

It was not over.

Rolling to her side, she came up off the ground with a quickness she didn't think possible. Shelly wanted to fight. "I have a life. I'm not dead," she yelled, stumbling. "Josie's waiting for me. I know she's waiting for me." She continued to lurch a few steps forward. "She can't go on without her mother. She can't turn into me." As she lost her footing, her view of the horizon swung to the left. She fell, hugging the ground.

John had said the road was a sick game, and she was foolish to think they were alive. In his view, seeing Josie float between two worlds had been the road making her dance for its own amusement, nothing more. Was this really their existence forever?

Shelly looked up to the top of a hill where the road intersected with sky. As darkness spread over the rising earth, she fought to an upright position again. Time to move.

Chapter Forty-Nine

A bend appeared in the forest, like an elbow. Less like a road and more like a logging trail. Shelly knew she never would have driven in such a place—it was too treacherous. The trees were thick on both sides, arching overhead. The ground, rough with gravel, gleamed like the backs of a million beetles shuffling in unison, the meager light catching their glossy shells. The incline grew steeper, and she trudged on, her sluggish feet scraping through the rocks underfoot. This was the longest stretch of road she had been allowed to wander without interference.

Soon, the light of the moon overhead was met by the color red, which intensified in the distance as crimson rhythmic bursts broke up the night sky. An atmospheric change not brought on by violence, for once.

"John!" she yelled, peering into the woods. "Are you there?" Silence. The way he had shut her down and discounted their chances of survival still tasted bitter on her tongue. Had he been right?

Shelly's pace slowed. It wasn't a game. There had been signs, memories of emergency lights and being surrounded by people, images of Josie thrashing on the hospital gurney. They did not exist as apparitions of the road lurking and stalking her. Tears had come, flowing over the pain of unhealed injuries. And Josie. Had she been swallowed and discarded there while she slept? If so, Josie moved through dreams far more than her mother. Then Shelly's blood went cold. All those moments, the lost time, and the visions haunting her daydreams opened a door while she slept.

It's you—your creation. This isn't any place for a child.

A wave of guilt flowed over her. Josie could not exist in this way, being constantly yanked back and forth, away from Paul and her youth. There had to be something she could do to cut ties and free her. Josie wouldn't live like she had—not if she could help it.

As Shelly rounded the top of the hill, her heart dropped. The car rested below, flipped onto its roof with the hood open, all sides were bent in, and the windows had shattered. The red brake lights fired on and off through the steam floating over the wreck. The smell. She recalled the acrid aroma inside the car, the vapor of gas, and the whine of the engine slowing. Amazed, Shelly walked down the embankment. The accident looked as if it had just happened. The sheared-off paint exposed twisted chrome in silver flashes. She stepped back, remembering the impact: orange safety lights flashing, John's body flipping up and over.

Moving along side of the mangled Audi, she saw pieces of the bike lodged in the tire well. More parts of bent-up metal were on the ground, alongside shredded tires. The bike spokes radiated from the frame like a dead bird's wing. A man's sneaker rested on the ground, just past the littered shards—evidence of John's last moments strewn all around.

"John," Shelly said quietly. She touched the passenger door but ripped her hand back. Pain seemed to hang off the surface of the metal. John's pain.

Acid from her stomach spilled into her mouth, as she realized the force it had taken to propel his body into the air. Shelly moved to the driver's side. The door was ajar. The airbag had deflated and drooped like a lifeless tongue. The glass appeared as a wound, milky white in some smashed areas, red smears in others. Shelly winced when she saw body fluid, a web of sharp lines through the blood.

"How could anyone survive this?"

Something small caught her eye, swaying subtly at the edge of her vision. Next to the chewed car door, a glossy purple tulip stuck up from the ground. Odd, considering the torn landscape. Shelly couldn't help but lose herself in the rich plum petals, which looked like they could be plucked and held to her chest. This thought, this sliver of weakness, rose without resistance, beckoning her to lie down next to the flower and wreckage, and meet death. Or meet it, again. Heaviness swooped over her skin, welcoming her toward the soil, toward the flower. Without thinking, she extended her hand.

Something flashed. She jumped back and gripped the car. An orange light flickered in the distance. Abandoning the tulip, she ran toward the glint, the mud loose under her feet, sticky around the soles of her shoes and reminiscent of her sudden entombment. Going closer to the light, she made out a figure in the grass.

"John?" she called weakly, hoping he'd be there. But she heard no reply, saw no movement. A shadow on the ground flashed orange then black. The intense smell of freshly cut grass mixed with the whiff of plowed earth, and then a new odor wafted through her sinuses, sulfurous with a hint of metallic.

A crumbled body lay at her feet, but not in sleep. "Oh, God, no." The shock of his condition sank in. Red flesh, bone, missing teeth. Shelly slapped her hand over her mouth as she gasped, then moaned in agony. She reached out her hand, then pulled it back in anguish, lowering her head against the mud.

"He can heal. He can come back from this," she cried.

No. She could feel it. Nothing lingered under the skin, no brewing energy to reconstitute the flesh.

"John! I don't know what to do."

He lay on his back, lifeless and brutalized, with one side of his face looking up at the sky. The other side, where his eye, nose, mouth, and jaw should have been, was a yawning hole of hanging skin, shredded muscle, and part of his tongue. An ear ripped from his head and rested on his shoulder. His jawbone protruded to the side, and some teeth were scattered in the grass next to him. Blood oozed, seeping into the grass and pooling around him. Shelly's stomach flexed, gagging at the sight of his mutilated remains.

Death had been denied to them. They had not felt pain unless it was a punishment. Yet, John had met his end, even on this endless road. And now Shelly felt more alone than she had thought possible. She didn't want to see more. Looking up would bring more sadness, more fear. But for some reason, she raised her head. Resting near John's hand in the grass, was a gun.

Part 4

Chapter Fifty

Shelly was taken back into surgery. The team loaded her up quickly and fast-tracked her out the door. Their haste rubbed off on Paul, and his muscles twitched. Shelly's pale face and lethargic features were mere shadows of the wife he once knew. Under normal circumstances, her expressions were soft, and she often appeared unsure, but her intention and devotion were clear: You felt her love if you were graced with it.

The uncertainty of the next hours and days preyed on his mind. There were so many things he wanted to say, failures he needed to make amends for, but his chances seemed to be slipping away. Standing in the middle of an empty hospital room, Paul put his hands behind his head and cradled his skull, unable to find relief from the ache in his chest.

What am I going to tell Josie if her mother dies?

He went to the waiting area where he dropped onto one of the benches next to the window, feeling overwhelmed and disconnected. He tried to fight off anxiety-ridden scenarios.

"Paul?"

Olivia appeared before him in a black sweatshirt and jeans, her hair pulled up into a bun. The large sweatshirt dwarfed her frame, and she wore glasses that appeared dated and out of place perched on her nose. The outfit was clearly meant to downplay her appearance, although her beauty still shone through. The thick, horn-rimmed glasses couldn't hide her striking eyes.

"Olivia." His shoulders dropped. The woman extorting him and forcing his hand against his employers was suddenly the only person who knew everything.

"We should talk." She gave him a once over.

"Yes, I agree." His body seemed empty, and it surrendered to the circumstances, whittled to the nub. In hindsight, Paul knew Shelly hadn't pushed him into bed with her.

She dug her hands deeper into her pockets. "I can't use anything I have because the source has already been threatened." She peered out from the hood of her sweatshirt. "This is bigger than you think. I can tell you more, but not here. Someone might recognize me. Let's take a walk."

They strolled down the long hallway. Paul pressed the elevator button, but Olivia flicked her eyes at the cameras above. "The stairs," she said, and he followed her.

In the close stairwell, a sense of indecency pressed in. All over again, he was waking up to the dingy smell of almond-scented cleaner and old tobacco. The taste of Olivia's body and stale whiskey on his lips. Regret intensified with each step.

Paul felt heat rising and stopped mid-step. "Why do you need me?" he asked. "If you have shit on the doctors and the hospital, then use it. Go to the press, go to your attorneys. Hell, I don't care if you take me down too."

She stopped and looked back at him.

"I love my wife," he said bluntly. "I wasn't looking for a fling, or a way out of my marriage. Things have been hard, but I love my wife." He thought about Shelly, fighting for her life in surgery, as he followed this woman into a basement.

I'll take care of the hard stuff like I always do, he remembered Shelly saying.

Olivia's expression softened. "Does she know about—?"
"Yes."

"Good," she sighed. "And bad, I guess. I imagine you've blamed yourself more times than you've taken a breath."

Paul gripped the stair rail.

"I wasn't to blame for my son dying," Olivia continued. "My body isn't flawed. I had to tell myself that a thousand times. But I'm a good person." She nodded slowly "No one deserves to be hurt or have an accident, but in my case, at least I know who is to blame."

They continued down to the bowels of the hospital. Paul remained uneasy walking with her. Around every corner, he waited to be discovered by Will or an administrator. The basement smelled of rubber and gasoline and was semi-dark even with the overhead lights. They exited the corridor, and the door slammed behind them. A doctor—or maybe a nurse—stood smoking a cigarette in the corner by a black Jetta. He puffed on his smoke with narrowed eyes. He wore standard-issue scrubs with a blue fleece vest and a stethoscope, an anonymous look—a quality Paul envied at the moment.

Olivia kept moving, but Paul hung back at the sight of the man, realizing the exorbitant amount of trust he was putting in her. She might be leading him to the wolves, and Shelly might be dying while he snuck through the hospital parking lot with a blackmailing one-night stand.

Olivia signaled Paul to come closer. He stared at her, but his feet stuck to the ground. She walked back to him.

"That man was in the operating room," she said. "He sent me the letter."

Paul followed, almost dizzy with anticipation. A witness? Olivia approached the man, who held a tense posture. His eyes were suspicious.

"Paul, this is Dr. Sachs," Olivia said.

Paul reached to shake the doctor's hand, but the gesture was not reciprocated.

"She's got you by the balls, doesn't she?" he said instead.

"Ed!" Olivia said.

"Well, you do! That's the only reason he's here."

Paul shook his head and started to back up.

Olivia grabbed his arm. "Hold on." She turned to the doctor. "Ed. He's in! That's what's important."

"Everyone who was in that room knows what happened!" The doctor stepped closer to Paul. "We documented it right. All the facts are there."

"Those records," Paul said, "are Swiss cheese. The interviews with staff were as vague as fuck."

The doctor laughed. "Yeah, guess why? We were all taken aside individually. One of the nurses there that day was threatened in an elevator. They approached me right here in the parking lot." The doctor looked around then back at Paul. "Some of the staff are on work visas. They threatened to pull their status. Like I said, they got to each one of us."

"Who are *they*?" Paul asked.

"Leadership!" Ed erupted. "Will Gerald, the administrator, and the VP of legal, Dan Howard. Not to mention the attending."

Paul's whole body tightened, and the hair on his neck spiked. "Will? What does Will have to do with this?"

"Are you kidding me?" The doctor threw up his hands, walking backward. "This is typical. You assholes keep your head down, avoid the signs. Same bullshit." He squared his shoulders and stared Paul dead in the eyes. "These guys are dirty. They blackmailed us—look the other way or lose our licenses."

Paul took a deep breath. "How many staff are we talking about?"

"Seven, including me."

Paul paced, overwhelmed by what he was hearing, the lengths taken to stifle the whole crew. "The chart on Twin B is—"

"Julian," Olivia said, her face still cloaked in large glasses and head concealed by her hood.

~ 276 ~

"Julian," the doctor said, "was hypoxic and seized shortly after birth. We took him and offered treatment. Two nurses, an anesthesiologist, myself, and three members of the respiratory team were there." The doctor paused, focusing on Olivia. "He died from an overdose of phenobarbital." He placed his hands on his head. "Fucker! He miscalculated. Babies who get that sick don't process medication. Your son died within twenty-eight minutes of birth."

Olivia's hand found her mouth, and tears spilled from her eyes. Though her hood concealed her face, her erratic cries were audible.

Then she dropped her hand. "You see. Twenty-eight minutes old. They fucked up, and he died." Her words were muffed by her emotion.

"He couldn't own up to it." The doctor's words echoed around the concrete of the underground parking lot. Ed's eyes fixed on Olivia. "He should have told the hospital, admitted that he made a mistake, but he couldn't. He has plenty of friends, though." The doctor bit his bottom lip. "His friends huddled around him, and we all got pinned."

"That's why he reached out to me in secret," Olivia said.

"I'm the only one who doesn't have an agenda." Ed put his hands up. "But I can't access anything, and I'm worried they'll destroy information if I try."

"Who's your boss?" Paul asked.

"Dr. Ramsey."

"I'm so sorry," Dr. Sachs said to Olivia.

Paul couldn't help but see two victims of that grievous December twenty-eighth. Dr. Sachs had been forced to compromise his ethics by those whom he had pledged loyalty, only to have it abused. As for Olivia, she had been passed over so the arrogance of the physician could be preserved.

Ed leaned against the black car behind him. "Dr. Ramsey said he'd sign statements alleging we falsified the tests, or our hours. Also, he'd show that we engaged in documentation and billing falsifications. I should have just let him. I was a coward."

Olivia's face turned red. "You see," she said to Paul. "Every time I questioned things or complained, they painted me as crazy. Oh, she's after money, they'd say. But I never was. I'm not crazy! I knew something was wrong. This has been an old-boys-club cover-up from the start."

Paul stood in silence, then asked the question that gnawed on his gut. "How does Will fit in?"

"Will and Dan were friends with Dr. Ramsey's father, a substantial donation source, and a doctor himself. It was Will who blocked the charting and chopped it up. Dan falsified the documents he was holding to send to the medical board. I've seen the letters. They have Will's signature."

Paul circled on the concrete, stunned. "Do you have proof it goes that high?" he asked.

"We need you to get the records," Olivia said. "We need a reason to investigate the higher-ups." She glanced at Paul. "A wrongful death claim or a murder charge."

A wash of cold flooded his body; blood retreated from the surface of his skin. The pieces were falling into place, and he held the last of them. But he also didn't. "I can't access the records," he said. "They locked me out too."

"Shit." The doctor banged a fist against the car.

Olivia's features wilted. It was the only time he'd seen her crack, her shell chipped away slightly.

"Hold on, let me think." Of course, Paul had considered alternatives already, some options that were by-the-book, and some that were not.

His gut twisted. It seemed he was caught in the middle between two opposing forces. Could he be the one Will picked, the one they thought would miss all the clues? *I'm their recruited lackey.* Or did Olivia manipulate him, through sex, and capitalize on his fear to push him where she wanted?

"I think I might know how to get the records," he said. "I'll need some time." Quickly, he headed towards the exit sign. He had to get back to the second floor.

Chapter Fifty-One

Paul wanted to run down the hallway and ram his head into a wall. A cover up. A dead baby, and it was not about the money.

Tension coursed through his chest, and his knee bounced as he watched Josie sleep. Shelly was in surgery, Josie's X-rays were pending, and there had been no news for several hours.

"I'm heading home, Mr. Blake. Just wanted to check one last medication order."

Paul looked up, and Miranda was at the door. During his other visits, she had slid in and out like she'd been smeared with butter. Today, she had a brighter expression; ready to finish her shift, she wore a light jacket, and a bag hung from her shoulder. She checked Josie's vitals, readjusting the monitor and jostling with the mouse. Eventually, she logged in. Paul took greater interest as boxes popped up on the screen.

Sweat collected around his hairline as he watched her. If he were going to ask her for help, this would be the time. Who knew what the next days would be like if there'd be—Paul stopped his mind from going there.

After five painful minutes, Miranda glanced at Josie, then rummaged in her bag. Paul inched closer to the edge of his chair and said the words in her head without letting them out of his mouth. With one last toggle of her finger, Miranda stopped and looked over.

Paul believed they were in a telepathic dialogue, speaking through stares and nods. She directed him with a bounce of her eyebrows and a wave of her head toward the computer, still up and running with a chart open. He read her body language: This is what you need. They won't know it's you. I was never a part of this. Don't fuck this up.

He looked at the screen, then nodded, holding his hands in a prayer-like gesture of gratitude.

"I'd like to visit Josie, even though it's my day off tomorrow," Miranda said, "if that's okay."

"Yes. She trusts you." He touched his daughter's forehead, smoothing her hair.

Miranda stepped closer to the bed and crossed her arms. "I do believe her, you know." Her chin quivered slightly. "I believe a multitude of truths are possible. Over the years, I've seen things you would not believe." She observed Josie for a few moments, then turned to leave.

"Miranda," Josie whispered.

Paul looked down at his daughter.

"I have to ask you something." She gestured for the nurse to come closer.

***

Miranda bent down to hear what the girl had to say. Her back strained, but she ignored the shooting, dull pain.

As color returned to Josie's face, her blue eyes sparkled, and a small grin crept across her lips. "Have you been to Florida?" she asked quietly before her mumblings turned into yawns. "Keys, what are the keys?"

Paul glanced nervously between them.

Miranda's tongue cemented to the top of her mouth. The last and only time Florida existed for her was the day Eli died. Since then, the place had been cast from her consciousness.

Eli was buried close to his parents at the request of his mother. "I will take him home to Florida," was how she'd put it. Miranda was not united in law to Eli, so she had no choice. She had no legal rights to bury the man she loved, no claim on his body, only the right to grieve. She remembered his black casket covered in beautiful flowers, followed by the family down the long aisle. There was no invitation for her to attend anything after the church service, and she never heard from them again.

"Florida, Dad," said Josie.

Miranda's mind flooded with questions and things she wanted to tell Eli: *What did he look like in your dream, Josie? What did he say? Was there pain? Is he happy? I'm still here and alone. I'm sorry. I wanted it to be me. I love you.*

"They won't believe me," Josie said.

Miranda looked at Paul. "Who Josie? Who won't believe you?"

"Everybody, like my dad." A single tear traced the end of Josie's nose.

Miranda extended her finger, gloveless and chapped from disinfectant, to catch it. "I believe you, but what's in Florida?"

"Eli. He's in the water."

Miranda felt like an electrical current had plugged into her center. A familiar image raced back: Eli's body, suspended in blue water, the blood billowing. He's in the water, she thought. No, he's buried. He's home.

"Josie, stop! I don't—" She started to shake.

Paul stood. "Sweetie, I think Miranda needs to get home and rest."

Josie ignored her father. "Eli helped me. The water was pulling me in the pond." She rolled herself tighter into the blankets. "Eli helped me out of the dream, but he's still in the water."

Miranda stood in place; her chest refused to expand with breath. *It's not true. She trusts me. She's picking up signs, gossip.*

"Who is Eli?" Paul asked.

"Eli wants you to visit," the girl said. "The water wasn't for me. He's waiting for you." Josie yawned, unaffected by her story.

"Waiting? Josie, what do you mean?" Miranda leaned down as

tears crested over her lashes and onto her cheeks.

"Stop now, Josie," Paul said.

"Maybe you could help him," Josie said. "You're a good nurse to me." The girl started to doze. "You could be good for him too."

***

After Miranda left, Paul stood breathlessly in the middle of the room. The nurse had rushed out, saying little after the odd exchange with his daughter. Josie hadn't been to Florida, and he wasn't sure they'd even talked about visiting. His hand found the back of his head.

Paul couldn't worry about Miranda. Obviously, the nurse had some inner demons of her own. The computer would time out within minutes if he didn't act quickly. In smooth zigzags across the screen, he moved the cursor to Client Search and then over to Archive Patients. He entered Twin B—Julian's—client ID, a number he had memorized. His eyes widened as the data spread across the screen from respiratory, nursing, Dr. Sachs, Dr. Ramsey—everyone's notes on the death. Everything filed and available. His hands shook over the keys.

Dr. Ramsey's notes described the baby's condition, interventions, and orders. The nursing notes indicated concern about blood levels and whether to check the serum of phenobarbital.

RN18: Noted critical PNB levels. Sent to provider for review.

RN18: Order clarified; dosing appropriate with planned increase. Send serum levels to the provider for second review. The provider affirmed dosing and indicated urgent due to seizure activity.

The doctor had been notified but kept pushing the dose.

Dr. Sachs: Neonate with provider, respiratory depression, bradycardia.

Dr. Sachs: Neonate coding. CPR, respiratory on site.

Dr. Ramsey: Monitoring Code of twin B.

Everything about Paul's next step was illegal, a violation of privacy and a thousand other laws. For the first time in his career, he plotted stealing client records from a hospital, a breach of confidentiality. At any moment, he could be discovered. The shift was about to change, and new nurses would come in. He worked as fast as he could to gather information before it disappeared without a trace.

Administration above Paul's paygrade had signed off on an incomplete chart and passed along blatant signs of missing data. Then they threatened staff, and in a series of charades, passed this to an auditor. They banked on Paul lacking the motivation or skill to pursue the inconsistencies, at least long enough for further tampering to be completed. If his hypothesis had weight, their lock-out only affected a select few. Miranda had clearance, but he didn't. He remembered something she had told him. She worked in Emergency, not Labor and Delivery, and she'd been on leave when it happened.

Will.

Dr. Sachs was right. Paul would be proven careless and burned out, someone who would look the other way without question, move the players along, and neglect the details.

They must have been secretly pleased when his wife and daughter were injured. More distractions! All this time, he thought he'd concealed his jaded attitude well enough. Yet, they had picked him, pushing all obstacles out of the way. They organized his family onto one floor of a hospital and paraded him around for the lawyers to see, hoping for a quick signature. Maybe the bosses were right to choose him. Nothing had mattered to him before the accident. Not even his marriage.

He clutched the mouse, transferring all the documents to his work email. Sweat formed on his back as he fell deeper in with Olivia and Julian.

Paul whispered to the screen. "I got you by the balls, now." He cleared out the boxes and notes, closing the chart and logging Miranda out. Checking his phone, he confirmed the files were in his inbox.

What now?

Chapter Fifty-Two

A combination of smells permeated the atmosphere. The smokiness and spiciness of bourbon, sweetened with a hint of caramel, his mother's sweaty odor, and a hint of mold. Her screams reverberated through the house. Standing in the doorway of the bedroom, rage pulsed through John's veins.

Joanne remained splayed on the floor where she had fallen, and the boy sat against the wall, hands wrapped around his knees. The glossy whites of his eyes popped from behind his legs. A dark wooden chair lay on its side.

The paint-chipped bed with disheveled covers was cockeyed, rather than snug in the corner. A man of John's height lay sprawled, his shirt pulled up to expose his bloated fat and stringy strands of perspiration-soaked hair. Richard, his father, extended his arms on either side, like an obese, drunk Jesus on the cross. One of his shoes had been cast off, the other pulled loose from the heel.

Even through adult eyes, John saw his father as menacing. A sinking feeling burrowed through his body as he stared at the sleeping giant and relived violent memories—slaps or kicks without warning or being yanked out of bed by his foot in the middle of the night. John's hand slowly moved to his head behind his right ear and smoothed his hair, soothing the ache of abuse that throbbed in his memory.

On the floor next to his father's shoe, a whiskey glass lay on its side, tipped over, Jameson or Bushmills clouding the bottom. There was something rather odd about the color, a smeared butterscotch tone.

John's head felt cloudy, and a steady warmth hung on his limbs like an early rush after a shot of tequila. He found the courage to take a few steps, but each one sucked his energy. Pieces of wood from the door frame crunched under his feet, causing him to pause and watch for a reaction.

"I hear you!" Joanna sputtered. "Satan child! God help us. You brought him into this house. You came from sin, and sin is what you are!" She crawled along the wall into the corner, her eyes bobbing side to side. She couldn't see him.

The little boy did not react to her words of damnation. The pistol, a black revolver, had landed near his scrawny left foot, halfway between him and Joanne. The size of it made the child's hand look tiny.

"It's too heavy," the boy whispered.

John stopped, surprised. "Do you see me?"

"Yes," he said. "I saw you with the policeman too, with Ashley." The boy's face remained expressionless.

"You see," his mother howled, moving toward them. "He appears to you. Boy, I knew this would happen. Son of Perdition! You will exist in pain. Tormented. That whore brought hell on us all!" Joanne curled into a trembling blob, shifting into a prayer pose with hands held to her lips. She murmured a string of pleas for salvation and protection, professing a love for *Our Father*.

The sight of it made John's lip curl in disgust. Like a wolf in sheep's skin, she called out for help when she had been the one lurking in the dark, inflicting pain. He wished he knew his mother's thoughts as she cowered before him. Would there be true repentance?

As quiet as a moth fluttering against a window, the boy had calmly moved to John's side, extending a hand as he'd done in the forest. John stared at it, uneasy about his intentions. Up close, the boy appeared sickly, withered and wasting away.

"Where will this take me?" John crumpled forward as the fire in his gut grew. The boy said nothing as he stared with glossy eyes. There were no other choices; one path or the other would lead to pain, as all had before. He took the boy's hand.

"She said it would only make him sleepy," the boy said.

John froze in his place, tethered to the ground as his mother and the boy repositioned before him.

The chair had spun upright. After another few seconds, his mother and the boy exited, flowing backwards, swooping and side-stepping in an instant re-play. Then everything stopped, and everything went dark.

The sound of his mother shuffling around the room woke him up from his daze.

John's view of the space had changed. The room now swayed like a carnival funhouse, and he became immediately, intensely dizzy. The roof of his mouth tasted metallic and chalky like old aspirin, a vinegary sting on his taste buds, coating his teeth and tongue. John blinked repeatedly, desperate for the swaying to stop. A mattress under him, the ratty blanket, and the foot of the bed were in his eyeline.

Something hard and smooth fell from his hand, and he heard a hollow thud and clank, then an object rolling on wood. It was a glass, like the one he'd found at his father's feet.

John knew that, once again, he'd embodied another; he saw through Richard's eyes now, as he had with the boy.

Richard was scared, and John, incarcerated within, felt his fear.

Enraged rants echoed through a prison corridor and into John's consciousness.

You fucking bitch. I'll ring your fucking bell. When I sober up, I'll make you eat that gun.

Richard began to fade, like going underwater only to resurface with less air above. Images distorted and blurred, colors smearing into streaks.

John had always known the truth. Lying dormant for years, the answer lived past a curtain in his mind. She'd planned this. The glass, pills in the drink. Put them in, and he would feel better. Joanne had told him it was okay.

She approached and grabbed Richard by the hair.

"Mom, don't hurt him. Please." The young boy pulled at her dress, which she answered with a backhand to the face, causing him to fall backward. Joanne yanked up her husband's head, his drooping lids and glistening brow visible to John in the sheen of her glasses.

"You think you can bring your incest bastard into this house?" She threw his head back against the pillow.

The words echoed with a force John could hardly absorb. Richard moaned, but nothing more came out.

"John, Mommy is sorry." She picked the boy up from the floor, and he whimpered under her. "But I need you to help Mommy, now." Her tone had changed to the sickly, sweet version—she wouldn't take no for an answer.

Chapter Fifty-Three

John could only compare the sensation of leaving Richard's body to pus being expelled from an abscess—pain, then relief. Once free, he rolled around on the floor, with a burn on his chest and stomach rolling.

"Okay, Johnny, you help Mommy. You'd do anything for me, wouldn't you?" Joanne stood holding the young boy.

"Mom, I don't want to. Mom—please!"

"You know what he's like, the hitting, the yelling." The boy started to pull away, but she regained control. "Everything will be better for us. You want that too, right?"

The promises—empty promises of less abuse. After Richard's death, the beatings intensified. Joanne hated everything about John—about them both. Nothing had changed. The abuse worsened when he was the only one left to take it.

Young John yanked his hands like they were caught in a bear trap and cried softly. Joanne struggled to keep a hold of him. The boy raised the weapon as tears dripped from his chin. His arms trembled, but Joanne's were straight as an arrow.

John didn't remember the police at the house, or the funeral. His mind closed off all those details. But John remembered—they shot him together. The road wanted him to remember it all.

Joanne put something in his father's drink. In thinking it over now, putting drugs into his system would have been tricky, could have made him unpredictable. He didn't remember his father taking pills. Alcohol sure, a concession on the rules they breached often, but they were Mormon, after all, drugs were against their values. Maybe the drugs didn't work, and she went to get the gun. Was it her plan all along for John to shoot him?

Maybe Richard deserved to die. He was a mean, abusive man. Dying again could make up for his horrendous sins—right there in front of John. Perhaps John had prevented so much pain and abuse. Perhaps not.

The gun—the black glossy cylinder and rounded barrel—floated less than a foot from Richard's temple. Muscle memory surfaced, and John knew how it felt, understood the sulfuric spray over his bare skin.

Joanne's grunts and protests moved more of his memories to the front of his mind. The image of brains across the bed and floor, and the deafening blast of the gun with the shell casing spinning and clanging around.

"What have you done?" Joanne had hollered that night. Her hands suddenly in the air, the innocent victim. She pulled him into the hall and locked him in his room, screaming and filling his head with shame and guilt.

In the days that followed, she whispered in his ear, continually dispelling any thoughts that she was to blame, instilling fear that authorities would come for him.

What you put me through, John thought. What I lost. The brainwashing, the blame. Always my fault. John paced back and forth. The sequence of his life jumbled into a disorganized timeline, but a consistent theme emerged, like spirits lurking in a cemetery: *Ouch my ear, please I didn't mean to. I'm hungry. I'm sorry. Please don't, that burns. please. I don't want to leave, Mom. Sophia, I'm sorry. I love you. I didn't mean it. I'll be good. Love me.*

"You stole everything from me," he screamed at Joanne, drawing little reaction.

A twist. A change. Neither of them was aware of John's presence, his voice snuffed out, part of the road's twisted control.

Enraged, John grabbed the gun from the boy's hand before he could fire. Joanne stumbled over her own feet, holding up her hands in defense. He turned to her, without feeling, the way he'd approach a shelf of cameras, and his body relaxed with a sensation of pleasure and freedom. Slowly, her features began to melt, and her mouth opened wide. The strain of hate and loathing loosened from his brow, and the rubber band fibers clinging to his skull, once taut with tension, drifted from consciousness. His decision was made; John breathed in deeply—a rush as good as cresting the tallest hill on his bike. Then he lowered the gun to her head.

Joanne's eyes enlarged, and her body twisted away from him.

"Killing you is the reason I'm here," John said. "Everything started with you—the hate, the beatings. The coddling you demanded and love you'd never show. Not once did you tell me you loved me. You had me believe I came from your body, why? Why didn't you let me go?" The gun trembled forward until it was centimeters from Joanne's clammy skin.

"If the devil lives in me, you invited him," he told her.

John pulled the trigger. The impact blew out the back of her skull. Gray matter and red spray hit the wall behind her, and her body fell to the ground.

Richard let out a huff from his drug-induced stupor. Calmly, John leaned over, put the gun to his head, and shot him. His father's head jolted, and a pool of crimson seeped through the bed linens under him. A dark stain formed on his pants and moved out onto the sheet; he soiled himself at the point of death.

John looked back and forth at the bodies, numb. The seeping pools oozed, bubbling out of their skulls. Before him was an impressionistic painting of death—deep red splashed over the muted honey oak floor and the taupe of bed linens.

Whimpering sounds came behind him. The boy cowered in the corner, clutching his head. John walked over, the gun still in his hand. For a split second, he thought of shooting the boy to end his future suffering and trauma.

A mirror on the wall caught his reflection, and John stared at himself. The person wore a mask he didn't recognize. Black circles against pale skin, splatters of blood across his cheek and neck. The image stalled his breath.

With a violent pain, the skin at the back of his head split. Blood poured from his opened wound. The pain grew at his temple, a searing agony behind his eyes as if a fist had pushed up through his throat into his head, driving through bone and muscle. John dropped the gun.

The healing faded, and the injuries of the accident emerged. His leg grew ineffective; the bones ached, grinding with each step. One long bone shot through his muscle, sending him to the floor screaming. Sweat poured from him, and his breath found no satisfaction, only more hunger for air.

His mother's corpse lay across from him, her eyes rolled up as blood pumped from her head.

"Why did you make me do it? I was a little boy!" John screamed. "All I wanted—" His whole body shuddered as he waited for the next transition. "I wanted Ashley," he said.

He longed to leave the road and return to life —bike rides and cherry blossom trees, even his job.

The little boy moved from the wall and picked up the gun. "Do you think things could be different? You trusted her over everyone." Through squinted eyes, he looked at Joanne's body, crumpled on the floor.

"Trusted?" John choked. "I didn't trust her." He rolled into fetal position, the agony in his head blocking the vision in one eye. "She's nothing but a lying monster."

The boy leaned down, and John watched him. For the first time since their meeting, his younger self was filled out, with meat on his cheeks, and smooth, rosy skin. John caught a blurred view of the boy's chest—still bare, but no burns. He pulled himself up.

"Nothing but a lying monster," the boy mocked, "but you made a choice to believe her, to trust the hate she gave." He set the gun down and cocked his head to the side.

Feebly, John groped for the gun but failed to reach it. In another attempt, he hooked the edge with a finger. "Why didn't Ashley fight?" he whimpered. "This is her fault. She shouldn't have left me—us!" John hugged the firearm, to his chest.

The little boy turned away, walked toward the door, and opened it slowly. Looking back, he shook his head then disappeared.

John lay surrounded by death, abandoned by his own spirit and will to live. He touched his face and found tears mixing with the blood and sweat. Red-tinged droplets dotted the floor under his lowered head.

Looking one last time around the place where his misery had originated, he slowly placed the gun into his mouth and with a steady hand, fired a single shot.

Chapter Fifty-Four

"John!" Shelly yelled at his body, too afraid to touch him. With each flash of reflector light, his injuries showed brilliant and gruesome. There were awkward bends in his legs, and bone appeared through muscle where his skull and face spread apart. The grass cradled John's body in tall shoots, bent over him like a weaved basket, smeared red. Wisps of smoke floated overhead as if his spirit was dissipating into the air.

Suddenly angry, Shelly snapped into a frenzy. "John, wake up. Please. I don't know what this means. You can't stay in this place. The road—it's nothing but suffering. Tell me we don't go out like this. You've left here and returned. So do it again." She inched closer to him. "We can help each other and try to get through this. I know how hard it is, the abuse and hurt. Let's do it together. Heal. John, please. Heal, and we'll get through to the other side." Shelly grabbed his hand. It was as cold and lifeless as the kitten in the closet. She clamped her eyes shut, tugging at his hand, willing a profusion of life's blood. "We shouldn't stay here, John. I can't stay."

His eyes were slit, trancelike, void of energy or light.

Shelly dropped his hand and drove her fists into her eyes. "I told him to hope. There were signs, but now I don't know what to believe. I'm so sorry." She had no solutions, no reason, no faith.

She wondered if he had found answers or validation, any proof that the road existed as only a cruel joke or a trap. She wished for him to be free. Perhaps if he regained peace, so would she.

A hush of wind shattered the stillness, ruffling her hair.

The choices are endless here.

Shelly fell back, squirming away from the voice.

Not again. She couldn't take it anymore. The reflector on John's body still blared across the field into the darkness. Her heart pounded in her chest. A gunpowder scent mixed with the metallic gases of the car flavored the air around her. Shelly scanned the field. *Is it my turn to die?*

She heard rustling in the grass. Frantically, she pulled herself up the hillside, past John's body and into the field. She wanted to drag him with her but couldn't. He'd drifted beyond the road to whatever was next.

As she moved up, the rustling grew louder and came from all directions, melting into a radio-like static. Shelly spun in circles, anticipating the coming pain. Glimpsing the dark forest ahead, she slipped over loose dirt and grass as she tried to escape. *Get up. It's coming for you. The road killed John.*

Each step felt increasingly useless, and fury boiled in her gut. Once again something stood over her, more powerful and with greater control.

"You killed him," she screamed into the night sky. "He was right. It's a game—a fucking game!" A tree limb caught the edge of her shoe, and again, she fell.

Shelly.

Her name echoed in the night, hung above the grass, and filled the canopy of trees.

Shelly.

She curled up on the ground, empty and resigned. Rocks and undergrowth crunched under approaching footsteps, and she used what little energy she had left to lift her head.

Blood dripping from her hands, Red stood above her, wearing the same ragged clothes. Next to her was a little boy—bruised, barely clothed, and chewing on something. He seemed sickly and weak, and he swayed on his two feet, which were bare and filthy. Shelly had no memory of the boy but couldn't stop looking at him. A part of her wanted to comfort him, but another part knew better. He was more than a neglected boy in a field, just as Red's dynamic force had greater depth and power.

"This place is filled with choices, Shelly," Red said, her face devoid of emotion. But her bloody shirt and hands, the remaining injuries on her swollen face, and her split lip spoke for themselves.

"Life is a two-way street," the little boy said, almost casually. "Coming or going, forward or backward, wrong direction and the right one. Full of choices."

Shelly, covered in sweat and blood mixed with the mud of a freshly dug grave, didn't believe them; her nightmare seemed to end only one way. She waited for their assault, but the pair was calm as she gripped the earth, mourning John, and mourning her life with Josie and any chance of restoring Paul's love for her.

"What's your choice, Shelly? Coming or going?" Red watched her, while the boy chewed noiselessly.

Shelly felt weak, tired of the endless war. "Was this how John died?"

They looked at each other and then back at her. "We aren't talking about John," the little boy said, his eyebrow raised.

Red nodded. "John had his own road." The childlike expression and mannerisms remained; her head bounced as she spoke, and the bun on her head flicked with each word.

"What choice do I have?" Shelly asked. This question relaxed her somehow. Like a weight lifted from her shoulders, the tremble in her body and flutter of her gut quieted as she leaned into a new uncertainty. Maybe she did have a chance.

"We try to help you along the right path, but it's not easy." The boy continued eating—she could see now it was a waffle. "Reasons to live come with as many reasons to die. John decided for himself."

The children looked at her intently, and Shelly couldn't look away; she knew they were an important part of finding her way through the road's maze, finding Josie. Red had been lurking in Shelly's dreams and now, here. The children extended their hands. Shelly took a long inhale and let them pull her to standing. Their hands pulsed in hers.

She looked around at the dark sky, the weakening colors of the forest, and the road that only led to nightmares. "My past is haunting this place. I don't want to live here anymore. I want my daughter and Paul. I don't want to live this way."

Red nodded; her mouth set in a resolute line. "Come with us," she said.

Chapter Fifty-Five

A sudden shiver ran down her spine as Shelly stood on the hard concrete porch of the house where she'd grown up. Deep cracks and uneven surfaces marred the floorboards; empty flowerpots were scattered about, some tipped over and forgotten. The sight of the wilted roots was a stark reminder of how life withered to death.

Red and the little boy stood on either side of her. Shelly paused, pulling at the little boy's hand as a mother would tug a toddler.

"Did you belong to John?" she asked the boy.

He made a *mm-hmm* sound and grinned. The answer brought sadness for Shelly—he seemed to be a child without an anchor, even as he stalked amidst the shadows.

"What happens to you now, with John gone?"

The boy didn't flinch. "I'll be waiting."

"Waiting for what?"

The smile vanished from his lips. "Can't tell. Depends on who comes." The words bounced in the air, and he shrugged as if the answer should have been obvious.

"Others are coming?" she asked.

His smile returned. "This place is full of so many." He let go of her hand. "Bye now."

She watched him walk away, back to the dark road. Confused, she turned to Red, who now appeared weakened, like wood left out in the rain through a winter season. The grip of her hand grew lax.

"Can I live through this?" Shelly asked. She didn't know the right path; she needed a sign that her efforts were worth it.

"You've already done that, Shelly. You need to ask better questions." Red released her hand and darted into the house.

Panicked, Shelly followed. Inside, fear circled in the air, more ominous than the trees whispering on the road or the mist rising from the fields. *You'll be found. It's not safe.* Her mind tried to overrule her body's urge to cower, retreat to the bed, and wait. Wait till the yelling stopped.

"Mom, talk to me. What should I do?" Images of her mother moved into her brain. Shelly envisioned the rocker thrown and her mother tumbling backward, taking the impact of a kick to her abdomen, only to be picked up and thrown against the wall. She watched the vision of her mother hitting her head and crashing to the ground, over and over.

"How did it end, Mom? I remember you here. I remember the fighting."

The kittens. Oh, God, he's coming. The wood is breaking. The blood. Oh, Mom, the blood. I tried. We were leaving for good. You promised we would leave for good.

A light flashed in the hallway. In this place, everything seemed to hold meaning.

The light. The hall. Remember.

Flash. *Running. Yes. That's where I went.*

Flash. *I ran. I got away. I saw them.*

Flash. *Toward the bedroom.* Flash. *Mom and Dad. Mom and Dad. I hid.*

Under the cover of the mattress, she watched as he surged on her mother, hands balled into fists.

Shelly tried to take a step toward the light, yet something held her back. An unmistakable pull anchored her, as if on a rack, her arms stretched on either side by unseen binds. Her head grew dizzy, and her vision blurred. She tried to call out, but her mouth was held shut. She heard only useless gasps and moaning deep in her throat. Her legs squirmed.

I don't understand. I need to walk through. To the bedroom, where I hide.

Why? Why are you stopping me?

The living room, previously dormant but foreboding, came to life. The rocking chair and other items vaulted toward the walls and windows, glass breaking. From her vantage point, harnessed to the ceiling in the corner of the room, what Shelly saw next brought more recollections from the past: her father, tall and stocky, a tee shirt torn around the collar and jeans with a chain hanging from the side.

She remembered the clanking of the keys against the chain, the sound he made coming down the hallway that served as a warning to disappear. It was impossible to predict the state he might be in—agitated, neutral, or even violently drunk. Rounded shoulders, his midsection shaped like a barrel, and a nose shaped like a parrot's beak—the wholeness of him reconstituted before her.

A scream. In seconds, Shelly found its source. Red dangled under his arm. As in her nightmares, his enormous arms and hands were dragging her away. He held Red around the torso while she screamed and kicked with everything she had.

As he turned, Shelly saw something that turned her core to ice. A large knife, tinted red, guarded by his closed fist.

Since childhood, she had never dreamt of her father, but now, she could no longer avoid him. She had to confront him, the room, and the smells and the sounds she had pushed down and run from her whole life. The poison he leaked had been locked away and held there, buried in her mind. Only his mark lingered, and that mark grew like a cancer, slowly taking over.

Still unable to speak, Shelly whimpered. The blood on your chest. The knife. He followed us with the knife. *I can't*, she thought. *I can't see this again.* She started hyperventilating, her mind firing off rounds from the past.

My father pulled me out, she yelled from her mind to the unseen spirits, or whoever was there to judge her. *He threw me across the floor. Do you hear me? I remember. Mama, you jumped on his back! You saved me.*

Shelly tossed her head side to side, her hair breaking out of its binds and falling onto her shoulder. The next images—her daughter—dug into her core and pulled at her ribs as if the anguish would climb out through her chest.

If I could see Josie again, I would give up and die. Is that what you want? Let me see my little girl, and I'll go. Shelly closed her eyes, quaking. *I'm so weak. I hid, but you fought for me. Mama. It's my fault. I have to see Josie and tell her it's not her fault that I died. Please.*

As her mind spilled its secrets, it was Josie now under her father's arm, her beautiful face contorted and pinched into screams. Shelly's mouth opened to scream; her entire body flexed. Every inch of her ached for her daughter, dangling, face drenched in terror. How could she save Josie? The unseen binds squeezed her tighter.

No. No. I'm asking the wrong questions. Red. We've already lived through this. Closing her eyes, she concentrated on slowing her panic, breathing in and out. *You lived.*

She took deep breaths. Then she hooked onto something Dr. Frazier-Velli had told her, something whispering in the back of her mind out of reach. Shelly tried harder to center herself, to calm her breathing and heart rate. *Breathe, breathe. Light, window, chair. Breathe. Green. Road, dark. Sky, gray. You created this place, Shelly. Breathe.*

"I've already survived. I created this place." She inhaled and exhaled, and as her body loosened, the force relaxed its hold.

"This life is no different from the one I've been living, evading things I've already survived."

Josie's thrashing fell to the background as Shelly sought the right path through her nightmares.

"Is there something I need to do?" she asked the room, herself, or the road. She couldn't tell what, but she needed to allow something to take over. Allowing the story to be retold was the only door left. She couldn't fight it any longer.

The images in her mind slowed, and her surroundings softened. She saw her mother standing over her, kissing her forehead, brushing her hair to the side, and smiling—a time in Shelly's youth when there were no injuries or panic. She tried to focus on her mother, tried to keep the image as if she were right there. Hold on to the joy. Listen to her.

It started to come back—the calm, the love. Her feet touched the floor as they gently came to the ground.

Chapter Fifty-Six

There was no quieting the world around Paul. The clock ticking, the ventilator running, and feet stomping outside the door—everything booming like a freight train. Even the chatter in the hallway felt like an assault. He hadn't slept or eaten for what seemed like days.

He tried to hold his focus on the two doctors updating him on Shelly's status, but his mind kept gravitating to differing points of sensory arousal.

The surgeon leaned against the bedrail, delivering his speech. Words filled the air, language about brain function, swelling, and pressure, which Paul diligently tried to comprehend. He looked at the doctor's mouth, the formulation of words and her tone, but he was distracted by the obnoxious squeaking of the metal rail against the metal frame.

When the other physician spoke, spit accumulated at the corners of his mouth, opaque and growing larger with every syllable. The pair performed over an invisible orchestra in slow motion, hands spinning and shoulders shrugging. Paul pretended to listen. They were speaking about optimism, but followed by saying that Shelly's situation was *touch and go*.

"I'm sorry. I'm trying to understand," Paul interrupted. "You relieved the pressure in her skull, and she will have an opening there until the swelling declines." His stomach twisted with the image of her exposed brain.

"Yes, this will keep the damage to a minimum while she improves."

His eyes widened. Damage to a minimum. The words hung in the air.

"Most of the time," the doctor continued, "we can keep ahead of this. We see mortality less than thirty percent of the time." The doctor massaged his lower jaw.

"One in three—people die." Paul's body crushed inward like an empty pop can.

"Now, she's had extensive injuries to other parts of her body, and her leg is also something ortho is monitoring. Overall, we have a long month ahead."

After the two doctors left the room, Paul went to Shelly's side and sat down.

"Oh, Shell." He exhaled and looked at her hand, no longer wearing her wedding ring, which had been removed due to swelling. An indent remained. A thin divot in the skin, lighter in tone, an imprint of their years.

Tears formed in his eyes. "Shelly, please get better. Even if I'm not part of the equation anymore. For Josie—please." He pressed his hands against his eyes, wiping away the tears. "Josie says you're somewhere else while she's dreaming." He moved closer. "Maybe you'll listen to her and come home."

His phone vibrated. He looked at the screen and saw it was Olivia. Calming himself, he answered the phone.

"Hey," Olivia said. "Everything okay?"

"Where are you?" Paul said.

"I'm at work. I got the files."

His pulse quickened. It had finally arrived, the moment his career would end. Sending the files would doom his professional journey.

"Before you do anything with the records," he said, "can you let me talk with Will?"

She exhaled loudly.

"I need to see if he has a soul. You have all the records, and you're ready. I need to own this one, give him a face to loathe. He might throw more people under the bus. There's no way upper leadership didn't know if donations were thrown their way. This could go further than you or I think."

"You have twenty-four hours," she said before he heard a click.

Paul sent a text to Will, asking him to meet at the hospital. He needed to do this in person.

***

Miranda hit the button on the elevator, holding a gift and a card. Not much had changed for her since leaving the hospital, just a shower and new scrubs. Her eyes never closed overnight, and she found herself googling Florida, pulling up articles about Eli's death and the beach where he had launched.

She replayed Josie's words over and over. Eli was in the water. The tip of her finger hit the up button again, this time with more force, trying to speed up her movement and distract her from her thoughts. But the walls seemed to shrink in on her, trapping her in place until the doors opened, whisking her towards the next floor and further into a stranger's darkest moment.

In her hand was a dreamcatcher, something she'd purchased right after Eli's death. She thought of it like a cross or sage, a gesture to ward off spirits for a little girl who saw only abuse. Miranda had put a lot of hope into the dreamcatcher's powers; maybe it would keep away the night terrors and calm Josie to sleep.

Finally, the doors opened. Miranda went into the hallway and saw Josie standing at the entry to her mother's room. The hospital gown hid any hint of the child's frame and extended to her feet. Josie looked like a stick figure in the entryway, blond hair against the pale dress and the wall's muted paint casting an eerie, lifeless collage that drew Miranda's breath from her lungs.

She looked down the hall for any staff. "What are you doing out here, Josie?" She scanned the girl from top to bottom.

"Mama," Josie whispered, looking straight ahead. Then, her

breathing started to quicken. "He got me, Mama. I can't get away." Her eyes grew huge, and she screamed. "Mom. I can't leave you!"

The shriek made Miranda's pulse leap, and she fought the instinct to move away.

As the words left her mouth, Josie dropped as if the air had been let out of her frame. Miranda caught her before she hit the floor. "I need help down here!" she yelled as Josie's head rolled to the side.

Alarms blared in Miranda's left ear indicating a change in life function. She lowered Josie to the ground and ran into the room, slamming her fist into the wall control, calling for extra staff. Time slowed as a flood of staff arrived. The monotonous tone of the heart monitor only meant one thing—Shelly was flatlining.

Chapter Fifty-Seven

Paul walked down the hallway towards Josie's room. He heard his name and turned to see Will standing in the hallway. His jaw clenched.

Will looked around. "I had no idea they were this bad." He rubbed his head.

"Let's take a walk," Paul said, trying to hide his rage. He pulled his phone out, hit record without Will seeing, and put it back in his pocket.

He walked toward a family visiting area but pulled Will into the office next door.

"What's going on?" Will's voice rose.

Paul closed the door and glared at his boss. "How high does it go?"

"What?"

"Don't give me that shit. The baby, the death—you knew. You knew from the beginning."

"I don't know what you are talking about." He shifted back on his feet, looking over Paul's shoulder at the door. "The baby case? I told you we'd transfer that to someone. We have that in the works." He moved to leave, but Paul blocked him.

"You know exactly what I'm talking about," Paul said, pressing his finger into Will's chest. "The baby died of an overdose. The whole thing got blocked, which triggered the insurance to throw it out. Was the money too good to pass up?" He stepped in closer. "How did they cover it up? The records, the missing charts. Who else is involved?" Paul let his rage erupt. "Did you think I'm so burned out I'd push the case through, no questions asked? Will—I have the records."

Will blinked; his thoughts seemed to churn.

"Tell me!" Paul yelled, causing Will to jump.

Rapidly, Will told his side, making self-serving accusations about coercion, bribery, and the strong arm of upper management. The hospital looked the other way rather than hold the doctor accountable—in this case, the son of a significant financial backer. Not only that, but it actively concealed wrongdoing to save the relationship.

Paul stepped closer, eye-to-eye with his boss. Will's suit, the smell of stale tobacco, his wrinkled pants and faded jacket, were on a whole new level of disgust now.

"I need you to listen to me." He pointed again, pressing his finger roughly into Will's chest. "I'm going to burn you for this—and anyone else, for that matter." Finally, he was on the right side of things, for the first time in years.

"Wait a minute." Will's voice steadied as he recovered somewhat.

"You are going to resign," Paul said. "Dr. Ramsey will be reviewed by the medical board, and all the VPs involved will go before an ethical committee. If not, this heads to the media."

Will shrugged. "Your accusation has no proof. It's still her word against ours."

"I have all the labs, all the notes. I have a history showing the amendments and deleted images. I have enough to explain unethical behavior, tampering with medical records, and negligence on the part of Dr. Ramsey. I have you by the balls." Paul watched as his boss seemed to run through scenarios.

"There's nothing to link this to the doctors," Will said. "That's how it will play out. We have letters. The staff under him pulled it together, and the doctors had no idea. Sure, we can squash the bill, but nothing else will come from this," He spread his hands out. "Paul, if I go down, you will too. Do you really think they'll believe someone who drinks on the job and takes kickbacks from reps? That's how I'll spin it." He stepped closer. "I tried to help keep you sober, keep you employed. Sad that it took a tragedy like your wife and daughter to highlight your weaknesses. That's how it will look, anyway. The word of a drunk against mine."

Paul's throat ached. He had been selfish, ignoring Shelly and Josie, and all for this man. He'd come so close to losing everything for useless ambition in this unethical job. He took his phone from his pocket and tapped the screen, ending the recording. As Will watched, he sent it to Olivia.

"Like I said, we have you by the balls. Behavior reflects leadership, Will." Paul held the proof up, and the color drained from Will's face. "I'd put in your resignation," he said. "It's all coming out." He opened the door and walked out.

Still buzzing with adrenaline, he found Josie's room empty. The IV pole had been knocked over. He quickly backed out, hurried to the nurses' station, and noticed a commotion in front of Shelly's room.

"Rapid response," a robotic voice bellowed over the speaker. "Rapid response."

Chapter Fifty-Eight

Released from the power controlling her, Shelly stood in the living room of her childhood home, analyzing the space. Her breath fluttered in and out.

Red emerged from the hallway and looked at her with curiosity and a familiar calm. "Do you remember?" Her eyes narrowed. "Do you remember the choice he made before he died?"

"Who are you? Who are you really?" There were elements of her younger self in Red, but she went deeper than skin and expression. "I see you, but you're not me."

"Shelly, you left me behind with him. I tried to let you forget, but there's so much here in this house. So much pain. I couldn't keep the bad thoughts from finding you." She hoisted herself taller, which appeared to take significant effort, and pointed toward the kitchen. "It's up to you now to close up this house."

"You wanted to let me forget, but you were in my dreams, all those times." Shelly swallowed hard. "You were there to help me? But I fought you," she said. "I didn't want to see it. I never wanted to come back here." She dropped her head, unclear if she felt shame or betrayal.

"He made a choice. You can't run away anymore. Walk through, Shelly." The words had barely escaped before Red began to change.

As Shelly watched, Red's skin drained of color, and her eyes shrank deeper into her skull. In a single movement, Red lowered her shoulders, deflated her chest, and folded her small body into itself. In the end, she looked like skin over bone, like a corpse. Shelly's face fell into her hands. Red had so much trapped inside her that needed to come out.

"Will we survive?" Shelly asked, desperate to know if Josie would live on without her.

Red looked in her eyes. "I don't know." In a moment, she was gone.

***

The road permitted her to be an observer, no more shaking lamps or flickers of light. Perhaps she had appeased it enough. Walking freely, Shelly followed the drops of blood and shoeprints leading to the kitchen. For so long, something had governed her, a message she had avoided since childhood, a pain that had kept her from living. Now she would follow a new path, back to her family to confront her fear and fight for survival, back to a life with Josie through healing.

Moments ago, her father had stolen the vision of Josie and fled, splattering red along the way. Shelly felt compelled to find Josie but knew this wasn't about her daughter. Josie was being used to lure Shelly toward a specific message.

A commotion to the right snapped her head around. Events reversed as she stood stationary. Josie appeared through the door like a video playing backward, still wiggling and screaming under her grandfather's arm. Frozen, Shelly watched the scene settle and begin again. With a jolt, she was ready to react, to pull Josie from his arms; instead, she stayed calm and analyzed the situation. *Where are you leading me?*

Josie's cries filled the room. "Mama, he's a bad man. Please, Mama. We need to wake up!"

With that, Josie vanished, replaced by Red, who fought his grip until she managed to wiggle free. Her father stumbled and fell to the ground on all fours, like a dog. Shelly took a few steps forward, hands extended as she mentally moved the playing pieces of her parents' death.

"I remember. I ran and left him here." She spoke to the room and to herself, a soft and methodical narration of her thoughts. "My mother was down the hall. You hurt her. You hurt her and wanted to take me away." Shelly's eyes widened as she stared at her father. He crawled on the floor, his hands stained red and sweat beading on his brow. His shirt clung to his wide shoulders.

"It was you," she said. "Everything leads to you." The knife had fallen to the floor and lay a few feet from his grip, the steel covered in rust-colored swirls. Shelly had an overriding desire to grab the knife and drive it deep into his skull. But something other than violence must come from this.

"What have I done?" He pulled himself up on one knee. "You were going to leave me. I couldn't let you. Someone had to take care of me. I couldn't let you abandon me here, leave me alone." His face filled with dark color. "You're mine, both of you! No one's going to poison her mind, make her hate me. You stupid bitch. You made me do it." With frantic movements, he scrambled to his feet and sprang toward the backyard.

"That's where you found the gun," Shelly said, following him. "The hunting shed. That's where you kept the drugs too." With each step, she rebuilt the path back in time. "We were leaving, maybe for good. The first time she'd asked me to pack—she must have had enough. It was all about *your* loss, not mine. Never what you took from *me*."

Shelly entered the shed; this time it didn't lead her to Dr. Frazer-Velli but instead to a dark, simple room with four walls and a door. Light filtered in behind her. "Red held you back," she said. "She kept you contained." An aroma of mold and whiskey mixed with sweat hit her instantly. Her father sat on the floor, crying and mumbling, spit dripping from his lips. In his lap was a pistol with a silver barrel and black handle. He looked over at Shelly. Her thoughts instantly thought of John, as he raised the gun.

Without dropping his gaze, her father lifted the gun to his temple. Shelly shielded her face. "No!" The blast of the gun drowned out her scream. She closed her eyes; she had enough images of tragedy in her mind already. The sound made her ears ring.

Shelly opened her eyes and saw Red behind her, appearing steady and not withered as she had been in the house. "My father has been kept here since that day? Trapped by the road?"

"No, in your mind," Red replied.

"I don't understand."

"You survived their death. There's strength behind survival. It's hard to witness such tragedy and live through it. So, we waited. Only, our father took up too much space and kept returning. Shelly, I tried to help, but it became harder."

The thought that her father had clung to her subconscious drove a chill down Shelly's back. *This is a world you created*, she thought. You already lived through this. You lived.

"It's where you go inside, where he takes you," Red's lip turned up, and there was empathy in her expression.

Shelly's father lay in a heap against the wall of the shed, blood issuing from his mouth. Behind his head was a splatter of red and tissue two feet in diameter. As they watched, the dripping blood started to diminish, and the color of the skin surrounding his mouth no longer blackened. The wetness and globs of brain matter flowed back into his skull.

This couldn't be happening. Shelly rediscovered the hate of a seven-year-old, back when he broke his fatherly promises one by one. She felt her body tense, ready to jump and beat him down with her fists. It hadn't occurred to her, up until he began healing, that she could find relief in his passing, and upon his return, anger. The road. It was not done. There was more to endure. *Endure? No. Learn.*

Regenerated, her father looked down at his hand holding the gun.

His shoulders hung in defeat.

"Shelly," he whispered.

The hairs on her arms and neck stood up. So much time had passed; his voice sounded unexpected and unfamiliar, not low and dominant but flat and nasal.

"I can't seem to die." He drew a chuckle. "No matter how many times I've tried. This gun is never empty, but my life never fades." He looked up at her.

Regret tightened Shelly's throat as she looked at his pitiful body. "I want to say I'm glad you're dead, and I never think about you. But that isn't true. You're taking over my life." She inched closer, and a rush of energy flowed up through her feet. "God, I wish I could be scrubbed of your existence. Do you realize what you meant to us? You could have been my protector, but instead, you shredded that privilege with a knife while I watched. You killed my mama."

For the first time, her eyes blurred with tears. As they rolled down her cheek, Shelly touched her face and gasped, crying harder, unable to stop the cascade.

"Dad?"

"Yes," he said, still looking down.

"Look at me!" she yelled.

He sat up, finally meeting her gaze.

"I watched you kill her," Shelly said.

He nodded and looked down again at his gun. "She was taking you away."

"You beat her! What else could we do?" Shelly towered over his diminishing frame.

"When I died, I finally saw how weak I was." He shuffled, his defeated manner not at all what she'd expected. "I died and came here," he said. "Not hell or heaven, just this place, this shed at the back of the house. Here, I relive what I've done, but instead of my pain, it's your pain I relive—in that room, watching me hurt her." He closed his eyes. "Hell is ours to make, and my hell is failure. It's mine to walk forever, stuck here.

Shelly's body stiffened, a mix of pleasure and shame. "I didn't do anything wrong!" she yelled. "Are you hoping for pity after your abuse?" She stared at his decrepit frame as he avoided her eyes.

"No, Shelly. Sometimes I wish I could fully die and descend to hell. But I always come back. I can't run, and so I wait here for something to be decided for me. Then, you came." He looked up at her, his face calm but hesitant. "I know there's nothing I can do. What's done is done. I experienced your fear over and over every day. My punishment is a life sentence, lost in your memories with no way out."

Shelly scoffed. "We create our hell? No. We've lived the same hell, but I have power. I know that now." She stood up and looked down on him. "The past has haunted me for too long. You don't have control over me anymore. I'm still here, and I choose the space you hold in my brain. You won't haunt my dreams anymore. Whether heaven, God, or hell exist, if I live through this, you will no longer control who I am."

Her father dropped the gun with a thud. He extended his hand, empty, still massive. "I'm sorry."

"Mom and I are leaving you now. This is the end." Then Shelly watched as her father diminished into thousands of drifting particles that whirled like a cyclone until he vanished altogether. Without looking back, she walked toward the house to find her mother.

Chapter Fifty-Nine

Shelly knew her mother would die—but stopping it wasn't the reason she'd come.

She entered the house and walked through the living room, which was now in shambles. Again, the road had regained control. She was a child. She was Red. Her clothing was tattered, and her feet were bare and childlike, covered in blood.

"Mother's blood," she said, as her toes moved over the tacky fluid. She followed the rust-colored tracks through the living room to the epicenter of fear, nightmares, and the sessions with Dr. Frazier-Velli. Finally, she'd made it into the hall and up to the bedroom, where handprints of red covered the door. It was cracked open—always locked until now.

Shelly could barely hold still to grip the doorknob; her young primal brain was terrified and longed for shelter with her mother. Light shone from the ceiling fan fixture. Her mother was sprawled on the floor, encircled by a dark puddle, wearing the same dress she'd worn at the water's edge. Blood soaked through the left side of her chest, fanning through the cotton fibers and growing by the second. The posture was heartbreaking—one leg turned to the side, the other pointed straight, and hands by her face as if still defending her body from attack.

Then it hit Shelly. The stench of urine penetrated her nose. Covering her face, she reeled backwards. The hammering of her heart filled her ears. Shelly's senses overloaded between the sight of her mother and the decayed ammonia.

No. Coming or going, it was time to make a choice. She'd come too far and there would be no going back. *I must walk through.*

Confronting the noxious odors of the room, she stared ahead, prepared for the end of the story. But a sight made her pause. Next to her mother's head, a glass jar had tipped over, with remnants of amber liquid inside. Under the edge of the bed, more jars.

"Of course." Her mouth dropped open, stunned, realizing the coveted secret her mind had chosen to conceal. "All this time, it was the smell from my hiding place. Urine in jars. It was mine; I was too scared to leave the room."

A dark pool of blood and urine wetted her mother's hair. Her eyes were fixed, staring at the ceiling. Next to her were broken pictures, fractures of wood, and a backpack with its contents poured out. Shelly had witnessed parts of her mother's demise so many times through nightmares and flashbacks, but never in its entirety. The account of her mother's last few minutes came through the eyes of a seven-year-old, with a little girl's pain. Yet, as Shelly slowly moved to her mother's side, the road released its grip, and she returned to her adult self. The memory of her mother's passing was no longer a child's burden.

Shelly touched her mother's head, careful of her fragility, but trying to soothe her. Her mother's mouth opened partially, the color in her cheeks and lips fading to bluish as life drifted.

"Mama." The words fought their way out. "I know why I'm here." Shelly tried to make eye contact, although her mother was fading, and her eyes were dark and distant. "I wish I could take this all away from you." She choked up. "So that you never lived with pain. Mama, you saved me. I lived because of you. You will always be in my thoughts, always. But I need to say goodbye. There was so much inside me I wanted to push away. I started to push my whole life away. Josie became my obsession, and this life—" Shelly looked around the room, the origin of so much anguish. "I need to say goodbye to you and this place, to release its hold on me so I can love my family and be free."

She sobbed into her bloody hands, overcome with emotion. Through cries, she continued. "I love you. I love you, Mom." Shelly pulled her mother close, hugging her with all she had, supporting the slack weight of her mother's body in her arms. As she let her down to the floor, her mother lifted a hand to Shelly's face, softly touching her cheek with the last of her strength. As it made contact, Shelly's mind filled with memories, not dark or violent, but visions of happiness and laughter. She watched as light moved through a large window, and her beautiful mother danced in the living room. The sight took her breath away.

In the glow of her mother's warmth, Shelly's euphoria was boundless. She fought through the inescapable grief, but in a bittersweet moment, realized her mother finally would be free, no longer stuck in the dark space between worlds.

With great effort, her mother's mouth opened, and Shelly moved closer.

"Dance in the daylight," she said.

Shelly looked down to her blood-spattered cheeks as her mother healed before her. Her wounds sealed, and brightness returned to her eyes.

"How you fill up your house and your mind is up to you," she continued. Her mother's fingers stroked Shelly's head gently, and with a final stroke, her body disappeared, leaving behind a blinding glow that filled the space.

Shelly's body floated, then repositioned on a flat surface. Again, there were shadows all around. Her mouth was dry, and a gagging sensation pierced her throat. And pain returned.

Chapter Sixty

Someone was pounding on her chest.

The lights dimmed, and the sensations in Shelly's head were tingling and sluggish. She tried to speak but couldn't make a sound.

Josie. Did she make it out?

Shelly pushed against her paralyzed limbs to no avail. It was as if she was confined in a dark box as each limb tried to press upwards, desperate to be free. With one last thrust, she broke loose from whatever held her and floated above, looking down. It was freedom, like a child in a swing, only floating a moment before rushing back to ground.

From above, she could see that the doctors were working on her body, thrusting over and over, pumping breath into her mouth. The scene tore at her heart, knowing she may soon meet her death after all.

Something twitched in her ear, and she heard a familiar voice outside the room, sad and regretful.

"Paul?"

Shelly listened, and her body responded. She passed into the hallway lined with rails, hospital beds, and hustling nurses. She heard his voice grow louder, more emotional and pleading. She moved through the hall effortlessly.

Is this how you say goodbye? Is this how death works? You're prepared for a grand departure, but instead, it's painful, powerless against other forces, directionless. She looked back at her body. *I was alive the entire time on the road.* It must be a space between, for the lost and wandering. The little boy's words resonated. Others were coming.

The voice continued to pull at her, and she continued down the hall. Paul sat on the floor of the waiting area, his face in his hands.

"I'm so sorry," he cried, overcome with emotion. "I broke us all—my bitterness did this."

Shelly hated seeing him in pain, taking everything upon himself. She reached out to touch him but was unable to make contact from behind the boundary of whatever death dream she was in.

"It's not your fault." She knew he couldn't hear her, but she didn't want him to live with such a burden. "I gave up on myself, on the idea that I deserved to be better and that others loved me despite my past. For so long, I thought you wouldn't accept all of me, only the strong parts. I wish I would have invited you in." Her hand extended towards him. "I wish I had more time to live for you and not hold you back."

Then she felt pulled by each foot toward the earth. Without warning, her body shot backward with a rush of energy, leaving Paul and the waiting room. The pain returned all over her body, and the lights blared above. Her world went black.

A cold assault ravaged Shelly's bones as she struggled through water, and her tightly clenched mouth tasted salt. Her body spun with the enormous pressure of the waves. The ocean.

Desperate for air, Shelly held back the urge to breathe, and the water finally gave up her body, expelling her onto the sand. Shelly felt her breath against the cool shore; she was drained of fight. She opened her eyes, which blurred and stung from the brine. She could make out some light from the moon. Another rush of water passed over her, pushing her forward. How nice it would be to lie there and be still.

What does it want from me now?

Getting to her feet, she stared in either direction. The wide beach expanded between the surf and the hillside. The water stretched out before her, and in each fade of surf, it left a sheen of diamonds. The scene was an experiment of color, with blue and rose mixing into the froth of sea. A Monet painting of the night sky. A cool breeze flowed through her clothes and more waves hit her feet, while marine-air sulfur drifted past her nose.

Shelly took a deep breath, let it out again. All was still.

"Maybe this is where the story ends. Finally, peace. I hope Josie is free with Paul." Shelly closed her eyes and listened to the water.

Someone took her hand. It was Josie, smiling, uninjured. On Shelly's other side, Red appeared and grabbed her other hand. A new warmth filled Shelly's core. Red gave her hand a squeeze, and her mouth turned up into a smile. The small being who filled her dreams, her protector, slowly vanished.

Shelly hugged Josie, together in the calm of the beach. "I don't know how much time we have," she said as her heart quickened. "No matter what happens, you brought me through this, through to you." She stared with longing into her daughter's blue eyes. Blue like her mother's, blue like the sea.

Josie started crying against her mother's neck, her fingers clutching at Shelly's arms and hands, pulling her closer as hair stuck to her wet cheeks. "Mommy, please come home with me. I can't leave you here. You have to come back. Please, let's go." Josie pulled at her arm.

Helplessly, Shelly watched her daughter's efforts. She knew it was time and pulled her daughter closer. "Don't be frightened, baby. Either way, home is where you are, and I'll be there. We will never be apart because love holds us together. Even if—" Shelly inhaled quickly, the grief stalling her words. "Even if I die. We'll be together through love." She inhaled Josie's sweet scent and moved against the softness of her warm cheek, wanting the embrace to last forever.

"I love you so much, Mommy." Josie cried louder, shaking under the embrace.

Shelly felt the strength in the little girl's shoulders, the warmth in her body. "I wanted nothing more than to be your mom. So, I've lived a wonderful life. You gave me that. No regrets, Josie. Live free, baby."

If only she had more time. If only.

There was the blast of release, an energy leaving Shelly's chest, and she knew Josie had disappeared. She crouched in the sand, with water gently lapping at her feet. As she took a deep breath, she smelled the last, sweet scent of her daughter. She was ready, as ready as she'd ever be, for the road to lead her home—whatever version of home awaited her.

Without thought, her body pulled forward, knowing what to do.

Chapter Sixty-One

Shelly's body lay on the hospital bed with the blankets and sheets torn away, exposing her to the room. Her gown was draped carelessly across her naked body. The monitor blared a steady tone, indicating that her heart had stopped. Staff members gathered around, each winding down from the flurry of action. The doctor had challenged them to hold compressions, but Shelly's blood pressure and heart rate had flatlined.

The air in the room was heavy, each member winded from trying to save the patient. The staff slowly moved away from the body, shuffling equipment. No one spoke.

Miranda pulled Shelly's gown up to cover her breasts, a gesture of decency. But it was just another death, like countless other times she had stood beside a body. Wasn't it? No. Miranda stood next to Shelly this time. A patient named Shelly, with a family she now knew. Miranda let the grief wash her head to toe, understanding the impact it would have on Josie.

A tightness clenched her throat, something a hardened nurse would bat away, swallow, and move through. Grief wasn't allowed. There were rules, and she understood them. Letting each loss and tragedy grab hold of you would surely take a person down. Miranda stared down at Shelly—broken, lifeless, her head turned to the side. Still bruised across the scalp from the accident.

Josie's dreams, the stories of her mom fighting to get back to her, were vivid in Miranda's mind. Those thoughts tightened the lump in her throat. Shelly had been a young mom at the start of a path with her daughter, learning her anchors and touchstones in life. Miranda shut her eyes. More pain would hold space for Paul and Josie. Why did this have to happen—the question she could never answer. We do all this work, take in all this pain, and people die, leaving us behind.

"I don't want to be left behind anymore." Miranda's eyes brimmed with tears, powerless to stop them.

She put her hand on the tube at Shelly's lips but hesitated. Eli came to her mind, stopping her movement. He'd never made it this far; he'd been scooped out of the water, leaving his soul behind.

"Hard one," a voice said. Dr. Stevens had walked up to the bed.

She dropped her eyes and tried to resume her work.

"Sorry, didn't mean to interfere." He looked at her. "How long since we called it?" He glanced at the clock on the wall.

Miranda stared at his face, irritated by his callousness. "I don't know what time. Check the fucking scribe."

He blinked. "Sorry. I know you've worked with both patients. I can tell the family." He turned to walk away.

"Seven minutes ago," she whispered, tears streaming down her face. "We called it at twelve thirty-seven." She leaned over the code cart, holding on to its sides. Unable to hold back now, she started crying—crying for Josie and crying for Eli.

"Listen." He moved toward her; his eyes were kind.

Suddenly, a monitor beeped behind Miranda. The vitals machine started to move, flowing blue and red lines, ebbing with a pulse. The oxygen saturation registered again, and the blood pressure was on the rise. Everyone in the room stood and stared at the body—Shelly—as she showed active signs of life. Nurses lined the room, holding tubing, bags, cords, but motionless and gawking in those brief, shocking moments.

Miranda took a step toward the bed. Throughout her entire career, she'd never seen a return of spontaneous circulation after so much time with chest compressions had failed. There had been stories sometimes, early in her career, of the Lazarus patients, but she'd rejected those stories. She stared at the monitor—which now, without a doubt, showed heart rhythm and blood pressure.

Miranda snapped into action and rushed to the bedside. She looked around the room at the frozen, wide-eyed staff. Even Dr. Stevens stared at Shelly as if the air had been sucked from his lungs. "Fucking move!" she hollered. "She's not done!"

Epilogue

Shelly recalled every detail of her awakening.

She had opened her eyes to a blinding white light. A warmth caressed her skin, and a sweet, floral scent passed through her nostrils. Lilac. Death, finally. Heaven, maybe. She waited, fully comfortable, expecting movement into a great void. Was there such a place? The question hung as if dangling from a piece of lace. She wanted to see more. If it was heaven, she'd meet it with her eyes open, without fear.

Instead, her vision swirled on a halo of light around two spheres: one big and one little. Could it be another dream? Please, no. Shelly didn't want to dream. She wanted to live.

In a test of faith, she squeezed her eyes shut. Pain. Tears. The signs of life emerged, and her vision reconstituted to see Josie's bright smile and Paul's tear-soaked face.

Eighteen months had passed since Shelly reawakened in that hospital bed. And now she found herself in a familiar chair across from a familiar man. Enough time had passed since the accident, and Shelly had wanted to see the good doctor again, to put one more aspect of her previous existence to rest.

"I've thought about you often," Dr. Frazier-Velli said. "I'd hoped we'd get a chance to decompress—if that's a way to say it." He leaned forward, hands together in his lap. His notepad was closed on the table next to him. "What's your world been like?"

Shelly inhaled slowly. The doctor she'd met on the road wasn't the man seated before her—she knew that. Although that figure had been merciless and cruel, perhaps his accusation that she'd created her own hell had been the key she needed—with Red providing the final piece of the puzzle, of course. Either way, she was a survivor.

Shelly didn't know what to tell him. With all his training, maybe he would understand the function of the road, the dark place she had journeyed to and somehow, lived to remember. Or maybe he'd want to lock her up in a psychiatric ward. Who could really understand her journey?

John.

She hoped that in future sessions, they'd have a chance to work through who John was and why they may have journeyed the road together. So many questions remained. Why had she made it out, while he succumbed to the road? They had been linked, drawn together somehow, both battling the demons of their past. In the newspaper article about the accident, she'd read about some of John's background—two sisters, a father who'd died tragically by suicide. But his coworkers at the camera shop respected him, and he'd recently been promoted, just as he said.

When they interviewed John's mother, she'd vowed to sue Shelly for the accident. Based on the things John had said about his mother, her bitter words made sense. Shelly waited for a letter from an attorney, but nothing ever came. The insurance investigation found the crash was caused by issues with the car, a piece of metal popped the tire, and then the steering failed—an "unexplained mechanical failure." It was an accident. A random, horrible accident. But Shelly knew better. The road operated with purpose.

"It's been way too long." Shelly's words ran together slightly; she was still working through some paralysis on the right side of her face and weakness in her arm. Her lips continued to be slower than her mind. "I'm glad we were able to make the appointment," she said.

They spent most of the fifty minutes updating each other on her recovery. Shelly shared that her mobility had gone from bedridden to the use of a wheelchair, to walking with a cane in twelve months. For the past six months, she attended weekly strength training sessions.

Josie had recovered fully and went back to swinging on monkey bars as if the accident had never happened.

"And Paul?" The doctor's tone dropped.

"Marriage counseling." She gave a small smile. "I think we are making progress. After the lawsuit and settlement, Paul started his own consultation practice. He's trying to help people now, and we smile more."

"That's wonderful, truly."

At the end of the session, he walked her to the door. Down the hall, Josie waited, grinning and full of energy, in her father's PSU sweatshirt. But with one look at Dr. Frazier-Velli, her hands rose defensively, and her expression hardened. The girl's eyes shot from him to her mother as if searching for context.

"Baby, it's okay. This is my doctor." Shelly put her arm around the girl. "And this is my Josie."

The doctor bent down. "Well. I've heard a lot about you, my dear," he said. "Nice to meet you finally."

Josie said nothing at first, her eyes quivering with analysis. Shelly's hair prickled on the back of her neck. Even though Josie had no lingering physical challenges, there had been changes. Before the accident, she'd rarely stop moving. Moments of concentration were brief unless harnessed by play, television, or her teachers. After the accident, Shelly would find Josie sitting quietly, staring through a windowpane, or standing under a tree studying its branches.

One time, Shelly discovered her daughter sitting on the tile floor of the bathroom, fully clothed, gently running her hand over the surface of water in the tub. When asked about these episodes, Josie would talk about the wind, smells, sounds, and the currents of water with the detail of a poet. Josie remembered the road. She remembered the accident, and details of their time between worlds. She remembered Red but shied away from the memories when asked directly. When she did talk about it, she only discussed Red.

"I'm glad she's safe now, Mommy," Josie said once at the park, leaving Shelly frozen. "Red needed to get some sleep. Her mom can help her now."

And now, Josie seemed to be processing something from the road as she looked at the doctor with narrowed eyes. "We met already," she said finally. With another glance at her mother, she turned and ran down the hall to where her father waited.

Shelly turned to Dr. Frazier-Velli and studied his face as his smile faded into confusion.

"I don't remember—"

"She's mistaken," Shelly said. "Kids mix things up sometimes." She gave the doctor a warm embrace and said she looked forward to seeing him in a couple of weeks. Shelly walked toward Paul and Josie in the lobby. Shelly released her tightly held breath, and as she deflated, the tension in her shoulders loosened. The plan was lunch and the park. As her strength returned, her bandwidth for activities blossomed.

Slowly, Shelly passed the receptionist desk, pausing to reposition her bag on her good side, as she'd come to call it. A woman stood checking in, and near the door were Paul and Josie. Shelly's attention snagged, and her gaze floated back to the woman. The woman was petite, and she wore Converse high-tops, jeans, and a gray hoodie that covered part of her black hair. Something in Shelly fluttered. It was a sensation of worry, or grief, connected to nothing. She'd felt good today. Her husband and daughter were there with her. The wounds and limitations of her body were healing. Yet the gnawing continued, and she proceeded down the hall.

The woman shuffled through her wallet and slid documents over to the receptionist. Shelly noted her pale skin and youthful profile as she tucked a stray strand of hair behind her ear. She didn't recognize this woman, but a sense of a connection nagged at her.

The receptionist gave back the woman's documents with a snapping sound on the counter. "Thank you. Ms. Proctor," she said.

The woman bundled her license and cards together and put them back in her wallet. "Call me Ashley," she replied. "Ms. Proctor makes me think of my mother."

Shelly shrugged and walked out of the office with her family. She didn't know any Proctors. Maybe the young woman reminded her of someone else. She put her arm around Paul's waist. "Ready?"

***

The heat of the tropical sun warmed Miranda's shoulders. There was sand between her toes and waves lapping at her heels. She'd kept her promise to Josie, and to Eli.

She pulled out the baseball hat tied to a fishing weight. She hadn't been able to find the homeless man to bribe him for the original. This was a new hat, one Eli might need in the hereafter.

The horizon was beautiful. Blue sky met clear blue water, with a breeze that smelled of salt. Miranda moved into the surf, and the sway of the tide pressed against her torso. When she was waist deep, she paused, closing her eyes. Eli would have loved the sky, the waves. *He would have loved me forever.* Tears ran down her cheeks.

Raising the hat and catching hold of the tear-drop-shaped weight of metal, she threw it as far as she could. She watched it land, drift slightly at the water's surface, then drop out of sight.

Miranda floated there a while, letting the undulating current support her body. She heard her own breath in her ears, as the water muffled the world around her.

A warm current flowed over her submerged shoulders, swooping over the ridge of her neck. It grew under her, like a pillow of energy, an embrace, coming up under her knees, her hips, holding her. Threads of heat caressed her stomach, her cheek, moving like fingers.

There was no fear, only peace. Miranda's eyes filled with tears. She looked up at the blue sky as the sunrays formed circles overhead. Together she floated with Eli, the waves rising and falling as though they shared breath again, as they had all those mornings. It was a gift from the water, from Eli, from Josie. If only she could stay there forever, feeling his presence.

Eventually, she walked back to the beach. Wiping her chest and face with a towel, she stared out at the water.

Solid, warm arms encircled her, and she leaned into the curve of the man's torso as she hugged him. She recalled her efforts to keep from ovulating around him. But in the excitement of Shelly's miracle awakening, they'd fallen into each other's bed, gushing over life and death, their past and future.

"Hey there—" Chuck hummed in her ear, pushing against her; his erection was obvious.

"I told you we were here on business," she said. Guilt encircled her throat, with Eli fresh in her mind. She'd not been entirely honest with Chuck about what she was doing in Florida.

"You're right. I'm sorry." He dropped his hands. "I'm glad you asked me to come."

Turning, she moved her fingers over his bare chest, rough with dry sand. Coming up on her tiptoes, she kissed him. "I want you here," she said. "I want you." She smiled, catching his eye.

"You're a bit young for me," he said, returning his hands to her skin.

Miranda laughed, knowing he had her by a slim five years. "Your appetite for the nurses was often college-aged, so that's a big lie, Doctor."

He kissed her. This time, it was firm and confident. "Can I keep you?" he asked, bringing a flutter of electricity to her stomach. Was the predatory bachelor asking for a commitment after a few, short months? The thought excited her. Scared her?

Miranda smiled, leaning back to study him. "About that—"

"What?"

"You might have to make an honest woman out of me."

"Meaning?" he asked.

She swallowed, then let the words rush out like the tide. "Well, how do you feel about babies?"

Acknowledgments

Stephen King said it best: "No one writes a long novel alone."

First and foremost, I wanted to express my gratitude to my mother. I would never have put pen to paper or finger to the keyboard without her sacrifice and influence while growing up. I am truly thankful.

To my husband and daughter, who supported me. Allowed me to ignore soccer games and laundry while I curled myself over a laptop night after night. They are my anchor to the real world, love, and inspiration.

Also, this book comes from healed wounds—healing that wouldn't have been possible without my best friend and her family, who welcomed me in, flaws and all. As well as my sister, who will never let me forget ... I'm older than her.

An acknowledgment wouldn't be complete without recognizing my publisher. Mary Vensel White and Type Eighteen Books gave this book a chance and nurtured it to life.

ABOUT THE AUTHOR

Kathleen Rhodes was born and raised in Oregon and has worked in the healthcare field for eighteen years. As a therapist then Registered Nurse and finally, a Psychiatric Mental Health Nurse Practitioner, her experiences working in outpatient clinics, jails, emergency rooms, and addictions services have provided invaluable insights into the human psyche. When she's not writing or deep into a book, Kathleen enjoys Oregon's wine country with her husband and daughter.

Printed in the USA
CPSIA information can be obtained
at www.ICGtesting.com
JSHW021148170824
68167JS00001B/6